PRAISE FOR
FRANCES MENSAH

'One of my go-to heart-warming authors.'

Dorothy Koomson, best-selling
author of *The Ice Cream Girls* and *I Know What You've Done*

'The characterisation is so good that I was on the edge of my
seat . . . presses the comfort-reading buttons for me.'

Katy Moran, author of *Wicked by Design*

THE
SECOND
TIME
WE MET

THE
SECOND
TIME
WE MET

Frances Mensah Williams

LAKE UNION
PUBLISHING

Text copyright © 2022 by Frances Mensah Williams
All rights reserved.

Published by Lake Union Publishing, Seattle

www.apub.com

Amazon, the Amazon logo, and Lake Union Publishing are trademarks of Amazon.com, Inc., or its affiliates.

ISBN-13: 9781542038867
ISBN-10: 1542038863

Cover design by The Brewster Project

Printed in the United States of America

For my large, loud and always loving family

PROLOGUE

Cara braced herself as the coach jerked to a stop, grabbing the seat in front to avoid banging her head again. Thankfully, Kensington was the last pick-up point for volunteers before the coach was to deposit them at their allotted patch for food parcel distribution, and she leaned back, irritated by the confines of her window seat. The headrest had already flattened the back of her loose Afro corkscrew curls while her Doc Martens only just slotted into the space above the foot rack.

After a cursory glance at the new arrivals trooping down the aisle, she turned back to stare gloomily through the window. The grey November skies reflected the steady dip in her spirits since boarding the coach outside Kensal Green station forty-five minutes earlier. *Why the hell did I let Ashanti talk me into this?* Not that her best friend had given her much choice.

'Cara, I know this time of year reminds you of he-who-must-not-be-named, but I'm not going to stand by and watch you spiral again,' Ashanti had declared. 'Rosie and I have given you space, but you've missed two girls' nights out and there's only so much Netflix anyone should be watching. I've signed you up as a volunteer for a charity called Parcels of Hope, and you're starting on Saturday.'

Flatly refusing to take no for an answer, Ashanti had pressed a brightly coloured flyer into Cara's hand while pointing out that volunteering would get Cara out of her own head as well as her tiny top-floor flat. Not to mention, she'd added virtuously, helping the lonely and underprivileged.

'Um . . . sorry, but is this seat taken?'

Cara's heart sank at the sound of an unmistakably plummy accent, and she turned away from the window. Although the coach had been filling up steadily at each pick-up point, she had hoped to keep the seat beside her free and not be drawn into conversation with a random volunteer.

A broad-shouldered man in a well-cut, dark wool coat brushed back a floppy blond fringe and gestured towards the empty seat.

'Bloody stupid question really, isn't it?'

Despite the posh enunciation, his smile was so warm that his greenish-grey eyes crinkled at the corners, and, despite her reservations, she found herself smiling back and nodding. 'It's fine . . . I mean, it's free. There's no one sitting there.'

He raised a dark-blond eyebrow and Cara burst into giggles at her equally ridiculous response. He slid into the seat and his bulk immediately filled the space. To her horror, the moment Cara felt his muscular thigh press against hers, a frisson of excitement darted through her. *What the hell, Cara! Get a grip!*

With the coach on the move again, Cara shifted in her seat to break the contact between them. Seconds later, he sat back in his seat with a satisfied sigh and spread his legs a little wider, touching hers once again and setting off another spark of electricity down her thigh.

'This is all pretty cosy, don't you think?' Her new neighbour tilted his head towards her, and she smiled in response to the teasing note in his voice. The space was so cramped it was hard to blame him for occupying what little there was, although her body's reaction to his proximity was disturbing. Meeting attractive men did not feature among her reasons for agreeing to volunteer, and this posh-sounding, fair-haired stranger was definitely not her type.

'Yeah, you have to wonder who designed these seats,' she agreed. It would be rude not to respond to his friendliness, and besides, she reassured herself, any physical reaction on her part was simply a biological response to being squashed against a man.

'I'm Henry, by the way.'

'Cara.' She nodded.

'It's good to meet you, Cara, and I have to say the plus side of this . . . er . . . rather snug seating is that I'm close enough to see your gorgeous brown eyes.'

Cara gasped, a rush of warmth shooting up her face, but he returned her outraged glare with such an innocent expression that she couldn't help grinning.

'You've got some front, I'll give you that,' she conceded, and Henry chuckled.

'Okay, I'll stop embarrassing you now, I promise,' he said with a mischievous smile. 'So, how long have you been volunteering?'

Suddenly feeling at ease with this virtual stranger, Cara relaxed. 'This is my first time, actually,' she confessed. 'I hate this time of year and, if I'm being honest, it was my best friend who signed me up to stop me turning into a Netflix addict – her words, not mine. What about you?'

Henry shrugged, and the sensation of his shoulder rubbing against hers sent Cara into a spin. *What the hell is wrong with you? Stop acting like you've never sat next to a man before!* She was so busy berating herself that it took her a moment to focus on his reply.

'—exactly what you mean. I'm a corporate lawyer, so volunteering is a great way for me to do something more useful than making more money for people who already have enough. I travel a fair bit, so I try to help out whenever I can.'

Before Cara could comment, the crackle of the loudspeakers indicated that Nigel, their team leader, was about to speak. Sure enough, after a couple of taps of the microphone, his slightly nasal voice carried around the coach.

'Alright, folks, now we're all on board, I want to run through the process. Once we get to our stop, you'll each get a bag and a list of the people you'll be delivering your parcels to. Now then, a couple of rules to keep in mind. One, don't get caught up in conversation. Some of these people haven't seen another face for weeks and they'll try to keep you chatting for as long as they can. Don't fall for it. Drop the parcel, say a few words, and move on to the next one.'

Cara grimaced and exchanged glances with Henry, who looked appalled. 'He sounds more like a regimental sergeant major than a community volunteer,' he whispered, sounding so horrified Cara couldn't hold back her giggles. Nigel was still in full flow, and she tried to concentrate on his words and ignore the tingling in the thigh resting against Henry's.

'Two, make sure you're back here on the coach by 16:55. We'll be leaving at 17:00 hours – no excuses. If you're not here in time, you'll have to make your own way back.'

'Yes, *sir*!' Cara muttered under her breath, wondering if Nigel *had* been drafted in from the Army. Henry chuckled and within moments, like naughty schoolkids, they were taking turns mimicking their leader. Henry's impressions of Nigel's bossy tone were so accurate that Cara creased up and it felt like only minutes later that the coach arrived at their destination.

The driver switched off the engine and Nigel took up the microphone again. 'All right, team!' he bellowed. 'When you leave the coach, form a single line and I'll hand out the goody-bags and your lists.'

As the volunteers stood up and made for the door, Henry turned to Cara, suddenly serious. 'If you get back before me, save my seat, okay?'

His face was so close to hers that she could feel the warmth of his breath as she stared into the green-grey depths of his eyes, and she shivered at the sudden intensity she saw there.

'Will you, Cara?'

Her heart gave a little wobble and she nodded slowly, as if hypnotised. 'Yes, I will.'

◆ ◆ ◆

Cara looked at her watch and tried not to show her impatience as Gertie narrated the story of her first encounter with her Bertie for the third time. By Cara's reckoning, she had already broken Nigel's first rule, and if she couldn't get Gertie to stop reminiscing about her dearly departed husband, she was in danger of breaking the second and missing the coach. *Not to mention my promise to Henry.*

With Gertie as the final recipient on her list, Cara had ignored her team leader's instructions and agreed to the cup of tea the old lady had wistfully offered her. Once the tea had brewed and Cara had politely sipped the weak, milky concoction, her attempts to leave had been thwarted with a steeliness that belied the elderly woman's soft, twinkly eyes. Cara's agonised glances at her watch apparently sailed right over the garrulous pensioner's head as she regaled Cara with yet another rendition of when Gertie met Bertie.

It was only when Gertie reluctantly conceded her need for the loo – 'That's the trouble with tea, isn't it, love? It goes right through you.' – that Cara was able to seize the opportunity to jump to her feet. A quick check of her watch showed the time as 4:45 and it would take her at least ten minutes to make her way back.

'I'm so sorry, Gertie. I've got to run now, or I'll miss the coach!' Grabbing her coat and backpack, Cara gave the old lady a hug and muttered goodbye before dashing outside. Darkness was falling, and without even the anaemic rays of winter sun to warm the air, it was freezing. Cara shrugged on her coat as she hurried up the quiet street, too anxious about the prospect of missing the coach – and Henry – to even stop to put on her gloves.

In the dusk, the street looked unfamiliar and, panicking, she pulled out her phone and tapped open the Maps app. She groaned as it dawned on her that she was heading in the wrong direction and, heart pounding, she turned on her heel and sped back up the street. Her fur-lined parka weighed on her as she ran and, despite the icy temperature, she could feel the sweat prickling down her back. Finally spotting the railway bridge she had crossed after leaving the coach, she sent up a prayer of thanks and glanced at her watch. She squealed with horror. 4:59 p.m.

The memory of Henry's eyes staring into hers flashed through her mind as she raced over the bridge and down the road. To her relief, the coach was still there, lights on and engine humming. Gasping for air, Cara slowed down. And then, with a roar of its exhaust, the coach began to move.

'Hey! Wait for me!' Cara yelled, sprinting along the pavement with as much speed as her heavy boots would allow. Her chest was burning and the vehicle was at least a hundred metres away, but even as the coach picked up speed, she kept on running until she couldn't catch her breath and was forced to stop.

She bent over, panting furiously, her hot breath clouding in the cold air. Cursing herself for not exchanging phone numbers with Henry when they had the chance, Cara watched in despair as the bus continued down the road, plumes of smoke from its exhaust whirling up into the air and disappearing into the darkness.

1

Falling . . .

'Cara! If it's not too much trouble, perhaps you wouldn't mind giving our lowly team meeting a tiny moment of your attention?'

Paula's saccharine tone did nothing to mask her sarcasm, and Cara snapped to attention. Annoying her boss wasn't a good idea at the best of times, and it was a seriously bad one when Paula was leading the Monday morning team briefing.

Apparently satisfied that Cara was listening, Paula announced, 'Betsey took a tumble down her stairs at home on Saturday and has broken her ankle. It's the worst bloody time to lose one of my best event managers, so you lot will have to pick up the slack and you'd better not mess up.'

She glared at the assembled group for a moment to underline the implied threat, then looked down at her notebook. 'Cara, you'll have to take over the Intellectual Property Lawyers' event.'

'You can't be serious! Why do *I* have to do that God-awful conference?' Cara protested. 'I've still got loads of prep for the Hadlow music festival and you know how much time that takes!'

She tried to stare down her boss but, true to form, Paula was unmoved and her expression didn't waver. 'The IP Lawyers'

Convention is one of this company's bread-and-butter events and, without Betsey, you're the only one with enough experience to take over.'

'But—'

'No buts, Cara. All Betsey's notes as well as the costing spreadsheets and delegate lists are on the system – thank God she's as meticulous about her record-keeping as everything else. Now, you'll need to set up an appointment with Elaine Hanlon, the conference manager at the Rosebank Hotel, as soon as possible. Make sure you're up to speed on everything first, and don't forget to confirm the breakout rooms – they almost double-booked us last time.'

◆ ◆ ◆

After three weeks of meetings and almost a hundred emails back and forth, the conference part of the IP Lawyers' Convention was finally over and the gala dinner about to begin.

iPad in hand, Cara stood inside the doorway of the hotel's magnificent banqueting hall and allowed herself a small smile of satisfaction as she surveyed the sea of white dining tables topped with spotless silver cutlery and sparkling crystal glasses. After a day spent shepherding loquacious but obliging lawyers into meeting rooms to deliberate over trademarks, patents and international copyrights, and stopping only to soothe anxious conference committee members, she savoured the silence. In a few minutes, the space would be packed with legal superstars, all of whom, Betsey had warned in her handover notes, could put away copious amounts of food and drink.

Despite her indignation at having it dumped on her at short notice, the convention had proved to be the smoothest event Cara had ever handled in her five years at Westbrook Events Management, and a world away from the projects that usually came her way. The meetings with Elaine over coffee and pastries had been infinitely more civilised than trudging across fields with farmers and battling with promoters and musicians over long lists of ridiculous green room demands.

'Is everything okay?' Elaine's pleasant voice carried a hint of anxiety as she came up to Cara.

Cara nodded, her loose dark curls bouncing in emphasis. Scanning the room, she tapped on her iPad to triumphantly tick off the last item on her checklist before giving Elaine a reassuring smile.

'It all looks fantastic, Elaine. Oh, and thanks for sorting out the extra microphone. You'd think this lot would have done enough talking for one day, but Geoffrey looked fit to explode when I told him we didn't have another one for the top table.'

Elaine's expression relaxed into a grin. 'Most of the committee members are lovely, but Geoffrey takes his position as Chair very seriously and he can get quite scary. I usually leave it to Betsey to deal with him – she's managed this event for so long that nothing seems to faze her.'

Cara tried not to pull a face. It was bad enough having Paula sing Betsey's praises daily without another reminder that her colleague practically walked on water.

Elaine cast a look around and then leaned in and confided, 'You know, I used to think lawyers were a quiet bunch, but it's the same every year. Just wait until later this evening when they've knocked back a few and you'll see what I mean.'

She paused. 'Don't take this the wrong way, but you're very . . . different from Betsey. To be honest, I wouldn't have thought this event was quite your thing.'

Cara stiffened, but Elaine didn't appear to notice any change in her demeanour and carried on, 'I mean, let's be honest, this *is* all rather stuffy, isn't it?'

Cara released her breath as she took in Elaine's friendly expression. The woman clearly didn't mean her comment as a dig, and, in all fairness, Cara's black satin waistcoat, long floral skirt, mustard tights and Doc Martens was probably not an obvious look for someone managing a black-tie function.

'To be honest, Betsey usually handles the corporate-y events. I tend to run the ones that are more . . . well, more on the creative side,' Cara conceded. If creative meant muddy festivals, dodgy-themed high-end parties, and tightly budgeted literary events, then that sounded about right.

'Well, please don't quote me, but . . .' Elaine looked around again before continuing, 'it's been a *lot* more fun working with you. Betsey can be a bit—' She stopped herself with a guilty titter.

' . . . Uptight?' Cara suggested.

'She's very good, don't get me wrong,' Elaine protested. 'Very professional and everything – and, as I said, she doesn't take any nonsense from Geoffrey. But she . . . well, you know, she's not the most approachable person, if you know what I mean?'

Cara did, but the sudden stream of people in formal evening wear entering the banqueting hall prevented her from saying so. Taken aback by the speed with which the room was filling up, Cara craned her neck and scoured the room for Ben. *Where the hell was he, and what was the point of bringing back-up if he kept disappearing?*

Cara suppressed an irritated sigh and squeezed Elaine's arm. 'I'm sure it will be a great evening. Well, here goes!'

Gripping her iPad and fixing a professional smile into place, she moved forward to help direct the people trying to locate their seats. Feeling somewhat self-conscious after Elaine's comment, Cara experienced a rare moment of regret for ignoring Paula's command to wear a black dress and heels. She had been far too busy chasing caterers, errant speakers and IT technicians throughout the day to worry about her appearance, but now, surrounded by immaculately made-up women in glamorous evening gowns and sleek updos, Cara's colourfully patterned Zara skirt and sturdy boots felt distinctly out of place. Shrugging away the pang of self-doubt, she beamed at a bewildered-looking elderly man fiddling with his bow-tie and, checking his name on her list, gently steered him towards a table near the stage.

Searching the room again, Cara finally spotted her missing colleague and beckoned him over impatiently. The free drinks were already loosening tongues and when Ben eventually navigated his way through the crush of lawyers at the bar, Cara had to drag him aside to be heard above the hubbub of well-bred voices.

'Where the *hell* have you been?' she fumed, with a withering glance at his smooth quiff. 'No, let me guess – in the Gents faffing around with your hair!'

Ben was lobbying furiously to be promoted from his role as assistant events manager, and, unlike Cara, he had taken Paula's instructions to heart and was in a smart black suit. With his pale cheeks and red hair, he could have been Tintin without the dog.

'Come on,' she added. 'Help me round up those stragglers at the bar and get them seated. We're already behind schedule.'

Unmoved by Cara's scolding, Ben scanned the packed banqueting hall and gently patted the wiry red hair he had just tamed with a generous dollop of gel. 'It'll take forever if I have to go around the whole room. Tell you what, I'll make an announcement over the microphone and—' His eyes widened, and he hissed urgently, 'Uh-oh . . . *move!* Geoffrey's coming over!'

Two hours after Geoffrey had gamely made it through the heckling that accompanied his speech, the party began in earnest. Elaine's warning rang in Cara's ears as she watched sober lawyers transform into rowdy ravers on the dance floor. Tossing aside dinner jackets, the men were whooping loudly to the thumping music while the women, elegant gowns hitched up, gyrated wildly with moves more suited to a Rihanna video.

A heavy-set delegate punching his arms in the air on his way to join the dancing barrelled past Cara. She ducked to avoid his clenched fist and lost her balance, stepping back to save herself from falling. Her boot came down hard on something much softer and she heard a yelp from behind her, immediately followed by a muffled curse.

'Oh my God! I'm so sorry!' Mortified, Cara whirled around to see whose foot she had damaged and immediately caught her breath. As she later described it to Ashanti and Rosie, one look at the muscular, fair-haired man hopping on one foot in barely suppressed agony instantly launched an invisible orchestra of violins.

Omigod, it's him! She'd have known that out-of-control blond fringe anywhere. After all, she'd seen it in her dreams for months before she'd reluctantly consigned the brief encounter on the coach to history.

2

Blind Love

'Henry . . .?'

   'Hmmm . . .?'

   'You need to move. I can't feel my arm any more!'

Henry raised his broad shoulders off the pillow, allowing Cara to slide her slender brown arm out from under him. She winced as the blood slowly flowed back and then propped herself up on one elbow with a happy sigh to inspect the man lying in her bed.

   'You have the most amazing eyes,' she marvelled. 'The colour's really hard to describe . . . sort of, well, a bit mossy green with a touch of grey and a layer of cobwebs—'

   '*Cobwebs*! Bloody hell, Cara, is that really the best you can do?' He pulled himself up to sit against the headboard, pushing away the fringe which immediately settled back onto his forehead.

   Cara grinned and snuggled against his chest, inhaling the lemony scent of his cologne as he wrapped an arm around her. 'Well, I never claimed to be a poet, did I? Trust me, I wouldn't be organising events if I had what it takes to be the next Shakespeare.'

   He stroked her arm and her heart rate accelerated at the sensation of his fingertips grazing her skin. They traced a slow path up her shoulder to caress first her neck, then her face and then, as she knew he would, he threaded his fingers through her curls and wound a lock of hair around his forefinger.

'I love your hair.'

Cara gave a good-natured roll of her eyes and smiled. Henry's fascination with her hair never ceased to amuse her. Much less funny were the endless hair battles she'd fought over the years. After her initial disastrous attempt to straighten it, in a bid to look more 'corporate' when she'd first started job hunting, Cara had tried every hairstyle from long braids and short locs to straight weaves and everything in between. Finally, fed up with spending hundreds of pounds on hair products and endless hours under the ministrations of hairdressers specialising in Afro hair, she had decided to leave her hair in peace. Spared any intervention other than rich conditioners and her own fingers, her hair had grown out into a cloud of loose ringlets which framed a heart-shaped face the colour of honey with huge brown eyes and high cheekbones.

Cara pulled away. 'Yeah, and it also needs a wash.'

He laughed, and she looked at him enquiringly. 'What's so funny?'

'You are. I don't know any girl who'd admit that so readily, unless of course it's to get out of a date.'

'Dearest Henry, you don't know *any* girls like me, full stop.' Cara smiled, reaching up to brush the hair off his forehead. 'But you'll soon learn that one of the many joys of going out with me is I know when my hair needs washing.'

He trailed his lips over her shoulder and then pulled her into his arms and nuzzled her neck. 'Remind me again of some of the other joys . . . *Damn,* I can't believe I've only properly known you for three weeks! Think of all the time we've wasted being apart thanks to that sodding idiot, Nigel! I begged him to delay the coach for a few more minutes and, when he refused, I was *this* close to throttling him.'

Cara giggled, entranced by Henry's clipped vowels. Even in the throes of passion, he still sounded as if he was addressing a judge.

She pulled the crumpled sheet up over them. 'I'd given up hope of ever seeing you again. Imagine if I hadn't landed on your toes that evening. You were *so* sweet about it.'

'My darling, even if I hadn't already fallen for you on the coach, you looked so horrified it would have been churlish of me not to have accepted your apology. Besides, you looked so sexy in that black waistcoat that I forgot all about the—'

Her mobile cut him off and Cara groaned. 'For fu—' She caught herself in time. ' . . . goodness' sake, it's Saturday! This had better not be Paula because I do not have a single event on this weekend,' she grumbled, reaching over Henry to pick up her phone from the bedside table.

Glancing at the screen, she grimaced and scrambled upright. 'Dex, what's up?' she demanded impatiently.

The voice squawking through the phone didn't sound pleased. 'Where the hell are you?'

'At home. Why?'

'What do you mean, *why*? I've been waiting for ages for you to get here so we can go and buy Mum's birthday present! Don't tell me you forgot?'

Cara gasped and covered her mouth, only just catching herself before the expletive slipped out. Since the last telling-off from her mother, Cara had been trying extra hard to stop swearing. She glanced guiltily at Henry, no slouch himself in the casual sweary department, but seeing him focused on twirling a lock of her hair around his finger, Cara turned her attention back to her brother.

'Dexter, I'm really sorry but it completely slipped my mind. This week's been so crazy! I crashed out early last night and . . . um . . . I'm still not up yet.'

The squawking grew louder and more intense. 'Cara! What the hell? What do you mean it *slipped your mind*? It's almost twelve o'clock and Ozzie's got tickets for me and him to go to the football this afternoon. You promised we'd buy her gift together before the lunch tomorrow!'

Oops! The trouble with being besotted with the new man in your life was that your brain didn't think anything else mattered. Her mother's birthday lunch had also slipped off Cara's to-do list and she maintained a prudent silence until Dexter finally ground to a halt. 'Are you still there?'

'Yes,' she said shortly, and then switched to a more conciliatory tone to stop him launching into another rant. 'Look, Dex, I'm really sorry. Tell you what, I'll go shopping this afternoon and get something from both of us. You can pay me back tomorrow.'

'Thanks, Sis, you're a gem! Oh, and Ozzie probably hasn't got Mum anything yet, so can you buy something biggish and we'll all chip in, yeah? I'll tell him you're sorting it.'

Cara swallowed the momentary flash of resentment at the all-too-familiar phrase before ending the call. *Why is it always me who sorts it?*

'I take it that was Dexter? He didn't sound very happy,' Henry remarked.

'Which is nothing new these days,' she said, sliding back down. She draped an arm around his comfortingly solid chest, enjoying the feel of the light sprinkling of hair against her cheek. 'Since he and Ashanti decided to take a break, Dexter has turned being moody into an art form. Although, to be fair, I suppose he has a point this time. It's my mum's birthday tomorrow and I promised him ages ago we'd go shopping together for her present, but—'

'You forgot because you're with me.'

'I suppose so,' she agreed, reluctantly. 'But I just love us being in our own little bubble. Anyway, Mum's not exactly the easiest person to shop for.'

'Why not?' Henry sat up and fixed a mock-stern expression on his face. 'You know, you really haven't told me very much about her – or about any of your family, for that matter. All I know is that you've got three brothers and a sister, and your parents live in Cricklewood.'

Cara giggled at the precise way he pronounced the name of the North-West London suburb where she'd grown up and a world away from the well-heeled parts of town Henry frequented.

'Because my family is officially crazy, so I'd thank my lucky stars if I were you. We could probably film our own reality show, except nobody would believe that's how we really are.'

'Okay, but you still haven't told me what your mother's like.'

'Mum's lovely; a bit scatty, mind you, but really, *really* sweet. Which is part of the problem. She hates us spending money on her because she says she's already got everything she needs. She's a food writer and does loads of demos on healthy eating at schools. Schoolkids seem to love her, which probably explains why they actually eat the weird recipes she comes up with.'

'Since we're finally talking families, you do realise I don't know anything about yours either, except that you've got two sisters and your parents live in Gloucestershire?' She stumbled slightly over the word, and Henry grinned.

'I doubt we're interesting enough for a reality show. My father's a . . . er . . .' He hesitated for a fraction too long and she squinted at him curiously, wondering why he suddenly looked so furtive.

'A what?' *Drug dealer, professional hitman, or . . . please God, not an accountant!*

' . . . a farmer, I suppose, now he's retired from the City. Mother does a lot of charity work and helps run the local croquet club. My sister Imogen's a . . . ' He frowned, then shrugged. 'Actually, I don't remember what she is this month. I can't keep up with her constant career changes. Fleur's the youngest; she lives at home and goes to the local school.'

'Well, that's a start,' Cara said, feeling somewhat dazed by the flood of information. From the moment they'd found each other again, she and Henry had been inseparable, peeling themselves apart only long enough to go into their respective offices and to shop at the local Tesco Express for Henry to cook the dinners she was enjoying getting used to. Up until now, as if by unspoken mutual consent, they had stayed in the present and avoided discussing families or pasts, and Cara was in no rush to let the outside world in.

'Okay, so now we've got that out of the way, how about we stop talking for a while?' She moved her hand below the sheet with a teasing smile, reaching behind him to stroke his back. Her fingers paused as they encountered a ridge of skin.

'What's the story with this scar?' She had noticed the lattice of faded silver lines at the base of his spine a few times but had always been too distracted by the sight of Henry's muscular nakedness to delve into their origin.

'War wounds from playing rugby,' he replied smoothly. 'That game can kill you, you know.' Flipping her onto her back, he tickled her until she squealed, effectively ending the discussion. Just as things were starting to heat up, her phone rang again. Although sorely tempted not to answer, she hauled herself upright.

'Yes, Ozzie, what is it?'

'I just spoke to Dex, and he said you're buying Mum's birthday present, yeah?'

'Yes, but—'

'Great. I haven't had time to get her anything, so I'll chip in for whatever you buy, if that's okay?'

'Oz—'

'Thanks, Cara, you're a star! See you tomorrow. See, I knew you'd sort it!'

Of course you did! She put the phone down, bristling with indignation. Who needed brothers? Those two lazy bastards had somehow managed to manoeuvre things so she was stuck with doing the work yet again while they went off to watch the football!

'Your brother, Ozzie?'

Cara nodded, not trusting herself to maintain her no-swearing policy if she opened her mouth.

Henry threw back the sheets and jumped to his feet. 'Come on! It looks like we've got a birthday present to buy, so let's get busy.'

Cara sat bolt upright as he pulled on her kimono-style dressing gown and headed for the door. 'Hold on a minute! Are you saying you want to come shopping with me?'

Henry showed no sign of self-consciousness as he wrapped the scarlet silky gown that barely reached his knees around him. 'Well, it's Saturday, I don't have to go into the office, and I don't want to leave you. So, yes, I want to go shopping with you.'

Cara beamed. 'I've never dated a man who actually *wants* to go shopping.'

As if mesmerised by her smile, Henry returned to the bed and leaned over to kiss her, offering no resistance when she pulled him on top of her.

Eventually Henry pulled away. Raking back his dishevelled hair, his face as flushed as the robe that barely covered him, he firmly retied the belt she had just undone.

'Stop teasing, Cara, or we'll never leave the room.'

Cara smiled. 'Okay, fine! You go ahead and shower while I find something to wear.'

As Henry left, Cara wrapped her arms around her knees and hugged herself with joy. How could she ever have thought he wasn't her type? Henry Fitzherbert was the best thing that had ever happened to her, and she still couldn't believe her luck at literally stumbling across him at the gala dinner. Before the night had ended, he had invited a dazed Cara to lunch the next day. Lunch had been followed by dinner the following evening, after which they had ended up in Henry's flat for a coffee that never quite got brewed.

For the next three weeks, abandoning her best friends and neglecting her family, Cara had barely registered Ashanti and Rosie's texts and phone calls. Her vow to never forget what had happened the last time she opened herself up to someone was shelved as she found herself caught up in the glow of long walks hand in hand with her new boyfriend, cuddling on the lumpy sofa in her flat watching movies, and lying in bed eating pizza while listening to him talk about his day and make even copyright law sound fascinating.

Henry's off-key singing from the shower jolted her out of her reverie. Hopping off the bed, Cara rummaged through the mix of market stall purchases and high street bargains that made up her wardrobe and invariably provoked the side-eye and scathing comments from her fashion-conscious best friend. But while Ashanti's views on Cara's dress sense was water off a duck's back, Cara did occasionally wonder what Henry, whose most bohemian item of clothing was a Ralph Lauren polo shirt, made of her offbeat taste. She pulled a black skirt out of the closet and plucked a sleeveless white cotton top with a slashed neckline from the pile of folded clothes stacked on a chair, and when Henry emerged from the bathroom, she gave him a quick kiss before heading into the steamy room. After a speedy shower, she dressed quickly and applied a touch of lip gloss before giving her hair a generous spray of conditioner. Peering into the mirror, she sighed and gave her curls a final fluff; her hair really did need a wash, but it would have to do for now.

She stepped back from the full-length mirror to take a proper look at herself. The long, fitted skirt with a front slit revealing her slim legs skimmed her hips and she wished yet again for a bigger bust – or at least one that matched the promise of her rounded bottom. Sitting on the bed, she slipped on a pair of socks and tied the laces on her black Converse trainers. Unlike Ashanti, who'd graduated from baby bootees straight to stilettos, Cara and high heels rarely went together.

'Ready?' Henry stood in the doorway. Not knowing how long he had been watching her for, she smiled a little self-consciously and reached for her bag.

'Ready.'

Strolling down the road to the train station, her hand held loosely in Henry's, Cara's heart felt full to bursting. She hadn't been looking for love, but feelings she had thought were gone forever were blooming into life again. Basking in the warmth of the sun shining high in the clear blue sky, even the honks of irritated drivers struggling to get through the temporary traffic lights outside Kensal Green station couldn't poke a hole into the blanket of happiness wrapped around her. She looked up at Henry in his open-necked shirt, chinos, and a lightweight navy blazer, and squeezed his hand with elation.

'You know, I've been thinking,' Henry said, his eyes meeting her gaze.

'Careful, you could hurt yourself.'

But instead of joining in her laughter, he pulled her to a stop to face him, and Cara's smile slowly faded. 'What is it? What's wrong?'

Henry nodded as if he'd reached a decision. 'Hear me out, because this might sound a little crazy, but it's just dawned on me that, well . . . as I'm helping to choose her present, I'd really like to meet your mother – and your family.'

While Henry smiled expectantly, Cara's jaw dropped. She scrambled for something to say, but the words refused to come. *Who in their right mind wants to meet someone's family after only three sodding weeks!* What was Henry *thinking* and how the hell had that tiny sharing of information about their families galvanised the man into wanting to meet hers?

Cara's sinking heart slowed her light step into a miserable plod as she cast around for a convincing excuse. Suddenly the sun seemed a lot less bright. That's what comes of ignoring vows, she reminded herself grimly. How could she explain what a terrible idea this was without mentioning – well, *him*.

Her family was used to her being single and she knew without a shred of doubt that taking Henry home was going to set the cat among the pigeons. *I know they'll wonder if he's just a replacement and, oh God, it's going to bring everything up and . . . I'm just not ready*!

If a man asking to meet her family was what every besotted girl was supposed to want, Cara thought darkly, she was definitely the exception. Instead of euphoria, all she felt was a deep sense of foreboding.

3

Outside the Bubble

With Henry by her side, Cara walked through the garden gate and down the terracotta-tiled path leading up to the house. At the sound of screeching car tyres, they both swivelled round to see a dark-blue Audi pull up. The driver reversed skilfully into a small gap between the parked cars that lined the street of Victorian houses and, moments later, two men spilled out and raced each other to the gate. Cara couldn't help laughing as she reached into her bag to pull out a large pink envelope and a Biro, holding them out to the man sprinting up the path towards her.

'Good timing! You guys can sign Mum's card before we go in.'

She handed the envelope to a tall, athletically built man with smooth brown skin almost the same shade as Cara's. He bent to kiss her on the cheek with a muttered, 'You're a diamond – love you, Sis!'

Sliding the card out of the envelope, he perched it on his raised knee and tried to keep his balance as he wrote.

Shaking her head, Cara turned to Henry.

'This, by the way, is my brother, Dexter,' she said dryly.

After scribbling a few illegible words and signing off with a flourish, Dexter examined Henry with narrowed eyes. Then, still clutching the pen and without saying a word, he raised his hand and Henry awkwardly bumped the fist on offer.

The other man, who had stopped by the gate to catch his breath, was now approaching. With tousled wheat-blond hair, razor-sharp cheekbones and the tiniest glimpse of a tattoo peeking out from under his tight white t-shirt, he looked like a walking advert for the blue jeans that clung to his muscular thighs. Nudging Dexter aside, he wrapped his arms around Cara in a tight hug, only releasing her when she squealed in protest. He grinned at her before turning to openly inspect Henry.

'So, who's this, then?'

Cara slipped her hand through Henry's arm possessively. 'This is Henry, my *boyfriend*.' She emphasised the last word with defiance and watched the two men exchange a startled look. Having expected a reaction, she decided that her best strategy was to ignore their obvious astonishment.

'Henry, this is my other brother, Ozzie.'

'Your *brother* Ozzie?' Henry echoed, bemused.

Ozzie exploded into laughter, earning an evil glare from Cara. 'Okay, technically, he's my step-brother,' she conceded, 'but we don't use those terms in our family because it would be far too confusing.'

Passing the birthday card along with pen to Ozzie, Dexter eyed Cara. 'So how come your *boyfriend*,' he stressed the word exactly as she had a moment earlier, 'doesn't know anything about your family?'

'That's a good question,' Henry murmured. 'I've been asking her the same thing myself.'

Dexter pursed his lips before glancing at Ozzie, who was engrossed in writing what looked like a short essay on the blank

24

side of the card. With no help forthcoming from that quarter, Dexter cleared his throat.

'Okay. It looks like *I'd* better give you a quick intro to the Nightingale-Grant family before we go in.' Not waiting for a response or even seeming to draw breath, Dexter continued. 'Right, so Ozzie's dad is married to our mum – I mean, Cara's and my biological mum, yeah? Dad – that's Ozzie's dad – and our mum also have two kids together.'

Henry nodded. 'Right. I've got that . . . I think.'

The look he shot Cara suggested otherwise and she shrugged. 'To be fair, Henry, we don't exactly spend a lot of our time talking.'

At that, her brothers whistled and high-fived each other, while Henry flushed a fiery red. Cara hugged his arm in reassurance. 'Relax. You don't have to impress this lot. Honestly, we're a pretty easy-going bunch. All you need to remember is that my mum's name is Bev, Dad is Gerald and—'

Suddenly the front door was flung open and a massive shaggy dog that could have come straight out of a paint commercial emerged in a frenzy of barking and tail wagging and, panting heavily, leaped up at Dexter.

'*Logan!* Get down, you foolish dog!' Pushing the excited animal back inside and into a narrow hallway, Dexter walked in and stooped to high-five a lanky teenaged boy standing just inside the door.

'I could hear you talking outside! Why didn't you ring the bell?' he demanded. His faded blue t-shirt fell loosely over the battered jeans hanging from his narrow hips, and his hair, a mop of black curls cut low at the back and sides, emphasised wide hazel eyes set in an oval-shaped face.

Cara and Henry went through, ahead of Ozzie, who slammed the door shut just in time to thwart Logan's attempt to dash outside. Moving the unruly dog out of his way, Ozzie bumped fists with the younger boy, throwing an affectionate arm around his shoulders as they followed the others into a large sunny living room with magnolia-painted walls and huge bay windows bracketing French doors that looked out on to a mature garden. Books threatened to spill off crowded shelves that had been built into high nooks on either side of an open unlit fireplace, and a huge plasma television screen dominated the wall space in between. A chaotic mix of brightly coloured cushions, half-open magazines, recipe cards and schoolbooks were scattered along the length of two squashy L-shaped grey sofas. In one of two matching armchairs was a plump cat with grey-striped fur that blended comfortably into the fabric. As they trooped in, it lazily opened one eye to check on the source of the commotion, then closed it again and stretched out languorously.

Cara tossed a pile of magazines from one sofa to another and gestured to Henry to sit down. 'Sorry, it's a bit of a mess. Have a seat while I go and look for Mum.'

She turned to the teenager who was openly studying Henry and held her arms open with a smile. 'Seriously, have you grown taller in just a few weeks?'

The boy hugged her distractedly and Cara released him with an impatient sigh. 'Stop staring, Thaddeus, it's rude! This is Henry. Henry, this is—'

'Seriously, Mum, it's not *fair!*'

A slightly built girl wearing a thunderous expression marched in through the open door. Barely acknowledging the people in the room, she threw herself into the vacant armchair and scowled furiously.

'Life is not fair, young lady, so deal with it!' said the petite, dark-skinned woman who was following close behind. As her eyes fell on the crowd assembled in the room, she gave a shriek of excitement.

'Oh, my word! I didn't hear the doorbell! When did you all get here?'

Dexter was the first to reach her, swinging her into the air with a loud whoop. 'Happy birthday, Mum!'

Her feet had hardly touched the ground when Ozzie squeezed her into a bear hug. 'Happy birthday, Mum! I swear you don't look a day over seventy!'

Clutching onto his arm to steady herself, she aimed a mock blow at him. Then her gaze moved past Ozzie to land on Henry, who had sprung to his feet to stand beside Cara, and her eyes widened.

'*Caramia*! You didn't say you were bringing someone. Who is this handsome man?'

'Happy birthday, Mum!' Cara hugged her mother and took Henry's arm, trying not to sound as defensive as she felt. 'Mum, this is Henry. My boyfriend.'

The woman blinked and took a deep breath as if she needed to compose herself, then smiled warmly at Henry. Her thick salt-and-pepper hair was twisted into locs that grazed her shoulder as she tilted her head to look up at him with sparkling brown eyes.

'It's a pleasure to meet you, Henry.' She shook Henry's out-stretched hand and clasped it between both of hers. 'I'm Beverley, but you can call me Bev. I'm Caramia's mother, as you've probably guessed, and you're very welcome to our home.' She stopped speaking to glare at the young girl now engaged in a tug-of-war with the dog as she attempted to pull a magazine from its mouth.

'Manon! Will you control that wretched dog of yours? And, Logan, for the hundredth time, *stop* eating my magazines!' She marched over and, despite her tiny build, grabbed the glossy publication with one tug before tossing it back onto the sofa. 'Excuse me while I check on lunch. Dad should be back shortly, and then we can eat.'

'Cara*mia*?' Henry whispered, taking a step closer to Cara.

'Mum was learning Italian when she was pregnant with me,' Cara said, keeping her voice down in the hope the others wouldn't hear.

'Manon?'

'She'd moved on to French by then.'

'Okay, then, let me guess. Thaddeus . . . Greek? Latin?'

Cara laughed. 'No, he's named after Dad's – Gerald's – father. He died the year before Thad was born.'

The sound of the front door slamming was followed almost immediately by the appearance of a tall man carrying an armful of newspapers. His thinning blond hair was neatly slicked back from his forehead, and he stood in the doorway for a moment surveying the room and its occupants with a wry expression. 'Is my house getting smaller or is this family growing?'

'*Dad*!' Cara sped across the room, and he dropped the papers onto a side table and held her close for a long moment before releasing her.

'We haven't seen you for quite a while, young lady.' His wide smile belied the admonishment and brightened an angular face with dark-blue eyes and high cheekbones reminiscent of Ozzie's. Just as Bev had done moments earlier, he looked straight past Cara and fixed a quizzical gaze on Henry.

'And would this gentleman be the reason why?'

Cara flushed and pulled Henry forward. 'Dad, meet Henry. Henry, this is Gerald, my—'

'Father, I know. Good afternoon, sir. It's a pleasure to meet you.' Henry held out his hand and returned Gerald's firm handshake confidently. 'I really hope you don't mind me barging in like this, but I wanted to meet Cara's family and I pestered her until she gave in.'

'You're very welcome, although I can't promise you'll leave with your sanity intact,' Gerald said with a broad wink, before moving on to hug his waiting sons. He then turned to a disconsolate Manon who had curled up in the chair, a deep frown marring a pretty face with the same light-brown complexion as Thaddeus. Her black leggings and white trainers accentuated long, thin legs and, in contrast to her brother's closely cropped back and sides, Manon's hair was caught back into two thick braids hanging past her shoulders.

'And what's the matter with you, Miss Manon?' her father asked gently.

'Dad, you *have* to talk to Mum!' she pleaded. 'She won't let me go to Alonzo's party next Saturday. *Everyone* is going and I'll look like a baby if I'm not allowed!'

Gerald scratched his chin and studied her stormy face thoughtfully. 'Who's Alonzo? I don't think I've heard his name before. Is he one of your 249 Facebook friends?'

Despite herself, Manon giggled. '*Da-ad!* I've got loads more followers than that – and *nobody* uses Facebook anymore. Alonzo goes to my school – he's in Year 10 and really fit!'

Dexter and Ozzie exchanged glances, and Ozzie spoke first.

'You're in Year 7, so why would you be going to a fifteen-year-old boy's party?'

Manon pouted, looking mutinous. 'Everyone in my class—' She took one look at her father's raised eyebrows and carefully reframed her sentence. 'Okay, *some* of the people in my class are going, but Alonzo invited me *personally* on the group chat.'

'Yeah, well, Mum's right,' Dexter said bluntly. 'You're too young or he's too old. Either way, it's not happening.'

'*Dad*!' Manon wailed. 'It's not fair! At least I'm asking . . . Cara used to sneak out and go to parties when she was at school. She *told* me!'

'Manon! Don't tell fibs!' Cara glared at her sister while doing her best to avoid Gerald's pointed gaze. 'And even if I *did* happen to go to any parties, I was certainly a lot older than twelve!'

Desperate to change the subject, Cara turned to Henry who had been watching the interplay with fascination. 'Henry, would you like a drink? I—'

The doorbell rang and she looked around, puzzled. 'Are we expecting anyone else? Never mind, I'll get the door.'

Within moments she was back, closely followed by a short, elderly man in baggy blue jeans rolled up at the hem. His stomach sat comfortably outside his worn black belt and his bushy hair and beard provided a striking contrast to his chocolate complexion.

'Another brother?' Henry whispered.

'No, silly,' Cara giggled. 'He's our neighbour. Mind you, he's over here so often, he might just as well be.'

She pushed Henry forward. 'Uncle Floyd, I'd like to introduce my boyfriend, Henry.'

A momentary flash of stunned surprise vanished almost immediately, and the older man's craggy features relaxed into a warm smile. Holding out his hand, he gripped Henry's and pumped it up and down.

'Henry, you say? Well now, it's good to meet you, m'boy.' His strong accent was an immediate giveaway of his Jamaican heritage. 'Welcome to the family, son. It's a little crazy at first, but you get used to us pretty quick.'

As Floyd moved on to greet the others, Henry muttered to Cara, 'I'm confused. Your neighbour is also your *uncle*?'

She giggled and shook her head. 'Oh, Henry, you have so much to learn. He's not a *real* relative – it's just, well, a cultural thing to call older people 'auntie' and 'uncle'. You know, to show respect?'

Henry nodded slowly and Cara beamed at him before turning to address the room at large. 'Okay, now everyone's been introduced, I'll go and help Mum in the kitchen. Dexter, can you sort out drinks for Henry and Uncle Floyd, please?'

With her previous apprehension about their visit almost forgotten, Cara almost skipped across the corridor to push open a door leading into a spacious, steam-filled kitchen. All four burners on the large cooker were covered with huge stainless-steel pots and she sniffed appreciatively at the blend of rich, spicy aromas swirling around the room and suddenly making her feel very hungry.

Bev had been muttering under her breath while pulling out bowls and plates from a cupboard to add to a pile stacked on the island, and she looked up in relief.

'Oh good! Caramia, help me take these through to the dining room, will you? I'd get Manon to do it, but she's driving me crazy about some party and I'd like to enjoy my birthday without an argument.'

Cara picked up as many plates and bowls as she could carry and nudged open the sliding doors at the other end of the kitchen that led into the adjoining room, most of which was taken up by a huge pine dining table with matching chairs.

'Uncle Floyd's just arrived, so I'm setting an extra place for him,' she called while pulling out cutlery from the sideboard and laying the table.

As Cara returned to the kitchen, her mother stopped stirring the contents of a large pot. 'Why didn't you mention you were bringing your friend?'

Cara shrugged. 'I hadn't planned to, but Henry insisted he wanted to meet you. He helped me choose your present and . . . well . . .' She ground to a halt. 'It's not a problem, is it?'

Bev stared at her for a moment, then shook her head. 'Of *course* it isn't a problem . . . and you know that is not what I meant.'

Dexter came in to take a few cans from the fridge and Bev turned her attention back to the saucepan. 'Dexter, please tell everyone lunch is in ten minutes. I thought I'd try out a new recipe today: a spicy five-bean and coriander soup. *Don't* make that face, I promise you'll like it!'

4

THE CHILLI EFFECT

Half an hour later, squashed up against Henry as they sat around the dining table, Cara was doing her best to relax. *Nothing bad is going to happen*, she reassured herself, taking deep breaths to quell the anxiety masked by her calm demeanour. The first course was out of the way and, so far, her family had managed to behave reasonably well. While Henry's courtroom skills had been severely tested, he had held his own against the tide of questions coming his way from Thaddeus, the chief interrogator.

Not to be outdone by her brother, Manon had peppered Henry with questions about his work, not bothering to hide her disappointment when he reluctantly confessed that his clients didn't include armed robbers or murder suspects. However, minutes later, his approval rating had shot up when she spotted him petting Logan, who was hiding under the table.

Logan nudged her knee insistently, and Manon broke off a piece of the bread left on her plate and discreetly slipped it into his mouth.

'Manon! Stop feeding the dog while we're eating,' her mother scolded, not deceived by her daughter's stealth tactics. 'No wonder Logan thinks he's human.'

'Give him some of the bean soup. That'll teach him to stop taking food from our plates,' Ozzie muttered, earning a smothered chuckle from Dexter and a glare from his mother.

'Don't pay the boy no mind, Bev! The soup was great. Full of flavour,' Floyd said, leaning back in his chair to rub his stomach.

Ozzie grinned unrepentantly while Thaddeus looked gloomily into his bowl and swirled his spoon around the broth he was pretending to eat.

Gerald leaned across to pat his wife's hand. 'That was lovely, darling. What's next?'

The martyred tone accompanying the question didn't go down well, and Bev pushed back her chair with an audible sniff. 'Thaddeus, since you don't seem to appreciate your food, help me clear the plates so I can bring in the next course. I've made some spiced lamb, a chicken curry and jollof rice, which I hope you will manage to eat without comment.' Bev paused as though struck by a thought. 'Henry, you're not a vegetarian or anything, are you?'

Startled by the unexpected question, Henry paused in the act of stroking Cara's hand under the table. 'Absolutely not! I love meat. Eat loads of the stuff.'

As her mother left the room, Manon giggled. 'You're so posh, Henry!'

Cara groaned under her breath, but Henry's grin made it clear he wasn't in the least bit offended.

'I'm not really, you know.' He lowered his tone conspiratorially. 'I blame my school, because when your wretched teachers insist on what *they* call proper English then I'm afraid that's what happens.'

As if on cue, everyone's eyes swivelled towards Gerald, who frowned and stroked his chin.

'Well, as a teacher of almost thirty years and a headteacher for the past ten, I'm afraid I have to defend my profession against that slur.'

Gerald sounded genial enough, but Henry immediately looked aghast, and his face suffused with colour.

'Ah!' Momentarily lost for words, he cleared his throat. 'I didn't mean to imply . . . er . . . no, of course not, you're absolutely right there.'

Thaddeus returned to the table, sliding into his seat next to Floyd, his gaze shifting from Henry to his father and back to Henry.

Gerald chuckled, eyes twinkling with mischief. 'I'm just teasing you, Henry. Now, I'd better help my wife bring in the next course or we'll be here until supper time.'

He left the room, and, for a moment, there was silence.

'*Awk-ward*,' Thaddeus muttered under his breath.

Floyd nudged him. 'So, young Thaddeus, when you coming round for another Marley session? Those old records of mine could use a listening to, you know?'

'Is it all right if I bring my friend Jamie to yours, Uncle Floyd? He didn't believe me when I told him you've got more than five hundred *actual* records in your collection.'

'Sure you can, Son. The more the merrier. You know I like any excuse to play my vinyl.' Floyd looked across at Henry, who was surreptitiously playing footsie under the table with Cara.

'Henry, you like reggae music, man?'

A wary expression crept across Henry's face. 'Er . . . well, I'm not really that familiar with reggae. I mean, I know some of Bob Marley's music but that's probably about it, if I'm honest.'

Dexter rolled his eyes and Floyd gave a polite nod before turning back to Thaddeus, who was tugging on his sleeve and demanding an answer to his next question.

Cara patted Henry's knee reassuringly and scowled at Dexter, who pulled a face in response. Dex was always going to be the one most likely to give Henry a hard time, and Cara eyed her brother sternly, willing him to stop being difficult. The sticky moment was eased by Bev returning, closely followed by Gerald, with two large bowls heaped with tomato-red rice. Ozzie and Dexter immediately stood up to relieve their mother of the dishes, setting them in the centre of the table while she went back to the kitchen to fetch the rest of the food.

Gerald placed a large platter of sliced lamb next to the rice and a deep dish filled with golden-brown fried plantains in front of Cara and, as soon as their parents were seated, everyone piled in without ceremony.

'I *love* fried plantains!' Cara exclaimed. 'Henry, have you eaten them before? Here, try.' She scooped up a pile of hot plantains and deposited them onto Henry's plate before tossing a piece into her mouth.

'Mmm . . . It tastes *so* good!'

Amused at Cara's unrestrained joy, Henry speared a large piece of plantain and took a bite, almost spitting it out as the heat burned the roof of his mouth. He grabbed his glass and downed the contents with long glugs.

'*Christ*! Cara, your mouth must be lined with asbestos!'

She giggled as she watched his breathing return to normal. 'Sorry, I should have warned you they were just out of the fryer. I learned to eat plantain piping hot when I was little to stop the boys from stealing it off my plate.'

For a few minutes, the only sound was of cutlery against plates and murmured requests for the serving dishes to be passed up and down the table. Henry cut a piece of spicy lamb Cara had forked onto his plate and chewed it slowly, his expression wary.

'Caramia, pass Henry some of the jollof rice,' her mother instructed. 'Henry, I hope you'll like it. It's an old family recipe and my mother taught me to cook it just like they do in Ghana.' She pointed her fork at the bowl and added, 'I always like to put in a little Scotch bonnet chilli pepper to give it some bite.'

Cara spooned a generous portion of the rice onto his plate before turning back to her own. She was so engrossed in eating the pile of fried plantain she had loaded onto her plate that it took her a few moments to pick up on the gasps coming from beside her. Her eyes widened in horror as she watched Henry grip his throat as his face turned bright red.

'Henry! *Shi*— Oh my God, are you okay?'

The tears streaming down his face suggested otherwise.

'*W-water* . . .' he croaked, and Cara scrambled to her feet to seize the water jug, almost spilling its contents over him in the process. She poured a full glass and handed it over, watching anxiously as he gulped it down without pausing for breath.

'Wow, Henry . . . you've turned *really* red,' Manon said in wonder.

Conscious of Bev's alarmed expression and the eyes of everyone at the table on him, Henry cleared his throat several times and tried to speak. After the third try, his voice reappeared, albeit sounding somewhat raspy.

'Sorry about that. I must have bitten into some of that Scotch bonnet you mentioned.' He coughed again and waved a placatory hand at Cara. 'I'm fine, really. Oh, and um, the food's delicious, Mrs Grant.'

'Call me Bev,' she said absently, keeping an eye on him until his colour returned to normal.

Clearly eager to divert the focus of attention, Henry looked across the table. 'So, Dexter, Cara tells me you have your own delivery business?'

Dexter nodded, chewing slowly before answering. 'Yep. I started it five years ago. Built it up to a fleet of ten delivery vans.'

'That's impressive,' Henry remarked. He swallowed a mouthful of rice, following it immediately with a gulp of water.

Cara squeezed his knee in encouragement and Henry pressed on. 'Are you in the same business, Ozzie?'

Dexter replied for him. 'Nah, he works on construction sites.'

'Dex . . .!' Cara sighed in exasperation and then turned her ire onto Ozzie, who was laughing helplessly. '*Don't* encourage him! Henry, take no notice of them. Ozzie's a model and spends half his life traipsing around Europe and America doing fashion shoots for weird designers.'

'I *do* work on building sites between modelling jobs, so Dex is telling the truth . . . *ouch!*' Ozzie protested as Cara aimed her foot at his ankle under the cover of the table.

Gerald cleared his throat and frowned, suddenly looking every inch the headteacher. 'May I remind you we have guests, and that you are supposed to be setting an example for the younger ones?'

'Sorry, Dad,' Cara muttered with a final glower at both brothers.

The rest of the meal passed without incident, and Floyd was the last to finish eating. Dropping his napkin beside his plate, he licked his lips with satisfaction.

'Thank you, Bev. That chicken curry was wonderful! And you know how I love plantain. It always reminds me of my late Marcia's cooking.'

Cara pushed her chair back from the table. 'If we've all finished, let's give Mum her presents. I'll get ours. Thaddeus and Manon, you can go and fetch yours.'

'What about dessert? I thought we were having ice cream,' Manon whined.

Cara sighed impatiently. 'We will, but let's do the presents first because Henry and I can't stay too long.'

'What's the hurry, Cara?' asked her father. 'We haven't seen you for weeks.'

Cara turned to Henry, but his deadpan expression offered no support and she looked around the table fighting her sudden sense of panic. How could she explain that her intuition had warned her against bringing Henry here and that she was desperate to leave before things *really* went wrong?

'Fine,' she muttered. 'But I'm still giving Mum her gift now.' She stood up abruptly and headed back to the living room, taking deep breaths to calm her racing pulse.

The cat was lying prone in the armchair and didn't appear to have moved an inch since their arrival. Hearing the echo of Cara's footsteps on the wooden floor, it opened its eyes and stretched, before hopping off the soft cushion and padding across to meet her. Cara bent to pick up the plump tabby, burying her face in its soft fur.

'Oh, Lexie, what should I do?' she whispered.

Lexie purred lightly for a moment and then bared her teeth in protest and wriggled out of Cara's grasp, dropping lightly onto the polished floor, and slinking off in the direction of the cat flap beside the French doors.

With a sigh, Cara picked up the gift bag she had left by the sofa and returned to the dining room where Thaddeus and Ozzie were shouting over each other trying to relay their version of the same story to Dexter. She glanced at Henry, who was watching them with amusement, and then went over to her mother, breaking into her conversation with Floyd.

'Happy birthday, Mum. This is from me . . .' She looked at her brothers and waited for silence before continuing. 'And Dex and Ozzie. I hope you like it.'

Bev clasped a hand to her chest. 'Of *course* I'll like it, Caramia! You really didn't need to spend any money on me, but I love anything you kids give me.'

Peeling back layers of white tissue paper, she pulled a dark-blue rectangular box with orange edging from the bag and carefully pried it open.

'*Oh*, it's a necklace! My word . . . oh, look, Gerald! The stones are such beautiful colours. Thank you so much, my love!'

Beaming with delight, Bev held the box up for everyone to see. Dexter cleared his throat loudly and deliberately, and his mother burst into laughter. 'Yes, thank you, Dexter, and you too, Ozzie!'

'You're welcome, Mum,' Ozzie said grandly, sounding as gratified as if he had personally chosen and wrapped the gift himself. Cara rolled her eyes in irritation and took her seat next to Henry without a word.

Manon's high-pitched voice piped up. 'Cara, don't you think it looks a bit like the necklace you lent me for Becky's birthday party last year? You know, the one that Ryan gave you.'

The sudden silence was so stark that the sound from the clock ticking on the narrow mantelpiece seemed to echo around the room. Cara felt a surge of heat rise from her chest and spread across her face to collide with a wave of nausea. Even though she had been half-expecting something awful to happen, in that moment it felt like turning a blind corner and walking straight into a brick wall. For a few agonised moments her heart stopped pumping until her breath re-emerged in short, shallow gasps. She knew Henry must be wondering what was going on, but she couldn't get out a single word of reassurance, or even look at him, and instead she kept her eyes glued to the table while reaching blindly with shaking fingers for her glass and gulping down its contents.

Then, as if in response to a secret signal, everyone started speaking at once. As the torrent of sound spilled into the tense silence, Cara fought to regain control over her emotions. *I knew this would happen!* She had almost persuaded herself that nothing could go wrong but, in the end, it had been Manon, not Dex, who had spoken Ryan's name, opening the can of worms Cara had prayed would remain sealed.

'I'll bring the ice cream,' said Bev, springing to her feet. 'Caramia, come and give me a hand.'

Unable to speak, Cara nodded and followed her mother into the kitchen. Bev quietly shut the interconnecting door and turned to her daughter, who was leaning against the island, her face a picture of misery.

'You haven't told him, have you?'

Cara shook her head, her eyes suddenly filling with tears. 'We've been so happy, Mum, I didn't want—'

Her voice broke and her mother swept her into her arms, shushing her gently. 'It's all right, my darling. Henry seems lovely, and I can see why you like him so much.'

Cara stepped out of her mother's arms and wiped her face with the back of her hand.

'He really *is* lovely,' she insisted. 'It's been so long since— Anyway, I'm just so glad I found Henry. Mum, I *want* to be in love again . . . I want to be happy. You *do* like him, don't you?' She was almost pleading, and her mother nodded slowly.

'Yes, I do. But, Caramia, if you're serious about this, you have to tell him.'

Whatever Cara was going to say was cut off by Manon's entrance, her braids bouncing in indignation. 'Where's the ice cream? We've been waiting for *ages!*'

'Stop exaggerating, child,' her mother smiled. 'Take the tubs out of the freezer and put them on the table – and don't forget the scoop.'

Two helpings of birthday cake with chocolate ice cream and a mug of tea later, Cara stood up to leave. Overriding her family's protests by insisting she had to prepare for an early start the next morning, she hugged everyone and hovered impatiently while Henry shook hands all round and thanked her parents for lunch.

With a final wave, Cara closed the front door behind them with a sigh of relief and followed Henry down the garden path. Late afternoon was creeping into dusk as they strolled hand in hand along the Broadway to the train station, skirting around wooden stands displaying bowls of cut-price fruit, open cartons of yams and plantains, and stacks of plastic household items spilling out of the shops onto the pavement. The normally busy main road was quiet, and outside the bingo hall a group of boys whizzed up and down the pavement on scooters. Drinking in the scent of spicy curries drifting from the kitchen of a nearby Indian restaurant, Cara felt the tightness in her shoulders loosen as the tension brought on by Manon's innocent question slowly eased.

'Isn't this weather just glorious?' she said dreamily, raising her face to catch the last reluctant rays of sunshine. 'I love it when it's like this. You know, breezy but still warm.'

Henry's mind didn't appear to be on the climatic conditions when he stopped without warning to face her squarely. 'Cara, help me understand something.'

Alarmed, her stomach plummeted, but she gamely returned the laser stare trained on her.

'What?'

'Firstly, why did everyone looked stunned that you'd brought your boyfriend with you? Or that you even *have* a boyfriend?'

Cara hesitated before carefully picking her words. 'I told you I haven't dated anyone for a long time. I suppose my family was just surprised that I was . . . well, seeing someone again.'

A warm puff of air blew a stray lock of hair across her mouth as she looked up at him with wide eyes, willing him to believe her and silently begging him not to push it any further. After a moment, Henry nodded. Relieved, she made to turn away until his gentle grip stopped her.

'Well, that was my first question,' he said evenly. 'My second question is, who's Ryan?'

5

Interrogations

'*Cara*! Have you heard a single word I've said?'

Dragging her mind away from the troubling conversation with Henry, Cara sat up straight in her chair, chiding herself for letting her attention wander when Paula was in full-attack mode. She hated these Monday morning staff meetings when Paula delighted in casting a dampener on the week before it had even begun, publicly blasting those who had fallen behind in their admin – a fireable offence in Paula's opinion – and dishing out new assignments to the unwary. Paula's bite was far worse than her bark and, ignoring Ben's smirk, Cara tried to look penitent.

'Um . . . sorry, Paula. I *was* listening. I . . . er . . . just missed the last bit.'

'So then, you heard me say that you're in charge of the sixteenth birthday party booking that came in on Friday?'

The caustic tone went right over Cara's head as she stared at her manager in dismay. 'What! But I had to manage the last blood— . . . er, birthday party! I even got that awful woman to cough up a massive tip after assaulting the poor dancer in the middle of his act.'

Paula's eyes, two deep pools of inky blackness, didn't blink, and Cara added accusingly, 'You've said yourself that I'm too senior for events like that. Why can't Ben do it?'

'No buts, Cara.' Paula's tone brooked no argument. 'Until Betsey's fully back on her feet again, Ben's helping her with the Cartography Association conference. Besides, the party is only for sixty-odd kids; you can easily handle it yourself.'

Ben's grin grew wider, and Cara restrained herself from lobbing her Biro at him. Much as she liked Ben – and secretly admired his ability to drink all-comers under the table at staff parties – his constant sucking up to Paula drove her mad. Surely no promotion was worth the ridiculous number of *Of course, Paula* and *Such a great idea, Paula* that followed every interchange with their manager.

'So, what's the theme, then? If we're talking sixteen-year-olds, can I at least assume I don't have to deal with any more flipping strippers?'

Indifferent to Cara's sarcasm, Paula scanned a printed document while Cara watched in silence, wondering yet again why the woman insisted on wearing the shapeless black trousers that did nothing to flatter her tall, angular frame. Her age remained a mystery, as Beth in HR steadfastly refused all bribes to reveal the details of Paula's personnel file. Bets ranging from thirty-five to one hundred years were still open which, along with her manager's spiky black hair and waxy complexion, played deftly into Cara's theory of Paula's vampire origins.

Paula looked up from the form. 'It says here "wizards and witches", whatever that means. You'd better set up a meeting with the client and take a proper brief. Oh and they want fireworks as well, so have a word with Julio to see if he can do it. Once you've sorted out the budget, we can get our quote approved.'

'*Julio*! Why don't you just kill me now?' Cara groaned.

Ben was openly laughing now, and Paula pursed her lips. 'Julio's fees are a fraction of what the others charge, and we can't afford to jack up our prices in this market. In case it's slipped your notice, we're not exactly the only events company trying to win new business.'

Cara rolled her eyes in disgust. 'Julio's only cheap because he always messes things up and has to offer discounts to keep his clients.' She raised her hands in surrender at Paula's dour expression. 'Fine, okay, I'll do it!'

'I know you will. Anyway, you should be pleased about how we got the referral. The client's one of the lawyers that was at the IP conference you handled last month. She wanted to know if we did smaller events like parties, *and* she specifically asked for you because you did such a great job.'

Ignoring the incredulity in her boss's tone, Cara sighed inwardly. Westbrook Events' business strategy, at least according to their managing director, Malcolm Poretti, was to focus on big-ticket, high-margin events. Malcolm clearly hadn't aligned his thinking with Paula, who took on any event for which she could issue an invoice.

'I assured her that we'd be very happy to help,' Paula continued. She consulted the document again. 'Her name's Primrose Wynter. Take down her number and you can give her a call when you're ready.'

In Paula-speak 'when you're ready' translated into 'right this minute', and Cara reached for her notepad and scribbled down the number. With the meeting over, she headed back to her desk, pausing to tap Ben's shoulder with her pad.

'Good luck working with Betsey,' she hissed. 'You'll be laughing on the other side of your face when you see how late she makes you stay every day!'

◆ ◆ ◆

Half an hour later, conscious of Paula staring meaningfully at her from across the open-plan office, Cara reluctantly punched out the number from the call sheet and was immediately put through to a very elegant-sounding Primrose Wynter.

Cara cleared her throat and adopted her most professional voice. 'Hello, Ms. Wynter. My name's Cara Nightingale and I'm calling from Westbrook Events Management. I understand you contacted us to help you plan a sixteenth birthday party?'

'Ah yes, Cara! Thank you for calling back so promptly. Um . . . I'd quite like to get the ball rolling as soon as possible. Could we have a meeting to discuss the party – in fact, would you be able to come over to my office today? We're in the City and very easy to get to.'

Taken aback, Cara hesitated for a moment. Then, looking up to find Paula's eyes still fixed on her, she continued hastily, 'Yes, of course. What time suits you?'

'Well, there's no time like the present, wouldn't you say?'

Wondering for a moment if Primrose and Paula were related, Cara scribbled down the address, hung up the phone and reached for her bag. Slipping on the light jacket hanging over the back of her chair, she ran impatient fingers through her curls. The olive-green Lycra miniskirt she wore had ridden to the top of her thighs, and she tugged it down, conscious that Westbrook's relaxed office dress code was probably poles apart from that of the swanky law firm she had just been summoned to. *Well, I didn't ask for this assignment, so that's just tough!*

Leaving her frigidly air-conditioned office on such a lovely summer's day had its advantages, however, and despite her annoyance at Paula, Cara couldn't help enjoying the warmth of the sun on her face and bare legs as she made her way towards Hammersmith tube station. She was approaching the entrance to the tube when her phone rang, and she pulled it out of her backpack and grimaced as she saw the name on the screen. She could guess what was coming and she really didn't need it.

'Hi, Dex. I'm literally about to go into the Tube. What's up?'

'Why are you dodging my calls?' Dexter asked without preamble.

'Because I've been *busy!* I'm at work and I've just taken on a new event and—'

'And nothing. You just don't want to talk about yesterday.' He paused, and then exploded. 'Cara, what were you *thinking?*'

'Dexter, I— *Oof!* She glared at the back of a man who had just bumped into her without a word of apology, and hastily moved to the side of the pavement to avoid the oncoming people traffic. 'Sorry, some rude idiot literally ran into me. Look, don't ring me up simply to have a go. What do you mean, what was I thinking?'

'Cara, you haven't gone on so much as a single date since . . .' He hesitated. 'Well, for *years!* Waltzing in with a bloke no one's ever heard of and saying he's your boyfriend is hardly fair, is it?'

'Mum said it was fine, so what's your problem?' Cara retorted defiantly.

There was a moment's silence before Dexter spoke again. 'You know exactly what I'm talking about.'

Cara leaned against a shop window and closed her eyes for a few seconds to gather her thoughts. Her mum had been right; she should have told Henry before allowing him to be blindsided by Ryan's name. She was still shaken from the conversation with Henry after leaving her parents' house, although it shouldn't have been a surprise that he'd challenged her about Ryan. The man was, after all, a lawyer and well used to dealing with prevarication. But Henry's curiosity had been unnerving, and she needed time to process what had happened before explaining herself to anyone, much less Ryan's number one fan, Dexter.

'Have you told him about Ryan?' Dexter's voice jerked her back to the present.

'Dexter, for your information and *not* that it's any of your business, Henry knows Ryan is my ex-boyfriend and that we broke up three years ago. He also knows the two of you were close friends – which was why you were bordering on being plain rude! – and that because I hadn't told anyone in the family I was dating, you were all a bit shocked. I've made it clear to Henry that we both have relationship baggage we've kept outside the door until now and I'm happy for it to stay that way.'

'And that's all you told him?'

'That's all he needs to know! Ryan is history, or at least he would be if you lot didn't keep going on about him!'

She took a deep breath to quell her rising anxiety, but Dexter hadn't finished. 'If that's how you feel about it, then fine. But if you and Henry are so tight, how come he's clueless about your family?'

'Maybe because we've got better things to do when we're together than talk about you!'

'Come off it, Cara, he didn't even know your full name! He's a lawyer, and you do know no one trusts lawyers, right? The guy is well posh and obviously comes from money. He doesn't look like someone used to slumming it in Cricklewood. Are you sure that's the kind of man you want to be with?'

Cara spluttered in indignation. 'D'you see? That's why I didn't want to answer your calls or bring Henry home. I knew *you'd* start nit-picking and finding fault because he isn't your precious Ryan. Well, too bad, Dex! Henry and I are solid, and I *really* like him, so if you've got nothing better to do than piss me off, I'm hanging up!'

'Cara, calm down! I'm just trying to look out for you.'

'*Don't* tell me to calm down! You *know* how much I hate that! Thanks for your concern, but I'm thirty years old and I can take care of myself. And since you've brought up relationships, don't you think you should be dealing with your own instead of worrying about mine? When are you going to sort things out with Ashanti?'

There was a long silence and Cara waited it out, determined to get her brother to speak. When he did, he sounded grim. 'Stay out of it, Cara.'

She shook her head, forcing herself not to scream in frustration at his stubbornness. Then she looked at her watch and sighed. 'Fine, as long as you do the same for me.'

Emerging from Moorgate station thirty minutes later, Cara fished out her phone and tried to get her bearings. As most of her clients were in the creative sector and she rarely needed to come into the City, it took a few minutes to locate Primrose Wynter's office. The law firm of Lowell and Stephenson was in a towering steel and glass edifice with revolving doors that led into an imposing marble-tiled lobby. After signing in at the security desk, Cara found herself cocooned in a steel-lined lift with a man in a dark suit carrying a bulging briefcase. Pretending she hadn't noticed him ogling her legs, she tugged down the hem of her skirt and folded her arms across her chest.

The instant the lift doors opened onto the fourteenth floor, she headed towards the huge reception desk. The hushed environment was a far cry from the noisy chaos of Westbrook Events' reception area where Mandy Quinn's loud, piercing voice regularly harangued all-comers, whether they be couriers or staff members who'd forgotten to book meeting rooms.

The efficient-looking receptionist printed off a visitor's pass and handed it to Cara with a friendly smile, nodding towards a cluster of armchairs and sofas.

'Please take a seat while I let Primrose know you're here. She is expecting you, so she shouldn't be long.'

Cara smiled politely and crossed the pristine cream carpet to sit on a brown butter-soft leather sofa. The plush reception area, almost twice the size of her flat, had huge floor-to-ceiling windows providing a panoramic view of central London. Henry's law firm was also in the square mile, and although he downplayed his work as being terribly boring, she knew from a quick scan of their website that his firm was one of the top partnerships in the City, and Henry one of their prize litigators. Thinking of Henry brought Dexter's phone call back to mind and, as Cara gazed out at the aerial view of the city, she fiercely wished she could re-enter the happy bubble of life before last weekend. Sunday had ended gloomily, for while Henry had listened and appeared to accept her explanation about Ryan, for the first time that she could remember, he had returned to his flat alone, claiming he needed to prepare for an anti-trust case in Manchester. She knew Henry was disappointed in her for holding back information and she also knew she would eventually have to tell him the whole story. But it felt like a lot to dump on someone she had just met and the last thing she wanted was to risk her brand-new relationship. Ryan had ruined enough for her already.

'You must be Cara.'

Startled, Cara turned round to find a slim woman in a black suit accented by a cream wraparound blouse standing in front of her. Her blonde hair was twisted into a glossy bun and, although her face was long and rather mournful, the discreet make-up and single-strand pearl necklace with tiny pearl studs oozed an under-stated elegance.

Hoping her thighs hadn't stuck to the sofa cushions and fighting the temptation to adjust the upwardly mobile hemline of her clingy skirt, Cara jumped up, focusing on smiling and trying to sound professional as she shook the limp hand on offer. 'Hello, Ms Wynter. It's a pleasure to meet you.'

'Please, call me Primrose.' With a brief smile that didn't quite reach her light-blue eyes, the lawyer eyed Cara appraisingly.

'I understand from my manager that you were at the IP lawyers' event a few weeks ago?' Cara offered brightly in a bid to break the increasingly awkward silence.

'Yes, it was certainly memorable,' Primrose murmured, her gaze dropping to Cara's tiny skirt. Then, as if remembering her manners, she clapped her hands together. 'Let's go and have a chat in my office, shall we? It might be easier if I lead the way. This place can be bit of a maze.'

A few minutes and several security doors and winding corridors later, Cara found herself seated at a small table in Primrose's compact office clutching a paper cup of anaemic-looking vending machine tea while the lawyer settled herself into the chair opposite. Scrutinising Primrose, Cara had absolutely no memory of seeing the woman either at the conference or during the gala dinner, but then the event had been packed and there was no obvious reason Primrose would have stood out.

Cara took a sip of the tea and, trying not to grimace, set down the cup and pulled her notebook from the depths of her backpack.

'So, Ms Wynter – Primrose – perhaps you could tell me a bit more about the party and any ideas you have in mind?'

Primrose ran a hand over her perfectly coiffed hair. 'It's my niece Tabitha's birthday in a few weeks and I promised her a party as my gift. Tabitha is my brother's daughter and, between you and me, James and Bella are completely hopeless about this kind of thing.'

She flashed a toothy grin and Cara responded with an understanding smile.

'They're both terribly clever academics but have no idea what to do for a teenage girl. Now, I've got lots of ideas, but my job is very demanding and doesn't leave me much spare time, I'm afraid. That's why I thought getting your firm to organise something would be the best bet.'

Cara nodded. 'Paula mentioned you wanted to go with a theme of wizards and witches?'

'That's right. Tabitha has always *loved* Harry Potter! Anything like that,' she waved a hand vaguely in the air, 'would be perfect.'

Puzzled as to why a sixteen-year-old girl would prefer a wizard-themed birthday party to something more sophisticated, Cara prudently kept her thoughts to herself. She had no desire to incur Paula's wrath by putting off a new client, and she contented herself with scribbling down notes as she reeled off her own ideas.

'Well, we can certainly help with that. Let's see, there's a great venue we've used for a few parties. It's a converted barn and very spacious. I'll check if it's free for the date you requested. We could get it decked out with dark fabrics and papier-mâché trees and things, and bring in cauldrons for fruit punch. Oh, and I can arrange for party food with a wizard and witches' theme. Party bags, of course; we can suggest some ideas. Paula also mentioned that you want fireworks, is that right? Well, the barn I mentioned is next to a large field where we could set up a fireworks display, and there's a production company we use for special effects and entertainment that can handle that and take care of all the health and safety issues. Would you like us to organise the music, too?'

Primrose blinked a couple of times, looking dazed by the torrent of information coming at her. 'Er . . . yes, absolutely. I've no idea what young people listen to these days.'

Cara smiled. 'That's no problem. There's a DJ we use quite often, and we can find out your niece's taste in music nearer the time and make sure he plays her favourite artists. If it's helpful, I can also recommend a costumier for the fancy-dress outfits.'

After a few more minutes of discussion, Cara put down her pen. 'I've got all the information I need for the moment. Is there anything else you'd like us to include in the quotation?'

Primrose shook her head. 'No, that's it for now.'

'Great! I'll get a quote to you in the next few days and, once you've approved it, we can get started.'

As Cara reached for her bag, Primrose cleared her throat and Cara sat back in her chair and looked at her enquiringly. Primrose played nervously with the pearl stud in one earlobe, and then said, 'You know Henry Fitzherbert, don't you?'

Taken aback by the abrupt change in subject, Cara stared at the lawyer in surprise. 'Yes, I do. Why?'

'Well, his sister – Imogen – is one of my *dearest* friends. We were at school together. Pemberton Hall, you know?'

When Cara's blank expression made it clear she didn't, Primrose looked more than a little put out. 'It's a very well-known girls' boarding school in Gloucestershire.'

'Oh, okay,' Cara murmured.

'Anyway, Imogen mentioned the other day that Henry has a new girlfriend and that you'd met at the IP lawyers' dinner.'

From her tone, Primrose was clearly expecting an answer and Cara reluctantly replied, 'Yes, that's right.'

Discussing her love life with a stranger, and a client to boot, was not on Cara's agenda, and the woman's apparent desire for a cosy chat was starting to irritate her. Cara looked meaningfully at her watch, but Primrose didn't take the hint.

'I'm just curious. You see, Henry's family and mine are *very* close. Practically neighbours – although, of course, our house doesn't even begin to compare with the Fitzherberts' estate.'

'E-e-state?' Cara croaked, a prickle of shock running through her. Primrose now had her undivided attention. 'What – you mean estate, like, *land?*'

Primrose's eyes narrowed and she said sharply. 'Absolutely! Henry's family lives in a magnificent manor house, and they own over two thousand acres of prime arable land. Didn't he tell you?'

'He said his father was a farmer,' Cara said feebly.

Primrose let loose a high-pitched peal of laughter. 'Oh dear, Henry can be *such* a tease! I'm not at all sure Lady Isobel would describe herself as a farmer's wife.'

'*Lady* Isobel?'

'Yes, Henry's mother. She's the daughter of the Earl of Croton. Their title dates to the eighteenth century.'

Cara sat in stunned silence as Primrose prattled on. Her mind flew back over the conversations she'd had with Henry. Although his accent and upbringing were undoubtedly posh, and she knew from his company website bio that he'd attended a well-known public school, she was pretty sure she would have remembered him mentioning that his grandfather was an earl. She forced herself to tune back into the lawyer sitting opposite her and immediately wished she hadn't.

'So, how are you two getting along? I wouldn't have thought someone like Henry was quite your thing. You seem quite . . . you know, artistic, and lawyers aren't exactly the most exciting people.'

Wondering if Primrose had been talking to Dexter, Cara shrugged. 'We're getting on just fine, thanks.'

'It's still early days, though, isn't it?' Primrose persisted. 'Imogen says Henry seems quite taken with you. Not that he's giving much away.'

Cara's dark eyes narrowed as she took in the innocent expression on Primrose's face and her bullshit antennae instantly shot up. Something here was failing the sniff test.

'Is *that* why you asked for me to organise the party?'

'Oh, God, no! As I told the woman I spoke to, I thought you did a great job at the conference. The band was amazing, and we've certainly never had a fire-eater at our events before.'

Cara bit her lip. *The less said about that, the bette*r. The after-dinner entertainment had been another of Julio's mix-ups, but fortunately, Geoffrey had been too drunk at that point to remember he'd requested a comedian.

'Hmm, yes indeed,' Cara said, keeping her tone non-committal. 'Well, I'll get back to the office and start working on all this. If anything else comes to mind, please give me a call.'

She dug a slightly battered card out of her purse and handed it to Primrose, who scrutinised it carefully before handing her one from a box on her desk.

'Here's mine. You can email me directly.'

Primrose led the way back to Reception. 'It was very nice to meet you and thanks again for coming over at such short notice. I'll wait to hear from you.'

As soon as the lift doors opened on to the ground floor, Cara hurried across the lobby, still in a daze from Primrose's revelations. She had no idea how to feel about discovering her new boyfriend was not only incredibly wealthy, but also came from the aristocracy. It was obvious from Primrose's barrage of questions that she had been fishing for information, whether out of curiosity or to pass on to Henry's sister, and if Imogen was anything like her close friend

Primrose, that didn't bode well. With Dexter's disapproval looming over her like a dark cloud and Henry's uncharacteristic silence since the previous afternoon leaving her feeling unsettled, Cara desperately wished for the cosy bubble that had shielded Henry and her from complicated explanations, unsolicited opinions and prying eyes. With a nod to the security guard, she pushed through the revolving doors out of the chilly building and into the sunshine.

6

ARTISTIC DIFFERENCES

The music was so loud when she entered the darkened club that it took Cara a minute to adjust to her surroundings. With the air conditioning barely functioning, Mocktails was hot and muggy with an underlying aroma of stale sweat. Wrinkling her nose, she slipped off her leather jacket and scanned the room, immediately spotting the curvy brunette in a black dress standing and beckoning furiously from a table on the other side of the dance floor. Pushing her way through the group of people stationed inside the doorway, Cara squeezed past the crowded bar.

'She's *alive!*' Rosie squealed, face pink with excitement, as she flung her arms around Cara's neck in a tight embrace.

'*Rosie!* I can't breathe . . .' Cara gasped, her face crushed into her friend's thick, shoulder-length hair.

'She's not going to be alive much longer if you don't let go,' the girl sitting at the table remarked. Even in the club's poor lighting, she was stunning, with full lips and even white teeth that contrasted with flawless chocolate-coloured skin. Her thickly lashed hazel eyes, heavily lined with dark kohl, looked Cara up and down dispassionately.

'Well, well, well . . . and to what do we owe the pleasure of your company? I'm surprised you even know who we are.'

'Ha-ha, very funny, Ashanti. I take it you've missed me, then?' Cara grinned.

'Hardly noticed you weren't around,' was the swift response. Then, breaking into a grin, Ashanti stood up to pull Cara into a hug. Releasing her, she took her seat and crossed long, shapely legs.

'So how come you've suddenly realised we exist?'

''Cos Henry's away on business this week,' Cara said equably. 'Stop giving me evils, I'm just kidding! I've really missed my girls. Besides, you didn't think I'd forget you were singing tonight, did you? Especially after sending me at least thirty texts to remind me?'

'Nothing would surprise me after the way you've dumped us since getting yourself a man,' Ashanti said in a waspish tone.

'Well, she's here now and that's what matters,' Rosie intervened. Her deep, eyebrow-skimming fringe clung damply to her forehead and framed a pair of huge baby-blue eyes, and her rounded cheeks were flushed with delight as she sat down and beamed at Cara. Rosie had none of Ashanti's glamour and the only adornment on her freshly scrubbed features was a liberal sprinkling of freckles.

Cara draped her jacket over the back of her chair and dumped her oversized purse on the table before taking her seat. Looking across the table at her two best friends, she sighed happily. 'It's so good to see you! It feels like ages since we were together.'

'Yeah? And whose fault is that, then?' Ashanti muttered as she stood up again. 'What are you girls having? My set starts in twenty minutes, and I need a drink before I go on.'

Rosie's smile drooped. 'Can you make mine a vodka and diet coke, please? I've started a new diet to get into those stupid trousers I bought in the sale at Linzi's, and please don't ask why I bought skinny jeans when I've got an arse the size of Denmark.'

'Don't be so hard on yourself, hon,' Ashanti said kindly. 'Personally, I'd have said it's more like, you know, the Isle of Wight?'

Cara giggled, and Rosie stuck her tongue out at Ashanti. 'Hilarious! You try sitting at a desk analysing spreadsheets all day. Besides, I tried taking them back, but the skinny cow behind the till said I couldn't return them because they don't do refunds on sale items.'

'You should have told her where to go,' Ashanti tutted. 'I'll take them back if you like.'

'No, no,' Rosie protested. 'I can do it . . . I will.'

Cara and Ashanti exchanged glances. Rosie had been at the back of the queue when the gift of assertiveness was handed out and she loathed any kind of conflict. The youngest in their year at school, Rosie had been notoriously unable to stand up for herself and she was the first to admit that without Cara and Ashanti's protection, she would never have survived the seven years spent in their North London comprehensive.

'Hold on, if you haven't worn the jeans, why should returning them be a problem?' Cara demanded. 'Isn't there some consumer law about refunds? I'll ask Henry, I'm sure he'll know.' She pretended not to hear Ashanti's groan. 'I'll have a rum and *real* coke, thanks. By the way, I love the hair – very glam. When did you get it done?'

Ashanti swished her long curtain of silky black hair from side to side with an impish smile. Smoothing down her fitted white bandage dress, she struck an exaggerated pose and tapped her nose knowingly. 'Aha! You see, *that's* what happens when you stay away. You miss out on the latest reinvention of my fabulous self.'

She dropped the pose to grab her bag from the table. 'I had it done last week. Colum reckons there'll be music agents showing up tonight, and I've got to look like a superstar if I want to get a superstar recording contract, dontchathink?'

Cara refrained from pointing out that superstar contracts were generally thin on the ground in Kilburn nightclubs and instead watched as Ashanti tottered off in her white stilettos towards the bar. As if by magic, the crowd parted to clear a path for her.

Cara shook her head in bemusement. 'Just like Moses and the Red Sea . . . I don't know how she does it,' she said under her breath.

Rosie looked at her curiously and Cara raised her voice to be heard above the music. 'I said, I don't know how she does it. It's really not fair how she gets to be beautiful *and* have a great voice!'

'What are *you* complaining about? You're not exactly Shrek – more like Shakira with those gorgeous hips of yours . . . and I'd kill to have your legs!'

Cara laughed and leaned forward to rub her friend's arm affectionately. 'I've missed you, kiddo. How's the Spaniel, by the way?'

'You can ask him yourself – he's over there at the bar talking to Colum. No, don't turn round,' she hissed belatedly as Cara waved cheerily at a tall thin man with a mop of hair perched on a bar stool. After giving Cara an enthusiastic thumbs up, his eyes fixed longingly on Rosie like a starving man confronted by a juicy steak.

'Oh, go on, Rosie, give the Spaniel a chance,' Cara giggled.

Rosie stared at him for a long moment and, undeterred by her frown, the man continued gazing at her, his expression nakedly pleading. Giving him the tiniest smile, Rosie returned her attention to Cara. 'Don't encourage him! Can you believe he had the nerve to start singing outside the house at three o'clock in the morning last Saturday? I mean, who *does* that? Dad was ready to strangle him. And he would've if Mum hadn't stopped him!'

Sean Strakey – more commonly referred to as the Spaniel – would have been a shoo-in for the title of World's Most Persistent Suitor. As skinny as Rosie was curvy, Sean had been madly in love with her since school and after Rosie's latest short-lived relationship had crashed and burned, he'd been desperate to catch her eye before she moved on to the next. In the hope that big romantic gestures might do the trick, he'd launched his campaign on social media, posting pictures of himself in front of a series of London landmarks holding a hand-written poster with the words '*Rosie, pleeze go out with me!*' After the pictures had garnered almost two hundred thousand likes and her account had been inundated with people sharing the images and voicing support for Sean's efforts, he had reluctantly abandoned the cause when the usually placid Rosie threatened to have all his accounts suspended.

Cara tried not to laugh at Rosie's outraged expression. Despite his penchant for the dramatic, Sean was a lovely guy, and it would do Rosie good to go out with someone with a kind heart instead of the good-looking charmers she invariably fell for and who predictably dumped her after a few weeks.

'Why don't you do the poor man, and the rest of us, a favour and go on one date? At least that way your dad can get a good night's sleep. I know the Spaniel can be a bit of a muppet sometimes, but he's so sweet, not to mention handy. I mean, who else happily drops everything he's doing to come and help you out when you've been to Ikea?'

'Just 'cos he can build a Billy bookcase doesn't mean I should go out with him. He is *not* my type,' Rosie said implacably. 'And besides, there's no way I'm dating a guy with a smaller waist than mine.'

Cara couldn't hold back her laughter and, after a moment, Rosie smiled. Leaning forward, Cara touched Rosie's arm gently. 'Look, if you want, I can—?'

'*No!* I mean it, Cara, this isn't something for you to fix. I don't *want* to go out with Sean Strakey, I'm *not* going to go out with Sean Strakey and, for Christ's sake, can we *please* stop talking about Sean bloody Strakey!'

Cara stared at her, open-mouthed. Rosie was invariably good-natured about being teased and yet, after her initial excitement at seeing Cara, she seemed uncharacteristically on edge.

Ashanti sashayed back to the table, closely followed by a man in tight black jeans and a dark t-shirt trying to balance three tall glasses on a tray. He deposited the drinks carefully on the table and Ashanti flashed him a grateful smile, fluttering her lashes coquettishly.

'Thanks a million, um . . . Jack, was it? You wouldn't mind taking the tray back to the bar for me, would you?'

Nodding like an eager puppy, Jack wedged the tray under his arm and made a beeline for the bar. Watching him go, Rosie's scowl vanished and she laughed.

'Ash, you're impossible! The poor guy's tongue was practically hanging out of his mouth!'

Ashanti took a sip of the blue liquid in her glass and shrugged. 'Hey, it's not my fault if he thought he was in with a chance.'

Cara snorted derisively. 'Nothing to do with you batting that extra row of eyelashes at him, then?'

Ashanti narrowed her eyes and Rosie jumped in. 'All right, you two, don't start! We haven't been together for ages. Can't we just have a good time?'

'Rosie, stop trying to play peacemaker all the time,' Ashanti said irritably. 'Cara can't help being a bitch— *Ow!*' She rubbed her arm where Cara had elbowed her and glared at her.

'Good!' Cara said in satisfaction. 'Don't come for me. Now then, what's been going on with you two?'

'Not a lot,' Ashanti muttered. Then, brightening, she sat up straight and flicked her hair back. 'Actually, I take that back. Guess what? No, don't bother, I'll tell you. I've finally finished the new songs for my demo! One of the guys in the band I sang with last month has a friend who manages a studio and he can get mates' rates. So his friend has booked in a day for next week *and* he's agreed to produce the demo for me. Isn't that amazing?'

'That's awesome!' Ashanti had been chasing a record contract for years and had spent months working on her new portfolio. 'So, what's all this about Colum and music producers coming here tonight?' Cara took a sip of her drink and tried to hide the scepticism that went hand in hand with anything involving Mocktails' owner, Colum O'Shea.

After ten years of running a pub in Dublin, a huge win at the tracks had netted Colum enough to sell up and move to London. With his winnings, he had taken over the lease of an old pub in Kilburn which was even dingier than the one he had left behind. But, after a few licks of paint and the installation of a piano and a brand-new cocktail bar, Mocktails had been born – along with Colum's unshakeable conviction that it was where the next global singing sensation would be discovered. The fact that his clientele preferred Carlsberg to Cosmopolitans hadn't dented Colum's optimism and, having no doubt that talent scouts and record producers would soon haunt the club, he'd set up Mocktails' Thursday Night Live to make their lives easier.

Ashanti glanced at the chunky silver watch on her wrist and slid off her stool. 'I'd better check they've set up the backing track properly. See you guys later.'

◆ ◆ ◆

Ashanti's distinctive voice soared effortlessly around the club. The punters had fallen silent at the first low-pitched husky note, and after twenty minutes of soulful love songs and jazzy up-tempo numbers, the last notes died away to rapturous applause. Seconds later, Colum clambered up onto the stage to seize the microphone, almost falling straight off again in his excitement.

'All right, everyone, would you give it up for the beautiful Ashanti!' he yelled above the whistling and appreciative foot stamping. '*What* a voice, eh? Any music producers here, don't be shy! This girl's a superstar in the making.'

Taking a final bow, Ashanti grinned and stepped down from the stage, rushing over to her friends, where Rosie pulled them all into an exuberant hug.

'Oh my God, you were amazing!' Cara exclaimed. 'I love your voice and I can't wait for you to get your music out there.'

'Me neither! You almost had me in tears with that last song,' Rosie added, disentangling herself from Ashanti's silky locks.

They had just settled back in their seats when Colum appeared. His ruddy face was shiny with perspiration and his eyes bulged with excitement under thick, bushy brows. Twenty years in the hospitality business had yet to persuade him that crumpled baggy trousers and short-sleeved Hawaiian-patterned shirts were no one's idea of fashion, and Cara had long since given up coaxing him to update his wardrobe. He was accompanied by a tall man with narrow shoulders dressed in dark trousers and a sports jacket.

'*Ashanti!* So, what did I say, eh? What have I been after telling you all this while?' Colum bellowed, his Irish brogue even more pronounced in his elation. 'This fella here is Elliott Robbins. He's a record executive at Nine Elms Records, would you believe it? He loved your set!'

Cara, Ashanti, and Rosie looked up at Elliott in stunned silence. Ashanti was the first to react, jumping up and sticking her arm out to shake his hand.

'*Omigod!* You really liked it?' She grinned and Elliot stared at Ashanti through round blue eyes as though mesmerised by her sparkling smile.

'What's Nine Elms Records? I've never heard of them,' Cara demanded suspiciously. Years of managing events had made her a stickler for details and she always found it best to double-check things, particularly if Colum was involved.

'We're an independent label based in London. We specialise in discovering and nurturing original musical talent,' Elliott replied. He spoke with a slight stutter and barely spared Cara a glance.

'Sure, and would you be after signing her up today, then?' Colum's voice was almost cracking with eagerness as he tugged on Elliott's sleeve, oblivious to the look of distaste on the agent's face.

Elliott jerked his arm away with an impatient tut. 'First things first.' He turned back to Ashanti. 'I'd like to arrange a meeting at our offices and listen to your demo – you *do* have a demo of your music, I take it?'

Ashanti nodded enthusiastically. 'Yes, or at least I will have by next week. I'm going to record it professionally, and it'll have some of my earlier stuff and all my new material.'

Elliott pulled out a battered wallet and extracted a card embossed with black lettering. 'When it's ready, I'd love to hear it. I'm in meetings all morning tomorrow, but give me a call in the afternoon and we can set up an appointment for later next week.'

Ashanti reached for the card, holding it reverently as she read the words emblazoned across it. Then she clasped it tightly against her chest, visibly restraining herself from hugging Elliott while, pink with pride, Colum beamed and wiped his face with a large handkerchief. With a curt nod, Elliott turned on his heel and stalked off with Colum close behind.

'Was that for real? Did that just happen?' Ashanti squealed, jumping up and down in excitement.

Cara squashed her instinctive feelings of disquiet about Elliott and flung her arms around her friend. 'I guess it did, you superstar!'

'*Group hug!*' Rosie screeched, throwing her arms around her friends. 'Ash, you're going to be famous!'

Ashanti sat down and replayed Elliott's words. 'Did you hear what he said? *Original musical talent.* That's me!'

She tossed back the rest of her drink and promptly choked, spluttering wildly as she tried to catch her breath.

Cara watched her warily. 'You alright? I can slap you on the back.'

'I don't care if I'm dying, slap me and I'll slap you right back,' Ashanti croaked.

'Right then, the next round is on me,' Rosie said quickly. 'Cara? Rum and coke again?'

Cara nodded. 'I've got a heavy day tomorrow, but what the hell— I mean, heck.'

Rosie set off for the bar and Ashanti burst into laughter. 'I see someone's trying not to swear. Don't tell me the new boyfriend's changing you already? Ozzie says he's really posh.'

Cara shrugged. 'Henry doesn't care if I swear – he's probably worse than me, actually. No, Mum's been telling me off about it for years, and she had a proper go at me last month and said I was setting a bad example for Manon and Thad.' She frowned. 'When did you talk to Ozzie? He only met Henry a few days ago.'

'Yesterday, when he rang me for the hundredth time to try and persuade me to call your other brother.'

Cara sighed. 'Don't you think it's time you and Dexter sorted things out? This "break" has gone on way too long.'

Ashanti pursed her lips and shook her head vehemently. 'Look, I've told you before and I said the same thing to Ozzie, *I'm* not making that call. Until Dexter's ready to apologise for what he did to Barry, we've got nothing to talk about.'

'Ash, I'm not defending Dexter, but Barry was a total tramp for trying to take your money when he knew he hadn't arranged a single venue, let alone the tour he'd promised. Even Colum was so livid when he realised he'd been had that he very nearly set Toby and the other bouncers on the man.'

'I could have dealt with Barry Sykes myself, Cara. I didn't need Dexter punching his lights out. Dex was bloody lucky the man didn't press charges!'

Cara sighed. Her big brother's temper was legendary and, as much as she hated Barry and his slimy conman tactics that had left Colum mortified at making the introduction and Ashanti hundreds of pounds out of pocket, Cara had been even more furious at Dexter for resorting to violence. Nevertheless, Ashanti and Dex had been a couple since they were teenagers, and their separation was taking its toll on everyone.

'Why don't you at least talk—?'

'No. Cara, can you please just accept that this is one thing even you can't fix! Dexter is funny and kind and he can be a total sweetheart and, yes, I know he thought he was trying to protect me, but he needs to stop flying off the handle so easily. It feels like ever since— well, you-know-who left, the Dex I fell in love with has slowly gone missing. Maybe you and I should have told him the truth about Ryan because I'm so tired of dealing with the fallout. Which means that until and unless Dex is ready to open up and deal with what's really going on with him, we've got nothing to talk about.'

They sat in silence until Rosie returned, holding three glasses in her small hands. She set the drinks down carefully on the table and looked warily from Cara's frown to Ashanti's set features.

'Now, what? Honestly, can't I leave you two alone for five minutes without an argument?'

'No one's arguing with anyone,' Cara retorted. 'Let's just say I knew no good would come of my brother and one of my best friends getting involved with each other. But then, no one listens to me, at least not until there's a problem I have to sort out.'

Clearly keen to change the subject, Rosie tapped Cara's hand. 'So, tell us more about Henry, then. He sounds wonderful and it can't hurt that he's loaded. He must be something special if you've finally decided to get back on the relationship horse again, not to mention ignoring your friends for weeks.'

'Yeah, really,' Ashanti interjected. 'What kind of girl dumps her friends just because a man comes along?'

'The kind that's getting *loads* of bedroom action,' Cara said with a cheerful, unapologetic smile.

'Well, whatever he's doing to you, you're definitely looking well on it,' Ashanti admitted grudgingly. 'Look at you all sparkly-eyed and bouncy. But I don't get how you've only just found out he's super rich. You've been holed up together for weeks! What were you guys talking about all that time?'

Cara shrugged. 'Everything and nothing, it's hard to explain. You know, big things like our hopes and dreams, and silly things like what our day at work was like, and sometimes complete nonsense . . . and, of course, having *tons* of sex,' she added.

Rosie giggled. 'Cara!'

'Well, it's true! We avoided talking about families and bringing all the baggage of our pasts into the room. To be honest, up until last weekend, it was like we were in our own little world and nothing outside was allowed in.'

Cara's expression switched from dreamy to exasperated as Colum rushed up to their table, almost panting with excitement.

'Did you get an eyeful of that one?' he said triumphantly, pulling up an empty chair. 'And aren't I always telling you that Mocktails is crawling with talent scouts? He'll be the making of us – er, I mean, you – Ashanti!'

'Isn't that what you said about Barry Sykes?' Cara said darkly.

'Sure, and wasn't that one an eejit, telling us all those lies about being a concert promoter?' Colum reddened with renewed indignation. 'No, no, this one's a proper record executive – you saw his card, didn't you? Take it from me, this time it'll be grand!'

Cara sighed inwardly. Ashanti had a wonderful voice, and it was only a matter of time before she got a break, but after the Barry Sykes fiasco, Cara was especially wary of sharks trying to muscle in on her talented friend. However, knowing how badly Ashanti wanted a recording contract and reluctant to burst her bubble, Cara concentrated on her drink and the performance poet on stage while Ashanti and Colum speculated excitedly about what signing with Nine Elms Records could mean.

Rosie had fallen into an uncharacteristic silence and when Colum finally took himself off to announce the next act, she took a long sip of her drink and cleared her throat loudly.

'Going back to the subject of friends who date our relatives . . . um, I really didn't want to say anything to ruin the evening, but I'd better come clean about my cousin.'

Cara and Ashanti turned in unison to stare at her and Rosie immediately flushed and ducked her gaze to avoid their eyes. Rosie was as transparent as an onion skin and as Cara took in her friend's obvious discomfort, the mild buzz from the two rum and cokes turned into a queasy feeling in the pit of her stomach.

Ashanti frowned. 'Rosie, I really hope you're not talking about who I think you are? You know the rules and that you-know-who isn't allowed as a topic for discussion.'

Rosie opened her mouth, looked up at Cara, and then flushed an even deeper red before dropping her gaze again.

Staring at Rosie's lowered head, Cara fought the impulse to shake whatever she was hiding out of her. The queasiness in her gut intensified and the volume of the music from the band that was now on stage seemed to fade.

'What the hell, Rosie! What's going on?' Cara's words came out through lips that suddenly felt as stiff as cardboard.

Rosie took another long sip of her drink and thumped the glass down on the table. Still unable to meet Cara's eyes, she stared down at the table and mumbled, 'Ryan called Mum yesterday . . . from Dublin.'

'O-kay . . . we know that's where he is. So . . .?'

Rosie gulped, her face crimson with guilt. 'The thing is . . . um, well . . . he's coming back to London.'

7

RURAL RETREAT

Cara slipped her fingers under the strap of the seat belt, silently cursing her decision to wear a silk dress. The whole point of wearing a smart frock and heels was to impress her boyfriend's parents and the last thing she needed was to arrive at Henry's family home looking a crumpled mess. With a sigh, she pulled the belt aside to relieve the pressure on the soft fabric. If making a good first impression came at the risk of being flung against the windscreen in the event of an accident, then so be it.

Henry took his eyes off the road briefly to give her a reassuring smile. 'Relax, we're almost there.'

She bit her lip. Being told to relax when you felt as tense as a cat facing down a rabid Rottweiler was almost as annoying as being told to calm down when you wanted to rip off someone's head. Trying not to let Henry's well-meaning advice make her feel more jittery, Cara stared dolefully out of the window at the scenery whizzing by. Since passing Swindon an hour earlier, the landscape had been one of endless rolling hills of green interspersed with flashes of purple and yellow fields. Although undeniably beautiful, the relentless openness of the English countryside without a Starbucks or a McDonald's in sight was a far cry from Kensal Green and more than a little unnerving. For just a moment, she longed for the vibrant, noisy high road outside her flat and the traffic-choked streets she had left behind. It wasn't that she hated the rolling hills of the Cotswolds or the miles of verdant countryside exactly, but it was all so far outside her comfort zone that she didn't quite know how to feel. Or how to control her apprehension at meeting Henry's parents. Not for the first time, she wondered why she had let her boyfriend talk her into this visit. She could barely pronounce Gloucestershire and didn't have the first idea how to behave around an earl's daughter. It was one thing watching *Downton Abbey*, but quite another going to stay there!

Cara ran a hand through her hair before realising what she was doing and hastily smoothed the carefully tamed curls back into place. *Christ, I can't even touch my own hair!*

'Why did I let you talk me into coming with you?' she grumbled.

'Well, it's only fair, don't you think?' Henry said equably, his eyes fixed on the road ahead. The sleeves of his pale-blue shirt were rolled back and revealed muscular forearms with a sprinkling of blond hair. 'I've met your family, and now my parents and sisters really want to meet you.'

'Yes, but *my* parents aren't millionaires and nobility,' she muttered.

Henry glanced across at her. 'Cara, my family aren't snobs, you know. And, in case you're wondering, they aren't racists, either.'

'Henry!' In her indignation, Cara forgot about her dress and leaned forward to peer at his frowning profile. 'I never suggested they were! No one as lovely as you could have been brought up by bigots. I just meant . . . you know . . .' She tailed off and then tried again. 'Let's face it, I'm not exactly the type of girl you've brought home to your mother before.'

'If it makes you feel any better, I haven't brought any girl home to my mother.' Henry grinned. 'So, look on the bright side, you'll be setting the standard for any future girls I decide to bring.'

Despite herself, Cara giggled and the tension in the car eased. 'Very funny, but seriously, have you never taken a girl home?'

'Not really, or at least not for ages. Mother can be a bit—' Cara looked at him with raised eyebrows.

'A bit what?'

Henry shrugged. 'I suppose she's a little overprotective of me sometimes. Honestly, I wouldn't worry about it, it's just her way. She's got her reasons, but I promise she's fine when you get to know her. Forget the nobility bit and just think of her as a mum.'

Well, my mum isn't called Lady Beverley, so that doesn't really help. Feeling not the slightest bit reassured, Cara sucked in a deep breath. 'I'm not usually the nervous type, but this is a big deal. What if she . . . they hate me?'

'Just be yourself, and they'll love you.'

The car picked up speed and Henry returned his attention to the motorway while she resumed her scrutiny of the green hills, feeling a little more heartened. It was also a relief to see Henry relaxed and back to his old self. He had made no further reference to Ryan and, since returning from Manchester, things appeared to be back to normal. While Cara was keenly aware she owed Henry the whole truth, she was already haunted enough by thoughts of Ryan without speaking him into existence. Rosie's bombshell announcement at the club had rocked Cara to her core, leaving her terrified of bumping into the last man she ever wanted to see. But after two weeks of skulking around doorways, she had forced herself to put him out of her mind. Ryan had already taken too much from her and the best place for him was in her Pandora's box of memories that needed to stay locked.

Bored of the scenery, Cara wriggled in her seat, manoeuvring around the seat belt to avoid strangling herself. 'Okay, take me through who everyone is again. I want to make sure I get their names right.'

'Mother is Isobel, Dad is Douglas. Sisters are Imogen and Fleur,' Henry recited obligingly, his eyes fixed on the road ahead.

Ah yes, Imogen. Cara had told Henry about her encounter with Primrose Wynter, leaving out Primrose's questions about their relationship. If, as Cara suspected, Imogen was behind Primrose's interrogation because Henry hadn't chosen to share much information about Cara, was that a bad sign? Leaning back against the headrest, Cara decided to leave Imogen out of it and settle for the safer option. 'Tell me about Fleur – how old is she?'

'Fourteen. She'll be fifteen a week before Christmas. She's a sweet kid and a bit of a child genius. Her IQ is phenomenal, and she runs rings around her Maths and Science teachers.'

'Oh,' Cara said, intrigued. 'Where does she go to school?'

Henry gave a short laugh. 'That's a good question and a bit of a sore point at home. Fleur goes to the local school, but her teachers say they can't give her the kind of push she needs, so my mother has signed her up for Imogen's old school.'

Pemberton Hall. In a flash Cara remembered the unconcealed pride with which Primrose had referred to her school.

'Why's it a sore point?' Cara wondered aloud. Primrose had been almost reverential about her alma mater, barely concealing her irritation when it was clear Cara had never heard of it.

Henry grimaced and tapped the steering wheel with his thumb. 'My little sister is horse mad and hates the idea of going to boarding school and leaving her bloody horse behind. Up until now, she's managed to wheedle my father – who's complete putty in her hands – into letting her stay at Lakeland High. But the school has

74

made it clear she needs to be on an accelerated Maths and Science track which they can't offer, and Mother's determined that she starts next term at Pemberton Hall. They've been at loggerheads over the whole thing for the past couple of months, with poor Dad caught in the middle.'

Henry fell into silence, and from beneath her lashes, Cara surveyed his profile and the small frown of concentration between his eyes. Being driven by Henry didn't involve pressing the invisible brake under her foot, which was her usual reaction whenever she sat in Ozzie or Dexter's cars, and despite the needle of the speedometer quivering around the 70mph mark, she felt completely relaxed. Was it Henry's solidity and self-control that made her feel so safe and taken care of, she wondered, or the smooth and controlled way he did everything? Well, not quite everything. Cara smiled, her mind flicking back to the previous night when Henry's demonstration of his wilder side had made waking up for today's early start incredibly difficult.

'Are we there yet?' Her thumb was sore from holding onto the seat belt and with each mile of countryside they drove through, her nerves were growing exponentially.

'You sound like a five-year-old.' He laughed. 'We'll be in Little Duckworth soon. That's our closest market town, and the house isn't too far from there.' Henry glanced at her with a grin. 'I bet you were one of those maddening kids that pester their parents on long drives.'

'We didn't exactly take long drives when we were kids,' Cara retorted. 'Unless you count getting the bus 189 to Oxford Street.'

He raised a disbelieving eyebrow. 'Are you serious? Didn't you take trips outside London when you were younger?'

'Only school trips. Oh, and years ago when Dad's – Gerald's – parents were still alive, we went to Cornwall a few times. Dexter used to drive us crazy on the way wanting to play "I Spy" all the time, and we had to keep opening the windows to stop Ozzie throwing up.'

'What about when your father was alive?' Henry asked gently. 'You don't seem to talk about him.'

Cara shrugged. 'I was only ten when he died and, to be honest, I don't really remember him that well. He was a musician and he used to tour a lot with his band, so even before the accident he was killed in, he really wasn't around that much. I still remember little things like how he'd sit on our beds and play his guitar to wake us up in the morning. Dexter remembers a lot more than I do, which is just as well since Mum hardly ever talks about him.'

She fell silent for a moment and reflected on the past. 'Sometimes I feel like I've blocked out a lot because losing him was so traumatic for everyone, especially Mum. After he died, she couldn't stop crying. I remember her hiding in my bedroom sobbing her heart out and thinking we couldn't hear her. I used to make her tea because that's what people did on the telly when someone was upset, but then she'd drink the tea and cry anyway. There was this one time when Mum was washing up after dinner, and she just sort of crumpled over the sink and started wailing, like, really loudly. She had tears pouring down her face and I still remember the water from the tap spraying everywhere.'

Cara stared out of the window, her mind latching onto the memory of the evening she had realised her mum wasn't invincible and even though she was only a child, it would be her job to hold things together. It had also been the moment when she'd finally understood that her father would never again stride through the front door of their flat with his guitar slung over his back, distributing toys with deep, hearty chuckles, and producing sweets from his pockets like a magician.

'Looking back, I really don't know how Mum managed. She was only thirty-six when Dad died and left her a widow with two kids to look after.'

'That must have been tough.' Henry gave her hand a sympathetic squeeze and returned his hand to the wheel to steer off the motorway.

'It was,' Cara said soberly. 'Mum's parents had moved back to Ghana a few years before it happened, and most of Dad's family live in Barbados. It all got a bit mad after the funeral with both my grandmothers competing to be the most supportive. Thelma, Dad's mother, refused to go back to Barbados and insisted on staying on to help Mum out. Which, of course, put Grandma Maggie's back up, because if anyone was going to be on hand for her daughter, it had to be her. The next thing we knew, she'd packed poor Grandad off to Africa and moved in with us as well.'

'Two grandmothers in one house? That must have been an experience.'

Henry chuckled. The road narrowed into a single lane, and he brought the car to a crawl as they approached a queue of slow-moving vehicles.

Cara laughed. 'Now, *that* I remember! When they weren't arguing with each other, they insisted on cooking. Honestly, it got to the point where they'd made so much food, we couldn't close the fridge door and Mum literally had to beg them to stop. Individually, they're lovely, but together . . . not so much. They both come over every year, but, after Manon was born, Dad got so fed up with their bickering that he threatened to walk out. So now, Mum makes a point of only letting one of them visit at a time.'

Henry inched the car forward. 'Your mother and Gerald seem very happy.'

Cara was silent for a moment. 'Gerald was a lifesaver in more ways than one. After our father died, Dexter started hanging around with a group of boys in the area.'

'You mean like a gang?'

Cara shrugged. 'They might as well have been. Most of them came from the same estate as us in South Kilburn and they called themselves the Boxers. It was all pretty harmless stuff in the beginning, mostly mucking about at the bus station and getting kicked out of shops. But one or two of the boys started to get out of hand and Mum was terrified Dex was going to get caught up in something. She began getting calls from school about his behaviour and it was constant arguments at home.'

'Did he get into trouble?'

Cara sighed. 'No, but it wasn't for want of trying. He was devastated by Dad's death, and he just felt angry all the time. I spent half my time dragging him away from fights, even though most of the boys were twice my size. One time, Mum had to go to work and she warned Dex not to leave the flat, but of course he snuck out anyway. I didn't want him to get into trouble, so I went looking for him. He was standing with some of the Boxers outside a school on the other side of the estate and, just as I got there, a couple of the other boys jumped this poor kid coming out of the gates and started roughing him up. So I start yelling at the boys to leave him alone and Dexter tries to pull me away before they start on me. At the same time, the other Boxers are jeering at Dex for not controlling his little sister. Then Dad – Gerald – who was a teacher at the school, comes out as all this is going on. The other boys vanish, but Dex is still trying to calm me down. So, at this point Dad's furious and gets Dex by the collar, demands to know where he lives, and insists on marching him home to report him to his parents. He hauls Dex back to the flat just as Mum gets home from work, but then he takes one look at her and completely forgets what he was there for. Six months later, they get married. Ta-da!' She waved her hand with a dramatic flourish.

Henry whistled. 'Wow, now *there's* a love story! What about Ozzie, though? How did he take to having a new family?'

'Ozzie's mum had died years before and he was an only child, so he couldn't have been happier. He's a year younger than Dex and he still worships the ground Dexter walks on – he's not very bright, bless him! After Mum and Dad got married, we moved out of the estate and went to live with Dad and Ozzie in Cricklewood. A few years later, Thaddeus was born, and soon after that Manon came along.'

Intent on relating past events, Cara had taken scant notice of the changing scenery until Henry made a sharp turn. He drove through two huge black wrought-iron gates into what was obviously a private road and her stomach plummeted with nerves. Lined with trees, the grey Tarmac ribbon of road wound its way through acres of woodland and open fields and, as Henry nudged the car up a slight incline, Cara couldn't help gasping at the sight of the house drawing closer by the minute. They drove up to a gravelled circular driveway and her eyes widened as they fell on an enormous water feature dominating the island in the centre of the driveway. She rolled down her window and stared in fascination at the delicately sculpted scales of a huge bronze fish captured in mid-leap with a steady stream of water gurgling from its open mouth.

Henry parked in front of the house and switched off the engine with a satisfied smile. 'Welcome to Oakley Manor, my family home.' His gaze met Cara's dumbfounded expression and his smile faltered.

'Hey . . . are you okay?'

'This isn't a *home*,' she squeaked. 'Henry, it's a . . . flipping mansion!'

He followed her gaze as if seeing the imposing stately house with its tall, elegant windows, flowering wisteria, and sweeping flight of stone steps for the first time. Then he shrugged, looking amused. 'It's not as big inside as it looks from out here. I'll show you around when we've said our hellos. Come on, let's go in.'

Henry opened the car door and swung his legs out, shoes crunching on the gravel. He took her small case and a black holdall from the boot before coming around to where she sat, but other than releasing the offending seat belt, Cara made no attempt to move.

Henry dropped the bags onto the gravel and poked his head through the open window.

'Are you planning to get out of the car at any point?' he asked, sounding genuinely curious.

Cara took a deep breath and then shook her head. 'Probably not.'

'Okay,' he said reasonably. 'Give me a few minutes and I'll get the family out here to say hello.' He picked up the cases and turned towards the house.

Cara squealed. '*Henry!* Wait . . . don't just leave me here!'

When he continued walking, she scrambled out of the car and slammed the door, heels sinking into the gravel as she chased after him. When he reached the shallow steps leading up to the house, he turned and waited for her to catch up and then leaned down to kiss her gently on the lips.

'Relax, sweetheart, they'll love you. I promise.'

Nodding at the reassurance in his voice, and praying that the back of her silk dress hadn't creased up like an accordion, Cara made her way up the steps, wobbling slightly in her unfamiliar heels. Even she knew better than to arrive at Henry's parents' house for the first time in a pair of Doc Martens.

Henry turned to Cara with a smile. 'Ready?'

As ready as I'll ever be!

She took a deep breath and nodded.

8

A Noble Affair

Henry rang a discreetly placed doorbell, disturbing a fat bumblebee which buzzed angrily between the huge stone urns potted with yellow and pink begonias standing on either side of the door. While they waited, Cara surveyed the beautifully landscaped gardens and well-tended flower beds abundant with colourful shrubs and blossoms, and breathed in the gently perfumed breeze wafting off the flowers.

'Henry, darling!' The door was flung open and a slim woman in a white cotton skirt and lacy knit top stepped out with arms extended and swept him into a hug. Henry returned the embrace, kissing her on both cheeks.

'Hello, Mother. You're looking very well – as ever,' he remarked with a smile.

Henry's mother was of average height, and beautiful. Her face was a perfect oval with high cheekbones and her eyes a shade of blue so deep, they were almost violet. With shoulder-length blonde hair held back from a smooth forehead by a blue hairband that matched the colour of her sweater, she projected an elegance that immediately reminded Cara of the actresses in her grandmother Thelma's coffee-table book of 1950s Hollywood.

'Mother, this is Cara,' Henry announced, urging Cara forward. 'Cara, my mother, Lady Isobel Fitzherbert,' he added with a grin, 'if we're going to be formal.'

Wondering if she had imagined the slight widening of blue eyes as Henry's mother turned towards her, Cara fixed a determined smile on her face. A slightly awkward pause ensued, and, taking her cue from his mother's silence that they were indeed going to be formal, Cara extended her hand politely.

'It's a pleasure to meet you, Lady Isobel.'

The handshake was firm, if slightly cool, and followed by a few moments of open inspection by eyes that were speculative but not unfriendly. Then Henry's mother gave an infinitesimal nod and turned to Henry.

'You weren't exaggerating, darling. She really is lovely.'

Lady Isobel's voice was low and melodic with the same clipped precision as Henry's, and Cara flushed, silenced by the unexpected compliment. As Henry led the way, she followed him, heels clacking against the polished dark-wood floors, into a circular hallway with creamy-white walls. In the centre was a marble table on which a tall crystal vase displayed an exquisite floral display that gave off a sweet, almost spicy, fragrance. It felt as grand as the lobby of an exclusive country hotel and Cara stared up in wonder at a huge glass chandelier hanging from the high ceiling. Across the hall, a few steps away from a wide, sweeping staircase that circled up to the first floor, stood an imposing grandfather clock with a bronze pendulum swishing back and forth.

Henry dropped the bags and looked around expectantly. 'Where is everyone? Isn't Imogen here?'

'Not yet, darling. She rang a short while ago to say she's on her way. Some last-minute errand she had to run for her boss who, I must say, sounds rather awful. I suppose we should simply be grateful she has a job although, quite honestly, I still don't understand what she does.'

Lady Isobel tweaked a flower in the already perfect display. 'Fleur's around, though. She went riding early today so she could be here to meet you. I expect your father will be home shortly. Max and Caesar were getting a bit restless, so he took them out for a run. He mentioned meeting Jenkins to talk about something to do with the estate, but hopefully that shouldn't take too long.'

Feeling as though she had suddenly stepped into *Downton Abbey*, Cara immediately pictured a burly gamekeeper in a tweed cap tugging on a forelock. With the flowers arranged to her satisfaction, Lady Isobel turned her attention back to Henry and her eyes softened. Watching her reach up to stroke his cheek, it was obvious to Cara that Lady Isobel adored her son.

'*Henry!* Oh my God, you're finally here!' A flash of honey-coloured brown hair and long legs in khaki jodhpurs suddenly exploded through the door and flew past Cara to land with a thump on Henry.

'*Christ, Fleur!* You nearly knocked me over!' Henry staggered back under the weight of the teenage girl clutching him round the neck. Regaining his balance, he hugged her and then gently disentangled himself.

'It's good to see you, you little monster,' he said with an indulgent smile. 'Say hello to Cara,' he added, taking his sister by the shoulders and swivelling her around to face his girlfriend.

Fleur was tall for her age and wore an outsized grey t-shirt that had seen better days, along with somewhat grubby riding trousers that she'd tucked into dusty boots. She had a pretty kitten-like face with a neat little nose and a pink rosebud of a mouth. In contrast to her mother's pale blondeness, Fleur's hair was a deep chestnut streaked with gold and hung thick and straight down to her waist.

Her blue eyes, however, were identical to Lady Isobel's and proceeded to subject Cara to the same scrutiny as her mother had done a few minutes earlier. Biting her lip to hide her amusement, Cara held her gaze steadily.

Without warning, Fleur lunged forward and seized Cara in a tight embrace. Taken aback by the unexpectedly warm greeting, Cara cautiously hugged her back, feeling the girl's strong muscles under her thin top and inhaling the faint aroma of what she hoped was mud.

'Gosh, you're so pretty! Just like Henry described you!' Fleur exclaimed when she finally released Cara. A sunny smile lit up her delicate features. 'I *love* your hair . . . I've always wanted curly hair!'

'Why don't we go into the drawing room and have some tea,' Lady Isobel interrupted smoothly. 'You must be parched after the drive down.'

She turned to her daughter with a frown of disapproval. 'Darling, do go and change first, you look such a mess. Oh, and please tell Mrs Soames we're ready for tea.'

Fleur's smile disappeared and, for a moment, she looked ready to argue. After a glance at Henry, however, she appeared to think better of it, and, with an exaggerated roll of her eyes and a toss of her hair, she stalked off.

'Henry, take Cara's bags up to the Yellow Room, would you?'

Henry raised an eyebrow, and Lady Isobel responded with a bland smile. 'Darling, you can do whatever you like with your sleeping arrangements when you're in London but do remember that Fleur is still an impressionable teenager.'

Cara watched Henry pick up the bags with an exasperated expression remarkably like Fleur's and she suppressed the giggle threatening to erupt.

As he disappeared up the stairs, Cara followed Lady Isobel into a large sunny room where a smaller version of the hallway chandelier hung from a high moulded ceiling. The walls of the room were painted a pale peach and were the perfect background for the gilt-framed landscapes and antique family portraits. As Cara took in the plush floral rugs, overstuffed sofas and polished sideboards topped with silver-framed photographs and china figurines, her first impression was that Lady Isobel certainly loved flowers. The drawing room was filled to bursting point with fresh flowers; some displayed in large vases while smaller arrangements were scattered between the photos and knickknacks on display. At the far end of the room, half-open glass doors led out to a wide stone terrace overlooking stunning views of rolling green lawns, tall blossoming trees and wildflower meadows.

Cara's heels sank into the soft pile carpet as she walked slowly around the room examining the photographs. Other than a formal portrait of the whole family and a large snapshot of two Great Danes, who she guessed must be Max and Caesar, the pictures were mostly of the three Fitzherbert children. Cara smiled at one of Henry in a graduation cap and gown sporting a huge grin. In the adjoining frame, he looked rather more sober in a dark gown and white wig, clutching a rolled-up certificate.

Lady Isobel, standing close beside her, remarked with a distinct note of pride, 'That was taken when he was called to the Bar.'

Cara spotted a large black-and-white picture on top of the oak sideboard, and gasped. Wearing a filthy rugby shirt and shorts, Henry was sitting on the shoulders of his equally muddy teammates holding aloft a large silver trophy and grinning triumphantly through mud-streaked features.

Lady Isobel followed her gaze, and a shadow crossed her face. 'He looks so carefree, doesn't he? I used to love watching him play rugby, although at times it could be quite terrifying. But Henry was so fast that whenever he had the ball, it was like watching a greyhound race.'

She sighed. 'Now all he does is work and I rather think he's forgotten how to enjoy himself after what happened.'

Lady Isobel looked at Cara for a long moment and, slightly unnerved by the woman's vivid-blue eyes, Cara fought the urge to deny any responsibility for Henry's workaholic tendencies.

Just as the silence was becoming unbearable, Lady Isobel continued, 'Although, that rather seems to have changed since he met you. He's been sounding more like his old self again. You know, before—'

She broke off at the sound of a soft knock on the door. A middle-aged woman carrying a silver tray laden with a large teapot, cups and saucers came in. She walked with a slight limp and Lady Isobel hastened to help her.

'Here, Mrs Soames, let me take that! You should have asked Henry to bring it in. You really shouldn't be carrying heavy trays just yet,' she scolded gently. Nudging aside a shallow bowl of white azaleas, she set the tray on a sturdy table.

'Mrs Soames, this is Cara Nightingale, Henry's friend. They'll be staying until tomorrow.'

Dressed in a cotton dress with short sleeves that revealed heavily freckled arms, Mrs Soames' equally freckled face crinkled into a warm smile that showed off large white teeth.

'Pleasure to meet you, I'm sure, miss.'

Lady Isobel swiftly set the teacups onto saucers. 'Mrs Soames lives in Little Duckworth and has worked for us for— how long is it now?'

'Oh, my goodness, it's coming on for thirty years, milady! Ever since Mr Henry was a young boy. Full of mischief, he was, miss.' Mrs Soames gave another smile. 'I'll just fetch the sandwiches and cakes, milady,' she added, heading back towards the door.

'Please have a seat, Cara. Let's have some tea while we wait for the others. Do you take sugar?'

Cara shook her head and perched at the far end of the sofa, wondering how to bring the subject back to what Henry's mother had been saying before Mrs Soames' arrival and which sounded like something she expected Cara to know. She watched as Lady Isobel poured a splash of milk followed by a stream of golden tea into one of the fine china cups on the tray, setting it down next to Cara before pouring herself a cup.

Just as Cara opened her mouth to clear up the mystery, Henry walked in carrying a large platter piled with sandwiches, scones and tiny cakes. 'I just rescued these from Mrs Soames. Cara, I hope you're hungry because there's a ton of food here.'

Placing the dish next to the teapot, Henry picked up a sandwich and took a huge bite.

'Henry!' His mother looked at him reproachfully. 'Where are your manners? Pass Cara a plate and offer her some sandwiches. Cara, please excuse my son, he really should know better.'

With an unrepentant grin, Henry carried the platter of sandwiches over to where Cara sat, before wolfing down the remains of the one he'd started and pouring himself a cup of tea.

Suddenly ravenous after the long drive and her earlier bout of nerves, Cara munched on a crust-free egg-and-cress sandwich, enjoying the serenity of the room. Bright rays of sunshine streamed through the open windows and Lady Isobel seemed happy enough to sip her tea in the comfortable silence, giving Cara time to take in the elegant drawing room.

The baby grand piano, gilt-framed wall paintings, crystal flower vases and heavy silver photo frames were in a different league to her humble Ikea-bought furnishings, and Cara tried to absorb everything, knowing her friends would demand details on her return. Leaving no room for doubt, Ashanti had already texted, *Make sure you report back on how the other half lives!*

9

Family Matters

Cara was on her second cup of tea when the thud of fast-approaching footsteps cut through the stillness of the room. A second later, the door was thrust open and a tall man with a shock of dark hair strode in.

'Dad!' Henry seized his father in an unselfconsciously warm embrace, and the older man patted his son on the back before turning his attention to Cara, who was doing her best not to stare.

'So, this is Cara!' She jumped at the unexpectedly loud voice and her teacup rattled nervously against the saucer. Depositing the cup safely on a side table, she stood up with hand outstretched, but just as Fleur had done earlier, Henry's father pulled her into a bear hug instead.

'Welcome to our home!' With the same muscular build as his son, and bushy, grey-flecked eyebrows that softened a craggy forehead above a patrician nose, Henry's father looked exactly as she would have imagined the lord of a manor, and he seemed so delighted to see her that she couldn't help returning his smile.

'Thank you, Mr Fitzherbert. It's very kind of you to have invited me.'

'Call me Douglas!' came the hearty reply. 'You're a lucky sod, Henry. She's every bit as gorgeous as you said!'

For the second time since her arrival, Cara flushed with embarrassment. Being told you wouldn't break a mirror was about as close as anyone in her family ever got to saying you looked nice.

Douglas went over to his wife and squeezed her shoulder affectionately. 'How are you, m'dear? Awfully sorry I'm late. It all took rather longer than I expected. The dogs got pretty wet down by the stream, and I had to give them a good rub down.'

Neither Henry nor his mother appeared to mind the volume as Douglas's deep voice thundered out a stream of patter. Barely pausing for breath, he picked up a sandwich, the delicate square of bread looking tiny in his large hand, and bit into it forcefully, finishing it in two bites.

'Jenkins is on the warpath and absolutely insists we fight the blasted council about that public access ruling. Says he's fed up with bloody hikers and ramblers wandering into the grounds from the footpath. If that's not bad enough, some of them act like it's some damned lovers' lane! Can you believe Jenkins caught a young couple going at it the other day? I mean, really, what—'

Douglas stooped to peer into the teapot and grimaced before continuing with his stream of verbal consciousness. Pacing up and down the room with all the calmness of a hurricane, he paused long enough to open a polished mahogany cabinet and extract a wide-bottomed whisky decanter. He poured out a generous measure into two crystal tumblers and handed one to his son before taking an appreciative sip from the other.

'Good drive up, Henry?'

'Not bad at all, Dad. Traffic was a bit slow on the motorway coming up to Swindon, but we were fine after that. The worst part was crawling past those roadworks after Gloucester. What the hell's going on there?'

Douglas tossed back the contents of his glass and scowled. 'It's all down to the local bloody council. Those bastards couldn't organise a piss-up in a brewery! It's causing a hell of a nuisance with getting the farm supplies in and out. Three of our lorries were stuck on the road for over two hours last week and Jenkins almost blew a bloody gasket! He's all for threatening them with legal action if they don't damn well get on with it!'

If Mum thinks my swearing's bad, she should meet Douglas, Cara thought as she finished off her tea, quietly impressed by the curses that flowed so effortlessly off Douglas's tongue.

Fleur bounded in, putting an abrupt end to Douglas's stream of invective. She had changed into a clean navy vest top and a pair of skinny jeans that emphasised her lean legs, and her eyes lit up when she saw her father.

'Daddy!'

Douglas beamed and set his glass on the sideboard, an inch away from the coaster his wife had quietly placed on the polished mahogany. He hugged his daughter and then retrieved his glass and returned to the cabinet for a refill. 'Jenkins said he saw you out on Caramel, Fleur. How did you get on?'

Fleur flopped into the nearest armchair. 'He's such a darling, Daddy. I took him out by the woods for some practice jumps and he was brilliant! I can't wait to see how he does in the competition next month.'

Her mother frowned. 'Fleur, I do wish you wouldn't go off into the woods by yourself. Surely you can practise your jumps in the field next to the stables. If anything happened to you out there . . . well, it's so far off the beaten path . . .'

Fleur's mouth tightened, and she stomped over to the table and picked up a sandwich, cramming half of it into her mouth and chewing fiercely before speaking.

'Caramel gets bored with jumping the same old fences. Honestly, Mother, being out in the woods is no big deal and, besides, I'm not on my own, I'm with Caramel.'

'A horse can't exactly call for help if anything happens to you, can it?' her mother murmured.

Fleur curled up in the armchair, finishing her sandwich. 'Well, I'm sorry if I'd rather ride my horse than play croquet all day. I don't suppose you'd have any problem with me if I loved that ridiculous game as much as you do!'

'Fleur, that's enough,' Henry said firmly. 'Mother's only concerned about you.'

His sister shrugged defiantly. 'All Mother's concerned about is her precious croquet. Caramel and I are competing in a few weeks, and we've got to keep practising to have any chance of winning the Junior Lakes trophy.'

'It would be rather nice if you showed this much enthusiasm for your education, Fleur,' her mother interjected.

Douglas cleared his throat loudly and poured yet another shot of scotch into his glass. Holding the decanter, he looked across at Henry with the hunted expression of one who knew that war was about to break out but was powerless to stop it.

'Er, Henry . . . another?'

Clearly unmoved by his father's silent cry for help, Henry shook his head and took Cara's hand to pull her up. 'No thanks, Dad. I think we'll take a walk. I promised Cara I'd show her round.'

Although she was loath to relinquish her front row seat to what was shaping up to be an interesting match between mother and daughter, Henry clearly couldn't leave the room soon enough and reluctantly, Cara allowed herself to be led away.

The drama continued with Imogen's arrival a couple of hours later. Tall and slim with a blonde beauty that echoed her mother's, Imogen's frigid demeanour was a far cry from her father and sister's

91

warm welcome. Everything about her screamed haughty; from the cream linen shift dress that could have come straight off the pages of *Vogue* to the cool, barely there handshake and ice-blue eyes that raked dismissively over Cara's creased dress, her expression clearly consigning it to the bin of high street quality. Primrose had doubtless relayed a detailed account of their meeting because from the initial quickly concealed flash of surprise on Imogen's face, high street or not, Cara's silk dress and heels were clearly not what the other girl was expecting.

After exchanging perfunctory greetings with Henry, taking a few sips of black tea, and reciting a litany of complaints about the drive from London, Imogen finally unbent enough to speak directly to Cara. From her barrage of questions, it was immediately obvious that Henry had told her very little about his girlfriend and after a few minutes, visibly irritated by his sister's inquisition, he unceremoniously shut her up.

'For Christ's sake, give it a rest, Imogen! Cara isn't here for a bloody interview.'

Imogen flushed defensively. 'Well it's not as if you bring a girl home every day, so you can't blame me for being curious.'

'There's curious and there's downright nosey!'

They glared at each other until Fleur, who had clearly had enough of her sister, jumped up.

'I'm taking Cara to see my trophies,' she announced. Before anyone could object, she hooked her arm into Cara's and led her off to Douglas's study. As Cara tried to keep up with Fleur's breathless commentary on the impressive display of horse-riding trophies, she couldn't help reflecting that the little she'd seen of the aristocracy in action was proving a real eye-opener.

10

Fine Dining

In her bedroom later that evening, dressed and almost ready for dinner, Cara gave her lashes a final coat of mascara and peered into the gilt-edged mirror on the dressing table, hoping she hadn't overdone the blusher. While the Yellow Room was gorgeous with buttercup-coloured walls and curtains and a cheerful daffodil-print bedspread, the discreet lighting was no help when applying make-up.

Oakley Manor was easily the biggest house she had ever visited, Cara reflected, unscrewing a tube of tinted lip gloss. Henry had walked her through two enormous reception rooms, each with marble fireplaces, heavy floor-length curtains, antique rugs and in one room, a huge tapestry that took up almost an entire wall. The tour had included a peek into a dining room with high ceilings, a huge, highly polished dining table, and the obligatory chandelier, as well as a spacious library with mahogany panelling, wall-mounted lamps, and bookshelves stacked with hardback volumes. Cara had tried not to gawp at the full-sized billiards table in the games room and had fallen in love with the brightly lit family den filled with potted plants and huge, squashy sofas arranged around a massive television screen.

As Henry had pointed out, Oakley Manor did feel smaller inside than appeared on first sight and, despite the grandeur of the antiques and artwork that filled almost every room, it was far more homely than Cara had expected. Away from the formal drawing and reception rooms, copies of Fleur's dog-eared horse magazines, school textbooks, and the occasional stray item of clothing strewn around the house, gave it a lived-in feel. While Henry's family had been welcoming – well, except the snobby Imogen – Cara felt distinctly out of her comfort zone. Even the idea of changing for dinner, a concept unheard of in her neck of the woods, was a reminder of how different her boyfriend's world was to hers.

With a sigh, she stood up to take a last look in the mirror and smooth down the long, black jersey dress Henry had suggested she bring along. Its wide, boat-cut neckline showed off her slim shoulders and the soft fabric clung to her breasts and waist. Plumping up her curls, she smiled, remembering Fleur's envious comments about her hair. Following their tour of her father's study, Fleur had announced that she was taking Cara to meet Caramel at the stables in the village before she left for London, an invitation Cara had warmly accepted, despite her misgivings about large animals. Fleur clearly adored Henry, and from their easy banter it was obvious they shared a strong bond and a markedly different relationship than with their other sibling.

Imogen was a different story altogether. She had remained stubbornly aloof all afternoon, ignoring all attempts to draw her into conversation. Eventually disappearing to sit on the balcony outside the family room to take multiple selfies to post on her social media, the only reminder that Imogen was still around was the occasional sound of shrill laughter punctuating her back-to-back phone calls.

Dinner was at 7:30 and, with less than five minutes to spare, Cara sprayed a quick blast of her favourite Jo Malone fragrance before making her way down the winding staircase. She held tightly onto the polished banister and was so focused on not catching her heels in the carpet running down the hardwood steps that she didn't see Henry standing by the stairwell until he gave a wolf whistle.

'Shhh!' she hissed, mortified. 'You scared the life out of me! Why are you standing there?'

He held out his arm and tucked hers under it. 'I thought you might like an escort into dinner.'

'I am *so* not used to all this formality! Why can't we just have dinner on a tray in front of the telly?'

'If you think this is bad, you're lucky it's only immediate family tonight. Imagine having to get through drinks and five courses at dinner while making conversation with a bunch of elderly relatives.'

At the look of pure horror on Cara's face, he dropped a light kiss on her nose. 'I'm only joking . . . well, sort of.'

She shook her head with a heavy sigh and looked around the hall. 'Where is everyone? I'm not late, am I?'

'Mother's in the dining room and the others should be down shortly. She's a stickler for punctuality, so I'm glad you're on time. You look gorgeous, by the way.'

They walked into the dining room and Cara stopped inside the doorway, only just holding in a gasp. The muted lighting on the mahogany-panelled walls set off the elaborately set dining table covered with white bone china plates and bowls, sparkling cut-glass tumblers, and polished silver cutlery. Three crystal vases filled with full-bloomed pink and white roses decorated the length of the table.

Lady Isobel, dressed in a navy velvet gown that fell in soft folds to her ankles, looked up from inspecting the table. 'Oh good, there you are!' she said crisply. 'Henry, you can both sit over on that side. Cara, you'll be next to Douglas. I'm keeping Fleur and Imogen on this side of the table. Although, with their constant bickering, putting them together is probably not a good idea . . .'

Right on cue, a red-faced Fleur charged into the room, closely followed by Imogen, ubiquitous phone in hand, looking stunning in a scarlet dress with a sweetheart neckline and tiny straps. Immediately launching into a heated exchange, the two girls only fell silent when a beaming Douglas strolled in.

'Shall we sit down?'

The sisters exchanged a final glare and chairs scraped across the wood flooring as they all took their seats. As if summoned by some magic signal, Mrs Soames appeared, carrying a tureen which she laid down in the centre of the table before leaving as silently as she'd arrived.

After polishing off the last of his vegetable soup, Douglas reached over to pinch Fleur's cheek gently. 'And how's my little flower this evening?'

Fleur pushed her empty bowl aside. 'I'm *so* excited about the championships, Daddy. You *will* come, won't you? I really wish you'd seen Caramel this morning. He went over all the jumps like a real pro!'

Her argument with Imogen clearly forgotten, Fleur's eyes glowed with excitement as she recounted Caramel's performance in painstaking detail.

'That's my girl!' Douglas interjected indulgently when he could finally get a word in. 'Of course I'll be there, and I'll bet my last bloomin' pound that you win!'

Imogen gave an audible tut and dropped her spoon into her half-eaten bowl of soup. 'I cannot understand what's so great about that ridiculous horse. It's all such a fuss about nothing.'

Fleur glared at her. 'Oh, really? Maybe it's because you do such amazing things yourself. Come to think of it, apart from living in Mother and Daddy's flat in London and taking loads of holidays just so you can show off to your Instagram followers, what exactly *do* you do, Imogen?'

Henry choked on the water he'd been drinking, earning a glare from Imogen. 'I don't know what *you're* laughing at!'

'Don't blame me if no one can keep up with your constant career changes,' Henry protested when his coughing subsided.

'Well, we can't all be a world-class lawyer and the perfect son to boot, can we? And for your information, Fleur, I happen to be the executive assistant to the CFO of a major advertising company, and it's a *very* important job.'

'Temp job, you mean,' Fleur muttered.

With the sigh of the long-suffering, Lady Isobel changed the subject. 'Henry, when do you and Cara plan to leave tomorrow? My ladies are coming over for afternoon tea and croquet and it would be nice if you could stay long enough to say hello. Arabella was asking after you the other day, and I'm sure she'd love to see you.'

Henry cast a glance at Cara, his expression unreadable. 'I'm not sure, Mother. We were planning to leave early and stop off at Little Duckworth on the way.'

A look of disappointment crossed his mother's face and Cara felt a stab of guilt. 'I'm sure we could wait and meet your friends first if that's what you'd like, couldn't we, Henry?' She looked at him meaningfully and he gave a non-committal shrug.

Cara turned back to Lady Isobel. 'Henry gave me a tour earlier, but we didn't get around to seeing your croquet pitch. It would be fun to watch a game.'

'Croquet *lawn*,' Imogen murmured, not quite under her breath.

Henry scowled at his sister and Cara flushed, sorely tempted to smack Imogen's judgemental expression off her beautiful face.

'Do stop slouching, Fleur,' Lady Isobel said sharply, her eyes resting disapprovingly on her younger daughter. 'I hope you pay more attention to your posture when you're at Pemberton Hall.'

Fleur pulled a face. 'I keep telling you, there's no way I'm going to that awful school.'

'Darling, please be reasonable! Pemberton Hall is an excellent school and you've been very lucky to get a place there. The teaching is first class and exactly what you need right now. Do you know how hard it is for even the best families to get their children in?'

'Well then, let someone else from a 'best' family go there. I like Lakeland High. I get to go to school with Jess *and* see Caramel every day. If I'm stuck at boarding school, I'll never see my best friend or be able to ride my horse!'

'You'll have plenty of time to do both during half-terms and holidays. You're the only child left at home, and you're on your own far too much. It will be good for you to make new friends and mix with people your own age.'

'You mean it would be good for *you* to have me out of the way,' Fleur muttered, her expression suddenly bleak. 'It's not like you wanted any more children after Henry and Imogen, anyway.'

'Oh, stop making such a fuss, Fleur!' Imogen said impatiently. 'For someone who's supposed to be so clever, you can be incredibly dense at times. Pemberton Hall is a great school. You'll get to play lacrosse and hockey and you can take piano lessons and meet loads of other swots. There's absolutely nothing wrong with that school. *I* went there, for goodness' sake!'

Fleur flashed a look of pure contempt at her sister. 'And look how well you've turned out.'

Imogen's nostrils flared, and her mother swiftly intervened. 'Fleur, that's enough! You have a place at one of the best girls' boarding schools in the country and you are going. Now, please remember we have a guest tonight,' she added, as Fleur opened her mouth to protest.

Cara bit her lip, trying hard not to smile. Fleur's outraged expression was a dead ringer for Manon's when she was in a strop, and social class apparently made no difference when it came to temperamental teenagers and their parents.

With dinner over, the family soon dispersed. Douglas disappeared into the library muttering loudly about some 'damned papers' he needed to sort out for 'bloody Jenkins', while Lady Isobel, pleading a headache, retired to her room. The others moved into the den where Fleur, ignoring a cackling Imogen who was once again back on her phone, chose a film before sprawling across one of the sofas. Cara sank down on another in front of the huge TV screen, kicking off her heels and tucking her legs up under her as she snuggled up against Henry. *Hmm . . . I could seriously get used to this,* she decided.

11

CRUSHES AND CROQUET

The next morning, after a leisurely breakfast served by Mrs Soames, Cara and Henry set off with Fleur to the stables in Little Duckworth to see Fleur's prized horse. The short drive into the market town took them past pretty cottages with trimmed hedges and neatly thatched roofs, and through farmland ringed with honey-coloured stone walls. The idyllic country scenes, rather than inducing panic this time, left Cara enchanted.

Little Duckworth further confounded her expectations. The market town, with its intriguing blend of old-fashioned period charm and modern convenience, was completely at odds with what she had imagined. Together, Cara, Henry and Fleur strolled down cobbled lanes with several old-fashioned inns adorned with ancient hanging lanterns and past bow-fronted tea shops displaying cakes and pastries. Popping into a chocolatier to buy a thank-you gift for Lady Isobel gave a giggling Cara and Fleur an excuse to tuck into the samples laid out on the counter. The narrow streets lined with quirky craft shops were clearly aimed at tourists, whilst the bustling high street a few minutes away was packed with stylish boutiques, chain stores and brand-name coffee shops. Little Duckworth hummed with activity as locals mixed with backpack-toting tourists and groups of sightseers spilled out of coaches parked on the lanes behind the busy market square.

Meeting Caramel was another revelation and, having never been at such close quarters to a horse, Cara was unnerved by the size of the animal. However, after some gentle coaxing from Fleur, Cara was soon stroking Caramel's velvety brown nose, even feeding the horse a slice of apple from her palm and flinching only a little at his large white teeth. After a walk through the surrounding meadows bordered with ancient stone walls, they wandered alongside a stream which ran down into woodland where Cara and Henry watched Fleur practise jumps over a series of log fences and ditches. Once Caramel had been wiped down back at the stables, Fleur hooked her arm through Cara's as they walked back to the car to return home.

'I'm so glad you've met Caramel. Now, you know why I love him so much. Some of the girls at school think I'm nerdy for spending so much time riding instead of gossiping about boys or being stuck on my phone all day like Imogen. Jess is the only one who understands why he's so important to me.'

'Everyone's different, Fleur,' Cara said reassuringly. 'I wouldn't worry too much about what your schoolfriends think. Pets can be amazingly good company, especially if you're on your own a lot. I talk to Lexie, our family cat, all the time. Although, to be fair, she mostly ignores me.'

'I knew you'd get it!' Fleur beamed.

◆ ◆ ◆

Bags packed and stowed in the car, the plan was to drop in on Lady Isobel's croquet game for a few minutes before leaving.

'Fleur has really taken to you,' Henry remarked, pushing open the door to the pantry and standing back to let Cara through.

'Well, it's mutual. She is such a sweetheart! She'd get on well with Manon. One's dog mad and the other's obsessed with her horse. I'm sure they'd find plenty to talk about.'

'I told you my family would love you.' He looked at her with a wicked smile, 'Fleur says you're the big sister she always wished she had.'

Cara choked back a laugh. 'Oh my God, I hope Imogen didn't hear that. Fleur really knows how to wind her up.'

Henry chuckled. 'So, now will you admit that my family isn't any different to yours?'

They walked through the pantry and into a room with a flag-stone floor and a damp, slightly musty smell. One side of the room was taken up with shelving holding garden tools and gardening gloves, while on the other, wellingtons, walking shoes, riding boots and muddy trainers competed for space. A couple of bicycles were propped up against the wall next to the door that led outside, and Henry bent to retrieve a pair of secateurs from the floor.

'Um, I'm not quite sure about that.' She gestured towards the wooden racks lining the walls filled with freshly potted plants.

'What *is* this room?'

'It's the boot room. It's where Mother arranges her flowers and we keep outdoor boots and things.' Henry shrugged.

'For most people, that's called the garden shed. I had no idea that boots actually get a room of their own.' She softened her words with a smile and tucked her hand into his arm. 'Come on then, I'm dying to meet the croquet posse.'

Henry laughed. 'I've never heard them called that before, and yes, let's get it over with. But . . .' He stopped to look her straight in the eye, adding sternly, 'To be clear, we're saying a quick hello and then we leave. Agreed?'

She grinned and reached up to brush his fringe off his face. 'Agreed.'

Out in the afternoon sunshine, the sky was a perfectly clear blue and, holding hands, the couple strolled past the staff quarters and through a kitchen garden filled with herbs, potatoes, lettuces, green beans and tomatoes. An ivy-covered gate at the bottom of the garden opened onto a gravel path.

Silently congratulating herself on her new-found ability to walk in thin-heeled strappy sandals without tripping, Cara listened as Henry pointed out several landmarks, including the large, pretty cottage where Jenkins and his family lived. As they went past manicured lawns and along the banks of a lake where ducks and birds flapped noisily across the surface of the water, Cara felt as if she was walking through a picture book. The path meandered through an orchard of apple, pear and plum trees and they stopped to examine a treehouse built into the branches of a large oak tree and now used, Henry explained, by Jenkins' children.

'See that clump of trees over there?' he added. 'When we were teenagers, my father had a tennis court built behind it because Imogen fancied herself as a future Wimbledon champion. In typical Imogen fashion, six months later she'd decided she hated tennis, and Dad turned that whole area into a golf course.'

'This must have been an amazing place to grow up. It goes on for ever,' Cara murmured, shading her eyes from the bright sun as she followed his gaze. 'How on earth do your parents manage all this? Mrs Soames is really efficient, but I can't imagine she does everything.'

'God, no! Mrs Soames does the cooking and oversees the house and Mother has a couple of girls who come in from the village to clean. We used to have a butler when we were younger, but Dad dispensed with him years ago.'

The gravel path narrowed, and Henry stopped to let Cara pass ahead of him. 'Oakley Manor is a working farm, don't forget. There's a whole team of people that take care of the grounds, and Jenkins has managed the estate for years. Actually, he deals with pretty much everything.'

'I've been meaning to ask you something,' Cara said hesitantly, and Henry looked at her enquiringly. 'Well, it's something your mother said yesterday – or at least, started to say. I got the impression that something bad happened to you?'

'She was probably referring to the accident I had a few years ago. It seems a long time ago now, but Mother is still a little overprotective.'

Henry squeezed her hand in reassurance, but, despite his off-hand tone, Cara was about to probe further when they turned a corner and she stopped dead in her tracks. All other thoughts were forgotten as she gaped at the exquisite patch of land a short distance away which was clearly Lady Isobel's prized croquet lawn.

'*Shi*— eesh! Look how smooth and just . . . *perfect* that grass is!'

Henry smiled at her awestruck expression. 'Mother takes her croquet very seriously.'

About the size of a tennis court, the mint-green turf was so smooth that each blade of grass could have been hand-trimmed with a pair of scissors. Vivid-white markings delineated a rectangular-shaped court with white and coloured hoops wedged into the ground at each corner of the boundary. Inside the court, a multi-coloured post in the centre was flanked by hoops on either side and, as they drew closer, Cara spotted a collection of wooden mallets on the ground along with an assortment of red, blue and black balls.

On the other side of the croquet lawn a group of women stood chatting around a large trestle table sheltered beneath a frilly green canopy and loaded with jugs of iced drinks and glasses. Around the trestle were several smaller tables with folding chairs. Feeling like she had inadvertently stumbled into a scene at a country house just before a murder takes place, Cara's eyes widened as she took in her surroundings.

'Most of these ladies have been playing here for years and some of them treat me like I'm still ten years old!' Henry said in a resigned tone. 'Okay, here we go . . . big smiles.'

He kept a firm grip on Cara's hand as the group of women suspended their conversations to watch with open curiosity as the couple approached. Feeling uncomfortably like a prize exhibit and relieved she had chosen to wear a relatively un-quirky black-and-white polka-dot skirt with a simple white top, Cara hung onto her pink clutch bag while trying to keep her heels from sinking into the soft earth.

Lady Isobel looked up from pouring a drink and her eyes lit up. 'Henry . . . Cara, just in time! We're having refreshments before we start the next game, so do come and say hello to everyone.'

Grasping Henry's hand like a drowning man clutching a rope, Cara smiled politely and murmured a greeting in response to the chorus of 'hellos' from the group. She counted twelve women altogether and although a couple of them appeared older, most were around Lady Isobel's age and casually dressed in a mix of flared skirts and loose trousers teamed with uniform light-blue blouses and flat-soled shoes.

A sprightly elderly woman with sparkling blue eyes and thin white hair scraped into a low bun marched up to Henry and grabbed his face between her hands. She kissed him soundly on both cheeks and tweaked his nose hard the instant she released him, forcing Cara to stifle a giggle at the appalled expression on Henry's face.

'My goodness, boy, you're looking well! Even more handsome than the last time I saw you,' she pronounced in an imperious accent.

Henry rubbed his nose and stepped back to put some distance between them. 'Thank you, Mrs Fortescue. It's . . . er . . . great to see you again.' He turned towards the other women with an apologetic smile. 'Good afternoon, ladies. We don't mean to interrupt your play, but Cara and I wanted to say a quick hello as we're just about to head back to London.'

Cara bit back a smile at the chorus of disappointed *Oh's* that followed and, as she scanned the faces, her eyes fell on a woman with short fair hair standing a few paces away from Lady Isobel. The woman's eyes locked onto hers with an expression of unmistakable hostility which she quickly concealed with a tight and not very convincing smile. Cara stared back in puzzlement; although she'd never met her before, there was something familiar about the long face and pale-blue eyes. The mystery was quickly solved as the woman put down her half-empty glass and flung her arms around Henry, forcing him to release Cara's hand.

'How lovely to see you, Henry! Why, Primrose was saying only the other day that getting hold of you now seems quite impossible. If I had heard sooner that you were coming home this weekend, I'd have suggested she come down so the two of you could meet up.'

Henry extricated himself from the embrace and ran his hands through his hair. 'Hello, Mrs Wynter. It's nice to see you too,' he said politely.

Of course! Cara examined Primrose's mother curiously as the resemblance immediately became apparent. The similarity didn't end there as she discovered when she shook the hand Mrs Wynter grudgingly extended and received the same limp handshake Primrose had offered.

'You two must at least have a glass of orange juice before you head off. I insist!' Lady Isobel declared, picking up a jug and quickly filling two tall glasses. Unlike the previous day, she appeared relaxed and animated and showed none of her earlier hauteur or the tension that coloured her interactions with Fleur. *Either she's warming up to me or croquet brings out the best in her*, Cara observed with amusement, depositing her handbag on the trestle table to take the proffered drink.

Mrs Fortescue had been scrutinising Cara and a mischievous smile emerged, causing wrinkles to crease around her eyes. 'It's a pleasure to meet you, my dear. Isobel has been rather singing your praises since we got here.'

Cara blinked in shock, but Mrs Fortescue had already turned back to Henry. 'Now, Henry dear, come with me,' she commanded. 'I need a word of advice before we start the next game. Since you're a fully fledged lawyer, you can clear up something for me about my will.'

Before he could protest, Mrs Fortescue seized his arm and pulled him off to one side. With the main attraction commandeered, some of the women went to retrieve their mallets and balls, while one or two offered Cara a tentative smile and an enquiry about her stay before returning to their conversations.

Taking advantage of the lull, Arabella Wynter moved closer. 'So, what do you think of Oakley Manor then . . . Cara, is it? It must be a big change for you after the inner city. I dare say no one would blame you if you found us all a little too . . . traditional out here in the countryside?'

The braying laugh that followed did nothing to disguise the spite behind her words, and Cara bristled at the woman's naked condescension.

'Not at all, I'm having a great time. Oakley Manor is a beautiful house and it's been lovely to see Henry's home and meet his family.'

Coming back to place an empty jug on the table, Lady Isobel interjected dryly, 'Fleur has developed quite the crush on Cara, Arabella. Mercifully, she's been so excited to have Cara stay with

107

us that we've had fewer tantrums than usual this weekend. Fleur even took Cara out to the stables this morning to introduce her to Caramel, and I can't think of anyone else she's allowed near that wretched horse.'

'High praise indeed.' Arabella pursed her mouth as though sucking a lemon and, picking up her discarded glass, she sipped on her drink, cubes of fruit bumping around her top lip. She continued to stare at Cara with stony blue eyes that radiated an intense dislike she made no attempt to hide. Suppressing the urge to stick two fingers up at the woman, Cara tried to ignore her and instead focused on describing Fleur's impressive riding skills to an attentive Lady Isobel.

Lady Isobel moved off to top up her guests' drinks and Arabella took a step closer to Cara. 'Well, you certainly seem to feel at home with us, which must be very reassuring for Henry. Of course, Lady Isobel is a very modern and *tolerant* woman and an extremely polite hostess, but it would be quite understandable if you felt a little . . . well, shall we say, out of your depth here?'

There was no mistaking the insinuation behind Arabella's words and Henry, who was approaching arm-in-arm with a beaming Mrs Fortescue, was just in time to catch them. He flushed with anger and his mouth tightened into a grim line and, for a moment, Cara thought he was about to rugby tackle Primrose's mother. But before he could speak, the older lady placed a silencing hand on his arm.

'Arabella, dear, is that how *you* felt after marrying poor dear Hector? Out of your depth, I mean?' Despite her saccharine-sweet tone, Mrs Fortescue's eyes blazed with contempt.

Arabella gasped and spun around, her face suffused with colour and her lips pinched tight with outrage. But Mrs Fortescue wasn't finished. Injecting a note of deep sympathy, she raised her voice theatrically. 'I suppose it must have been quite a challenge for you to deal with Hector's drinking, not to mention living with his ogre of a mother. She was quite the penny-pinching old tyrant, as I recall.'

A couple of women standing nearby tittered and Arabella turned a deep shade of crimson. She opened her mouth in indignation, but, before any words could emerge, Mrs Fortescue added kindly, 'Then again, marrying Hector was probably a relief for you after so many years of scrimping to get by. I can't imagine your job as the receptionist in Hector's surgery was particularly rewarding . . . financially, I mean.'

Visibly shaking with anger, Arabella stalked off without a word and Mrs Fortescue cackled. Picking up a clean glass, she held it out while Henry, shaking with laughter, attempted to fill it with Pimm's without spilling any.

'Take no notice of her, Cara dear. It's just a case of sour grapes because her daughter isn't the one on Henry's arm. Which is just as well because our wonderful boy here deserves to be happy and if that huge grin on Henry's face is anything to go by, you're exactly what he needs.'

Cara smiled weakly, her emotions still churning from Arabella Wynter's outrageous statements. Cara had met women like her before and, while Arabella's offensive words were wounding, unfortunately the woman's coded language was nothing new. Feeling saddened for Henry who had never experienced comments like that directed against someone he cared for, Cara forced a more convincing smile. It was no one else's fault that Primrose's mother had tried to poison what had otherwise been a lovely visit and Mrs Fortescue's sincerity helped soothe the sting of Arabella's remarks. But while Cara didn't doubt the older lady's good intentions, the incident, highlighting as it did the undeniable differences between her and her boyfriend, sowed fresh doubts in Cara's mind about her place in Henry's world. What if Arabella's only crime was saying what the other women were thinking?

Mrs Fortescue took a sip of her drink and then tugged on Henry's arm to pull him down for a kiss. 'Louisa and the others are waiting for me, so I'd better get on court. Thank you so much for your legal advice, dear boy, and I shall do exactly as you suggested. Now, do drive carefully on the motorways.' She shuddered. 'Personally, I much prefer going to London by train.'

With a warm smile at Cara and a final pat of Henry's arm, Mrs Fortescue picked up a mallet and set off to join the three women waiting on court, mallets in hand, to start the game. Two of them stood next to a pile of black and blue balls, while Louisa had commandeered the red and yellow ones.

Relieved not to pretend a civility she didn't feel towards Arabella, who was now seated alone at one of the tables with her back to them, Cara waved goodbye to the other women before following Henry and his mother back to the path. Lady Isobel was clearly distracted by the croquet game in progress, and, after a couple of minutes, she kissed her son goodbye and took Cara's hand in both of hers.

'It's been a pleasure to meet you, Cara, and thank you for coming to visit us.' While there was no kiss forthcoming, Lady Isobel's handshake felt considerably warmer than the one she'd offered Cara the previous day. *Well, at least I'm making progress.* Even if Henry's mother wasn't yet fawning over her, Cara had managed to get through the weekend without disgracing herself.

'I've had a lovely time and thank you again for having me.' She smiled. She slipped her hand into Henry's as they watched Lady Isobel hurry away to rejoin her team.

'Come on then, tell the truth. Meeting my family wasn't as awful as you expected, was it?' asked Henry.

Cara wrinkled her nose and grinned, nudging him playfully in the ribs. 'Okay, so you were right and there was nothing for me to get worked up about. Your family's adorable and everyone except that evil cow Arabella Wynter has been very nice. I'm still a die-hard city girl, but I will admit the countryside is a lot nicer than I thought *and* I got through the weekend without showing you up.'

Henry wrapped an arm around her as they walked back up the path and lowered his voice suggestively. 'Well, I can't wait to get back to London and make up for spending last night apart—'

He broke off as Cara stopped abruptly. 'What is it?'

'*Shi*— shoot. I left my bag on the drinks table!'

'Don't worry, just wait here and I'll—'

Henry was still in mid-syllable as Cara turned on her heel and sprinted down the path, her full skirt blowing up in the breeze.

'I won't be a minute!' she called over her shoulder as she raced back down the path and over the grass towards the trestle table. The croquet game was underway, and both teams were at the far side of the court where Lady Isobel and the other women were watching from the boundary line. Cara cut across the grass to the table and snatched up the forgotten pink clutch. In a rush to get back to Henry, she turned back and broke into a run.

'Cara, *no!*' Henry's cry of alarm came too late and with a sinking feeling Cara looked down to find she had run onto the croquet lawn. She froze in horror. *How the hell did I miss seeing the white markings?*

Henry's shout had alerted the women congregated at the far end and the players stopped to gaze open-mouthed at the petrified figure standing on the grass. Even from where she stood, Cara could see the wide-eyed horror on Lady Isobel's face.

A loud chorus of *Off the lawn!* from the players and spectators reached her and looking down at the grass, even the blades of the perfectly manicured lawn seemed to reproach her. Panicking, she cursed under her breath and hurried to obey the instruction. The combination of frazzled nerves and hot sun had her back prickling with sweat as she ducked her head and ran towards Henry. Through the chorus of protests from the outraged croquet players, she could hear him calling her name, but she was far too mortified to stop.

'*CARA!* TAKE OFF YOUR SHOES!' His anguished voice cut through the hubbub and once again she stopped in her tracks. She spun around and stared in horror at the previously pristine lawn, realising too late why all the women were wearing flat shoes.

It was easy to see where she had run. Her path across the velvety green lawn was vividly marked, courtesy of her spiky new heels, by a series of ugly black puncture holes.

12

Spanish Fly (In the Ointment)

Cara slammed the copy of Primrose's invoice into the box file on her desk and snapped it shut. After some spirited negotiations with Paula, the lawyer had finally agreed the budget for her niece's birthday party. While a part of Cara felt a sneaky admiration for Primrose's skill in whittling a ten per cent discount from Paula, who haggled over every deal as zealously as if she'd been raised in a Turkish *souk,* just seeing the name 'Wynter' brought the weekend's humiliation flooding back.

Pressing her lips tightly to suppress the groan that emerged whenever she recalled her fateful run across Lady Isobel's hallowed croquet lawn, Cara pulled her laptop closer, forcing herself to concentrate on the to-do list on the screen. *Stay focused*, she muttered to herself. The production, catering and music for Tabitha's birthday party, not to mention her other projects, weren't going to manage themselves. But thinking something wasn't the same as doing it and, seconds later, a muffled groan escaped her lips.

Ben's head jerked up in alarm and he craned his neck over the partition that divided their desks. Having satisfied himself that Cara wasn't dying, he threw a cautious glance across the room to where an unusually cheerful Paula was engrossed in a loud phone conversation. Reassured that Paula wouldn't notice him taking a break from his work – office chatter ranked high on her long list of forbidden activities – Ben's eyes swivelled back to Cara.

'What's wrong with you? Are you ill? It's not, you know, that time—'

'Urgh, just shut up! I'm fine,' she muttered irritably, annoyed at herself for losing control.

'Of course you are. It's totally normal to sit and groan as if you're being stabbed every few minutes.'

His sarcasm held an underlay of concern, but Cara was in no mood to confide her problems. It was mortifying enough to recall the disfigured lawn without sharing the cringe-making details. Her office phone rang, cutting off Ben's persistent questioning, and she seized it gratefully.

'Cara Nightingale speaking.' She flashed a reproving look at Ben to indicate that at least one of them was focused on their work.

'Sweetheart, are you okay?' Henry's voice momentarily threw her off-balance.

Ben's eyes were still trained on her and Cara ducked down into her seat, trying to pretend her colleague wasn't two feet away as she hissed quietly into the phone. 'Henry! Why are you calling me on my work phone?'

'Because you're not answering when I call you on your mobile,' he replied, sounding so reasonable and so *Henry* that for a moment all she wanted to do was curl up in his arms. But not even Henry could stop her agonised self-recrimination. Only minutes after taking a tiny step into Lady Isobel's good graces, Cara had taken two gigantic strides back by massacring the woman's precious croquet lawn. Henry's attempts to reassure her on the drive back to London had fallen on deaf ears and she'd been almost relieved when he'd left a little later for Brussels where he was representing a client in a competition claim.

'Shouldn't you be in court?' she whispered.

'The case has been adjourned until after lunch. I've got to join the senior partner for a meeting with our client, but I wanted to make sure you're not still torturing yourself over what happened.'

Cara glanced up, and, although Ben's quiff was no longer visible, she lowered her voice anyway. 'I feel *awful* when I think about it.'

'Then stop thinking about it,' came the immediate reply. 'It was an accident, and Mother really shouldn't have made such a fuss. Sweetheart, don't worry, she'll get over it. It's only a bit of grass, it's not like anyone died!'

'Henry, her lawn looked like I'd stabbed it to death!' Cara exclaimed. She bit her lip, holding back another groan while Henry assured her yet again that, no, her name wasn't mud as far as his family was concerned, yes, he would pass on her apologies to his mother once again and, yes, Jenkins had already arranged to have the lawn restored to rights.

The sound of another voice came through the phone and Henry broke off abruptly. 'Sorry, I'd better go,' he whispered. 'My senior partner's panicking about losing the case, and if he gets any redder, he's going to give himself a heart attack. I'll call you tonight – *please* stop worrying!'

She replaced the handset and Ben's quiff immediately reared upwards, his eyes bright with amusement. 'What *have* you been up to? Don't tell me you've managed to piss off his family on your very first visit to meet the parents?'

Silently cursing herself for confiding her planned weekend trip to Oakley Manor, Cara leaned over the partition.

'*Shush!* Keep your voice down!' she snapped, glancing over to where Paula was busy haranguing the new office junior. Today, instead of her usual t-shirt and cardigan, Paula had teamed her shapeless black trousers with a cherry-red top, a matching bead necklace, and a slash of red lipstick that emphasised her pallor.

'Why's she all togged up today?' Cara queried, momentarily distracted by her boss's makeover.

'Useless Dave got back from holiday this morning.' Ben snickered, and Cara shook her head in bafflement that her heartless, hard-nosed boss could be so taken with the disaster that was Dave Prentiss. It was impossible to understand why Paula, who was such a stickler for order and discipline, had such a man-sized crush on the balding deputy accounts officer who had never knowingly sent out a correct invoice or payment. It was an open secret at Westbrooks that Useless Dave was only kept on payroll because his best friend, a professional football player, was a ready source of free match tickets for the MD. The last few weeks of the football season were always an anxious time for Dave, who was only too aware that if his mate's team was relegated, thereby losing him access to Premier League tickets, he would be sacked from Westbrook Events faster than he could say 'bought ledger'.

'Don't change the subject! What did you do to upset lover boy's people?' Ben demanded.

'Mind your own *business*!' Cara retorted. There was no way she was telling Ben about her most embarrassing moment ever. Caught up in their bickering, neither of them noticed Paula approaching until she planted herself in front of them with her arms folded aggressively across her chest.

'I trust your work duties aren't interfering with your petty squabbles, and can I remind you both that the *only* business that matters in this office is Westbrook's. Ben, where's the revised budget for the Cartography conference? Betsey says she told you not to leave yesterday until you'd updated the figures.'

Cara's vengeful smirk disappeared as Paula swiftly rounded on her.

'Cara, have you booked Julio for the birthday party? Now that Wynter woman has shaved off a chunk of our profit, we'll have to use him for the pyrotechnics, so go over there and make sure he's clear about what's expected.'

Being forced to deal with Julio suddenly made Primrose's haggling skills rather less admirable, and Cara reluctantly reached for her bag. It was pointless trying to arrange anything with Julio by phone or email because if she didn't personally stand over him to make sure he'd taken down her instructions correctly, there was no telling what could happen.

'Okay, okay, I'm on my way.' She flashed a saccharine-sweet smile at Paula, clicked off her monitor and tossed her mobile into her bag. Walking past Ben, she deliberately bumped up hard against his shoulder, smiling with satisfaction at his startled yelp as she headed towards the lift.

Julio's headquarters in Shepherd's Bush was an airless two-room affair above a shop that doubled as a mini-mart and a barber. Cara knocked half-heartedly on the door marked 'Julio's Global Production Company' and walked straight in. Despite the open windows, the room smelled distinctly musty and most of the floor space was given over to stacks of cardboard boxes. The naked strip-lighting overhead highlighted cracks running along the edges of the ceiling and down the chipped walls.

Julio was slouched in a black-cushioned chair with a phone clamped to his ear and both feet planted on a desk completely clear of any equipment or papers. Deep in conversation, he spoke loudly in rapid Spanish and, although his eyes brightened when Cara walked in, there was no break in the words tumbling out. He blew her an extravagant kiss which she ignored, instead turning her attention to the other occupant of the room, a dark-haired girl with a sullen expression who offered a tiny nod of acknowledgement before continuing to fold a pile of brightly coloured fabrics.

Abruptly ending his conversation, Julio dropped his phone onto the desk and bounded to his feet in a single lithe movement, approaching Cara with arms outstretched. His large head was further magnified by a shock of long, black, curly hair, and when he smiled, his gleaming white teeth, reminiscent of a hungry lion, stood out from the surrounding dark stubble.

'Cara! *Cariña!*'

'Hi, Julio.' With a sigh, Cara submitted to the moist kiss on each cheek with good grace.

'I haven't seen you for ages, Cara.' He gave her a fond grin and thrust his hands into the pockets of his tight jeans.

'No, you haven't. Not since you sent me a fire-eater for my lawyers' conference instead of an after-dinner comedian,' she remarked dryly.

Julio chuckled and sauntered back to his desk. He pushed a wobbly swivel chair in her direction and waved at her to sit down. 'Cara, I swear that was not my fault! Monica gave me the wrong message. You know her English is not so good. I would have fired her, but she is my sister's daughter, so what could I do?'

Taking his seat behind the desk, he tried hard to look penitent. 'Monica, she has gone back to Spain.' He gestured grandly towards the girl who was now rooting through a box. 'Now, I have a new assistant, Gina. She speaks the English very well and we will have no problems.'

Gina didn't bother to look up, and after an awkward silence Julio cleared his throat noisily. 'So, sit and tell Uncle Julio what you need.'

Cara perched cautiously on the chair, testing her weight on it for a moment. When she was satisfied it wouldn't skid out from under her, she reached into her bag and pulled out her notebook.

'We've got a birthday party coming up for a new client and *Paula . . .*' she paused to make it clear that using him wasn't her idea, ' . . . suggested you might be able to organise a firework display to close the party.'

Although her tone was begging him to refuse the offer, Julio was back on his feet before she had finished.

'But of course, for you, anything!' He broke off to glance across at Gina, who was half-buried in a large cardboard box. '*Querida*, you can sort those flags later. Please come over here and take notes. Westbrook is a very important client for our business.'

Emerging with her ponytail askew, Gina wiped her hands down the sides of her jeans and, without comment, dragged a chair from behind a small desk in the corner and pushed it to sit a few inches away from Cara. Communication skills were clearly not a high priority for Julio's global organisation, Cara mused. The new assistant had yet to utter a word and, judging from the tiny smile she flashed at Cara before holding her pen in poised anticipation, that wasn't about to change.

'Right, so it's a sixteenth birthday party and our client wants a "wizards and witches" theme. What we'll need from you is . . .' Speaking rapidly and with the occasional glance at Gina as she scribbled away assiduously, Cara rattled through her list of instructions while Julio paced up and down the worn carpet, nodding his huge leonine head.

' . . . so, what do you think? Are you sure you can do the job?' Cara concluded, scepticism seeping through her tone.

Julio returned to his desk and picked up his mobile. 'What is the date of this party?'

'Fifteenth July.'

He scrolled through his phone to check the calendar and then looked up with a broad smile.

'No problem, *bella*! Uncle Julio will make everything very nice.'

'Seriously, Julio, don't mess this one up,' said Cara sternly. 'Paula will wring your neck if anything goes wrong again.'

His smile faltered at the sound of Paula's name. 'Have I ever let you down?' he asked plaintively, quickly adding before she could reply, 'Gina, you write everything down, no?'

Gina nodded and snapped her notebook shut. She pushed her chair back to her desk and returned to untangling a string of flags she had pulled from the box.

'Oh, and can you email me an itemised invoice by next Tuesday at the latest? Paula has to sign off on it, so don't bother trying to pad it out,' she warned.

Julio responded with a brazen wink, and, eager to escape the stuffy office, Cara picked up her bag and headed for the door, skipping down the narrow flight of stairs and out onto the street. The heavy traffic on the main road drowned the sound of her ringtone, but she could feel vibrations coming from her bag and she pulled out her phone. Seeing Ashanti's name on the screen, Cara frowned. Ashanti was due to sing at Mocktails that evening and generally avoided speaking before a performance to save her voice.

'Guess what?' Without waiting for an answer, Ashanti's words gushed out in an excited flow. 'No, forget it, you'll never guess! Elliott loved my demo tape! Did you hear that? He *loved* my songs. He says his record label is looking for a new sound and he's positive that I'm it!'

'Ash, that's *amazing*!'

'You're the first person I'm telling. Isn't it awesome that I've finally got a deal! Elliott's really keen to get me on board, and we're meeting next week at their office to go over everything and sign the contract!'

Stunned by the speed of events, Cara's trouble-spotting antennae vibrated furiously, and she scrabbled to find the right words.

Unlike the deluded talent show singers with zero talent and apparently tone-deaf friends and family, Ashanti was the real deal and deserved to work with the best. Judging from her first impressions of Elliott, Cara couldn't help wondering if settling for a deal with Nine Elms Records was really Ashanti's best option.

'That's brilliant!' Cara tried to sound enthusiastic but she couldn't ignore the alarm bells going off in her head. 'Why the rush, though? Don't you think you should take a bit of time to consider their terms and get some legal advice first?'

'*Cara!* For once, can't you just be happy for me?' Ashanti pleaded, her voice rising in frustration.

'Of course I'm happy for you! Don't get me wrong. Haven't I always said you're incredibly talented and that you're going to be a star one day? I just think—'

Ashanti cut her off with a wail of protest. 'Do you know how long I've waited to get a record deal? Who cares if it's a rush? I *want* to sign before they change their minds. Jeez, Cara, this is a *good* thing, okay? There's nothing wrong here that you need to sort out!'

Cara prudently remained silent, but Ashanti pounced anyway.

'Okay, forget about my contract – which I'm going to sign whatever you say. While I've got you on the phone, don't you think it's time we talked about you-know-who?'

'Why?' Cara kept her voice even and refused to rise to the bait. Ashanti had evidently decided that attack was her best form of defence and was trying to deflect from a question she couldn't answer by turning the tables back on her.

'What do you mean, *why*? Because you've been in denial ever since Rosie's confession and, let's face it, we all know the effect that man has on you.'

Taking a deep breath, Cara willed herself to remain calm. That was the trouble with confiding in people, especially those who had no qualms about using that information against you. Ashanti could try all she wanted to play dirty, but Cara was damned if she would give her the satisfaction of losing it.

'I'm not in denial. I just don't care!'

'Really?' Ashanti scoffed. 'And is that because you've suddenly forgotten everything that happened with him? Or do you need me to remind you that you were on your knees when he left, and no one's been allowed to mention his name to you ever since? Maybe it's also slipped your mind how you couldn't get out of bed for weeks and turned into such a zombie that I literally had to put you under the shower?'

Cara flinched at the harshness of Ashanti's words and was about to correct her, but, not wanting to give her friend further ammunition, said nothing. Then, as if regretting her tactics, Ashanti's voice softened.

'Hon, I'm not trying to upset you, but we need to face facts. You and Ryan were like Romeo and Juliet without the family aggro. From the minute he showed up at school with that stupidly sexy Irish accent, you were all over each other! It's like the guy is in your blood, and you can tell yourself you're over him all you like, but we both know different. You've got no backbone whatsoever when it comes to Ryan so if he's coming back, we need a plan of action.'

'No we don't! I've told you. *I. Don't. Care.*' Cara's exasperation overcame her strategy of silence.

Ashanti replied with a sceptical humph. 'Cara, this is me. Don't act like Ryan turning up again means nothing to you.'

'I'm *not* acting,' Cara protested hotly. *Careful.* She took a deep breath and cautioned herself. *Don't get angry.* She exhaled softly before continuing. 'Ash, I got over Ryan ages ago. I know it was hard after we split up but, honest to God, I'm over it! I'm with Henry now, and the past is in the past.'

Taking advantage of a strident exchange of horn blasts between two angry van drivers, Cara muttered goodbye and switched off her phone. She ran down the steps into the underground station still fuming at the call. Why was it so hard for Ashanti and Dexter, and indeed everyone in her family, to understand that she had consigned Ryan to her past? Her ex-boyfriend had taken enough of her time and tears, and she had no interest in wasting any more of either on him. All she wanted to do now was find a way past the humiliation of her visit to Oakley Manor and restore her standing with Henry's family.

Although finishing work early risked incurring Paula's wrath, Cara was in no mood to return to the office and face another inquisition from Ben. Instead, settling for some retail therapy, she headed to the market at Camden Lock.

Two hours later, leaving the station loaded with bags, Cara hurried towards her flat. She was cutting it close if she was to be at Mocktails on time, and she mentally raced through the logistics of changing clothes, refreshing her make-up, and organising getting to Kilburn within ten minutes. She turned the corner into her road and hurried down her pathway, coming to a halt as her eyes fell on a lone figure sitting on the doorstep.

All thoughts of a quick shower and booking an Uber vanished. Instead, her insides contracted as violently as if the air had been sucked out of her body by a giant vacuum cleaner. She stared at the man now standing and walking slowly towards her and her heart pounded painfully in her chest. For a surreal moment, she felt as if she was standing outside herself watching the scene unfold, and a single thought flitted through her frozen brain. *The past is in the past.* Wasn't that what she had so blithely assured Ashanti only a couple of hours earlier? *But what happens when the past becomes the present?*

'Hello, Cara. It's good to see you.'

The deep voice with its achingly familiar lilt shook her to the core, but she forced her expression to remain impassive and raised her chin defiantly.

'Hello, Ryan.'

13

Past Perfect

It's good to see you.

It would be much later before Cara conceded that it was those five words, and of course, her neighbour Mrs Aggarwal, that had been her undoing and allowed Ryan to instantly demolish the painfully constructed wall around her memories.

For despite her initial bravado, all Cara could do was stare at him, her gaze sweeping over his tousled dark hair and the sharp cheekbones any modelling agent would have scrambled to sign up. He was close enough for her to see the tiny diamond stud in his left ear and the faint sprinkle of freckles across his lightly bronzed skin – *how on earth had he managed to get a tan like that in Dublin?* – and she felt herself drowning in the dark-blue eyes that had haunted her for years.

'Cara . . . I know I should have called first. I didn't want to just show up, but . . .'

He took a step closer and she automatically stepped back, the movement jolting her out of her reverie and restoring her voice.

'But what, Ryan?'

She struggled to keep her tone even while she fished for the keys inside her bag to avoid his gaze. Bitterly regretting not taking up Ashanti's offer to devise a plan of action, her mind swirled in a haze of indecision. Should she let him in or make him stand out here and say whatever he had to say?

The outdoor option would have suited Cara just fine, had it not been for her neighbour. As much as she hated the idea of letting Ryan into the intimate confines of her tiny flat, the curious stares she could sense coming from the direction of Mrs Aggarwal's house were confirmed by the gentle twitching of the curtain in the woman's front window. Recently retired after thirty years with the local council, Mrs Aggarwal devoted an extensive amount of her new leisure time to keeping an eye open on behalf of the residents. Cara would have bet serious money the woman had spotted Ryan from the moment he'd arrived and had maintained a vigil behind her curtains ever since.

Picking up her shopping bags, Cara climbed the shallow steps to her front door with Ryan in tow. She unlocked it and then hesitated, the symbolism of opening the door and inviting Ryan into her sanctuary not lost on her.

'I'm sorry. Maybe I should just go . . .' His eyes silently pleaded with her to contradict him.

Then Mrs Aggarwal's front door opened and before Cara could reconsider, she opened the door and pushed Ryan inside. 'Oh, go on, get in before my nosey neighbour asks for an introduction!'

Pretending not to hear the '*Coo-ee!*' from the woman hurrying towards them, Cara slammed the door shut. Once inside, Ryan's height seemed to swallow up the narrow entrance and she quickly led the way up the stairs and into her flat, shepherding him straight to the living room.

'D'you know what, Ryan, I really don't have time for whatever this is. I should have been at Mocktails by now and I haven't even changed!'

'Look, I'll leave if you want me to, but there's something I need to say to you first. Go ahead and get yourself ready. I can wait.'

Cara didn't have time to argue. Leaving him seated on the sofa, she dived into her bedroom where she kept up a running commentary of angry self-recrimination under her breath. *You should have said NO to him, Cara, however awkward it was!* Slipping on a sleeveless black lace top, she fastened the front buttons of the flowing black skirt she'd picked up at the market with trembling fingers, keeping a wary eye on the closed door that represented the only barrier between her and the man who had just thrown a hand grenade into her world. After tying the laces on her black patent Doc Martens, she applied mascara and lipstick with lightning speed, muttering angrily at the face reflected in the mirror. Just as she was reaching for her phone to ring an Uber, it trilled loudly and, for a few seconds, Cara stared at the screen, desperate to speak to Henry, but even more terrified that her guilt at having Ryan in her flat would give her away. On the fourth ring, she hit the button and cleared her throat.

'Hi, sweetie! How *are* you?' Her nerves caused her voice to come out louder and higher than she'd intended and even to her own ears she sounded ridiculous.

'Are you okay?'

Cara shifted uncomfortably at Henry's puzzled tone, horribly conscious of the man sitting on her couch only a few feet away.

'Mm-*hmm!*' She injected a note of enthusiasm and nodded vigorously as if he could see her.

'Court's over for today and we're heading out for dinner with the client. I wanted to check in with you first, though.' He hesitated. 'Are you sure you're alright?'

The concern in Henry's voice was making Cara feel even guiltier. 'I'm fine, Henry. Honestly. I'm running a bit late for Ashanti's gig, but it's nice to hear your voice. I've missed you so much. How's the case going?'

'The lawyers for the other side are trying all manner of dirty tricks, but let's just say I've seen worse.' Henry sounded as if he was smiling and she giggled, forgetting for just a moment that Ryan was on the other side of the door.

'Well, I'd better let you go so you don't miss the show,' he said. 'I'll give you a call tomorrow. Have fun!'

Fun and Ryan didn't even begin to go together, she thought gloomily, wishing desperately that it was Henry sitting in the next room instead of the man she had once known better than herself. She sighed and gave her hair a last disconsolate fluff before booking an Uber.

When Cara finally emerged, Ryan was on the sofa, one leg casually crossed over his knee, scrolling through his phone. It felt surreal to see him there and, while Cara wished he wasn't, she also couldn't help wondering what had brought him back to London. The cab was due at any moment and Ashanti would murder her if she missed her set, which left no time to hear Ryan out. Torn between curiosity about his motives and an intense desire for him to be gone, curiosity won, and when Ryan suggested continuing their conversation on the way to the club, she found herself agreeing.

But once within the close confines of the smelly cab, trying not to breathe in, the journey was conducted in near silence. Desperate to project a composure she was far from feeling, Cara stared blindly out of the window, willing her body not to betray her by relaxing its guard against the familiar body next to hers. Then, once the cab had dropped them at Mocktails, it didn't make sense for him to leave when they had barely exchanged a word, and she reluctantly agreed to him coming in with her.

With word having spread, mostly by Colum himself, that one of his live acts had just secured a recording deal, it was more crowded than usual for Thursday Night Live at Mocktails, and Cara elbowed her way through drinkers standing almost five-deep around the bar, painfully conscious of Ryan following close behind. She peered around the dimly lit room for the table Rosie had texted earlier to say she'd bagged. Spotting Rosie standing by the stage, Cara made her way over and gave her a quick hug before turning to Ashanti, who was perched regally on a stool. The words Cara had been about to utter died on her lips as Ashanti stared straight past her with an expression of outraged disbelief.

'What the hell is *he* doing here?' Ashanti jumped to her feet, her kohl-lined eyes narrowed in disgust. She turned her gaze onto Cara. 'How did he get in? Do you want me to get Colum's boys to chuck him out?'

'No, it's fine,' Cara muttered in embarrassment, mentally kicking herself for not confronting Ryan earlier. Rosie had turned deathly pale and looked as wretched as if she were personally responsible for her cousin's existence.

For the first time, Ryan seemed to lose his composure as he sighed heavily and ran a hand through his dark hair. The gesture triggered a torrent of memories. She could almost feel the silky texture of his curls beneath her fingertips. After all, how many times had she caressed his hair, even trimming it herself when he was too broke to afford the barber's?

Ryan held up his hand in a gesture of appeasement. 'Look, Ash, I—'

'Don't you *dare* "Ash" me!' Ashanti snarled. 'You don't get to mess up my best mate *and* my boyfriend and then swan in here like nothing's happened!'

Before he could speak, Cara broke in gently but firmly, 'Ashanti, just leave it. It's okay; it was me. *I* brought him.'

Quailing at the ferocious glare now being shot in her direction, Cara continued bravely. 'Ryan showed up at my flat and I was running late, so he came with so we could finish the conversation.' She studiously avoided Ryan's eyes. 'He's not staying long, and you don't have to talk to him. In any case, you're on in a minute. Shouldn't you be getting ready for your set?'

Throwing Cara a look of mingled pity and disgust, Ashanti adjusted the straps of her skin-tight black leather dress. She stepped out from behind the table and walked up to Ryan, standing so close that in her heels their faces were almost touching.

'This isn't over!' she snapped before storming off, her body rigid with fury. With hostilities suspended, even if only temporarily, Cara released the breath she hadn't realised she was holding and sat down while Ryan hovered uncertainly.

'Why don't I get us all a drink? What do you want, Cara – rum and coke?'

She bristled at his assumption that he knew what she wanted. Annoyingly, he was right, but she had no intention of giving him that satisfaction.

'No, thanks, I'll have a lager.'

'Rosie?'

Still looking the picture of misery, Rosie glanced at the half-full glass in front of her and shook her head. They watched Ryan lope off in the direction of the bar and as soon as his tall frame was swallowed up in the crowd, Rosie rounded on Cara. Her skin went from pale to an angry red within seconds as she leaned forward and planted her arms on the table, much too agitated to notice the sticky stains on its surface.

'What the hell are you *doing*?' she hissed. 'I only warned you that Ryan was coming back so you'd be on your guard and stay out of his way. You know what you're like around him! You weren't supposed to actually *talk* to him, never mind go anywhere with him. And what were you *thinking* to bring him here, of all places?'

Cara sighed, feeling worse than ever. Now even Rosie, who had never knowingly said boo to a goose, was furious with her. *What was I thinking?*

Ryan, on the other hand, was giving every sign of having the best time, and if he felt any discomfort, it certainly didn't show. While waiting for Ashanti's set to begin, Cara watched him chat easily to the regulars who stopped at their table, his face creasing into smiles with every back slap, high-five and 'Good to see you, mate!' The only dent in his composure came when Colum wandered past their table. Shocked into an almost comical double-take, Colum had immediately thrown Ryan a filthy look before casting an enquiring glance at Cara. Touched by his concern, Cara gave a tiny shake of her head. She didn't need Colum setting his bouncers on Ryan, however much he deserved it.

By the time Ashanti took to the stage and settled herself behind the piano Colum had strategically placed under a neon 'Mocktails' sign, Cara's nerves were stretched to breaking point. Any curiosity about Ryan's return had been overtaken by the more pressing concern of how to prevent her best friend from murdering her ex-boyfriend once she came off stage. Ashanti was unpredictable at the best of times, and, after springing Ryan on her without warning, Cara knew better than to take her friend's threat lightly.

And Ashanti didn't disappoint. Up on stage, she belted out a husky rendition of 'Blackeye', singing the words 'dirty dog' with extra venom while looking straight at Ryan. Rosie was no better, sitting boot-faced throughout the performance and ignoring Cara's tentative nudges and Ryan's sporadic attempts at conversation. Cara chewed miserably on her lip, unable to blame the girls for their reaction when she was at fault for doing the unthinkable and bringing Ryan here.

'Will I get you another drink?' Ryan leaned in to be heard above the music and nodded in the direction of Cara's half-empty glass while flashing the lopsided grin that still had the power to set her pulse racing. Three years away hadn't erased the mischievous twinkle in his eyes and as the pressure of his arm against hers and the intimacy of his voice so close to her ear set her nerves jangling, Cara fought her body's natural impulse to wrap itself around him. Under the strobe lights, Ryan's hair glinted like sparkling coal and her traitorous fingers itched to touch the unruly curls. She swallowed to relieve her suddenly dry throat. *It's simply force of habit*, she told herself firmly, inching her chair away from his. She had no feelings for Ryan except curiosity and once that had been satisfied, she was perfectly happy never to see him or his twinkly eyes again.

She shook her head to his offer, and he turned back to watch the performance, seemingly oblivious to the malevolent glares Ashanti was directing at him from the stage. Ending her set to a raucous ovation, Ashanti returned to their table, her gracious smile vanishing as she settled herself back onto her stool and locked eyes with Ryan.

'So, you've been hiding away in Dublin all this time?' she asked without preamble, looking pained at having to initiate conversation with the enemy. 'And does Dexter know you're back?'

'Not yet. I wanted to see Cara first.'

'What? You haven't paid a visit yet to your "best mate of all time"?' Ashanti mocked. 'You remember him, don't you? The one you skipped out on without a word of warning or even a phone call just so he'd know you weren't lying dead in a ditch somewhere. The one you haven't bothered to call once in the last three years. Now, why doesn't that surprise me?'

'I'll explain everything to Dex when I see him,' Ryan said evenly. The muscle twitching at the side of his square jaw was the only indication that her comment had hit home, and he took a swallow from his almost empty bottle and slammed it back on the table.

Ashanti leaned in closer, her eyes glittering with hostility. 'Yeah, well, he might be a pushover where you're concerned, but don't think for a moment that goes for the rest of us.'

Cara winced, wondering how much more of this public flagellation she could stand. Ashanti looked like a crouching tiger ready to pounce, while Rosie was delivering a stellar performance of someone who'd lost her hearing. Cara had planned to use the evening to warn Ashanti against a hasty decision on Nine Elms Records, but all she wanted now was to extricate herself from the mess she had created.

'Come on, Ryan.' She stood up abruptly. 'I think it's time you left. We can walk down to the station. Girls, I'll see you later,' she said and threw an apologetic look at Rosie, who still wouldn't look at her or even acknowledge Ryan's casual 'See you later, then?'

For a moment, Ashanti looked like an animal deprived of its prey, and then she shrugged. 'Wish I could say it's been a pleasure, Ryan, but wherever you've been holed up, why don't you do us all a favour and go back there?'

Cara propelled him away from the table before he could respond and pushed him through the crowd to the door. Once outside, she took several deep breaths of the cool night air, immediately choking on the fumes from the smokers congregated on the pavement.

Ryan turned to face her and raised both hands in apology. 'Before you say anything, I'm really sorry about suggesting I come along tonight. I should have known it wouldn't go down well with your mates, and it wasn't fair of me to put you through that.'

Moving upwind of the cigarette smoke, Cara cocked her head to one side as she looked up at him. 'No, it didn't go down well, and it was stupid of me to let you come. But we're here now, so let's get this over with. Why *are* you back, Ryan?'

He pushed his hands into the pockets of his denim jacket and seemed to hesitate. 'Is it true you're going out with a posh rich boy?'

Stunned by his response, Cara shook her head in incredulous disbelief which instantly morphed into rage. She hadn't spoken to Ryan in years, so how did he know about Henry? And even if he knew about her boyfriend, how was that *any* of his business? How bloody *dare* he?

'What the hell are you talking about?' Cara spat, deeply regretting rescuing him from Ashanti.

'Was that him you were on the phone to when I was at your flat?' Ryan persisted. 'Look, it's not my fault I could hear you – don't you realise how thin those walls are? I'll tell you what, though, all that '*Hi, sweetie*' stuff didn't sound like the Cara I know.'

'*How* I speak and *who* I damned well choose to go out with is absolutely none of your bloody business! You lost that right a long time ago, Ryan, and you *don't* know me because I'm not that same person you left behind!'

'I do know you, Cara,' he said softly, returning her scorching glare with a look so intense that it took her breath away. His eyes were trained on hers as he took a step forward. 'No one knows you like I do. Whatever happened in the past doesn't change that and I don't care how rich or posh he is, no man will ever know you like I do.'

Cara shivered uneasily at the intensity behind his words. The guilt she had felt while on the phone to Henry returned with a vengeance, along with the unsettling realisation that by letting Ryan back in, she had unwittingly started something she might not have the power to finish. She had been furious at Ryan's audacity in showing up uninvited, so why on earth, after everything that had happened between them, had she harboured him in her home and then compounded the damage by allowing him to come out with her this evening? *What were you thinking?* And that, Cara thought sadly, was the problem. She *hadn't* been thinking, only feeling, because in truth, as much as she had wanted to slap him, for one crazy moment she had also wondered if he'd finally realised— *Damn, it, Ashanti was right!* When it came to Ryan, Cara *was* weak. Although nothing he said should matter anymore, even now a tiny part of her wanted to hear anything that would help her make sense of what he had done. *Stop it, Cara!* Ryan was her past and he had no business disturbing her present or making veiled threats about her future with Henry – and Cara had no business letting him. His eyes hadn't moved from hers and she had the eerie feeling he could read every word running through her mind. She raised her chin defiantly; one ruined evening was enough. There was no way in hell she was going to let him bring any further destruction into her life.

'Stop changing the subject, Ryan. I asked why you were here.'

'I'm not changing the subject. Rosie let slip to my mam that you were seeing this rich guy and it sounded serious.'

'So? What's it to you?'

The look of wry amusement that crossed his face was almost worse than the earlier intensity. 'Do I really need to say it?'

It had been growing chillier as they stood outside, but the night breeze couldn't cool the heat rising in Cara's chest. She felt her composure slipping, and her heart thudded mercilessly as she instinctively backed away.

'Cara, you know why I came back.' The deliberate, almost matter-of-fact tone was at odds with the determined set of his jaw and the fierce gleam in his eyes. She knew that look only too well. It was the same one he turned on anyone who tried to dissuade him from doing something he shouldn't. She'd lost count of the times she'd seen Ryan deploy that blistering stare and then coolly proceed to do exactly as he wished. Well, not this time.

'No, I don't know.' She turned away and when he reached out and pulled her back to face him, the touch of his hand on her bare skin set her chest pounding so hard that it hurt.

'Yes, you do,' Ryan insisted calmly.

His eyes narrowed as he looked down at her, refusing to let her drop her gaze. 'Stop it, Cara, I'm not fighting you on this. You know we belong together.'

She wrenched her arm out of his grasp. 'Oh? Is *that* what you think?' she demanded scornfully.

He shrugged. 'What do you want me to say? That I'm sorry? Well, I am. That I love you and I always will? I do – and you know that.'

She glared at him in silence, and, after a moment, he puffed out his cheeks and exhaled heavily, rubbing at the light stubble on his chin.

'Look, what happened, happened. I can't change that. I know I was a bastard, and honest to God, I'm sorry. But you know you're the only reason I came back. And you should also know there's no way I'm going to stand by and let another man take you away from me.'

What the hell?! Her breath came in furious gasps as she stared at him, outraged. *Why are you even listening to him, Cara? You have Henry now, and you're happy! For the first time in years, you're actually happy.* And she was. After what happened with Ryan, and barely surviving the darkest days of her life, having anything to do with him now was playing with fire and she couldn't afford to get burned again. Suddenly desperate to get away, Cara turned on her heel and bolted, the turmoil in her mind drowning out the sound of Ryan calling her name.

14

Wizards and Witches

A gangly-legged boy wearing a star-spangled cloak and with his hair gelled into blue peaks like an alien Statue of Liberty emerged from behind the bushes and staggered back towards the barn. Even the glow from the coloured lights strung around the building couldn't disguise his sickly pallor, and Cara swore under her breath, too frustrated by the unruly teenagers to heed her self-imposed swearing ban.

Ever since an eye-watering queue of luxury cars – she had counted at least three Bentleys, one Rolls-Royce, and several stretch limos – had swept up the gravelled driveway of the huge Hertfordshire barn and disgorged the teens, she had been tested to her party-organising limits.

Within half an hour the venue had been filled with a motley collection of witches, wizards, goblins and other unidentifiable creatures huddled together in small cliques with identical expressions of feigned boredom. The DJ's persistence had eventually paid off and the pulsating electronic beats brought them piling onto the dance floor, their plummy accents punctuated by high-pitched giggles and ear-piercing shrieks.

With one hurdle overcome, it was patently clear to Cara that another was looming. This was the second time in less than twenty minutes that she'd spotted Jasper sneaking out to throw up. Despite the alcohol ban boldly printed on Tabitha's invitation cards and plastered over the online party updates, Cara had known that any self-respecting teenager, particularly those of the rich, spoiled variety like Jasper – who had introduced himself on arrival, demanding to know if the food provided was organic – would attempt to sneak in banned substances. Which was precisely why she had drafted in Toby, Mocktails' burly bouncer, to put the frighteners on any guests trying their luck. Unfortunately, despite her instructions that he search everyone entering the venue for booze, Toby was failing spectacularly in his duties.

Watching Jasper lurch unsteadily towards the barn door, his long legs stirred up an image of Ryan in his favourite skinny jeans and Cara took a deep breath, cutting off her train of thought before it left the station. She needed all her wits about her to get through Tabitha's birthday party and she couldn't afford to think about the problem that was Ryan O'Hare. About to set off after Jasper, Cara stopped abruptly when another guest, a girl in a black wig only slightly shorter than her skirt, raced out of the barn with her hand clasped over her mouth and made a beeline for the area behind the shrubs that Jasper had just vacated.

More than ready to give her missing bouncer an earful, Cara spotted Toby laughing with a group of boys a short distance away from the door he'd been hired to guard. *What the hell was the point in being a strapping six feet four if you were going to let a bunch of adolescents run rings around you?* Judging by his expression, Toby was being royally entertained by the youngsters which, Cara thought irritably, was not what she was paying him for. At this rate, Toby's lackadaisical approach to screening was going to land her in serious trouble. *Do I have to sort* everything *out myself?*

'What's wrong with that boy?'

Cara wheeled around and her stomach contracted anxiously at Primrose's sharp tone and her look of suspicion. Drunken teenagers had not been among the requirements for her niece's birthday party, and it didn't take advanced detective skills to recognise a plastered schoolboy.

'Um . . . I think he just needed to get some air.'

Playing for time, Cara moved quickly to block Primrose's view of Jasper until he was safely inside the over-heated barn before steering her back inside and skilfully changing the topic.

'What do you think of the decor, Primrose? We were very lucky to get a brilliant young set designer who's making quite a name for himself in the theatre. He's done an amazing job, wouldn't you agree?'

Primrose craned her neck over Cara's shoulder and her eyes darted suspiciously around the crowded room. Seeing no sign of Jasper, she returned her attention to Cara and followed the sweep of her arm around the interior of the barn where tall shrubs and dwarf fruit trees had been cleverly draped with netting and black fabric to create the illusion of a dense forest. Strings of multi-coloured fairy lights hung across the ceiling and twinkled down the barn walls, illuminating the spooky scenery, and along one side of the barn were trestle tables covered with silver trays of black-iced cupcakes and a variety of witch-themed finger food now wilting in the heat. The waiters, dressed in black and sporting billowing black capes, circled the room with trays of soft drinks while periodically topping up several large cauldrons filled with fruit punch. To the side of the packed dance floor, the DJ gamely spun his tracks while trying to ignore the giggling girls taking it in turns to attract his attention.

Primrose nodded and shouted above the din, 'You've certainly put a lot of effort into things.' She turned to the girl who had moved over to join her. 'It looks quite marvellous, doesn't it, Imogen?'

Cara rolled her eyes and waited for the verdict. Imogen's unexpected appearance had been the biggest surprise of the evening and quite possibly the most challenging. Henry's sister had been the last person she'd expected to see emerging from the chauffeur-driven limousine ferrying Primrose and Tabitha. While Primrose had made the effort to wear a witch's costume, Imogen's short coral-pink dress offered no such concession to the party theme. Her smooth curtain of blonde hair and exquisitely made-up face had immediately left Cara conscious of her own shiny features and dusty boots.

But while Cara could have forgiven being made to feel a scruff, Imogen's open sneers and relentless carping about everything from the decor to the party food from the moment she'd set her Louboutin-shod foot at the party were harder to stomach.

Cara steeled herself as Imogen wrinkled her nose at Primrose's question. Her cut-glass vowels cut through the lull while the DJ switched the records on his decks.

'Well, it's all a bit . . . *provincial*, isn't it?'

Primrose looked alarmed. 'Darling! Whatever do you mean?'

Imogen shrugged, looking as cool as if she were in an air-conditioned restaurant instead of a barn with temperatures rivalling the tropics. 'I just don't get it, that's all. Why come all the way out to the sticks when you could have had the party in town and made it a bit more, you know, upmarket? Remember that amazing party Lucy Carrington-Hall threw at Blue Mist last year? She hired Marquise & Noble for the catering and the sushi was divine! She even flew in that yummy DJ from Cannes.'

Primrose stared at her doubtfully. 'But, darling, that was for Lucy's thirtieth. It's not quite the same for a teenager like Tabitha, is it?'

'Well, you asked my opinion!' Imogen sounded distinctly huffy, and Primrose hastened to reassure her.

'No, no, perhaps you're right. It *was* quite a trek to get here and maybe I should have used a bigger events company—' She broke off abruptly as her gaze wandered past Imogen. 'There's something very peculiar going on with those kids. What on earth is that boy *doing*?'

Silently fuming while the two women carried on their conversation as if she weren't standing right there in front of them, it took Cara a moment to realise Imogen was snorting with laughter. Cara spun around and cursed under her breath. The crowd on the dance floor had thinned while waiting for the music to start up again and a comatose Jasper, cocooned in his distinctive cloak, was clearly visible. He appeared to be fast asleep and had wrapped his long arms around the trunk of a papier mâché tree while his head rested snugly against a branch.

Cara signalled frantically to the DJ and the dance floor quickly filled up, but this time Primrose was not so easily distracted. Her cheeks flushed with anger as she glared accusingly at Cara.

'Is he *drunk?* You're supposed to be providing security checks!'

Cara bit her lip hard, for once lost for words and completely out of diversionary tactics. A glance towards the door where a laughing Toby was sharing a cigarette with a spiky-haired blond wizard didn't help the situation.

The tension was broken by Tabitha's nasal voice rising above the music. 'Aunty Primrose! When are we having the fireworks? Allegra and Cheska are getting bored and telling *everyone* they're going to phone for their cars.'

Although the birthday girl's whiny voice and bossy attitude was only slightly less annoying than Imogen's sarcasm, Cara could have kissed her for distracting Primrose. But Primrose, clearly flustered by her niece's belligerent questioning, immediately turned an accusatory glare onto Cara.

'When *are* you starting the fireworks display? And shouldn't it all have been set up by now?'

Cara scrabbled for an answer that would pacify the three sets of eyes trained on her, but being equally in the dark about when – or indeed if – the spectacular finale she had promised her client would take place, words failed her. Despite her repeated phone calls and increasingly desperate messages, there was still no sign of either Julio or his fireworks. Thanks to puking teenagers, an absent special effects man, a laid-back bouncer, and a now clearly hostile client, this was rapidly turning into the event from hell.

Openly enjoying Cara's discomfort, Imogen smirked and drifted off towards the drinks table. Taking advantage of the thumping music, Cara held up her phone and pointed to her ear and the door in quick succession, dashing out before Primrose could stop her.

Toby had disappeared once again. Silently cursing Paula for making her use Julio, Cara punched out his number and stared up into the night sky fantasising about the different ways she could murder him. This time, instead of going straight to voicemail, Julio answered with a cheery greeting on the second ring.

'Where the *hell* are you?' Cara snapped, even more annoyed that he didn't have the grace to sound embarrassed.

'I shall be there in five minutes, *bella*. It is not my fault, I swear. Gina, she gives me the wrong information and then my Siri, she takes me to another place.'

'Julio, I texted the address to you again this morning! How could you get it wrong?'

'*Chica*, don't be angry at Uncle Julio. I will arrive soon and make some nice fireworks for you—'

Exasperated, Cara cut him off and dialled another number. 'Please pick up, please please pick up,' she muttered feverishly as the ringing went on and on. Then she sighed with relief. '*Ozzie!* Thank God! Where are you? What's with all that barking?'

'Bloody Logan!' She could just about hear her brother's voice through the cacophony of yelps coming through the phone. 'Oi! *Shut up*, will you! Sorry, I meant the dog, not you.'

'What are you doing out with Logan?' Cara asked, curiosity momentarily overriding her troubles.

'Photoshoot.'

'With *Logan*? The only thing that dog could model is a hound from hell.'

Ozzie was clearly struggling to control the pet and after bellowing 'Get down!' twice more, he came back on the line. 'Sorry. I'm in the pick-up and the stupid mutt keeps trying to climb through and sit in the front. We needed a dog for the shoot I was on, so I slipped Manon a tenner for Logan. It was going well until he decided to chew the photographer's lens cap and— *Oi!* I said, SIT DOWN!'

A rubber-faced ghoul rushed out of the barn and towards the bushes and Cara ran a hand through her hair and tried to marshal her thoughts. Tabitha's guests were dropping like flies and there was no way she could handle this on her own.

'Ozzie, I need your help, and I need it now! I'm running a sixteenth birthday party near Hatfield. Half the guests are pissed out of their minds and bloody Toby's gone AWOL. I can't even distract the kids with fireworks because the muppet who's supposed to handle the display hasn't showed up yet.'

'No problem, Sis. I was taking Logan back, so I'm still up north and it shouldn't take me long. Text me the postcode and I'll be there as soon as I can.'

Despite Logan's incessant barking, her brother's reassuring words came through clearly and Cara breathed a sigh of relief. She needed help to find the illicit alcohol and she could count on Ozzie to be somewhat discreet, unlike Dexter who would have waded in with his size tens and made matters worse.

She had just finished texting the address when a dirty white van with a grinning Julio behind the wheel appeared out of the gloom and shot up the gravelled drive. Bringing the vehicle to a screeching halt, he leaped out, an impressive move in light of his skin-tight distressed jeans. He also looked remarkably cheerful, further enraging Cara, but with Primrose on the warpath there was no time to waste.

'Julio, for chrissakes, get a flaming move on! You should have been here ages ago and I can't put off my client much longer.'

He grasped her by the shoulders and kissed her on both cheeks before she could protest. 'Do not worry, my beautiful Cara! I am a professional. We shall get this show on the road very quick, no?'

Moving to the back of the van, he unloaded a pile of metal racks and coils of tangled cables, and, carrying the equipment over to the empty field, carefully arranged the racks a few inches apart from each other in semi-circular tiers.

'Are you doing this whole thing on your own?' Cara called over, with an anxious glance towards the barn door from where she fully expected a raging Primrose to come charging out at any moment. 'Can I do anything to speed things up?'

'No, *bella*. You leave everything to Uncle Julio, no?'

Cara watched impatiently as he lugged cartons from the van, broke open the boxes and planted coloured sticks into the holders on the racks, silently praying that he knew what he was doing. She flinched when he dropped a boxful of Roman candles on the ground before using his bare hands to shove cardboard-encased rockets onto the racks.

'Julio . . . um, are you *sure* you know what you're doing? And shouldn't you be wearing protective gear?'

He finished his task without comment, then returned to the van to extract a hard hat which he jammed onto his head. Strapping on a pair of round goggles, he walked up to her with a wide grin that exposed teeth glowing eerily white in the darkness.

'Are you worried for Uncle Julio?'

Cara's response was cut short as Tabitha came running out of the barn, cheeks scarlet from the heat.

'What's taking so long?' she demanded, her voice squeaky with indignation. Tabitha's pretty cornflower-blue eyes didn't quite compensate for her limp mousy hair or teeth that were just a little too big for her mouth, while her energetic dancing in a heavy black witch's gown had melted away her make-up to reveal painful-looking acne.

'We've been dancing for *hours*! When are we getting the fireworks? Everyone is *totally* fed up with waiting.'

On the verge of issuing a sharp retort, Cara saw the girl's lower lip wobble and she bit back her words. This overpriced party was clearly her route into the in clique of girls she had invited, and her bossy exterior barely concealed an anxious teenager terrified of alienating the popular girls. With no sign of her parents, it was clear Tabitha wasn't popular with her own family either and recalling how Primrose had dismissed her brother and his wife as hopeless, Cara suddenly found herself bristling with indignation on Tabitha's behalf.

What kind of people can't be bothered to show up for their own daughter's sixteenth birthday party? Manon's last birthday had been a riotous event packed with friends, family, and neighbours, along with an excited Logan kitted out in a frilly collar for the occasion. Without an expensively decorated barn or a high-priced canapé in sight, her little sister had experienced more fun that day than tonight's lavish celebration was bringing Tabitha.

Cara touched the teenager's shoulder. 'We'll be starting the fireworks show very soon, I promise. Tell everyone we'll be ready to go in fifteen minutes, okay?'

Tabitha's eyes lit up in relief and she gave an unexpected grin that transformed her sulky face into one that came close to being pretty.

'Cool!' She turned on her heel and Cara watched her scoot back inside. If pacifying the party girl had been easy, her aunt was a different matter. Just as Tabitha rushed in, Primrose strode out of the barn with Imogen following close behind.

'Cara!' Primrose stalked up to her, almost breathless with annoyance. Her once-sleek, bouncy bob was visibly wilting, and damp tendrils of hair clung to the back of her neck. 'This is just not good enough! The firework show should have started—'

She broke off as her gaze fell on Julio hurriedly erecting additional stands and her eyes bulged in disbelief at the combination of hard hat, goggles and skin-tight jeans. Following her gaze, Cara sighed. It was hard to fault Primrose's reaction; the sight of Julio in protective gear wouldn't have inspired her with much confidence either.

Imogen snickered loudly, but before she could speak, the roar of a pick-up truck had them whirling around in surprise.

15

ROCKET FIRE

The white pick-up bumped up the gravel track and came to a stop, and the three women watched the driver's door open and a tall blond man hop out, his athletic build emphasised by dark tailored trousers and a thin black turtleneck sweater. Even in the gloom, it was easy to make out his perfectly chiselled features as he strolled casually towards the assembled group and bent to kiss Cara's cheek before flashing a slow and devastating smile at the two gawping women. Primrose gulped visibly, while Imogen appeared frozen and, for once, speechless.

Cara grinned with relief at the welcome sight of her brother. 'Thanks for coming, Oz. I really appreciate it.'

'That's okay.' Ozzie looked around curiously and gave a low whistle as he took in the imposing barn. 'Wow, this place is amazing! Okay, Sis, what do you need me to do?'

'*Sis?*' Primrose croaked.

Cara slipped a hand through the crook of Ozzie's arm. 'Oh, Primrose, this is my brother, Ozzie.' She glanced at Ozzie, who was clearly relishing Primrose's shocked reaction. 'And this is Primrose Wynter. My client.' She stressed the last word meaningfully.

'Your *brother*? But you're— he's . . .' Primrose tailed off with a frown, her gaze swivelling from one to the other in disbelief.

'Yes,' Ozzie agreed cheerfully.

Imogen suddenly found her voice and sprang into action. Tossing back her hair, she shoved Primrose aside and offered Ozzie her hand and a dazzling smile.

'Well, *hel-lo*! I'm Imogen, Henry's sister,' she said, her clipped vowels suddenly transformed into a purr. 'It's lovely to meet you. Henry mentioned that Cara has an, um, interesting family and as you're her brother, well . . . gosh, that makes us practically related!'

Cara's smile faded at the sight of Imogen preening like a beautiful blonde cat waiting to be stroked and not, she thought sourly, in a sisterly way. Not that her brother seemed to mind.

'It's a pleasure to meet you too . . . erm, both of you.'

The last bit was clearly an afterthought as Ozzie seemed in no hurry to release Imogen's proffered hand, and Cara stared at him with mounting dismay. This was no time for him to go into seduction mode. She had a crisis on her hands and even if she hadn't, the prospect of her womanising brother flirting with Henry's sister sat right at the top of her list of very bad ideas.

A series of howls from the back of the truck broke the spell, and Ozzie turned towards the vehicle, stuck two fingers into his mouth and emitted an ear-piercing whistle that made them all jump. Logan whined once more, and then fell silent, and Cara used the opportunity to tug her brother to one side and whisper in his ear. 'Half the kids here are loaded and puking up all over the place. You need to get in there, find the source of the booze and seize anything you come across!'

Ozzie's lips twitched with suppressed laughter, but one look at Cara's expression made it clear she wasn't joking. Shaking his head, he strode towards the barn, immediately followed by Imogen. Not to be outdone, Primrose smoothed down her hair and hurried along after them, with Cara following in the hope of distracting her brother's new fan club long enough for him to find and confiscate the contraband alcohol.

The instant Ozzie marched into the barn, several of the witches and wizards on the dance floor stopped to stare. Paying no attention, he cast a thoughtful look around and made an immediate beeline for the nearest cauldron. Having failed to steer Imogen and Primrose away, Cara joined them, holding her breath as Ozzie scooped a ladle of the contents into one of the black plastic cups stacked alongside, took a cautious sip, and grimaced before placing the cup back on the table.

'There's your culprit,' he pronounced firmly.

Cara stared at him in horror. 'But . . . but that's supposed to be a non-alcoholic fruit punch!'

'Unless vodka is a fruit, someone's been spiking the drinks. I'll check the other cauldrons, but, from the strength of this one, it's no wonder everyone's off their heads.'

Imogen waited until he was out of sight before dropping her smile. 'I thought you were meant to be keeping an eye on all this, Cara.'

'Yes indeed, Cara!' Primrose echoed accusingly, her eyes as hard as blue pebbles in her heat-flushed face. Her long-sleeved costume had not been designed for the barn's near-sauna conditions and her fringe lay in limp strands over her damp forehead.

'I'm so sorry, Primrose. I'll sort it out – I promise!' Trying not to sound panicked, Cara injected a note of soothing reassurance into her apology. She grabbed one of the waiters passing by and pointed to the offending cauldron. 'Look, could you tip everything out and fill it up again with a fresh batch of fruit juice. I need it done now!'

Picking up on the urgency of her tone, he nodded and waved over another waiter and Cara waited until they'd dragged the cast-iron cauldron outside. Then, taking a deep breath, she marched over to the DJ and seized his microphone with a gesture to turn off the music. As soon as the ensuing chorus of disappointed protests died down, she announced in her loudest and sternest voice: 'Right, listen up, you lot! I want everyone – and I mean *everyone*, girls and boys – to bring your bag and put it over there in that corner. No one gets theirs back until the party's over!'

Ignoring the disgruntled murmurs, she handed back the mic and walked over to stand guard while the sullen-faced teens trooped across the room to deposit their designer label bags. Someone shook Jasper awake and he staggered up on legs that looked ready to fold at every step. When he eventually dropped his bag onto the rapidly growing pile, the clink of glass was distinctly audible, and Cara shook her head. No wonder Jasper seemed so much more incapacitated than the others.

The owner of the last bag to be surrendered was a leggy blonde in a tight black dress and a silver necklace spelling out the name Allegra. Judging from the awe with which Tabitha had greeted her late arrival, Allegra was clearly the queen bee of the group, and she scowled as she placed her diamanté-studded clutch bag on top of the pile of expensive leather.

'God, this party is so *lame*,' she said bitterly before stalking off to re-join her squad. Cara sent up a silent prayer that Tabitha wouldn't suffer too much from her intervention and looked around in search of her back-up. Ozzie, his detective duties completed, was propped up against a nearby wall laughing as Imogen smiled prettily and leaned in to whisper something in his ear. Primrose had given up trying to restore her hair to rights and stood watching them, looking so dejected that Cara almost felt sorry for her. *It's like watching a preview of Allegra and Tabitha in fifteen years.*

Julio chose that moment to swagger in, jeans clinging to him like a second skin and goggles atop his head. Spotting Cara, he grinned and sauntered over. '*Querida,* I search for you everywhere! I am ready to start the show.'

Anxious to get the fireworks over before the convoy of luxury cars returned to collect the guests, Cara shooed everyone outside, stopping to help up a drowsy Jasper who'd been sitting on the floor with his back against the wall. Almost fizzing with excitement, Tabitha dragged Primrose outside while Imogen disappeared to the loo. Taking advantage of Primrose's temporary absence, Cara elbowed Ozzie in the ribs.

'You *do* know you're here to help me out and not to flirt with my clients, don't you? For God's sake, Ozzie, she's Henry's *sister.* Stay away from her!'

'Calm—' Ozzie caught himself just in time and smiled sheepishly. 'I mean, sorry, Sis. We were just talking, I promise. But you've got to admit she's a looker . . .'

Cara narrowed her eyes in warning, and he raised a hand in surrender. 'I'm *kidding*! Come on, let's get out there before those tanked-up little horrors set fire to themselves.'

Outside, Julio's goggles were back in place as he tried shooing everyone away from the racks of fireworks. 'Move back, MOVE BAA-ACK!' he bellowed. But each time he repelled one wave of curious teenagers, another would move in.

At this rate, they would be here until midnight, Cara sighed, glancing at Ozzie who obligingly stuck his fingers in his mouth and let loose another ear-piercing whistle. Taking advantage of the stunned silence that followed, she cupped her hands around her mouth and yelled, 'EVERYONE STAND WELL BACK, PLEASE! Fireworks are dangerous and we can't start the show unless you move back!'

The witches and wizards reluctantly followed her orders and Julio cast a last aggrieved look around before lighting a long flare and approaching the first set of racks. A rocket instantly took flight with a loud *whoosh!*, sending up a brightly coloured flame that exploded with an enormous bang. Within seconds it was followed by a volley of thunderous booms as spears of multicoloured light pierced the night sky.

'*Oooh!*' The teenagers murmured appreciatively, and Julio immediately let loose a bombardment of Roman candles which cannoned upwards with loud hums and crackles before scattering into stars of light. Warming up to his task, he set off a rack of fountains, earning a roar of approval from the bystanders that was almost drowned out by the bangs and whistles that followed the shower of sparks.

Despite the din from the fireworks, Cara could feel the stiffness in the back of her neck begin to ease. Things were back on track and the excitement from the partygoers was almost palpable. Through the splashes of light from the fireworks, she could see Tabitha jumping up and down in excitement, all pretence at sophistication forgotten.

Julio was clearly in his element. His wide grin sparkled white in the darkness as he bounded up and down with his flare, setting off rockets, carousels and spinning wheels like a crazy conductor. Egged on by his audience, he let loose a stunning cascade of sky-rockets which shot up into the sky accompanied by ear-shattering crackles.

Tabitha ran over and pulled excitedly on her arm and Cara smiled at her radiant expression. At least one of her clients was happy, she thought ruefully, feeling the first glimmer of goodwill towards Julio that night. He might be a complete numpty, but he was clearly giving the kids a magnificent show.

Much later, she would remember that as her last coherent thought before all hell broke loose. Spurred on by the excited 'oohs' and 'aahs', Julio lined up his big guns for the finale. He sped from one side of the rack to the other to set alight several enormous rockets and mortar shells, jumping back just in time as streams of coloured stars shot upwards, followed by deafening bangs that were easily the loudest of the night.

Suddenly, with the anguished howl of a dog who had been pushed beyond its limits, Logan broke free from his restraints in the back of the pick-up and bounded down into the crowd. His shaggy white coat streaked into the horde of teens whose panicked shrieks sounded even louder than the high-pitched whistles from the exploding fireworks.

As they attempted to dodge the mass of barking fur on the rampage, the kids tripped over each other, tumbling into the muddy grass. Ozzie dived into the melee to rescue his enraged dog and, desperate to keep Ozzie in her sights, Imogen dashed after him and missed her footing, falling heavily into a spiky bush from where her piercing screams added to the cacophony.

Logan, meanwhile, sped towards the racks of spent fireworks and was clearly set on destroying the stands that held the infuriating banging objects.

Julio blanched and then bellowed, 'Get that dog away from my *theengs*!'

But Logan was incensed beyond measure and hurled himself against the nearest rack.

'Get back!' Julio screamed furiously. Too late, he rushed to stop Logan, but the dog whisked past him and streaked away in a pale blur. Cara watched in horror as one rack slowly tipped over before toppling the others like a row of dominoes while Julio raced around the smouldering equipment screaming furiously in Spanish.

'*Logan!* You stupid mutt, come HERE!' Ozzie roared, sprinting after the dog who promptly ploughed back into the group of children, deftly dodging the grasping hands reaching out to pin him down until finally Ozzie managed to grab his trailing lead. Keeping a tight grip, he fell to the ground and secured the exhausted dog between his legs, both panting furiously.

With Logan captured, the crowd fell silent. Cara surveyed the muddy teenagers sprawled across the damp field and the carnage caused by Logan's run in dismay. The metal display racks, some with tapers still smouldering, lay on their sides like abandoned iron babies, while bits of coloured packaging and spent fireworks were scattered in every direction. The party was officially a disaster. Poor, poor Tabitha! Primrose was going to kill her, and what the *hell* was she going to tell Paula?

'Aww . . . look at that *darling* dog!' A high-pitched drawl cut through the silence, and Cara watched in astonishment as Allegra tripped across the trampled grass in her designer heels to where Ozzie was soothing an indignant Logan. Her scornful expression had melted into a beatific smile and the other girls immediately crowded around her, eager to endorse their leader's seal of approval.

Tearing her eyes away from the unlikely sight of Tabitha sitting next to Allegra as she crouched on the grass petting Logan, Cara looked across to where Julio was muttering furiously while dousing the remaining fireworks and trying to retrieve his possessions. Deeply contrite that her dog had sabotaged his show, she went over to help. Unfortunately, Julio's mad scramble to save his equipment had stressed his heavily distressed jeans and, as he leaned over to pick up a rack, the trousers split at the back with a loud rip. Cara stopped in her tracks, her mouth falling open at the silky scarlet briefs on display.

A group of teenagers standing nearby immediately began screaming with laughter. 'Love your knickers, mate!' one cried, making kissing noises that convulsed his friends and set off a chain of drunken jeers and wolf whistles.

Julio turned as crimson as his underwear. Filling his arms with whatever they could hold, he stormed off angrily towards his van.

Tossing the equipment into the back, he climbed in and slammed the door. With a loud crunching of gears, he shot off down the road, sending shards of gravel flying out from beneath the van's spinning tyres.

Minutes later, a black Rolls-Royce rolled majestically up the drive, closely followed by a fleet of limousines.

'Oh, *crap!*' Cara felt a knot forming in her stomach as the cars drew up in front of the barn. A young girl's birthday party had been ruined thanks to contraband booze, a mad dog, and a temperamental special effects man. Julio's inadvertent underwear display was the final nail in the coffin of a calamitous evening, and she had run out of time to redeem herself.

'Cara! *Cara!*' Tabitha was tugging insistently at her sleeve and Cara's heart sank. But instead of a tirade of teenage hysteria, Tabitha looked ecstatic, and her blue eyes were sparkling.

'Oh my God, Cara, that was *brilliant!* It was such a great idea to bring the dog. He's *so* gorgeous. Look at everyone!'

Cara blinked as she followed Tabitha's gaze to where a laughing Ozzie was holding onto Logan, who was now surrounded by a crowd of admirers. The bored young sophisticates that had arrived earlier that evening had been transformed by the dog's antics into animated giggling teenagers. Even Primrose, who stood a couple of feet away, was smiling for the first time that evening, while Imogen had manoeuvred herself into standing beside Ozzie, who was keeping a tight hold on Logan.

Feeling as though she had landed in a parallel universe, Cara returned Tabitha's excited hug before shooing the guests inside to collect their party bags and reluctantly head off to their waiting transport. A few minutes later, the luxury cars rolled away into the night with shrieks of 'Bye, Tabitha!' and 'Great party!' drifting out of the open windows.

The last limo to depart was the one ferrying Primrose, Imogen and Tabitha home, and Primrose had already taken her seat when Cara came to say goodbye. Still flushed and bubbling with excitement, Tabitha gave Cara an exuberant hug before jumping into the car to join her aunt. Imogen unpeeled herself from Ozzie's side and slipped her mobile phone into her tote bag with a coy smile before sliding gracefully into her seat.

Primrose stuck her head out of the car window and although her face was beetroot-red and without a trace of make-up, her smile was still in place.

'Thanks, Cara.' She beamed. 'All's well that ends well, eh?'

Cara nodded dumbly and stood back, watching the car bump its way down the drive until its red tail-lights receded into the darkness.

Logan gave a deep bark as if to say good riddance, and Cara turned to her brother and exhaled with relief. 'Thank Christ that's over!'

Ozzie released his hold on Logan and followed Cara's gaze around the smouldering remains of the firework display. 'I'm really sorry Logan messed things up, Sis.'

Cara shrugged. '*Shi*— stuff happens, what can you do?' She flashed him a grin. 'I'm just glad you were here and although I never thought I'd hear myself say this, thank God you brought Logan with you! Who knew those little rich divas had a human side, eh?'

She bent to hug the dog and ruffle his fur affectionately and Logan barked in appreciation and wagged his tail. 'Nice one, Logan. I think it's safe to say you saved the day.'

Cara glanced up at Ozzie with a rueful smile. 'I hope Primrose doesn't come to her senses and sue us, but at least Tabitha enjoyed herself in the end.'

She grimaced at the debris scattered around the field. 'I'd better pack up the rest of Julio's stuff and take it back to him because I doubt he'll ever set foot here again. Although how I'm supposed to look him in the face after seeing his rear end in scarlet undies . . .' She shuddered.

'Come on, let's clear this mess up,' Ozzie said. They worked fast to bag Julio's equipment, eventually bringing a semblance of order back to the grounds. Once the caterers and the waiters had left, Logan was shooed into the pick-up, and they were about to drive off when Cara noticed a sudden movement in the grass. She placed a restraining hand on Ozzie's arm and gestured to him to turn off the ignition.

Jumping out of the truck, she strode towards the bushes with Ozzie close behind her and gasped as the torch on her brother's mobile lit up a pair of long, lanky legs. The legs twitched again, accompanied by the sound of a deep snore. Although the head was hidden by foliage, Cara knew exactly who it was.

'*Jasper!*'

16

LEGAL EAGLE

'How on earth did you get him back home?' Henry was laughing so hard he could barely get the words out.

They had finished their main course and the dark-suited waiter with an accent even posher than Henry's had just taken their dessert order. Cara looked around warily as her boyfriend's guffaws rose above the hum of discreet chatter in the restaurant. She half expected them to be taken out quietly and shot for breaching the well-bred-low-volume threshold, although to be fair no one appeared curious about why the man sitting across from her was convulsed with laughter.

Taking no chances, she leaned across the table and lowered her voice. 'Well, luckily for us, Ozzie managed to wake him up long enough to find out where he lived. Which was just as well because he passed out again and we had to drive back with him propped up between us.'

Henry tried unsuccessfully to choke back his chuckles and she gave a reluctant smile. It might sound funny now, but the late-night drive to Chelsea with a comatose teenager had been no joke. She had been terrified of being stopped by a suspicious police officer and accused of intoxicating or, even worse, kidnapping a minor.

Henry wiped his eyes and shook his head in disbelief. 'He's bloody lucky you found him. Can you imagine if you'd left him behind?'

Cara shivered at the thought of poor, drunk Jasper lying in the grass all night. 'I still can't believe his parents weren't crazy with worry – the kid is fifteen! Ozzie had to ring the doorbell three times when we got to Jasper's house before they finally woke up and opened the door. I can't imagine Mum and Dad letting Thaddeus go to a party and then going off to bed without a care in the world.'

'No wonder the poor kid has turned to drink.' Henry's smile faded. 'Just goes to show that it doesn't matter how much money you've got if no one gives a stuff about you.'

It was time to change the subject, and Cara smiled and nudged Henry's foot with hers under cover of the table, her eyes sparkling with mischief.

'This is a very upmarket restaurant you've brought me to, Mr Fitzherbert.'

She glanced around at the wood-panelled walls hung with traditional landscapes of the English countryside and up at the vaulted ceilings with glittering chandeliers reminiscent of those in Oakley Manor. Her first impression that the restaurant shrieked opulence had been confirmed by one look at the prices in the leather-bound book the waiter had handed her with a reverential bow. Her second thought as she scanned the elaborate menu was that a meal here would cost her a week's rent.

Henry looked at her uncertainly. 'I know it's a bit old fashioned, but the food is good. Don't you like it?'

'Oh, no, it's lovely!' she hastened to reply. 'It's just, well, it's just not . . . you know, somewhere I'd normally eat.'

When his frown didn't budge, she added, 'But there's nothing wrong with trying new things and you're right about the food. My rack of lamb was absolutely delicious.'

Relieved to see him smile, Cara mentally kicked herself for sounding ungracious. It *was* a lovely place, even if the potatoes came in every form except chips and the ketchup was called tomato sauce. If she was feeling awkward, it was probably more to do with her black dungarees and Doc Martens and the red leather jacket the cloakroom attendant had taken off her. She pushed away her sense of disquiet and tried to enjoy the experience. After all, she was here now and after a hectic week at the office it was a joy to be away from Paula's eagle-eyed supervision and Ben's endless ribbing about the party.

Henry was back in full conversational flow, looking relaxed and at ease. *And why wouldn't he?* This was, after all, his world. Wood-panelled rooms, rich tapestries, English watercolours, linen napkins, clipped accents. Unlike her, he had grown up surrounded by these things and he had no reason to feel out of place.

Irritated by the direction her thoughts were taking, Cara gave herself a mental shake. *Snap out of it! If you want to be with Henry, you need to compromise and get comfortable in places like this.* Henry couldn't change who he was any more than she could, and, given the choice, there wasn't a single thing she would have wanted to change. She loved how Henry wore his self-assurance in an understated way that never veered into a sense of entitlement, and she appreciated the old-fashioned courtesy he showed her by opening doors and walking on the car side of the pavement. She loved the way he listened intently, the little frown between his eyes showing his concentration even when she went off at a tangent. She loved that he was a superb cook but never criticised her limited culinary skills, and that he could be serious one minute and laughing with unselfconscious abandonment the next. She loved the way his eyes

160

lit up whenever he saw her, but most of all she loved his kindness, and how he could never walk past a homeless person on the street without offering a cheery greeting and leaving some money.

It doesn't help to go looking for problems where none exist, she told herself sternly. She took a sip of the vintage wine in her glass *– but seriously, how did they justify charging over a hundred pounds for a single bottle!* – and tried to focus on her boyfriend's account of the legal case his team had just won. Describing how the trial had been so dull that even the judge had fallen asleep, Henry's eyes danced with amusement, and she dismissed her negative thoughts and laughed along with him.

Just then, her bag began to vibrate, and Cara reached down to slide out her phone. Glancing at the screen, she felt her nerves tighten. This was the tenth call from Ryan today and, just as she had done with the other nine, she punched the decline button to send it straight to voicemail. She knew it was only postponing the inevitable and giving Ryan the opportunity to leave yet another message begging her to talk, but she was in no mood to let him ruin her evening.

Henry finished recounting his story and leaned in closer, his eyes looking straight into hers. The flickering flame from the candle on their table added a fiery intensity to his gaze and she shivered deliciously as his foot rubbed gently up and down her leg.

'I'm delighted you've enjoyed your meal, Ms Nightingale, although it was nowhere near as delicious as you are,' he murmured. His gaze slid down to her full lips and she flushed at the naked lust in his eyes, desperately wishing they were alone and not in the middle of a busy restaurant.

The spell was broken by the waiter arriving with their dessert. Cara picked up her spoon and broke into the perfectly bronzed crust of the crème brûlée, exclaiming as the smoothness of the vanilla custard melted on her tongue. Restraining herself from scraping out every scrap of the creamy concoction, she watched Henry spoon the last of his sticky toffee pudding into his mouth.

'How's your mother, by the way?'

'You mean, how's her croquet lawn?' he smiled, not fooled in the slightest by her nonchalance.

Cara looked sheepish and Henry dropped his napkin and placed a reassuring hand over hers. 'Sweetheart, I've told you a hundred times that it's fine. It's only grass, for pity's sake! Jenkins has dealt with it and even Mother says you'd never know there'd been any damage. Now will you *please* stop worrying about it?'

While she doubted if she would ever forget the image of the roughly punctured lawn now seared into her brain, Henry was right. The damage had been repaired and there was nothing more she could do about it. Her thoughts turned to the other issue on her mind; if Imogen, who clearly had Primrose wrapped around her little finger, would somehow persuade her to change her mind and declare Tabitha's party an unmitigated disaster. Plagued by fear all week and in blatant violation of Paula's strict post-event client evaluation process, Cara still hadn't plucked up enough courage to contact the lawyer.

'Um, has Imogen said anything to you about Tabitha's party?' she murmured, desperate for any clues about his sister's state of mind.

Henry raised an eyebrow at the change in topic, and then shrugged. 'Not really. I thought it was a bit weird that she went in the first place since she hates kids, but, when we spoke the other day, she sounded like she'd rather enjoyed herself.'

Which was a relief, although she suspected Imogen's enjoyment had more to do with a certain Ozzie Grant than the birthday party, and she made a mental note to remind her brother to back off where Imogen was concerned. She had spotted him handing back her phone before she left, and Cara hadn't been taken in for a second by Ozzie's innocent smile at being caught in the act. She briefly considered telling Henry about the flirtation between their siblings but decided not to bother. Ozzie was the total opposite of the upper-crust types Imogen was used to dating, and she had hopefully forgotten all about him. As annoying as Imogen was, even she didn't deserve to be the next victim of Ozzie's infamous track record with women.

Cara's phone buzzed again, and she forced herself to ignore it. There was no way she was letting Ryan intrude into her life or ruin what she had with Henry.

Henry signalled for the bill and, moments later, the waiter arrived with a leather-bound folder which he placed on the table and nudged discreetly towards Henry. He offered Cara a bland smile which she returned through gritted teeth, torn between feeling offended that he obviously didn't think she could afford it and relieved that Henry was the one paying for the overpriced meal. It must be nice not to worry about money, she mused, watching Henry whip out a gold credit card. Her job at Westbrook Events didn't command what anyone would consider a massive salary, and even though she bought most of her clothes from vintage market stalls and high street shops, clearing her credit card was still a pipe dream. Watching Henry pay the exorbitant bill without flinching was depressing and it set her wondering yet again if she would ever feel comfortable in his affluent, upper-class world or if he would ever truly understand hers? In that moment, she couldn't help wondering if Dexter was right and she was wasting her time not facing reality.

They left the restaurant and walked hand in hand down the quiet Fulham side street. Happy to be out of the stuffy restaurant, Cara breathed in the evening air and, as it slowly filled her lungs, she felt lighter and more relaxed.

Without warning, Henry stopped and pulled her to him, wrapping his arms around her. His eyes were so close that she could see tiny flickers of light reflecting the glow from the streetlights overhead.

'I'm sorry.'

She stared at him in bewilderment. 'What for?'

Ignoring the irritated tut from a passer-by forced to walk around them, he pulled her even closer. 'For taking you to such an old-fashioned, boring restaurant. I honestly don't know what I was thinking.'

She disengaged herself and stared at him with a straight face, keeping her voice deadpan. 'You mean, you just assumed that I would love to go wherever you used to take Annabelle or Camilla or Bunny . . . or . . .?'

Henry looked aghast until she grinned cheekily. 'Gotcha!'

He exploded into laughter and she squealed loudly as he slipped his hands beneath her jacket to tickle her through the thin cotton vest under her dungarees.

'Okay, stop, I'm sorry . . .!' she gasped, helpless with laughter and trying to catch her breath.

He kissed her hard before releasing her. 'You scared the hell out of me. I really thought I'd offended you!'

'It takes a bit more than a pricey meal at a fancy restaurant to do that,' Cara giggled, reaching up to stroke his hair away from his eyes.

Just then her phone trilled loudly, and she froze. There was no point pretending she couldn't hear it ring, and yet she couldn't move.

'Aren't you going to see who it is?' Henry looked mystified by her reaction.

Her heartbeat had accelerated into a tattoo, but not answering the phone would only invite unwelcome questions. She reluctantly fished the handset out of her bag and released a slow breath of relief when she saw the name flashing on the screen.

'Ash! Hi, what's up?' The excited squeaks coming over the line had her wincing. 'Slow down, I can't hear a word you're saying!'

After a few more squeaks, Cara shook her head in exasperation. 'Look, I get that you want to sign a deal with them, but why's it all happening so fast? Are you sure Nine Elms Records is the right label for you? You're so talented, you're bound to—'

She held the phone several inches from her ear as Ashanti's voice rose in indignation. '*I'm bound to what?* Get a recording contract? How long are you going to keep telling me that? For God's sake, I've been playing grungy pubs and bars for years and still not got anywhere! How many more gigs do you expect me to keep doing at Mocktails for agents that never show up? I'm almost *thirty*, Cara! That's ancient for a singer these days. If I don't take this deal, who knows when I'll get another one.'

Ashanti took a breath and then lowered her voice. 'Cara, why does there *always* have to be a problem with you? Why can't you just be happy for me?'

'Okay, fine, so what does Rosie say?' Cara countered, knowing Rosie shared her misgivings about Elliott Robbins.

'I phoned her, but the sneaky cow said she couldn't talk because she's on a date with Sean bloody Strakey! She's a dark horse, that one.'

'Well, well . . . she kept that quiet! Wait till I see her.' Remembering the reason for Ashanti's call, Cara's tone sobered. 'Look, Ash, let's talk about this before you go ahead—'

She sighed as Ashanti's voice reverted to squeak mode. '*No!* Elliott says if I'm serious, we need to sign the deal by the end of next week, and he needs to know now if I'm on board before they put out a press release. They're only taking on three new artists this year so they can focus their resources on them, and I'm meeting the other two people on Thursday when we're all signing.'

After a short pause, Ashanti added, 'Cara, I didn't ring to ask your permission. I just wanted to tell you, and I stupidly thought you'd be happy for me.'

But all Cara could think about was protecting Ashanti from her own impulsiveness. Everything about Elliott Robbins felt shady, and she couldn't ignore the nagging feeling that he was railroading Ashanti into an agreement. But before she could speak, the phone line went dead, bringing the conversation to an abrupt end.

'What's happened?' Henry asked.

She shrugged and gave him a potted account of the offer from Nine Elms Records. 'I don't understand why they're in such a rush to make her sign their deal. Ashanti's an amazing singer, but she's so desperate for a recording contract that she's not thinking straight and keeps falling for con artists. Under normal circumstances, I'd call Dexter to talk some sense into her but *they're* still not speaking after the way he behaved the last time someone tried to rip her off. I'm really worried about her, Henry.'

'Look, entertainment law isn't my area of speciality, but I'd be happy to look over the contract for her if that would help put your mind at ease.'

Cara couldn't hide her relief. 'Would you? Thanks, Henry, that would be amazing. I'll tell her, and I only hope she isn't too stubborn to accept the offer.'

He smiled wryly. 'You worry about everybody, sweetheart. Why do you feel it's your job to sort out everyone's problems?'

Cara shrugged, trying not to feel defensive. It wasn't as if she enjoyed taking on other people's issues, but it was impossible for her to walk away when someone she cared about was in trouble.

'It's just who I am. My life hasn't been as easy as yours, Henry. I had to grow up early. I don't know . . . between getting Dexter out of scrapes and trying to help Mum out, I suppose the habit has just stuck.'

They walked along in silence until they reached the taxi rank by the station. Cara had come straight to the restaurant from work and the plan was for the two of them to go back to hers for the night.

'So, what are you going to do, then?' Henry asked as they joined the short queue.

Cara sighed and pulled her jacket tightly around her. Ashanti's call had dampened her spirits and the perfect summer evening had suddenly lost its warmth.

'I don't have a clue.'

17

CLOSE ENCOUNTERS

'Right, I've got a job for you!'

Paula strode into the room clutching a sheaf of papers and marched up to Cara's desk. Her uniform black trousers were teamed with a lime-green blouse, while the vivid slash of red lipstick signalled that Useless Dave was in the building.

Caught off-guard, Cara quickly slid her phone under an open file, hoping her gimlet-eyed manager hadn't seen her using it. Making personal phone calls during office hours was high on Paula's long list of no-nos and winding up her supervisor with a second infraction within a week would have been pushing it. Cara was still smarting from being read the riot act after being forced to admit the post-event evaluation for Tabitha's party Paula had been fruitlessly searching for didn't exist. A stickler for rules – *'What do we have if we don't have good processes?'* – Paula had been apoplectic.

'Is that a new top you're wearing?' Cara observed, forcing an ingratiating smile.

Paula glanced at her suspiciously and ignored the comment, waving the sheets of paper impatiently. 'I've just had a meeting with Malcolm, and for some reason he wants you to take the lead on this event. I told him that if I had my way, you wouldn't be starting *any* new project until I was sure you understood the importance of our processes. Not that he's much better,' she sniffed. The MD's relaxed attitude to procedures irritated Paula even more than his frequent threats to consign Useless Dave to the unemployment line.

'But as he's the boss,' she reluctantly conceded, 'I suppose I've got no choice.'

'Oh? What's the job?' Cara asked curiously.

'You're in charge of setting up a *fun*,' the word seemed to stick in Paula's throat, 'team-building away day for an advertising agency.' She flipped to the bottom of the last page and her eyes widened.

'Well, at least they're up for spending some decent money. Let me see your concept ideas as soon as possible – and don't come up with anything too weird!'

Before Paula could walk away, Ben's quiff reared up across the partition, his eyes bright with curiosity. 'Advertising? That sounds interesting. Can I work on it with Cara?'

Ready to dismiss the suggestion, Cara held her tongue. After the birthday party debacle, it mightn't be such a bad idea to have some back-up next time. Furthermore, with Ashanti having grudgingly agreed that Cara could accompany her to the signing ceremony at Nine Elms Records later that week, Ben could provide her with useful cover while she snuck off.

'That's not a bad idea, Paula,' she said casually. Sounding too enthusiastic was a sure way to make Paula refuse on principle since actively enjoying work was another no-no on her list. 'Ben used to work in advertising, and it would be good to have his input.'

Paula nodded and dropped the papers onto Cara's desk. 'Fine, I'll let Betsey know. But, Ben, that doesn't mean you get to slack off on your other projects, and you, Cara, don't forget to fill out the project forms and input *all* the quotes this time. Between the two of you, let's see if we can get this event handled properly for a change.'

Just managing to stop herself from rolling her eyes, Cara smiled sweetly, and they watched in silence as Paula strode back to her desk.

As soon as she was out of earshot, Ben leaned over the partition. 'Okay, so what was that about?'

'What do you mean?' Cara said innocently.

'Don't give me that! How come you didn't fight tooth and nail to keep me off the job? Everyone knows you hate collaborating.'

'So, maybe it's time I was a bit more, you know, open to other ideas.' Cara flipped through the sheets that Paula had left and raised an eyebrow in shock. '*Bloody hell!* I mean, my goodness, have you seen the size of this budget?'

Three hours later, having dutifully responded to emails, filed Primrose's reassuringly glowing testimonial, and set up appointments to view potential venues for the ad agency's away day, Cara left the office and Paula's eagle-eyed scrutiny. Henry was in Leeds for a few days, and she was looking forward to a quiet evening in front of the telly doing nothing more demanding than eating Pringles and catching up on her missed TV shows. Even the angry honking of drivers caught up in the never-ending roadworks outside the station couldn't dent her enjoyment of the late summer sunshine. Debating whether to pop to the Tesco Express for a bottle of wine, she rounded the corner to find Ryan sitting on the steps leading to her door flicking through a battered copy of *Metro*.

'This is getting to be a very bad habit,' she said frostily. She stepped past him and climbed up the steps to get to her front door while scrabbling in her bag for the key.

'Maybe if you answered my phone calls, I wouldn't need to do this.' He tossed aside the newspaper and stood up, bringing their eyes level, and she tried not to flinch as he leaned towards her, his dark-navy eyes dangerously close. Despite what felt like a hundred butterflies fluttering in her stomach, she was determined not to let him see that he still affected her.

'Well, *maybe* if you took the hint, you wouldn't need to waste my time and yours.'

Apparently unperturbed by the shortness of her tone, he smiled, and she forced her eyes away from his endearingly crooked side tooth.

'Ryan, I've had a long day and I don't need this. I've got a ton of things to do this evening and we've said everything that needs saying.'

'You mean *you've* said everything you want to say,' he corrected.

She slipped her key into the lock and pushed the door open with her foot still on the top step. Her happy mood was rapidly seeping away and Ryan standing so close was making her jumpy. But if he thought she was inviting him in, he had another think coming.

'I don't know what makes you think you can just show up here whenever it suits you and act as if the past three years never happened.'

'I'm not trying to pretend I didn't mess up,' he replied patiently. 'I was an immature prat, and I didn't appreciate what a good thing I had with you when I took off. But I'll do whatever it takes to prove I've changed. Look, I know I let you down, but you've got to believe me, no one else does it for me like you and, no matter what's happened, I know you still feel something for me. Come on, Cara, you and me, we're—'

Drawing on her anger was far better than acknowledging the turmoil raging inside her, and she turned on him furiously.

'Don't say it, Ryan,' she warned, her eyes blazing. 'Don't you dare say it because it isn't true and we're *not!* You have no right to come here and try and mess me up again. We have *nothing* left to say to each other and I wouldn't believe a word you said anyway because you're so full of *shi*— So full of it!'

'Cara, calm down!' The minute the words left his lips, he stepped back and raised his hands in alarm. 'Okay, sorry. *Sorry!* I meant . . . I'm honestly not trying to piss you off. Please, just hear me out.'

'Is everything okay, Cara?' A small dark-skinned woman in a dusky-pink sari hurried down the path. 'Do you need help? I saw him sitting on your step earlier.' She squared her shoulders and looked ready to launch herself on Ryan if needed. 'I was wanting to call the police, but you let him inside your house the other time, so I thought it was better to wait.'

'Thanks, Mrs Aggarwal,' Cara said evenly. 'Ryan is . . . an old friend and he's just leaving, aren't you?'

Her eyes challenged him to argue, and Ryan stared back thoughtfully. Then, ignoring Mrs Aggarwal, he reached for Cara, and she gasped in shock as she came up against the hard warmth of his body. She tried to pull away from his strong grip but, holding tight, he bent his head and swiftly kissed her lips. She immediately stiffened in angry protest and then her mind went blank as the soft familiar lips moved against hers. Her traitorous body was on the verge of giving in to him when alarm bells louder than twenty smoke detectors going off sounded in her head.

'*Ryan!* What the *hell*—!' Furious, she wrenched herself out of his arms and scrubbed at her lips with the back of her hand as if it would wipe away his touch. It was only the presence of her visibly intrigued neighbour that stopped her from slapping him hard across the face.

Ryan exhaled as raggedly as if he'd been running and ran his fingers through his hair. But instead of apologising, he simply shook his head.

'I'll go if that's what you want, but it's not over between us. You know it, no matter what you say. You and me—'

She tried to stop him, but he placed a gentle finger on her lips to silence her and spoke slowly and deliberately. 'You and me, Cara, we're destiny.'

18

DIVAS AND DEALS

As the train ground to a halt, Cara wearily pulled open the door and was immediately accosted by a blast of torrid air. The recent heatwave was showing no signs of abating and the high temperatures, combined with her guilt over Ryan's kiss, had been the cause of several sleepless nights.

She glanced at her watch, and with a hasty 'See you later!' to Ben battled her way through the mass of people spilling out of the train onto the platform. The manager of the venue they had been scouting for the advertising agency fun day had insisted on showing them every inch of the luxurious premises, including dragging her into the Gents for a quick inspection, and now she had little more than half an hour to get to the record company's offices. She still hoped to persuade Ashanti to delay signing the deal, which meant forking out for a taxi if she were to have any chance of winning her over before the meeting started at 3:30. Having coached Ben until he was word perfect, she was counting on him to convince Paula that a sudden bout of food poisoning from a dodgy prawn sandwich was the reason Cara hadn't returned with him to the office.

It was blisteringly hot and even the short walk through the station left her dress clinging damply to her back. To her mounting frustration, she arrived at the taxi rank just in time to see the last cab pull out. A glance at her watch further ratcheted up her anxiety and the instant the next cab pulled up, she scrambled into the back, horribly aware that it would take a miracle to get to Battersea in time. Fortunately, the sleepy-eyed driver behind the wheel perked up at the urgency in her voice and pressed sharply on the accelerator, bouncing his cab over the speed ramps and out onto the main road.

Feverishly rehearsing her pitch for begging Ashanti to reconsider her decision, Cara pretended not to notice the cab driver watching her through his rear-view mirror. Having apparently concluded that his passenger was on a life-or-death mission, the cabbie pressed down even harder on the accelerator, darting randomly between lanes of traffic. Taken aback by the sudden speed but in no mind to argue, Cara held on tight as the cab raced down back streets and spun around corners until it screeched to a halt in front of a grey building on a busy main road.

'We're here, miss. That there's number 271,' the driver declared.

Cara looked doubtfully at the betting shop in front of them and pulled out her phone to check the address in Ashanti's text: 271 High Street. She paid the driver and jumped out, even more perplexed when the cabbie gave her a knowing wink and tapped the side of his nose before pulling away.

It was only as she approached the bookies that Cara spotted an adjoining green door numbered 271a with 'Nine Elms Records' printed below the entryphone buzzer. She wrinkled her nose in distaste at the peeling paint and the dirty shoe prints tattooed across the door sill. As the headquarters of a company supposedly creating great opportunities for Ashanti, it hardly inspired confidence.

Despite the cab driver's mad dash, it was just gone 3:30 and Cara was too late to deliver her speech. The meeting would probably have started, but if she could get up there and at least glance at the paperwork before her friend signed her talent away, she might be able to spot anything dodgy. Her finger was poised to press the buzzer when she heard her name and Cara turned to see Ashanti running towards her in dizzyingly high white stilettos, furiously waving a voluminous white bag.

'Hold on! Wait for me,' she gasped, leaning against the door of the betting shop while she tried to catch her breath.

'Tube . . . took forever . . . had to . . . run . . .' she panted, frantically fanning her face with one hand. Her sleeveless white wrap-around dress clung to her curves and her hair fell in loose curls around an expertly made-up face. She retrieved a tissue from her bag and carefully dabbed her forehead and upper lip.

With no time left to adopt the diplomatic approach she had originally planned, Cara took advantage of Ashanti's temporary weakness and dived in.

'Ash, you know I'm here to support you, right?'

Still out of breath, Ashanti nodded.

'Okay, so will you *please* just take a second to think this through before you go rushing up there to sign with these people?' Encouraged by her friend's silence, Cara plunged on. 'I mean, look at this place. How many successful record companies do you know with such dingy offices?'

Ashanti abruptly stopped fanning, and her eyes flashed pure anger as she pointed an accusatory, scarlet-tipped finger at Cara, her words emerging between pants.

'*You* . . . said you wanted to come and watch me sign the deal, not sabotage it. I don't know . . . *any* successful record companies, Cara, and that's the point! I've sent demo tapes to . . . a ton of places and none of them showed the slightest interest. So, if Nine

Elms Records wants me, why the hell would I say no, hmm? Tell me *that*.'

'Look, I understand you're excited about this, but it's a big step. I've told you Henry's offered to review—'

'Just 'cos you're going out with some hot-shot lawyer doesn't mean I'm stupid! I don't have time for lawyers to wade in and go back and forth on this. I've already read through the contract and for your information they're offering me a five-album deal. Get that? *Five albums!* Look, if you don't want to be part of this, Cara, then just go home, because I'm telling you now that I'm going to sign that bloody contract today, with or without you.'

Tossing the tissue into her bag, Ashanti sucked her teeth impatiently and nudged Cara out of the way. She jabbed the entryphone button with a sharp nail and almost immediately a loud buzz sounded. Her face set, she pushed hard at the door, which refused to budge. After a moment's hesitation, she kicked the area plastered with footprints and the door gave way.

Ashanti stepped inside and then turned and blocked the doorway to prevent Cara from following her. 'Well?'

They glared at each other for a long moment before Cara shrugged in defeat. There was clearly no reasoning with her, but Ash was her best friend and she'd just have to swallow her misgivings and support her.

'Fine, let's do this,' she conceded.

Ashanti nodded and led the way up a steep flight of stairs to the first floor where Elliott stood waiting on the landing.

'Ashanti! Great to see you again, and you look fabulous!' His broad smile and white tombstone teeth reminded Cara of a hungry wolf spying its next meal.

Elliott's smile faltered when he spotted Cara. 'Ah, I see you've brought your friend along.'

When neither girl responded, he pressed on gamely. 'Well, it's a big day for you, so why not, eh? Come in and meet our other two new artists. Now everyone's here, we can get the show on the road!'

Elliott ushered them through to a surprisingly spacious room with pale-blue walls, high ceilings, big sash windows, and a large desk on which sat an open laptop. Even with the windows flung open, without air conditioning it felt warm and stuffy. Elliott shooed them towards the corner of the room where a squashy blue sofa that had clearly seen better days and a couple of brown fold-out chairs had been arranged around a glass-topped coffee table. The mismatched furniture did nothing to dispel Cara's doubts. *I wouldn't sign a cheque in here, never mind a career-making record deal.*

Ashanti nudged her sharply in the ribs and Cara turned her attention back to Elliott who was introducing the two people hovering by the sofa.

'. . . and Will, this is Ashanti and her friend. Will here is an absolute genius on the guitar and writes the most incredible lyrics,' Elliott gushed.

Will, Cara decided, had to be the thinnest man she had ever met. He was so pale his skin looked translucent, while his navy polo shirt revealed bony arms and wrists so delicate that it was a wonder he could carry, let alone play, a guitar. His jeans were belted tightly at the waist and hung loosely around legs that looked almost skeletal, and his doe-like eyes, framed by long lashes, reminded her of Bambi.

'And this is Angie. She'll be the youngest artist that Nine Elms has ever signed,' Elliott concluded.

In a short pink denim skirt with a matching sleeveless top, and pink flip-flops, Angie couldn't have been much more than eighteen despite her heavy make-up and thickly glossed lips.

'The three of you are going to be the next mega music stars, believe me,' Elliott promised. 'You each bring something unique to the market and we're investing a lot of money in your careers. Once we've finalised everything today, the next step will be getting you set up to work with the best producers in the business.'

Glancing around the room, Cara pursed her lips and looked suspiciously at Elliott. She might not know much about the industry, but this room didn't look like the kind of place where anyone could make music.

'So, where's all the recording equipment and, um, record-making stuff?'

Elliott looked pained. 'This is the *head* office. We hire recording studios and production teams as we need to.'

Angie, who had been staring at Ashanti as if trying to place her, jabbed a finger at her excitedly. 'I *knew* you looked familiar. I've heard you sing! You did a set at a club in Kilburn a couple of months ago and you were bloody brilliant!' Her accent was pure East End with a touch of gravel.

Ashanti beamed with pleasure and perched on the arm of the sofa. 'Oh, wow, thanks! This is a bit of a coincidence, then.'

'I know, right? I was trying to get a regular gig there and I met the bloke who owns it. He was really bigging up the place and going on about how he always gets loads of agents there checking out artists. But it's miles away from Leytonstone, and I didn't fancy the travel.'

'I hate to break up the love-fest, but we need to get the contracts signed,' Elliott interjected, looking a little put out that the conversation had moved on without him. 'Mr Hetherington,' Elliot said the name with such reverence that Cara couldn't help rolling her eyes, 'our founder and the owner of Nine Elms Records, is really excited about today. I'm going to take you through to his office now.'

Ashanti was on her feet before Elliott could finish his sentence and Angie grinned excitedly. Will, however, turned ashen, and for a moment he looked ready to bolt.

'Are you okay?' Cara whispered as Elliott led them towards a closed door at the other end of the office. Will nodded with such a wobbly, trusting smile that Cara began to regret her insistence on coming. She would have bet any money that neither Angie nor Will had vetted the contracts they were about to sign and watching the wide-eyed innocents trail behind Elliott Robbins felt like witnessing lambs being led to the slaughter.

Elliott knocked tentatively and a deep voice growled, 'Come in!'

Pushing the door open, Elliott stood aside to let Ashanti, Angie and Will go through before falling in behind them and leaving Cara to bring up the rear.

If Cyrus Hetherington was excited to see them, he was doing an excellent job of hiding it, was Cara's immediate thought. While he wasn't quite tapping his fingertips together and stroking a white cat, Elliott's boss's closely cropped dark hair, deep bushy eyebrows, and heavily lined, unsmiling face wouldn't have looked out of place on a Bond villain. Looking up from his laptop, he remained seated behind a massive desk as they trooped in.

Cyrus's office had clearly been set up to impress. The wall behind his imposing desk was crowded with gilded records in frames bearing labels too small to read, as well as pictures of a smiling Cyrus standing next to pop stars and instantly recognisable celebrities from the music industry. Having stretched out the silence, he gave a cursory nod and a twitch of his lips, which could have been interpreted as a smile, before standing up to shake hands with the artists Elliott urged forward. When it came to Cara's turn, Elliott's stutter reappeared as he explained she was there to support Ashanti. Feeling not in the least bit intimidated, Cara returned the fish-eyed stare Cyrus gave her, bristling at his rudeness as he took his seat without a handshake or a word of greeting.

Despite Elliott's assertion, Cyrus clearly didn't do excitement. With a deadpan expression, he pulled out a sheaf of bound papers from a folder on his desk and signed them quickly with a gold fountain pen. Any hopes Cara harboured of scrutinising Ashanti's contract were quickly dashed as Elliott gathered the three musicians around the desk and hovered over them as they each dutifully signed two copies of the documents. For the first time, Cyrus appeared to be something approaching animated as he handed them each a copy.

'I take it you've all given Elliott your demo tapes and any other material, as we agreed?'

Ashanti, Will and Angie nodded in unison and Elliott ducked his head in agreement. He was clearly in awe of Cyrus, showing none of the haughty confidence he had displayed at Mocktails. Cyrus turned back to his computer, making it clear the meeting was over, but, when Elliott tried to shoo them out of the office, Cara refused to budge.

'So, what happens now? What exactly is your marketing strategy for Ash? Do you have gigs lined up or studio time arranged for her to start recording?'

Elliott stopped in his tracks, visibly aghast at the cheek of anyone questioning his boss. Ashanti nudged her, hard, but Cara ignored her friend's furious glance and stood her ground. Angie raised her eyebrows, plainly impressed by Cara's boldness, while Will had the grateful look of someone who wished he'd had the courage to ask the questions.

Unmoved by the challenge, Cyrus shrugged his broad shoulders and pushed the papers aside. He stared at Cara with hooded eyes and drummed his thick, stubby fingers on the desk. For a moment, the rhythmic tap of his gold signet ring against the wood was the only sound in the hush that had descended.

Undaunted, Cara stared back, and when Cyrus finally spoke, his voice was flat and emotionless. 'We've got big plans for our new artists, and it's all set out in the contracts they've just signed.' He leaned forward and clasped his fleshy hands together. 'I'm putting a lot of money into the three of them, and I don't make investments lightly,' he added, sweeping a glance over them that was almost menacing.

That still doesn't answer my question, Cara thought huffily, but it seemed Cyrus had said all he intended to and before anyone else had the temerity to ask a question, Elliott hustled them from the room and straight through the main office into the corridor. Waving them off with a hearty 'I'll be in touch soon', he watched from the landing as they made their way downstairs.

Out on the street, Ashanti, Will and Angie excitedly exchanged numbers while Cara obligingly took group photos on everyone's phone. After waving the others goodbye, Cara and Ashanti linked arms and skipped down the main road towards the station, singing along to one of Ashanti's songs.

Ashanti broke off in mid-chorus to crow loudly, 'I've got a recording contract!'

Ignoring a couple of startled passers-by, Cara grinned at her friend indulgently. 'I'm really happy for you and I can't wait to hear your music being played everywhere.'

'Elliott says I've got enough material to start working on an album straightaway. I gave them the songs on the demo, and he's already got the tapes from my performances at Mocktails and my other gigs.'

Cara brought the skipping to an abrupt halt. 'Hold on a minute, have you given them *all* your stuff?'

Ashanti snatched her arm away impatiently, but it was too late to conceal the flicker of fear that crossed her face. Suddenly struck by a thought, Cara stared at her in horror.

'Ashanti Duncan! Please don't tell me you've given them your *notebook*?'

Ashanti's notebook was a thick, battered A4 book that she had painstakingly filled over the years with poems, snatches of writing and, most importantly, the lyrics to all her songs. It was easily her most precious possession and, other than her cat Nutmeg, it was the one thing she would rush into a burning building to rescue.

Ashanti tightened her lips and tossed her hair back defiantly. 'For God's sake, Cara, will you get over yourself! You heard what Cyrus said. They need to see *everything* so they can select the best material for my first recording. Don't look at me like that, it's honestly no big deal. I've got an appointment with Elliott next week to discuss next steps, and I'll get my notebook back from him then.'

With that, she seized Cara's arm and pulled her along the crowded high street, singing at the top of her voice and cutting off any further conversation.

19

Secrets and Pies

Having decided to avoid the rain-soaked streets of Kensal Green on a Saturday morning, Cara sat in her little-used kitchen, perched on a stool and lost in thought. With each day that had passed since kissing Ryan – or rather, as she reminded herself, being kissed by Ryan – her guilt levels had steadily risen, leaving her feeling unsettled and jumpy. While she hadn't invited or wanted it, she couldn't ignore the fluttery feelings she'd experienced when Ryan's lips had met hers. Even more disturbing was the realisation that she couldn't stop thinking about that moment and how she had so nearly kissed him back. *What is wrong with you Cara? How can you even* contemplate *anything with Ryan after what he did to you?*

To make matters worse, there was no one with whom she could safely share her mixed-up feelings about Ryan. Talking to Ashanti was out of the question, assuming she would even pay attention. Since signing with Nine Elms two weeks earlier, she had been closeted away working on updated versions of her old material and rehearsing new songs in readiness for the recording sessions Elliott had promised. Studio hire was expensive, he had pointed out, and until Ashanti was ready to lay down tracks, there was no point in wasting the time of the top-quality producers and session singers earmarked for the project. Ashanti had been in no mood to entertain Cara's observation that surely the whole point of working in a studio was to try different song treatments and mix the best results. But even if Ashanti had been available, Cara would have hesitated to confide in her. Her friend's hostility towards Ryan ran so deep that she would go ballistic on hearing that she'd kissed him – or rather, Cara quickly corrected herself again, had been kissed by him. And Rosie, who could usually be relied on to provide a level-headed shoulder to cry on, would just give her the wounded look that conveyed her deep disappointment in Cara.

Rosie, in any case, had been mysteriously absent lately and would deftly change the subject whenever she was pressed for details about the status of the Spaniel. While it was understandable that Rosie would hide information about Sean Strakey from her father, who was still bitter about the night-time serenading fiasco, her refusal to dish the dirt to her best friends was unacceptable.

Cara swallowed the cold dregs of coffee in her mug and shivered as a chilly gust of wind blew in through the open kitchen window. After nearly three weeks of sweltering temperatures, the prolonged heatwave had finally broken and several days of heavy rain had brought an almost autumnal coolness. With Henry coming over later in the afternoon, the miserable weather was the perfect excuse to road test her mother's lamb and potato pie recipe. It was one of several new dishes Bev was planning for her Food Technology classes in the autumn and, as she had bluntly explained when she handed over the recipe and a pie dish, if Cara managed to follow the recipe, her students would have no trouble.

Hopping off the stool, Cara dumped her mug beside the sink and retrieved the printout of the recipe she had stuck under her Eiffel Tower fridge magnet, skimming through the ingredients and the lengthy set of instructions dubiously. However, triumph overcame doubt an hour later when she carefully slid the borrowed pie dish brimming with mash into the oven.

Disregarding the pile of dirty saucepans waiting in the sink, Cara leaned against the counter and, like a curious tongue seeking out a wobbly tooth, her mind went straight back to the kiss. After brooding for a few more minutes, she straightened and reached for her phone. It was no use, she simply *had* to talk to someone about it. If she couldn't confide in Ashanti or Rosie, it didn't leave her with many options. She didn't want to worry her mum, and, after briefly considering calling Dexter, she just as quickly dismissed the idea. Dex had already welcomed Ryan back with open arms, no questions asked, and there was no point expecting impartial advice from that quarter. Her brother was so blinded by loyalty that if Ryan had been accused of murder, Dexter would probably insist the victim must have hurled himself onto the axe. Which left Ozzie.

When he answered on the third ring, she could hear the unmistakable sound of Adele playing in the background.

'What's going on over there? Am I interrupting something?' Cara demanded. Romantic ballads were hardly Ozzie's music of choice.

'Nothing that can't wait,' he said smoothly. 'Hold on a minute.'

The sound of a door closing cut off the music and a few seconds later he was back on the line. Too preoccupied with her own thoughts to dig any further, Cara quickly related the events leading up to the kiss. Fully expecting Ozzie to be outraged at Ryan for taking liberties, she was taken aback when he simply asked, 'Did you like it?'

'What do you mean, *did I like it*?' she squeaked. 'I told you, he grabbed me and kissed me before I could stop him. It's not like I encouraged him. I was telling him to get lost! I'd have belted him if my nosey neighbour hadn't been standing right in front of us.'

'I don't get why you're so shocked. This is Ryan we're talking about. He always does what he wants and gets away with it.'

'But I'm with Henry now. Hold on a minute, why aren't *you* shocked?'

Ozzie's shrug was almost audible. 'Look, you and Ryan had a huge thing going for ages. If he's saying he wants you back, then he's obviously going to do whatever it takes to break you and Henry up. But he can't do that unless you let him, so . . . did you like it when he kissed you?'

'No!' she protested, almost shouting in frustration. Suppressing the memory of the fluttery feelings, she took a deep breath to steady her voice.

'No, Ozzie, I did *not* like it and I just wish he would go away again. I dread coming home now in case I find him sitting on my doorstep. Even though I haven't done anything, I feel guilty all the time as if I'm cheating on Henry and I can feel myself pushing him away.'

'So then, talk to Henry about it.'

'It's not that simple, Oz. Every time I pluck up the courage, I'm scared I'll say the wrong thing and give him the wrong idea. Ryan's like a bad habit I thought I'd broken, but it's like when you've quit smoking, even a whiff of smoke makes you think about smoking again. I just need Ryan not to be here and you lot should stop encouraging him by making him feel so welcome.'

'Whoa, don't blame me, I've hardly spoken to the guy! Dexter's the one who still hero-worships him even after he buggered off and left him in the lurch. And good luck trying to get Dex to give Ryan the cold shoulder. You and I both know it's impossible to get him to say a bad word against the guy.'

Cara sighed and peered through the glass door of the oven. Relieved the pie wasn't burning, she sat back down on the stool.

'So how come you don't get pissed off about it, Oz? You've always managed to be there for Dex with no excuses.'

Ozzie went quiet for a moment. 'Cara, you can't change people. Dex is who he is, and Ryan's his friend. End of. Besides, Dexter and I are brothers, it's not a competition.'

'I suppose you're right. But none of that helps me. Okay, well I'd better go before I burn this stupid pie I'm making for Henry's lunch.'

Ozzie snorted with laughter. 'It must be love if you're actually cooking. Does the poor man know what he's letting himself in for?'

Cara sniffed indignantly and was about to hang up when a thought occurred to her. 'By the way, have you been in touch with Imogen? Don't think I didn't see you putting your number in her phone at Tabitha's party. Imogen is Henry's sister so if you've got any funny ideas about her, drop them.'

Ozzie laughed. 'Well, since you're asking—'

Cara cut him off before he could continue. 'On second thoughts, forget I brought it up 'cos I really don't want to know.' She had enough on her plate without Ozzie adding further complications.

She ended the call and peeked at the pie bubbling away in the oven. The mash looked a little brown, but, having forgotten her mother's strict instructions to set a timer, she had no idea how long the dish had been cooking for. As she pondered her next move, the phone rang, and she glanced at the screen and blinked. *Was the woman psychic?*

'Hi, Mum. Guess what? I'm making the lamb pie!'

There was a moment's silence. 'Are you, love?'

Bev sounded subdued and Cara's trouble-seeking antennae shot up. 'Mum? Is something wrong?'

'Caramia, what's going on? I've just spoken to Dexter, and he says Ryan's desperate to get back together with you. I thought you said you were happy with Henry.'

'I *am* happy with him. In fact, I'm ecstatic! Ryan's just being a pain in the— Look, Mum, it's fine. Everything's under control.' Cara grimaced and stared up at the ceiling. This was precisely why she had avoided discussing her dilemma with her mother, and she was furious at Ryan for upsetting her.

'Cara, do be careful. The two of you have so much history that even after everything that's happened, it would be so easy to . . .'

'Mum, it's okay. I mean it. I am not going back to him.'

'Alright, my love. If you're sure.' Her voice grew more animated. 'So how did you get on with the recipe? I meant to call and remind you yesterday, but I've been so distracted lately that I keep forgetting half the things I've planned to do.'

'Why? What's wrong?' Cara asked, relieved to change the subject.

'I wish I knew. There's so much going on, it's impossible to keep track of whether I'm coming or going. You can't imagine how much paperwork the schools make me fill out now for my cookery demos.'

Cara hugged the phone against her ear as she opened the oven door to check the pie hadn't burned. 'You've been working flat out for months, Mum. Maybe you need to take a break?'

'Now you sound like my mother,' Bev snorted. 'Beverley, you have to rest! It's not for you to do everything – are you a flag to follow every breeze? Don't you know that an overused pot ends up in pieces?'

Cara burst out laughing at Bev's wickedly accurate mimicry of her opinionated Ghanaian mother. Much as they all loved Grandma Maggie, her annual trips to London invariably tested everyone's limits, and none more so than Gerald's. Each visit left his nerves in shreds and strained his easy-going nature to breaking point. Her father was the first to admit that leading a school of twelve hundred students was nothing compared to the challenges of coping with both his legal and inherited mothers-in-law.

'Speaking of Grandma Maggie, isn't she due to come over soon?' Cara asked. 'Whose turn is it to lose their room?'

Hoping to discourage Grandma Maggie and Thelma's frequent visits, Gerald had converted the spare bedroom into a study, but the grandmothers had continued to visit regardless, forcing Thaddeus and Manon to take turns giving up their bedrooms.

'Manon moved out when Thelma came, so it's Thaddeus's turn to bunk in Dad's study. Thanks for reminding me, love, I'll phone Grandma to check when she's coming. I'd better give Thelma a call as well before she accuses me of neglecting her.'

'I do miss Thelma.' Cara sighed. 'It's funny how even though she lives in Barbados, we see more of her than Uncle George who's only in Wimbledon.'

'Yes, well, she certainly makes her presence felt when she's here,' Bev remarked dryly. 'The poor postman still can't look me in the eye.'

Once a beauty queen in her native Barbados and now in her late seventies, Thelma still loved wearing her stilettos and the latest fashions. She'd flatly banned her grandchildren from calling her Granny and was given to flirting at any opportunity, as Bev's postman had discovered. Opening the door one afternoon to receive a delivery, Thelma had responded to the postie's innocuous reference to the cold weather with a knowing smile and an invitation to come in 'for something strong to warm you up'. As the only thing the happily married man had been after was a signature for the parcel, it had been left to Bev to rescue both parties from a very awkward situation.

Cara giggled at the memory, and her mother joined in. After a moment, though, Bev's voice turned serious. 'Caramia, can we talk about Henry?'

'What about him?' Cara tried not to sound as defensive as she felt.

'If you two are getting serious, don't you think you owe him the truth?'

The buzzing of the doorbell gave Cara her reprieve. 'Can I call you back later, Mum?'

'But, Cara love, have you told him—'

'Mum, Henry's at the door! I'm sorry, but I have to go.'

◆ ◆ ◆

'Can we talk about Ryan?'

Henry was chopping carrots and green beans to accompany the lamb pie, and Cara, who had been sitting on the kitchen stool admiring his culinary deftness, froze like a deer confronted by a set of very unexpected headlights.

'Of course.' The change of subject was a bolt from the blue and feeling slightly panicked, Cara struggled to keep her tone neutral. 'What do you want to know?'

Henry stopped mid-chop. 'Look, I may have got this all wrong, but it just feels like you haven't been yourself lately. You seem a bit on edge and . . .' He shrugged. 'I don't know, slightly distant at times. Maybe it's not connected, but clearly something happened with Ryan, and since you never talk about him—'

'Henry, you don't talk about your exes either,' she cut in before she could help herself.

'I'm happy to tell you whatever you want to know about them, but that's not what I'm asking.'

The trouble with lawyers was that they were too used to inter-rogating witnesses to be distracted, she thought. Unlike Ryan who would switch off and grow bored or impatient if they talked for any length of time, Henry listened, paying attention to every word, spoken or unspoken.

'Cara, there's obviously history with Ryan and whatever it is, I don't want it to come between us.'

Her mother's earlier warning reverberated like a siren in her mind. *You owe him the truth, and this is your moment to tell him everything.* Cara took a deep breath, wondering where to start.

'Okay, so the thing is Ryan has been in Dublin since we split up, but he's now back in London. Our break-up was . . . was bad, but he's Rosie's cousin and he and Dexter are still close. I suppose I've been feeling a bit anxious lately because Ryan can be . . . Well, let's just say he can be disruptive when it suits him.'

Henry put the knife he was still holding on the chopping board, and his eyes searched hers intently. 'Why didn't you tell me sooner? Are you sure you don't still have feelings for him?' He hesitated and then said carefully, 'Cara, we haven't been together that long, but I've fallen for you . . .' He paused and shook his head. 'No, the truth is I'm crazy about you and if your heart's not in this, I need to know. Ryan's obviously important in your life—'

'*Was* important,' she corrected. 'I'm with you now and I'm pretty crazy about you, too. Henry, I *promise* you're the only one I want,' she added with a tremulous smile.

He leaned against the kitchen counter and eyed her quizzically. 'Cara, I know having your heart broken can sometimes leave you afraid of your own feelings. If you still need time to come to terms with what happened, I don't want you feeling any pressure from me. I just want you to know I'm here and I want to help, if you'll let me.'

Cara blinked back the tears she could feel prickling behind her eyes. What had she done to deserve Henry? She couldn't imagine

Ryan being so considerate of her feelings, especially when they might pose a risk to his.

Moving to stand in front of her, Henry stroked her cheek with a wistful smile. 'The first time I laid eyes on you on that coach, something inside me knew you were special. I don't want any distance between us and if anything's getting in the way, I want to know.'

Staring into Henry's eyes, the words trembled on Cara's lips but as much as she tried, she couldn't force them out. Instead, ignoring the wailing siren in her head, she reached up to pull him into a passionate kiss.

20

CLAUSE AND EFFECT

'Hi, you!' Cara grinned.

'Hi, you,' Henry echoed, tangling his fingers through her curls, and pulling her even closer.

They had eaten their way through more than half of the surprisingly delicious lamb pie and polished off most of the red wine Henry had brought. As the washing up had required more energy than either of them could conjure up, they'd collapsed onto the sofa instead, too stuffed to do anything more than exchange tipsy smiles. Cara winced as the hard edge of the sofa pressed against her hip and she shifted to get more comfortable.

'Easy!' Henry groaned. 'I'm too full to take your weight.'

'Are you calling me *fat*?' She flopped heavily against him in punishment and, seeking revenge, he slipped a hand under her t-shirt and tickled her until she shrieked with laughter and begged for mercy.

Lying contentedly in Henry's arms, Ryan felt a million miles away and even though she'd bottled the chance earlier to be completely honest with Henry, Cara's gnawing guilt over Ryan's kiss had receded. She hadn't invited it, she reminded herself, and all she cared about right now was enjoying the man beside her and the soft music playing in the background.

'Is that your phone vibrating or are you just happy to see me?' she giggled. After three glasses of wine, everything seemed hilarious, and Henry chuckled, pulling his mobile from his pocket to peer at the screen.

'Who is it?' Cara asked idly.

'It's a text from Fleur. She won the first leg of the junior horse trials this morning with a time that makes her the hot favourite to win the championship. She says to ask you to come and watch her ride in the finals.'

Cara raised her head in surprise. '*Me*? I'm hardly the horsey type. I wouldn't have a clue what was going on.'

'You don't need to. You just keep quiet while she's riding and then cheer like a lunatic once she's finished her round. You know she's taken a shine to you – which reminds me, I gave her your address so she can send you one of the village prints you were so keen on at the Sunday market.'

Cara smiled. 'That's very sweet of her. She's such a lovely girl.'

'Why do you sound so surprised?' he teased. 'I told you my family is as normal as yours.'

She snuggled deeper, breathing in the faint tang of lemon from his cologne. 'Ye-es, except that yours comes with a massive house, acres of land and a title that goes back to William the Conqueror.'

Henry sighed. 'Okay, so no one's perfect, but—'

Cara smiled up at him. 'Henry, you have a lovely family. But you must admit you've had advantages that most people never get.'

He frowned and sat upright. 'And is that a problem for you?'

Struggling to marshal her thoughts through a haze of red wine, Cara tried to frame her words carefully. She wasn't intimidated by Henry's wealth, exactly, but she also couldn't understand why *he* couldn't see the enormous gulf between their respective ways of life. No matter how friendly his family, Henry's upbringing and circumstances were a world away from what she had grown up with, and while none of that mattered cocooned in their own bubble, she wasn't naïve enough to imagine things would be quite so simple in the real world. But a mind clouded by wine didn't help as she struggled to voice her concerns without making them sound doomed as a couple.

Cara was spared the trouble by the insistent buzzing of her doorbell, and she frowned in dismay. Lazy Saturday afternoons with her boyfriend were not up for negotiation. Deciding to ignore it, the buzzing stopped, only for her phone to ring instead.

She answered it reluctantly, wincing as Ashanti shrieked down the line. 'Cara, I'm outside and I *know* you're at home. Open the door. NOW!'

The foggy wine haze was instantly dissipated by Ashanti's anguished tone and Cara's heart sank. Rolling off Henry and ignoring his quizzical look, she stumbled out to the corridor and pressed the entry buzzer. Seconds later, Ashanti raced up the stairs and burst into the flat. Dressed in a tracksuit she would never normally have been caught dead wearing outside her house, her normally sleek hair was dishevelled. She dropped her handbag onto the floor, and, taking one look at Cara, she burst into noisy sobs, shoulders heaving as tears streamed through the fingers covering her face.

Cara stared, horrified. In all the years she had known the tough-talking, take-no-prisoners Ashanti, she had never seen her in this state.

'*Ash!* What is it?' she gasped, gathering her friend into her arms and stroking her hair while trying not to panic. 'Ash, *talk* to me! What's happened?'

Henry appeared in the doorway of the living room, his eyebrows raised in silent query, and Cara threw him a helpless look. Ashanti pushed Cara away with a loud gulp and swiped her face with the back of her hands, drawing black streaks of mascara across her high cheekbones.

'The bastards! The absolute *bloody, sodding* bastards!' Furious, she let rip with a litany of curses that would have stunned a docker.

'Ashanti, stop!' Cara begged. 'What's going on? *Who's* a sodding bastard?' But even as she voiced the question, her gut already knew the answer.

'*Don't* say I told you so, Cara! Just don't!' Ashanti snapped.

'Ash, what's Elliott done?' Cara's expression darkened ominously.

'*Apparently*, I'm not allowed to sing at Mocktails anymore. In fact, I'm not allowed to sing *anywhere* unless Nine Elms gives me permission. Elliott says the contract I signed gives them ownership and they get to decide where and when I perform, and how much *they* decide to pay me! I can't even upload my performances onto my online channel without their say-so.'

Cara stared at her in amazement. 'But that's ridiculous! You never agreed to that, surely?'

'*Of course I didn't*! What kind of an idiot do you take me for? They said the contract was for a five-album deal and they would be paying for the recording and the marketing so I could concentrate on being an artist. They didn't say *anything* about having the rights to all my material!'

This wasn't the time to remind her friend that she had refused Henry's offer to review the contract, and Cara watched helplessly as Ashanti's eyes welled up again. Henry gently nudged Cara aside and took Ashanti's hands into his, waiting until she was calm enough to listen. 'Look, I'm not a specialist in entertainment law, but if there's anything I can do to help, I will. Do you have the contract on you?'

Ashanti took a shuddering breath and nodded. She rummaged through her bag, pulling out a bound sheaf of papers which she pressed into Henry's outstretched hand. He scanned the first page with a frown of concentration and moved slowly back to the living room as he leafed through the document.

Guiding Ashanti into the kitchen, Cara unscrewed the half-empty bottle of wine on the counter and poured out a generous measure, thrusting the glass into her friend's trembling hands before steering her to the living room where Henry sat engrossed in the paperwork.

Cara urged Ashanti onto the sofa and sat next to her, coaxing her to take a couple of sips before gently prising the wine glass from her friend's shaking hands, shocked at how cold and clammy they felt. Ashanti's earlier hysteria had vanished, and she stared dumbly at Henry, her eyes willing him to dispute Elliott's claims.

As Henry read through the lengthy agreement, Cara concentrated on rubbing some warmth back into Ashanti's hands and biting back her anger at her friend's predicament. It wouldn't help Ash if she started hurling insults at Elliott, nor would it ease her own guilt for not trying harder to protect Ashanti from herself.

'Well, this agreement gives them the exclusive right to produce, publish, sell and distribute her music, and contracts them to produce at least five music albums,' Henry murmured.

'Is that normal, though?' Cara asked dubiously. 'I've always thought it sounded a lot for a debut artist.'

'It is unusual,' Henry conceded. 'From what I know of entertainment contracts, a three-album deal would have been more likely—' He paused and whistled, his eyebrows rising high under his fringe.

'What is it?'

'Here's the kicker: *All song-writing and performing services shall remain under the exclusive control of the first party for the duration of the production of the stated output and all rights thereunto retained for life of copyright.* Well, that's just ridiculous!'

His expression darkened and Cara's palms grew damp. 'Why? How long is life of copyright?'

'The life of the artist plus seventy years,' Henry said, his voice grim.

'But that means—'

'Yes. Under these terms, they'll hold her copyright for years and she'll never own her own music.'

Ashanti moaned and her entire body trembled uncontrollably. Cara wrapped her arms around her, rocking her slowly from side to side and shushing her gently.

Henry shook his head. 'This gives them the right to put any of her material they choose on the albums and, that way, they get to keep control. They're even deducting all production costs from her advance and any royalties she earns. I can't believe the contracts these sharks get away with! This is just preying on innocent artists.'

He read on, then snorted with disgust and Cara's heart sank. 'What else is in there?'

'Well, I'm afraid it also says that they own the rights to any material she's written in the past.'

'They can't do that! That's . . . that's . . . *theft*!'

'It's certainly a very, *very* bad deal,' Henry agreed, flipping through to the next page. 'It can be a standard term unless the copyright to an artist's previous material has already been assigned. But, for a prolific songwriter like Ashanti, it means she's signed away rights to all her past songs *and* her next five albums. That's pretty vicious.'

Cara groaned. 'So, what are they actually giving her?'

'From the looks of this, it's an agreement for her recording services and a music publishing agreement for her song-writing services. Once a company has signed the artist and arranged for them to be produced, the company owns the output, in this case, all her future records. My guess is what they're really after is her song-writing ability, which makes this deal even more unfair.'

'Elliott's got my notebook, and he won't give it back. They really saw me coming, didn't they?' Ashanti said bitterly. She grabbed the glass from the side table and took a hefty slug of the wine. 'I was so bloody desperate for a recording deal that I've signed my life's work away to a crook and a sodding *tosser*!'

She folded her legs under her and buried her head in her hands and Cara's heart contracted in sympathy. 'I'm so sorry, hon.'

Henry leaned forward, his forearms on his knees. 'I'll be honest with you, Ashanti, it doesn't look great.'

Ashanti raised her head, and he kept his eyes trained on hers. 'But I have colleagues who specialise in entertainment law, and I'll see what I can find out from them and what your options are. I know it looks bad, but until we find out what we're dealing with, try not to worry, hmm?'

'I can't believe I was so stupid,' Ashanti said wearily. 'I put my whole life into my songs and now they're gone.' Instead of her earlier rage, she looked broken and as if all the fight had been beaten out of her as tears streamed silently down her cheeks and a pitiful sob escaped her.

'Don't, Ash,' Cara pleaded, throwing her arms around her. Ashanti was the toughest person she knew, and she had never seen her fall apart this way. But music was Ashanti's life and the only thing she had ever wanted in life was to write songs and perform. What if Ashanti really *had* lost everything to Nine Elms Records? What if they couldn't fix this?

As quickly as the thought entered her mind, Cara pushed it away and tightened her hold protectively. 'Please don't cry, hon. We'll sort it out. I promise.'

21

STALEMATE

Cara walked past the delivery vans and into the depot and was immediately greeted by a piercing wolf whistle. She turned and fixed the perpetrator, a short barrel of a man clutching a mug, with a withering look.

'*Piotr*! How many times must I tell you that it's sexist to whistle at women?'

Piotr didn't appear unduly bothered and put down his steaming coffee so he could hitch up his trousers and adjust the belt over his generous stomach. Moving with a swiftness that belied his size, he seized her hand and dipped her backwards over his arm, sending her black fedora flying. He rounded off the impromptu dance by pulling her upright into a crushing bear hug.

Cara disengaged herself and jammed her hat back on top of her curls in exasperation. Piotr's face was the picture of innocence as he met her glare with a shrug. 'I cannot help it. I see beautiful woman; I show appreciation for beautiful woman.'

He winked at her broadly and, despite her best intentions, her lips twitched as she fought back the giggles threatening to escape. 'Honestly, you're impossible!'

Piotr was Dexter's first recruit and the most reliable driver in the fleet. Although Dexter and the other drivers called him Pete, Cara always loved saying Piotr's name properly, rolling the word around her tongue with satisfaction. Originally a dentist in his native Poland, Piotr had been lured overseas by the prospect of earning good money, to the chagrin of the fiancée he left behind. After six months in Manchester, Piotr's English was still deemed not good enough to pass the professional dental exams and, with mounting bills to pay, he moved to London and signed up to drive for Dexter's start-up delivery business. After two years of waiting, his frustrated fiancée finally accepted she would never be a dentist's wife and married the local butcher, much to Piotr's relief. Free to work without the stress of Natalia's reproachful phone calls, he proceeded to clock up thousands of miles without complaint, zigzagging back and forth across the country on a steady diet of service station cuisine that had his waistline expanding along with the business.

'Is he in?' Cara gestured towards the closed door to Dexter's office. Piotr nodded, rubbing the bristles on his fleshy chin.

'He is giving Mick the bollocking for being late again. I tell him Mick's new baby is the problem. Mick is good worker and always first to do overtime, but I think your brother just needs excuse to bollock somebody today.' He spat in disgust. 'Yesterday he bollocked PJ for taking doughnut break!'

The door opened and a fair-haired man backed out. He shut the door and then leaned against it with his eyes closed and exhaled slowly. Opening his eyes, he spotted Cara and smiled.

'Hey, Cara!'

'Hi, Mick. How's it going?' Along with most of Dexter's staff, Mick was a long-server and a soft-spoken family man prone to whipping out pictures of his three daughters, accompanied by long-drawn-out descriptions of their latest antics. Despite his smile, he had the rumpled look of a man who hadn't slept properly in weeks.

'Can't complain,' he said with a wry expression. 'Are you here to see the boss?'

She noted his heightened colour and nodded with a sympathetic smile. 'I hear he's not exactly in a good mood.'

Mick stepped away from the door and lowered his voice. 'Been like a bear with a sore head ever since him and the missus had that last bust-up. Maybe you could have a go at sorting the two of them out? He nearly bit poor PJ's head off yesterday.'

'I wish I could,' Cara sighed, 'but I promised not to interfere. How are Eileen and the baby getting on? Juggling four kids can't be easy.'

Mick's tired features brightened. 'Oh, they're all great. The girls are beside themselves to have a brother and they don't leave him alone for a minute. He's a lovely lad but I'll be glad when he starts sleeping through the night. It's good to see you, love, but I'd better get back to work before the boss has another go.'

Piotr put down his mug and blew a kiss in Cara's direction before following Mick down the corridor. He obviously had no desire to run into Dexter in his current mood, and neither did Cara. But with Ashanti still inconsolable, it was time to fire the big guns and summon Dexter, even at the risk of incurring her friend's wrath. Following the Nine Elms ban on playing at Mocktails, Ashanti had refused point blank to pick up her guitar or write any music, fearing it would now belong to the record company. Furious with herself and bitter at the unfairness of her situation, she had fallen into a slump, rejecting Cara and Rosie's efforts to cajole her out of her flat. Instead, she spent her days watching daytime television and stroking Nutmeg until the poor cat would flee under the kitchen table in protest. Cara and Rosie's phone calls were either ignored or answered in hollow-toned monosyllables, and the emails from her temp agency were deleted unread. With Ashanti showing no sign of ever leaving her self-imposed prison, Cara had no choice but to call on the one person who could pull her out of her funk. Ash was far too stubborn to take the first step towards reconciliation, leaving it to Cara to try to persuade the equally stubborn Dexter to be the bigger person.

Taking a deep breath, she rapped twice on the door and pasted a determinedly cheery smile on her face before walking in. Dexter was sitting behind his desk, his handsome features drawn into a scowl which was replaced by a slightly less grumpy expression when he realised it wasn't another staff member in need of a bollocking.

'If you're looking for Ryan, he's out on a job,' he said flatly.

Cara's smile vanished and she stared at her brother in horror, all thoughts of her rescue mission fleeing like a burglar in the night. '*Ryan's* on a job! Have you actually let him come back to work here again? Dexter, are you insane?'

The scowl returned. 'He said he'd told you.'

'Ryan says a lot of things,' she replied scathingly. 'I thought you'd have figured that out by now. After the way he left you in the lurch before, I can't believe you'd trust him again!'

'Look, the man was going through a tough time, and it didn't help that you dumped him! I know Ryan can be a bit, you know, temperamental at times, but he's been a good mate for a long time and, well . . . bottom line? I trust him. So, yeah, I gave him back his job.'

She raised a sceptical eyebrow and Dexter sighed. 'Have a heart, Cara. Going off the way he did wasn't ideal, but we all do stupid things sometimes. He had his reasons, and you of all people can't blame the guy after what you did to him.'

Stung by the unfairness of the accusation, Cara glared at him, 'After what *I* did to him . . .! Did he happen to tell you his reasons for disappearing?'

Dexter eyed her warily. 'No, not really, but I know he was really cut up about what you did. Look, Ryan's a good guy and you should hear him out. Maybe if you sat down and hashed things out, you could find a way to make it work again.'

'DEXTER! Which bit of "I'm going out with Henry" do you find so hard to understand?'

'Listen, I've got nothing against the man, but let's not pretend he isn't a little bit out of your league. We're not fancy restaurants and country mansions type of people. You can shout at me all you want, but you know I'm right. You're probably a bit of a novelty for him, whereas Ryan's a good bloke. Solid. Comprehensive school, working class—'

'That's *such* an ignorant thing to say! I thought you were better than that.'

Her brother held up his hand in a conciliatory gesture. 'All I'm saying is that you and Ryan were very happy together and he still loves you – he's told me often enough. It wouldn't hurt to give him a chance to make things right.'

Cara drew a deep breath and bit down hard on her tongue. If she said any more, it could be far more than she intended, and this was neither the time nor place. She would deal with Ryan later, right now she needed to focus on why she was here. She perched on the chair opposite her brother's desk and tried to keep her voice neutral.

'Well, that's great advice, Dex. Ever thought of applying some of that yourself? Maybe if *you* sat down and hashed things out with Ashanti instead of terrorising your poor staff, they – and you – might be happier.'

Ignoring the reference to his employees, Dexter glowered at her. 'I thought we agreed you were butting out of it.'

'I'm not getting involved, I've told you already,' she protested. 'But this "we're on a break" business is making both of you grouchy and miserable and now . . . well . . .'

'Well, what?' he said irritably, and then his face cleared and he leaned back in his chair with a sigh. 'Just leave it, Cara. Ash and I are grown people and we'll figure things out for ourselves. Of course, I miss her like hell, but she told me to stay away and that's exactly what I'm doing.'

How did she tell Dexter and yet not tell him, Cara wondered? If she left it to Dexter and Ashanti to work things out, they would all be pensioners before that happened. She had promised Ashanti not to interfere in her love life, but her friend was far too traumatised to know what was good for her, and the contract fiasco demonstrated the dangers of letting impulsive divas make their own decisions. If Cara had stood her ground and insisted on Ashanti seeking legal advice before signing with Nine Elms, the girl wouldn't be in her dressing gown on the sofa watching re-runs of antique shows with a resentful cat.

She opened her mouth to spill the beans, when the picture of a bruised and bloodied agent flashed through her mind, and she hesitated. Dexter's response when those he loved were under threat was to strike first and ask questions later. As much as she hated Elliott for what he'd done, Cara couldn't risk another Barry Sykes incident. Injecting an overprotective Dexter into an already precarious situation could further complicate Ashanti's predicament. But then how could she persuade her lovesick brother to comfort his estranged girlfriend without telling him the truth?

'Look, Dex, she's going through a bit of a thing, and she really needs you. You should call her,' Cara urged. Even to her own ears, she sounded less than convincing.

'Yeah, right,' Dexter scoffed. 'That girl doesn't need anyone, *especially* me. She made that painfully clear the last time I tried to help her.'

'For God's sake, do you still not get it? Beating people up doesn't help anyone!' Cara exclaimed in exasperation.

'Why don't you *ever* give me any credit? I've told you a hundred times that *he* threw the first punch! I went there to give him a piece of my mind for ripping off my girl and when I threatened him with the police, he came at me and . . . well, at that point, I lost it.'

'That's exactly what I mean. I know all of this comes from a good place and that you're only trying to protect the people you love, but you need to know where to draw the line.'

'So, what was I supposed to do? Just let the bastard hit me and not fight back?'

'That's not what I'm saying!'

They sat in silence for a few moments and then Cara sighed. 'I don't get it, Dex, you are literally one of the kindest, most generous people I know. Your employees worship you and Mick's still made up about the extra time off and the bonus you gave him after his baby was born. You've always been a bit scrappy, but you're a fun, sweet guy – or at least you used to be. Ash reckons you changed after Ryan disappeared, and it took you back to how angry and abandoned you felt after our dad died.'

Dexter looked down but didn't say a word, and Cara added softly, 'You need Ash. You know you're hopeless without her, and she could really use your support right now.'

Dexter continued to stare at his desk, and, after a long silence, Cara jumped to her feet and pushed her hat down over her springy curls.

'Fine, I give up,' she said briskly. 'The two of you really *are* a pair.'

Opening the door, she paused on the threshold and then wheeled around. 'And, Dexter, when Ryan lets you down again, and trust me he will, *don't* say I didn't warn you.'

And with that parting shot, she marched out and slammed the door behind her.

22

STILL WATERS

With every passing day, Cara was growing increasingly distressed about Ashanti's state of mind. After two weeks of self-imposed solitude, her friend was no closer to coming to terms with the disastrous consequences of signing with Nine Elms Records. Now refusing to even listen to music, Ashanti had spiralled into a deep apathy spiked with periodic bouts of rage and tears.

Earlier that week, hoping to bolster her spirits and drum up some solidarity, Cara had invited Angie and Will over to Ashanti's flat. But after two large pizzas and a bottle of wine, when Cara had tentatively explained about the punitive clauses in all their contracts, Will looked ready to cry. Angie, after an initial lip wobble, had been surprisingly upbeat.

'I'm not worried. It will all work out, you've just got to 'ave faith,' had been her brave rejoinder, followed by an invitation to attend a service at her church where, she assured them, the Almighty would help them see their situation as just a temporary glitch. Momentarily stunned out of her despondency, Ashanti had listened open-mouthed to Angie's lecture on the importance of prayer, fasting, and trusting in God to sort out the unholy pickle into which Nine Elms had landed them.

Cara paced up and down the pavement outside her local Starbucks waiting for Henry and desperately hoping he had good news for Ashanti. When he arrived, linking her arm through his as they walked into the shop, she forced herself not to ask any questions until they were settled on a sofa with coffee and a sticky bun.

The scalding hot latte burned her mouth and she winced and set it down on the table before breaking off a corner of the bun. 'How was Stockholm?' she asked, eager to get the formalities out of the way.

Henry picked up a plastic knife and cut off a neat slice of bun, wolfing it down in two bites. 'Pretty hectic, but we won the case which is what matters. But I know that's not what you want to talk about.'

Not even trying to hide her anxiety, Cara looked at him with expectant eyes. 'So, what did you find out?'

He blew the steam from his Americano and took a cautious sip. 'It's not looking good,' he admitted. 'Those guys at Nine Elms might be scumbags, but they found a smart lawyer to draft their agreements. Two of my colleagues went through the contract with a fine toothcomb and they both agree that while a sympathetic judge might find some elements unenforceable, the bulk of it is water-tight. I've worked with Rowland and Chester for years and they're both experts on this stuff, so, if that's their opinion, I wouldn't fault it.'

The disappointment was so bitter Cara could almost taste it. She had wanted Henry to find a solution so badly that she hadn't dared consider the alternative. But if even his expert lawyers couldn't see a way out of the deal, then poor Ashanti, Will and Angie looked set to be Cyrus Hetherington's glorified cash cows for years to come, a blow that was sure to test even Angie's faith.

'But how is it even legal that they can take so much off the back of Ash's work?'

'I know it sounds absurd, but the reality is that it's the song-writer and not the performer who makes the real money. According to Rowland, a lot of record companies in the past used to work on a 50–50 split with writers, but these days the share of income between the music publisher and the songwriter can be structured much more in favour of the publisher.'

Henry took another sip of his coffee. 'As I suspected, Chester reckons what Nine Elms are really after is Ashanti's song-writing skills. Someone who writes across different genres, as she does, can be especially marketable and having her output under their con-trol could prove very profitable for them. What makes this deal even more unfair is that Nine Elms can let their other artists use Ashanti's material if they choose.'

Cara blinked, looking as dazed as she felt. 'So, what exactly does that leave her with? Is it just royalties?'

Henry hesitated and then sighed. 'To be totally frank, they've bought their way out of having to pay her very much of anything with this contract. All it offers her as the artist are royalties on any of her records sold after their financial outlay has been recouped. Which – until and unless she sells a ton of records – really won't amount to much.'

Cara finished her drink in silence. Her coffee had lost its taste and even her favourite iced cinnamon swirl looked unappealing. Try as she might, she could not fathom how she was going to break the news to Ashanti.

'This will destroy her, Henry,' she said slowly. 'She's devastated by what's happened and has been a complete basket case for the last two weeks. The only thing that's kept her going is waiting to hear your colleagues' advice. Oh God! *Why* the hell did I let her sign that stupid contract?'

'Stop it, don't blame yourself. It's not your fault. I don't think anyone can stop Ashanti from doing what she wants.'

'But I *promised* her I'd sort it out,' Cara whispered, clutching the empty mug.

'With the best will in the world, sweetheart, sometimes that's just not possible.'

Stricken, her eyes welled up. 'She's my best friend, Henry, I can't just stand by and let this happen to her. I swear, this will literally kill her!'

The tears trembling on her lashes spilled onto her cheeks and Henry put down his cup and hers and tenderly wiped them away. They sat side by side in silence for a few minutes and then he turned to face her. 'I've got an idea.'

Cara gazed at him with a tremulous smile, her eyes alight with fresh hope.

'It's a long shot,' he warned hastily, 'and if it turns out that these guys know the law, then we're on a hiding to nothing. But at this point I don't think we have anything to lose.'

'What's your plan?' Her new-found elation slowly faded. This wasn't sounding quite as promising as she had hoped.

'Lying,' he said, baldly.

She stared at him blankly.

'Okay then, bluffing,' he amended. 'If we can persuade them the contract is untenable, they might agree to void it.'

Cara frowned, not at all convinced by the idea. 'You said yourself that their lawyers must have been pretty savvy to make it so airtight. Besides, isn't there some penalty or other for lawyers who get caught telling porkies? I don't want you getting into trouble for violating your ethics.'

Tossing back the remains of his coffee, Henry put the empty mug on the table and relaxed into the sofa, pulling her back against him. 'If you swear faithfully to visit me in prison at least once a week, I'll take the risk,' he said cheerfully.

'Henry!' she protested, twisting round to look at him. He grinned and brushed a crumb of icing from her lips before kissing her.

'Cara, for once will you please let someone else try to help? I'm in Dublin for a meeting on Monday, but I can rearrange my schedule for Tuesday. The sooner we get this situation sorted, the better. Just trust me, okay?'

She gazed deeply into his eyes, close enough to see each strand of his enviously long lashes and then nodded. 'Of course I will.'

Henry's readiness to take a risk for her brought Cara's suppressed guilt about the kiss with Ryan rushing back to the surface, along with the nagging desire to confess everything and hope he would understand. But before she could voice her thoughts, Henry pulled her back against him and stroked her hair, winding a long curl tightly around his finger. 'Now we've got that issue out of the way, let's talk about something else.'

Cara tried to pay attention as Henry launched into the details of the latest drama between Fleur and her mother.

' . . . at this rate, I can see my mother being forced to enrol Caramel at Pemberton Hall.'

His laugh was so infectious that she couldn't help joining in. Sitting up on the sofa, she tucked a leg under her and leaned forward to smooth back his fringe.

'You don't know how lucky you are,' she sighed enviously. 'The worst thing you have to deal with is your sister making a fuss about attending one of the best schools in the country. Sometimes I try to imagine what it's been like for you. You know, having this amazing life where nothing ever goes wrong?'

Henry's smile faded and a shadow passed over his face for such a brief instant that she wondered if she had imagined it.

'Is that what you think?' he asked softly.

'I don't mean it in a bad way.' She shrugged. 'It's just that you didn't grow up poor and you've never had to deal with the type of tough situations that I did.'

This time she knew she wasn't imagining it. Henry's face shut down as if someone had swiped away any expression. Flummoxed by the sudden change in his demeanour, Cara laid a hesitant hand on his arm. 'What is it? What's wrong? I didn't mean to—'

Henry sighed heavily, a deep sigh that seemed to come from the very depths of him and he leaned his head back against the sofa.

'Perhaps I haven't been as open with you as I should have been, but it's tough to talk about,' he said, his voice suddenly sounding flat. 'I've told you before that I had an accident a few years ago. What I didn't say was that it was serious, and my spine was so badly damaged that I was paralysed for months. Maybe I didn't grow up poor, Cara, but I've had to deal with tougher situations than perhaps you can imagine.'

Cara listened in stunned silence, trying to process Henry's words. Instantly remorseful, she slipped her arms around him and laid her head on his chest, holding him tightly as he wrapped his arm around her.

'I'm so sorry, I had no idea. How awful for you,' she whispered, her guilt even more intense for having been so judgemental. 'I can't begin to imagine what you went through.'

For a few moments, they held each other in silence and then her phone rang. At first, she ignored it, but it continued to ring insistently, and she sat up and pulled it out of her bag intending to switch it off. One look at the screen changed her mind and she quickly tapped the green key.

'Cara, where *are* you?' Thaddeus demanded urgently.

'What's the matter, Thad?' she demanded. Her younger brother rarely phoned her, preferring to send texts instead. If Thaddeus was using his precious phone credit, then something serious must have happened.

'Grandma Maggie and Thelma are both here.' He paused for a moment so she could understand the significance of what he was saying, and then added '– *at the same time!*'

It took Cara a moment to find her voice. 'How the hell did that happen?'

'I don't know! Mum's been even more all over the place lately and keeps forgetting things! She was supposed to tell Thelma to come *next* month—' Thaddeus sounded impatient at having to waste time explaining the reasons behind the catastrophe. 'They've already started on each other, and Dad's furious! He stormed out saying he's going for a walk and doesn't know when he'll be back.'

Cara closed her eyes for a moment and took a deep breath. 'Where's Mum?'

'She's hiding upstairs, pretending to get my room ready for whichever one of them gets to stay.' His voice was thick with disapproval at his mother's disaster-management skills, and then, sounding more like four than fourteen, Thaddeus's voice rose into a pitiful crescendo. 'Cara, you need to come home *now* and sort it. *Please!*'

23

A Grand Mess

They were almost at the station when she heard the faint ring of her mobile. Worried that Thaddeus was calling to report that the grandmothers were now locked in a fist fight, Cara glanced apprehensively at Henry, who had insisted on coming with her, and fished inside her bag for the phone. Ryan's number flashed on the screen, and she groaned silently. Taking a phone call from an ex-boyfriend in the presence of a current boyfriend who had been confidently assured that said ex-boyfriend was ancient history wasn't a clever idea. Her resurgent guilt at the infamous kiss flooded her face with heat and she couldn't bring herself to look Henry in the eye.

'Is it Thaddeus?' Henry looked baffled by her reaction.

She shook her head, her brain scrambling in search of a plausible response. When none came to mind, she fixed a smile on her face and turned aside.

'What is it?' she muttered into the phone.

'And hello to you, too.'

She walked a couple of paces and hissed fiercely, 'What is your problem? I've told you not to call me!'

'Oh, don't be like that. Is this any way to treat an old friend? Listen, I'm on a job for Dexter and just a couple of streets away from your flat. Can I come over?' Despite the cajoling tone, he sounded so confident of her answer that she was immediately infuriated.

'No!' She moved even further away, taking advantage of Henry checking his own phone. 'Once and for all, just leave me *alone*! And don't think you can ignore me and come because I'm not at home.'

Ryan's voice took on a slight edge. 'So where are you, then?'

She closed her eyes in frustration, aching to scream at him to mind his own business but equally conscious of Henry standing less than a stone's throw away. A vision of her combative grandmothers flashed through her mind and she felt her agitation rising.

'I can't talk now. There's a crisis at Mum and Dad's and I need to go.'

The information tumbled from her mouth before she could bite the words back. She was supposed to be getting rid of Ryan, not giving him an opening to wriggle further into her life. Annoyed at her carelessness, she ended the call and linked her arm through Henry's, dragging him into the station before he could ask any questions.

The walk from Cricklewood Station to the house was completed in record time, galvanised by a mental picture of Grandma Maggie lying on the kitchen floor with the wooden hilt of a knife protruding from her chest and Thelma standing over her laughing maniacally. With Cara's fears intensifying by the minute, she pressed hard on the doorbell.

Against a cacophony of frantic barking from Logan, the door opened and a tall, heavy-set figure stood framed in the narrow doorway.

'*Caa-raaa!*' Grandma Maggie looked very much alive, and her plump arms jiggled as she seized Cara in a warm embrace laced with the faintest aroma of camphor.

'Come, come inside,' she commanded, shooing an excited Logan back and hauling Cara into the hallway. Since moving back to Ghana, Grandma Maggie had chosen to only wear traditional clothing and she was dressed in a brightly patterned long skirt and matching fitted top with a low neckline that showed off her impressive cleavage.

'Grandma, how have you been? You look amazing!'

Her grandmother patted the elaborately tied headscarf framing her broad face as she tried to look modest. Her gratified smile displayed brilliantly white teeth which contrasted against her smooth dark skin, and she took Cara's hands in hers and shook them excitedly.

'Ah, my sweet, beautiful granddaughter! It is *wonderful* to see you!' Twenty-five years spent living in London hadn't made the slightest dent in her grandmother's African intonation and she frequently burst into her own language whenever frustration rendered English inadequate to express herself. 'When will you come and visit us in Ghana? Your grandpa misses you all so much—'

'Is that Cara?' A loud, imperious voice with a lilting accent called out as the kitchen door opened and a woman emerged. Her cinnamon-brown features were lined but still beautiful and framed by glossy black waves that fell past her shoulders. She wore a fitted black dress that clung to her tiny but voluptuous figure, and she hurried towards them, walking easily in dizzyingly high-heeled black patent slingbacks. Despite the heels, her slight frame barely reached Cara's shoulders as she folded her into a long, loving embrace.

'Hello, Thelma,' Cara grinned. She kissed the older woman's soft cheek, relieved to see both grandmothers were still alive. 'Those shoes are wicked! How on earth do you manage to walk in them?'

Thelma ignored the contemptuous snort that escaped Grandma Maggie and gracefully kicked up one leg to display the narrow heel.

'Darlin', when you've been a successful model for as long as I was, you got a lotta practice wearing high heels,' she said, her accent carrying the distinctive cadence of her native Barbados.

Grandma Maggie sniffed. 'I'm surprised you can remember that far back, and you're asking for trouble wearing shoes like that at your age. One broken hip and you'll be in a wheelchair for the rest of your life,' she added hopefully.

Thelma pursed her lips and looked daggers at the other woman, and Cara quickly jumped in. 'I'm so glad you're here, Thelma, but to be honest I'm a bit . . . well, surprised?'

The shadow of a frown crossed her grandmother's face and Cara added hastily, 'But again, *such* a lovely surprise. It's just that Mum didn't say you were coming. Are you staying with Uncle Maurice?'

Thelma smoothed her hair back from her shoulders, looking somewhat put out. 'I don' know why everybody acting so shocked to see me! I told Beverley weeks ago that I was planning on coming to London. Maurice was expecting me, even if the silly boy sent a taxi to the airport instead of coming to meet me himself. Some foolishness about being too busy with Rebecca's family visiting from America. Anyone would think his scrawny wife and her people are more important than his own mother!'

Grandma Maggie ignored Thelma's grumbling and zeroed in on Henry, who was standing inside the doorway. She raised a pencilled eyebrow at Cara with a pointed nod in Henry's direction. 'And who is this young man?'

'This is my boyfriend, Henry.'

Henry smiled and Cara beamed at him with pride, completely missing Grandma Maggie's widened eyes and the tiny gasp of surprise that escaped Thelma's lips. Recovering quickly, Thelma pushed past Maggie to get to Henry, her face lighting up with a wide smile.

'Well now, isn't that just *marvellous*! Come and give me a hug,' she commanded, flinging her arms wide. Henry hesitated and she chuckled with a deep, throaty laugh at odds with her tiny physique. 'Come on now, boy, we won't eat you!'

He dutifully entered the outstretched arms and gently returned the older woman's squeeze. Clearly not wishing to be outdone, Grandma Maggie seized Henry's arm the instant Thelma released him and yanked him towards her, almost poking him in the eye with her stiff headscarf as she wrapped strong arms around him. After a few moments, Henry extricated himself and smoothed back his dishevelled hair, looking a little dazed by the lavish affection.

Grandma Maggie looked him up and down and nodded in approval. 'He's a big man. Handsome,' she pronounced. 'So, tell me, young man, what do you do for a living? You know my grand-daughter is very precious and we don't allow just anybody to—'

'Erm, sorry, Grandma, but where's Mum?' Cara interrupted. Tact was not one of her grandmother's qualities and, left unchecked, there was no knowing what would emerge from her mouth.

Her grandmother shrugged and Thelma piped up. 'I was just asking Manon the same question when you got here. Beverley's been upstairs for over an hour now – Lord only knows what she's doing up there. And why didn't she get my room ready before I got here?'

'*Your* room?' Grandma Maggie cut her eyes at her, and her full breasts heaved with indignation. 'Thelma, you know this is *my* month to visit and that I always stay here! You can go to your son's house since you're always boasting about the size of his mansion. I'm sure Maurice would be pleased to have you.'

Thelma drew her glossy lips into a sullen line. 'And *you* know I don't like to stay with Maurice when I come to England. So what if he has a big house? That boy and his skinny, stuck-up wife don't have no manners. Always telling me what I can and can't do like I'm a child and they're the grown-ups.'

'Maybe if you didn't act like you were twenty instead of well past seventy, they wouldn't need to,' Grandma Maggie scoffed.

Thelma's eyes flashed in anger, and Cara eyed them both warily. The nightmare scenarios she had entertained during the journey to Cricklewood suddenly seemed far less implausible.

'Henry, do you mind if I leave you with my grandmothers for a few minutes while I go up and find Mum?' She smiled at him apologetically, feeling like a mother abandoning her baby to ravenous wolves.

'Of course Henry don't mind,' said Thelma, waving her hand impatiently. 'You go on and see what Beverley is up to and give us a chance to get to know him.'

Which, Cara thought grimly, was exactly what worried her. But with her father missing in action and neither grandmother appearing inclined to relinquish their visitation rights, her mother clearly needed help.

Racing up the stairs, the sound of furniture being scraped across the floor led Cara straight to Thaddeus's room where Bev was pushing a neatly made bed back up against the wall. Cara looked around the spotless room and plain white walls in astonishment. The piles of clothing that usually decorated the floor had disappeared, along with the free weights and the stack of boxes filled with her brother's extensive collection of trainers. Also gone were the music and sports posters that had covered every inch of wall space and were now rolled up and stacked beside the heavy wooden wardrobe.

'*Mum!* This must have taken you ages! I can't remember the last time I saw this rug and I'd forgotten how big this room is. But why did you take down Thad's posters?'

'Can you imagine your grandmother sleeping with Stormzy and Cristiano Ronaldo staring down at her? She'd never stop moaning about it. Thaddeus can put them up again when Mama leaves.'

'But if Grandma Maggie's sleeping in here, what are you going to do about Thelma?'

'Oh, God, I wish I knew,' Bev groaned. 'She insists she won't stay with Maurice, not that he's even invited her. He's still furious that she made Rebecca cry the last time she visited. But if I don't let her stay, she'll go on and on about me forgetting about the Nightingales because I remarried and became a Grant. That woman can guilt trip me even more than my own mother.'

Bev ran a hand over the freshly ironed floral duvet cover and then sat on the edge of the bed, looking the picture of misery.

'But what happened, Mum?' Cara asked gently. 'How on earth could you have mixed their dates up? You promised Dad he'd never have to deal—'

'I know, I know!' Bev interrupted wearily. 'I'm not the most organised person at the best of times, but I told you my memory has been shocking recently. I don't know if it's . . . you know, the change, or if I'm just doing too much . . .' Her voice tailed off and she fell backwards onto the bed, staring up at the ceiling.

Cara's heart ached at the sight of her mother in distress. Bev looked exhausted and her eyes, usually bright with humour, were shadowed with lines of fatigue. For a few minutes, the only sound in the room was of Logan's barking floating up the stairs.

Bev broke the silence with a heavy sigh. 'Dad's furious with me,' she admitted wryly, her eyes still fixed on the pale-blue textured ceiling.

Cara shrugged. 'He'll get over it . . . he adores you. It can't be easy for him, though. Most men struggle with one mother-in-law, while poor old Dad's got to deal with two! Come on, let's go downstairs and see if we can talk some sense into one or other of them.'

'Sooner you than me, darling, I really can't deal with those two and their constant sniping. They're worse than the kids.' Her piteous expression looked uncannily like Manon's. 'Please don't make me go down there. Tell them I'm not feeling well.'

'Mum, you can't hide up here forever,' Cara said patiently. 'Besides, I've left my boyfriend alone with them and if I don't rescue him soon, they'll be fighting over who gets to feed him to death!'

This elicited a tiny smile and her mother sat up reluctantly. 'I just wish there was a way to make them see reason. They're so stubborn, they won't listen unless . . .' Her face lit up and she seized Cara's arm. 'I know!' she exclaimed with a triumphant smile.

'What?'

'I know,' her mother repeated. 'I know who can make them see sense. Quick, Caramia, go and fetch Floyd!'

Cara stared at her for a moment and then a slow smile crept across her face. She left the room without a word and tiptoed down the stairs. There was no sign of Henry or the two women, and hearing voices from the kitchen, she guessed her grandmothers were up to their old tricks. Poor Henry didn't stand a chance. Squashing a pang of guilt – after all, he *had* insisted on coming – Cara quietly let herself out of the house and crossed the low fence separating the front garden of the adjoining property. The sound of loud, pulsing reggae flooded out of the open windows of the house next door, and she clasped her hands together in a silent prayer of thanks before hurrying up the path to Floyd's front door.

24

CLASHES AND COLLISIONS

'Child! Come over here to your favourite grandma. I haven't seen you in such a long time.' Thelma beckoned Cara over and slipped an arm around her, squeezing her tightly. Thelma always gave the warmest, most loving hugs and Cara relaxed into her comforting hold and the familiar scent of Chanel No. 5.

Bristling at Thelma's provocative use of the word favourite, Grandma Maggie put the heavy saucepan she had been examining back onto the cooker and scanned the kitchen in search of a grandchild to cuddle. Thaddeus had already fled the house muttering about being late for football training, while Manon was at the far end of the kitchen, preoccupied with teaching Logan how to shake hands. With no one else immediately available, Grandma Maggie's gaze fell upon Henry, who immediately nipped past her to station himself safely behind Manon.

Visibly irritated by the giggling and whispering going on between Thelma and Cara, Grandma Maggie sucked her teeth loudly. When they both looked up, Grandma Maggie planted her hands on her hips and said brusquely, 'Eh, Cara, you are too thin!

You need feeding up. You know healthy fruit doesn't hang from weak branches. Beverley, don't you see she's too thin?'

Grandma Maggie swung her gaze from Bev to Thelma as if holding them both responsible for Cara's condition. Bev, who was on her knees hunting for canned tomatoes for her mother to cook jollof rice, raised her head long enough to roll her eyes before diving back into the cupboard without comment. Cara bit back the giggles threatening to erupt, far too accustomed to the personal observations and casually intrusive questions of her Ghanaian relatives to take offence.

Having unearthed a couple of tins, Bev stood up and huffed with exasperation at Logan, who was sniffing around the kitchen table laden with the sweet-smelling doughnuts and scones Grandma Maggie had brought from Ghana.

'Manon, would you please take him out of here? He's either getting under my feet or trying to eat the pastries,' Bev grumbled, pushing the over-excited dog out of the way.

'Come on, Logan, let's go to the other room and practise your handshake. We're obviously not wanted here.' With a martyred air, Manon seized Logan's collar with one hand, grabbed a scone with the other and marched out, the dog's paws skittering over the white tiles as he reluctantly complied.

Cara glanced at her watch anxiously. *How much more time does Floyd need to spruce up and come over?* As if her thoughts had conjured him up, Floyd poked his head around the back door which she had left ajar.

'Good afternoon, ladies! Can an ol' man come in and join you?'

Not waiting for an answer, Floyd ambled into the kitchen with an impish smile that lit up his face. Despite the summer heat, he wore tan corduroy trousers with a silky yellow and black polka-dot cravat tucked into a long-sleeved white shirt. He pounced on Thelma with a loud chuckle and kissed her soundly on both cheeks, leaving her flushed and giggling like a naughty schoolgirl.

Releasing her with obvious reluctance, Floyd rubbed his grey-flecked beard and loped over to Grandma Maggie. He seized her hand and lifted it smoothly to his lips with exaggerated courtliness before planting a gentle kiss that drove a tiny whimper out from between Grandma Maggie's lips. She looked almost sorry when he released her hand and then, visibly pulling herself together, she inspected him with critical eyes.

'You are looking well, Floyd, but maybe with a bit more middle than when I was here last, eh?'

She pointed towards his waist and his face fell. She smiled and added generously, 'But you are still handsome. Your necktie makes you look like – Thelma, what's the name of the old actor in that film we went to see?'

'You mean the one time we went to the cinema together all of ten years ago?' asked Thelma drily. She studied Floyd for a moment and then shrugged, before adding with a coy smile. 'I don' remember, but I always think he reminds me of James Earl Jones. You know, the one with the white hair and the deep, deep voice?'

Floyd ducked his head bashfully. 'Thank you kindly, Thelma. I can't complain 'bout that if you say so. Well, now, what a pleasant surprise seeing you lovely ladies. And both of you at the same time, too! I don't think my ol' heart can take so much beauty in one go.'

Thelma and Maggie tittered with undisguised pleasure while Cara tried not to cringe. Uncle Floyd was supposed to be saving the situation, not encouraging the women.

Grandma Maggie fished out a crumpled hankie that had been nestling deep in her décolletage and dabbed carefully at her face. 'Eh, Floyd, you are killing me! Woo, as for this weather, I've travelled all the way from Africa to find it is even hotter here!'

'The heat was terrible when I left home,' Thelma retorted. 'But then, some of us know how to handle hot stuff.' With an arch smile, she gave Floyd a flirtatious punch on his shoulder that drew an appreciative chuckle.

Grandma Maggie ignored the interruption. Thrusting her hankie back into its resting place, she picked out a food bag filled with little fried balls of dough, their golden-brown crust glistening with oil.

'Here, Floyd, you must have some of my special Ghanaian doughnuts.' Her tone brooked no argument as she held the bag out to him, and Floyd meekly accepted the gift with a courteous nod. He sniffed delicately at the aroma escaping from the bag and his eyes twinkled with merriment as he patted the gentle swell of his belly.

'Smells delicious, Maggie. But you know this won't help my – what you call it, my middle?'

'Personally, that's why I stay away from starch. That kind of food don' help *nobody's* middle,' Thelma said, giving Grandma Maggie's sturdy waist a pointed look that spoke volumes.

Floyd cleared his throat hastily. 'So, Thelma, how was your flight from Bridgetown? You certainly lookin' fresh for someone who's been on a plane for eight hours.'

Thelma opened her mouth to speak, but Grandma Maggie interjected. 'It's easy to look fresh when all you have to do is sleep and remember to put your wig back on when the plane lands.'

Bev ducked into the nearest cupboard, and Cara sighed. Far from solving the crisis, Floyd's presence was only serving to pour fuel onto the flames. Desperate to lighten the mood, she picked up one of the bags of pastries on the table and held it under her boyfriend's nose.

'Henry, you must try one of Grandma Maggie's doughnuts. She uses . . . what is it again, Grandma, cinnamon or nutmeg?'

Henry took in the naked entreaty in her eyes and without a word he picked out a doughnut and bit into the crisp, doughy ball. But while Cara was busy chewing her way through hers, Grandma Maggie was surveying Thelma's glossy hair.

'Don't you think you should leave it to the young girls to wear long wigs and tight dresses? It's time to start acting your age, Thelma. Telling the children not to call you Grandma doesn't make you a teenager.'

Everyone froze, and the room fell silent. Bev remained crouched on the floor with the look of one prepared to inspect the contents of the cupboard all day if she had to, while Henry and Floyd appeared ready to join her. Dismayed, Cara paused in mid-chew, clutching the last bite of doughnut. As strategies went, her mother's ploy to co-opt Uncle Floyd to solve their grandmaternal crisis was proving a non-starter.

Initially stunned into silence by the other woman's words, Thelma recovered herself with a gasp of sheer outrage. She quivered with indignation and drew her diminutive body up to its full height. Grandma Maggie folded her arms, clearly ready for battle, and Cara closed her eyes and braced herself.

'How *dare* you!' Thelma thundered, her accent even more pronounced in her fury. '*Who* you think you talking to?' Gesticulating wildly, she launched a fusillade of words at the other woman in a mix of Barbadian Creole and English, none of which sounded complimentary.

Grandma Maggie snorted indignantly. 'Listen to you! I am only speaking the truth, so why are you angry? All this emotion is not good for someone your age. As we say in my country, "A bad temper kills its owner".'

Giving up all pretence of hiding, Bev emerged from the cupboard in time to hear Thelma respond with another bombardment of Bajan. Goaded beyond endurance, Grandma Maggie retaliated with a tirade of English, heavily spiced with her own native tongue.

Cara attempted to intervene, but there was no cutting off Grandma Maggie once she got going. All anyone could do was wait and hope she'd run out of breath sooner rather than later. When she finally fell silent, the two women glared at each other, chests heaving as they prepared for the next round. Then Thelma sucked her teeth loudly and waved a dismissive hand.

'I can't even waste my breath on you, Maggie, you just a clown!' she spat. 'You always have something evil to say and I'm not taking any more of your—'

The doorbell cut her short. Loud barking from the hallway and the sound of running feet were followed by a shriek, and, seconds later, Manon raced into the kitchen screaming with excitement.

Ignoring her mother's exclamation and Thelma's alarmed, 'Child! What's wrong with you?' Manon rushed up to Cara and hugged her exuberantly, jumping up and down with elation.

'You won't believe who's here!' Manon's eyes sparkled and her words tumbled out of her mouth in an almost incoherent babble. '*Oh my God, oh my God!* Cara, did you know he was coming?'

Cara felt an icy prickle in her spine. *Oh no! Please, no!* Surely not even *he* would be so—

The kitchen door swung open, and Ryan walked in. Floyd's eyebrows rose almost to his hairline and the older women gaped. The sudden silence felt almost as loud as the earlier altercation between the grandmothers.

'Ryan! *Raa-yaan!*' Stretching the name out as far as it could go, Grandma Maggie tossed her rage aside as casually as litter by the wayside and raced towards him with an ear-piercing screech of delight. After submitting with good grace to her embrace for a few moments, Ryan released himself with a sheepish smile and shrugged his denim jacket back into place.

With a coquettish smile, Thelma wagged a finger at him. 'Well, well, well. Ryan O'Hare. This is certainly a day for surprises. You naughty, gorgeous boy, come here and let me look at you.'

Ryan dutifully kissed the proffered cheek and Thelma chucked his chin playfully. 'If I were twenty years younger, the girls wouldn't stand a chance.'

'If you were twenty years younger, you'd still be old enough to be his mother,' muttered Grandma Maggie waspishly.

Thelma paid no attention, her eyes still on Ryan who was striding past a frozen Cara to greet her mother. Bev took a half step back instead of moving into the arms he extended towards her, and Ryan dropped them awkwardly to his sides. They regarded each other gravely for a moment.

'Hello, Ryan,' Bev said evenly. 'Dexter mentioned you were back in London.'

For a moment Ryan looked uncertain and then a disarming grin snuck onto his face. 'Well, it's actually Dex I'm looking for. I spoke to him earlier and he mentioned he might be coming over.'

He glanced at Cara, who hadn't moved a muscle from the moment he'd walked in. 'Actually, I've been back for a few weeks. I thought Cara would have told you considering we've seen each other a few times.'

With a sharp intake of breath, Cara came back to life and cast an agonised glance at Henry. His expression didn't waver, and she wasn't sure if he had heard or was just giving a remarkably good performance of looking unconcerned. Her anger at Ryan, never far below the surface, flared up. *Does he think I'm a game he can play whenever he likes? How dare he come in here with his stupid insinuations trying to make trouble between me and Henry!* Ryan had warned her that all was fair in love and war, but just because he wanted her back was no reason for him to think she felt the same.

'I'd hardly describe a couple of brief conversations as seeing me a few times,' Cara said tartly. If the gloves were off for Ryan, then two could play that game. 'But the good news is that, since you're here, you finally get to meet Henry.'

Cara slipped her hand into Henry's with a proprietary air and lovingly threaded her fingers through his. She propelled him forward, her eyes meeting Ryan's with a defiant stare.

'Henry, this is Ryan. Ryan, meet Henry – my boyfriend.' She added the last in a saccharine-sweet tone, noting with satisfaction the involuntary twitch of the muscle along Ryan's square jaw and the tightening of his lips.

The two men sized each other up and the hostility felt almost palpable. Then Henry smiled and extended a hand and Ryan slowly returned the handshake, releasing the tension in the room like air from a balloon.

'Good to meet you, man.' Ryan nodded. He glanced at Cara, the faint smile at the corner of his mouth a rueful acknowledgement of her comeback. 'I've heard a lot about you,' he added, turning his attention back to Henry.

'Oh, really?' Henry murmured smoothly. He raised an eyebrow. 'I wish I could say the same.'

Ryan's eyes narrowed, but, before he could respond, Manon pulled the strawberry Chupa Chups lollipop she had been slurping out of her mouth and hugged him tightly around the waist.

He ruffled her hair affectionately. 'I can't believe how you've grown, princess. You'll soon be taller than Cara at this rate.'

'Why did you go away, Ryan?' she demanded, peering up at him with eyes filled with reproach. 'I was really sad that you'd gone. Thad and I thought we'd made you go away 'cos we were always making you take us swimming and down to the park. *Everyone* felt bad and Cara cried all the time.'

'*Manon!* I—' Cara stopped and inhaled sharply, not daring to look at Henry. Ryan flushed, Bev looked grim, and even Thelma and Grandma Maggie were stumped into temporary silence. Blithely unaware of the change in atmosphere, Manon prattled on. 'You didn't even say goodbye to Thad or me.'

Belatedly, Cara remembered her little sister's outsize crush on Ryan and how devastated she had been by his sudden disappearance. Yet another casualty of their failed relationship. *God, she could kill him!*

She watched sourly as he adopted a contrite smile that transformed Manon's frown into an expression of pure adoration. 'I'm so sorry, princess. I was going through a bit of a tough time, and I needed to go away for a while to sort my head out.'

He sounded so chastened and apologetic that both grandmas spun round to look at Cara, their eyes silently begging her to forgive him.

'You should have let Cara help you, then,' Manon giggled. 'She can sort anything out.'

Cara bristled, and Ryan, taking in her exasperated expression, prudently changed the subject. 'Talking of Thaddeus, where is he? I'd love to see him.'

Desperate to distance herself from their chatter, Cara took her mother's arm and pulled her to the far end of the kitchen where they could speak without being overhead. The problem of Ryan could wait; the more urgent problem was how to accommodate two elderly and very stubborn family members who couldn't be civil to each other for five minutes. Floyd appeared to have forgotten his mission and had joined the grandmothers who had surrounded Ryan, bombarding him with questions.

Logan circled the group a few times, his lead trailing along the flagstone tiles, whimpering as Manon hovered excitedly around the newcomer instead of taking him for his promised walk. Bored by the lack of attention, he nudged open the kitchen door and slipped out into the hallway.

A couple of minutes later, just as Cara looked up and realised Henry was no longer in the room, they heard frantic barking followed by the blaring of a horn and the sound of car tyres screeching. Manon looked around for Logan, spotted the open door and blanched. With a heart-rending scream, she raced out of the kitchen shouting his name. The front door was wide open, and Manon, closely followed by Cara, raced down the garden path to where a large van had stopped in the middle of the road.

Henry lay sprawled in the road, inches away from where black tyre tracks had burned into the Tarmac. Cara felt the blood drain from her face as she stared in horror at the figure lying prone on the ground, his blond hair stained with blood. Her heart thudded painfully in her chest as she pushed past Manon and sprinted to him just as he slowly struggled upright, ashen-faced and breathless and with one hand still clamped to the lead of a shell-shocked Logan.

'Henry! *Henry*! Are you alright?' Her voice was hoarse with fear as she knelt by his side, clutching at him and trying not to cry at the sight of the bloody shoulder exposed by his torn shirt.

'I knew playing rugby would come in handy one day,' he gasped, wiping a streak of blood from his forehead with his free hand and wincing as he moved his leg. The fabric of his trousers was shredded, and blood oozed from a gash on his knee. He peered at the van which was within touching distance and gave a heartfelt whistle.

'*Damn*, that was close!'

'Logan could have been killed,' Manon wailed as tears streamed unchecked down her face. She flung herself onto the shivering dog, showering him with kisses and almost smothering him with her cloud of hair.

'Oh my God, Henry, you saved Logan's *life*!' Manon cried. She buried her tear-stained face in Logan's fur, gently soothing the distressed dog until Logan's tail slowly wagged back to life.

The visibly shaken van driver had scrambled out of his vehicle and looked relieved to see both man and dog were still alive. As Henry made to stand up, the driver held out a steadying hand that shook almost as much as his voice.

'M-mate, take it easy! Are-are you sure you're alright? D'you reckon we should call an ambulance?' he stammered, as he helped Henry stagger to his feet.

Dizzy with relief that her boyfriend hadn't been crushed under the wheels of the van, Cara held onto Henry and turned on the driver angrily. 'Why were you going so fast, anyway?'

'It wasn't my fault! The dog just ran out into the road and if the gentleman here hadn't pulled him back—'

'Well, if you'd been driving at a reasonable speed, you would have had plenty of time to stop. This is a *residential* road! It's reckless drivers like you who cause accidents.'

The van driver backed away and raised his hands defensively. 'Now, look here, miss, just calm down.'

There was a collective groan from Floyd, Ryan and the grandmothers, who had gathered on the pavement outside the house along with some passers-by and several neighbours who had rushed outside on hearing the commotion.

The moment the driver's words were out, the colour drained from Cara's cheeks, and with the ferocity of a cork shaken loose from a bottle, she exploded into a furious tirade. Her words bumped up against each other in a hot tide of insults, only coming to an abrupt, panting halt when Henry placed a restraining hand on her arm.

Manon retrieved her lollipop from the pocket of her jeans and blew off the fluff before offering it to a chastened Logan, who licked it feebly. Looking up at the shell-shocked driver, she gave a nod in Cara's direction.

'You really shouldn't have said that. She totally hates being told to calm down.'

The man's eyes darted around the growing crowd of spectators, and he muttered something inaudible under his breath. After a final glance to reassure himself that Henry was still breathing, he clambered back into his vehicle and screeched away.

Floyd was the first to break the shocked silence as the van disappeared down the street. Staring in bewilderment at the open front door, he turned to Bev. 'How did that dog get out in the first place? Everyone knows he can't be trusted out on the road by himself.'

The women exchanged bemused looks and Ryan cleared his throat apologetically, reddening as all eyes swivelled in his direction. 'It's possible that it was my fault . . . I'm not a hundred percent sure I shut the front door properly after Manon let me in,' he admitted.

Manon was still on her knees with her arms wrapped around Logan, and she stared at him in disbelief. *How could you have been so stupid?* She didn't need to say the words because there was no mistaking her expression, which was mirrored by Floyd and the women.

Bev broke the accusatory silence with a clap of her hands. 'Okay, Manon, take Logan inside and give him some water. He's had a bad shock, but thankfully he's fine, and maybe he'll think twice before dashing out into the road again. Henry, I can't thank you enough for what you did. Let's go and take care of those cuts.'

With Bev and Cara on each side for support, Henry hobbled slowly back inside. A little later, with his wounds cleaned and a sticking plaster peeking out from under his fringe, he nursed a large whisky while half-sitting, half-lying on the sofa in the living room. A solicitous Manon fussed around him arranging soft cushions under his bandaged leg while a shocked Thaddeus, still in his football kit, examined the wounds beneath the torn strips of Henry's trousers with unconcealed awe. Refusing to be left out, a re-energised Logan, showing no ill effects from his near-death experience, woofed happily around Henry, swishing his tail back and forth in a frenzy of wagging.

Having allowed a decent interval to elapse, the two grand-mothers had resumed battle.

'Don't be foolish, Maggie. The man has had a shock,' Thelma was saying sharply. 'I can make him a nice plate of—'

'When you have nearly come face to face with the Lord, what you need is some hot pepper soup, not your tasteless dumplings,' came Grandma Maggie's withering interruption.

'Aren't you the one always warning the children that pepper has a beautiful face but an ugly temper? Why you want to torture the poor man when he's already suffering?'

Ryan, who had been sitting quietly in an armchair flicking through a magazine, tossed it aside with an impatient tut, visibly irritated by the bickering.

'Oh, come on, now! He's a big, strong lad, aren't you, Henry? You don't need the ladies to be fussing over you. He'll be fine in a few minutes if he's left in peace.'

'Shut up, Ryan!' Cara said sharply, searing him with a look that could have stripped paint. Her grandmothers might be annoying, but she was furious with Ryan for aiding Logan's escape and still smarting from her own encounter with the van driver. 'You're not helping in the slightest. Besides, if it's Dexter you're really looking for, he's clearly not here so there's no need for you to stay.'

Ryan's lips tightened angrily and the uncomfortable silence that followed was broken by Floyd clearing his throat and adjusting his cravat fussily. Satisfied he had everyone's attention, he clasped his hands together and spoke slowly, weighing his words with care.

'Thelma, Maggie . . . may I suggest a way out of this . . . situation? Why don't you two ladies put your . . . erm . . . differences aside and share Thaddeus's room? I've got a fold-out camp bed that I keep for my grandson's visits, and I could fetch it over right now. If you agree, that is?'

Floyd looked earnestly from Thelma to Grandma Maggie while the others held their breath. The two women exchanged a quick glance, sniffed in unison, and looked away, and Floyd threw his hands helplessly into the air.

'Please, Grandma Maggie . . . Thelma . . .?' Cara begged. 'Can't you try just this once to get along? Come on, you know we love you both.'

Manon piped up. 'Yes, please will both of you stay? Grandma Maggie, I can't wait for you to make your chicken jollof rice again. Mum's never tastes quite like yours.'

'And, Thelma, you *know* how much I love your curried fish thingy,' Thaddeus chimed in helpfully.

The women exchanged glances again and then stared hard at the wheedling teens who were flashing such sweet, winsome smiles that Cara almost retched.

Thelma was the first to crack. 'Okay, my darlings. If it means that much to you all, I'll stay. Although it's probably safer if *I* take the camp bed.' She scanned the other woman's sturdy build with pursed lips. 'We don't want no accidents now, do we?'

For once, Grandma Maggie didn't take the bait. Hands on hips, she beamed at Manon and nodded vigorously. 'As we say at home, "What is bad, we make good". Of course, I'll stay, my sweet grandchild, and you're right, nobody makes jollof rice like your Grandma Maggie.'

With hostilities suspended, the grandmothers sat side by side with a teenager perched on each arm of the sofa as they continued their charm offensive. Cara looked at her mother and, as their eyes met, they both struggled to keep a straight face. Cara's phone buzzed, and she glanced down at the screen. 'Henry, our cab's outside.'

She quickly kissed her grandmothers and gave Floyd a grateful hug, studiously ignoring Ryan's stormy expression and instead helping Henry to his feet. Bev hovered anxiously while Henry gingerly rested his weight on his injured leg and then half-walked, half-hopped his way out of the room.

As Cara left to help Henry into the car, she heard Thaddeus remark artlessly, 'I'm glad you two have made up 'cos I'd really like my dad to come back home.'

Settling herself next to Henry in the back of car, Cara couldn't help grinning at Thaddeus's lack of diplomacy. But then, as Grandma Maggie was wont to say, 'Once you have crossed the river, you can be rude to the crocodile!'

25

Checkmate

'*What?*' Elliott spluttered, his face puce with fury. 'You can't say that!'

'I just did,' said Henry calmly. 'And if the pair of you don't tear up this contract and return the material you've swindled out of this young woman, I will have you up in court so fast, you won't know what's hit you!'

Cara stared open-mouthed as easy-going boyfriend Henry was transformed into cut-throat lawyer Henry. Even the sticking plaster above his eyebrow, courtesy of his injuries from rescuing Logan, added to the air of menace he was giving off. This was hardly the subtle approach she had assumed would be the game plan. Cheered by the knowledge that his top-class legal mind was helping Ashanti, Cara had been anticipating some lawyerly approach to the negotiations and was dumbfounded by the blunt showdown Henry had used as his opening gambit. Perhaps they should have planned this a bit more carefully, she thought, watching him narrow his eyes and swing his gaze between an apoplectic Elliott and an unruffled Cyrus Hetherington because, judging from Cyrus's expression, the threat of court wasn't cutting much ice.

Reassured by his boss's composure, Elliott quickly pulled himself together. 'I don't know who you think you are, but you have no right to come here—'

'I'd hear him out if I were you,' Ashanti cut in, looking pointedly at Elliott before continuing to examine her freshly painted nails. Sitting in a chair facing Cyrus's desk with her legs crossed, she was struggling to suppress a grin and looked more animated than Cara had seen her in weeks. Despite the enormity of the stakes, Ashanti was clearly enjoying herself.

Which hadn't been the case when Henry and Cara had arrived at her flat a couple of hours earlier with instructions that she was to follow them and not say a word. Ashanti's first reaction had been one of disbelief.

'We're going to storm Nine Elms Records. What the hell does that even *mean*?'

Henry's repetition of his suggestion to Cara had been met with silence while Ashanti digested the plan. She frowned and scratched her untidy bun of hair and then asked him bluntly, 'Do you think it will work?'

'At this point, I'd say you don't have much to lose,' he shrugged. 'How much longer can you stay holed up in here not writing or performing? You're an artist, not a couch potato.'

Fully expecting dissent, Cara was stunned when Ashanti nodded. 'You have a point there,' she agreed. 'I'm going loopy sitting in this flat. I *was* sad, but now I'm just pissed off, so if you think it's worth a try, just give me a few minutes to change and put my face on.'

Ashanti's few minutes had been closer to an hour by the time she emerged in a clingy black dress and six-inch scarlet platforms. Flicking back her carefully tonged hair, she bent to stroke Nutmeg.

'Mummy will be back as soon as she's dealt with the naughty men who want to ruin her life,' she crooned.

Then she looked across to where Cara and Henry were sitting in silence and clapped her hands impatiently. 'Come on, then! What are you waiting for? Let's go and sort out my career!'

'You heard the lady, let's get a move on.' Henry hauled Cara to her feet, and she grasped his hands suddenly looking doubtful.

'Hold on a minute, guys. Let's think this through a bit more. Henry, if your colleagues don't think the contract is breakable, how—?'

Henry cut her off in mid-flow. 'Cara, just trust me. Please.'

Reminding herself that Ashanti had run out of options, Cara nodded, mentally crossing her fingers as she followed them out of the flat.

Getting into the Nine Elms Records office had been relatively easy. Hearing Ashanti's voice through the entryphone, Elliott had immediately buzzed her in, standing by helplessly as Henry and Cara filed in behind her. Caught off-guard, Elliott was too late to stop Ashanti from stalking confidently across the deserted room and marching straight into Cyrus's office with a cursory knock.

Pushing Elliott aside, Henry followed close behind, although once inside the office, he was momentarily distracted by the combination of celebrity photographs and ornate gilt furniture. Cyrus was sitting in a high-backed chair behind his huge antique desk, and he jerked his head up from the papers he had been studying as they marched in, his raised eyebrows the only hint of any surprise at their unceremonious entrance.

Without waiting for an invitation, Ashanti sauntered across the thick carpet to sit in one of the gilded visitors' chairs. Unlike the last time she had been in his office, she looked completely self-assured and returned Cyrus's frown with a cheery smile.

Judging from his casually rolled up shirtsleeves, their whiteness in stark contrast to his deep tan, Cyrus was clearly not expecting company.

'So, what's all this, then? Ashanti, it's good to see you again. You're looking very well,' he remarked, sounding as calm as if she had stopped by for afternoon tea and hadn't been in hiding for weeks.

Ignoring the other people in the room, Cyrus dropped the papers he'd been reading and leaned back in his chair. 'I'm assuming you've now seen reason and are ready to work with us? Hopefully you've also been using your time off to write some new material.'

Cyrus's arrogant tone had been the trigger for Henry's blunt introduction, and Elliott, who had sidled into the room after them, had been unable to restrain himself from his outburst.

Unnerved by Ashanti's breeziness, Elliott gave a nervous laugh and glanced at Cyrus, whose expression remained impassive. Elliott was patently eager to impress his boss and show he could meet fire with fire, and he plunged on.

'You're a fine one to talk about court,' he snarled at Henry. 'If anyone should be taking anyone to court, it's us! We've been very patient so far, but Ashanti signed a contract which we offered her in good faith, and she's done absolutely nothing to comply with it.'

Cara looked at Henry with apprehension. Having entered with all guns blazing, their plan now felt distinctly iffy. Ashanti appeared confident, but Cara's heart rate was speeding up alarmingly and she was beginning to regret going along with her boyfriend's idea.

Henry's eyes blazed with contempt. 'Go ahead, take her to court. This contract is not enforceable in law, and you know it.'

'What are you, a bloody lawyer?' Elliott sneered.

'Well yes, actually,' Henry said mildly. 'Intellectual property, patents, copyright, anti-trust . . . shall I go on?' He thrust a card into the agent's breast pocket and Elliott stepped back hastily, the disparity between Henry's solid bulk of muscle and his own slight frame clearly not lost on him.

'Listen, I don't care who you are. The contract she signed is the standard one for all our artists, and it's watertight!'

Ignoring him, Henry sat in the chair next to Ashanti and crossed his leg, resting his right ankle comfortably on his knee. Sounding relaxed, he kept his eyes fixed on Cyrus. 'If you're looking for a long, protracted and *public* court battle just to hold onto a hostile artist who's certainly not giving you any further material, then be my guest. But remember that you can't blackmail talent, and you'll be bloody lucky to get one decent song out of her, let alone five albums' worth. You might be able to gag her for a bit while you spend serious money litigating this in court, but I can promise you'll never get anything back on your investment.'

Elliott caught his breath, looking genuinely horrified at the prospect. 'Look, let's not get carried away here. Ashanti, we can talk about this . . . we *really* want to invest in you.'

He continued to bluster, his face growing redder by the minute, but Cyrus looked unmoved. Henry hadn't divulged the details of his strategy and Cara had no idea of his next move, but seeing Henry in lawyer mode for the first time, she couldn't help feeling relieved he was on her side.

Henry's eyes were still trained on Cyrus and his voice hardened. 'I would strongly suggest you have a word with those cowboys posing as lawyers that you employ and tell them an agreement like this one amounts to restraint of trade. And *you* should be aware that being party to an unlawful restrictive agreement amounts to conspiring, which is a serious criminal offence.'

Had it not been for the muscle working furiously at his jaw, Cyrus could have been a statue. Henry held his gaze without flinching and then, suddenly, Cyrus cracked.

'What the *hell* makes you think you can come into *my* office and talk to me like that?' He spat the words out furiously and stared at the three intruders in disdain.

243

'I can, because she's my client.' Henry looked unfazed, which seemed to stoke Cyrus's anger further.

'Well, then, tell your *client,'* Cyrus mocked, skewering Henry with a contemptuous glare, 'that she signed a contract. I don't care how fancy a lawyer she's managed to bag herself, she doesn't get to go back on it just because she's had a change of heart. That's not how I do business.'

His angry glance swept across to include Cara and she glared back scornfully. If Cyrus thought acting like some cut-price East End boss was going to intimidate her, he had another think coming. Henry stood up, his eyes chips of green ice. With the air of someone who had already wasted enough time, he pulled out a sealed envelope from inside his jacket and leaned across the desk to push it towards Cyrus.

'Well, then, let me tell you how *I* do business,' he said, his voice as dangerously smooth as a velvet-tipped sword. 'My client took no independent legal advice prior to signing this document and as any reputable lawyer would have told you, an artist must be independently advised on any long-term exclusive agreement. These outrageous terms are completely unenforceable, and I have no doubt that this so-called contract, not to mention your unscrupulous solicitors, will draw the immediate attention of the Law Society. Since you're not prepared to be reasonable, we'll see you in court.'

The atmosphere in the room was electric and Cara had to bite hard on her lip to stop the gasp that almost escaped. *What the hell!* Her agreeable boyfriend had turned into a barracuda faster than Clark Kent into Superman and, bizarrely, even though she knew it was all bravado, Cara believed every word.

Elliott had been growing progressively paler and by the time Henry finished his speech, his face was ashen. The lawyer's confidence also finally seemed to be getting through to Cyrus, who looked ready to explode.

'All of you get the hell out of my office before I do something you'll regret. NOW!'

The muscle in his jaw was working overtime and the end of his nose was pinched white with anger. Even his skin looked mottled beneath the mahogany tan.

Elliott tried to speak, but Henry held up a hand and cut him off, staring levelly at Cyrus. 'Oh, and by the way, once word of all this gets out and your other artists start suing to regain *their* freedom, you're going to find yourself spending a lot of time and money in court.'

Ashanti, who had been nodding along vigorously to Henry's words, chipped in. 'You heard my lawyer. I want that agreement torn up.'

Cyrus's eyes flickered from her unflinching stare to Henry's impassive expression and then back again. For an agonising moment, no one said a word and then he shrugged as if the conversation had suddenly become tedious.

'Fine, have it your way.' He gave a cursory nod in Henry's direction and added in a dismissive tone, 'We'll have a document sent to you tomorrow voiding the contract.'

'But, boss . . .!' Elliott's voice returned on a wave of indignation. 'You're not going to just roll over and let—'

'Shut it!' Cyrus growled, and Elliott paled, looking so frightened that Cara almost felt sorry for him. Elliott's boss made even Paula look good.

Swivelling his chair back to face Henry, Cyrus leaned forward and planted both hands on his desk. 'But let me be clear. If we walk away from this deal, it's on the express understanding that this remains confidential. I don't need you messing with my other artists. Have you got that?'

Ashanti stood up and smiled sweetly. 'Of course.'

Still in shock at Cyrus's abrupt change of heart, Cara didn't notice Henry getting up to leave until Ashanti jabbed a sharp elbow into her side. Jolted into action, she made to follow them and then stopped when Henry turned back to Cyrus and a chastened Elliott.

'Oh, and make sure I have everything – and I mean *everything* that belongs to my client – in my office by close of business tomorrow, or the deal's off.'

The moment they were out on the street, Ashanti hugged Henry so hard that he gasped for breath. With a triumphant whoop, she jumped on Cara and squeezed her fiercely and then broke into an impromptu dance on the pavement. Cara grinned, relieved to see Ashanti's sparkle back.

When she had finally calmed down, Cara asked curiously, 'By the way, did you mean what you said about keeping all this confidential?'

Ashanti sucked her teeth loudly. 'Are you kidding me? As soon as I've got my notebook and my tapes back, I'm warning Angie and Will to get themselves a lawyer, fast!'

26

STALKING HORSE

'Thanks, Ben. I owe you one.'

Cara sniffed loudly and added a couple of extra coughs for good measure before cutting off the call and grinning at Rosie. 'And *that's* how you get out of a day in the office.'

Standing in front of the bay window that overlooked the road, Rosie turned with an expression of censure mixed with admiration. 'You're awful, Cara. I'm surprised you still have a job sometimes.'

Unabashed, Cara jumped onto the sofa and tucked her legs under her. 'I promised my grandma I'd take her to get her hair done this morning and there was no way Paula was going to give me time off for that. Now I've sorted Thelma out, I've got the rest of the afternoon free, and what could be better than spending it at home with my besties?' She glanced at her watch and pulled a face. 'Where the flipping heck is Ash? I told her to get here for two o'clock. I swear that girl will be late for her own funeral.'

Rosie peered out of the open window and shielded her eyes with her hand as she squinted through the bright sunlight. 'Hang on, I can see her coming. She's carrying a load of bags which is probably what's kept her. Seriously, how does she even *walk* in those shoes?'

A few minutes later and breathless from climbing the stairs, Ashanti pushed open the front door and dropped a pile of shopping bags on the floor.

'Sorry I'm a bit late but I badly needed some new clothes now I'm back on the circuit. There's no way I'm getting a proper record deal if I don't look the part and I'm wearing stuff that's out of date.'

She hugged Rosie and turned to scrutinise Cara. 'Speaking about rubbish clothes, what the hell are you wearing?' She gestured towards Cara's outfit with a moue of disgust. 'Is that thing a dress or a sack?'

'It's vintage Prada and it wasn't cheap!' Cara protested. 'I got it in Camden a couple of weeks ago, so what's your problem?'

Ashanti eyed her critically. 'I won't lie to you, it's the sort of thing you should only wear in front of blood relatives.'

Rosie looked uneasily from one to the other, but instead of responding with a torrent of abuse, Cara simply laughed.

'Good to see you're back to your old mouthy self,' she said dryly.

'Before you two start on each other, who's for a cup of tea?' Rosie offered.

A duet of '*yes please*' followed her into the kitchen, and while Rosie put on the kettle and dropped tea bags into mugs, Ashanti broke the news about her special delivery earlier that morning.

'So, not quite the twenty-four hours that my lawyer demanded,' she concluded smugly, 'but at least I've now got everything back from those tossers. I called Henry to let him know, and guess what?'

Cara looked blank and Ashanti clapped her hands with glee, her words tumbling out in excitement. 'You'll never believe this . . . he says the lawyer at his firm who looked over the Nine Elms contract

248

was so disgusted with what they'd done that he's going to put in a word for me with one of his clients who is – get this – a *real* music producer!'

She whirled around, coming perilously close to knocking into the brimming mugs of tea Rosie was carrying out of the kitchen. Relieving her of one of the cups, Ashanti took a cautious sip before placing the mug on a side table and settling herself onto the sofa. She kicked off her shoes and crossed her legs before demanding without preamble, 'So, Rosie girl, stop hedging. How's it going with you and the Spaniel?'

Caught unawares, Rosie swallowed a huge gulp of her tea, spluttering as the scalding liquid burned her mouth and brought tears to her eyes. Turning a vivid red, she fanned her open mouth and glared at Ashanti.

'Look what you made me do!'

'Don't change the subject,' Ashanti said, briskly. 'Are you or are you not dating the man? Oh, and don't even *try* to pretend you haven't been secretly seeing him.'

'I'm taking it slow, if you must know!' Rosie huffed defensively. 'We've had lunch a few times and . . . okay, we went to the cinema one evening.'

Cara burst out laughing. 'About bloody time, too! So, what changed your mind?'

'You mean, apart from you two going on at me? I don't know – and I'm not even sure I have changed my mind,' Rosie sighed. 'He's such an idiot sometimes, but you guys are right – he's also incredibly sweet. But then, just as he does something lovely, he manages to balls things up again. Like last week, he literally begs me to go and see a film with him, buys the tickets and popcorn and everything, and then ruins the whole thing by telling me the ending halfway through!'

'You should be grateful he paid for the tickets,' Cara pointed out. 'Remember when Kevin McManus took you out to that posh restaurant and then made you put the bill on your credit card?'

Rosie winced. 'Don't remind me. Sean might be a bit of a numpty at times, but he's not pure evil like Kevin. I can't believe how crazy I was about that tight-arse.'

'And the Spaniel can't be any worse than Ethan Shawcross. Cara, d'you remember him?' Ashanti said.

'Sadly, I do. And what about that guy Brendan who could only spare enough time to go on two dates a month?'

'Ah, yes. Busy Brendan. The tosser who broke up with her on the phone because he was too busy to do it to her face.'

'And let's not forget Jared Shaughnessy!'

'Oh yeah,' Ashanti agreed, clearly enjoying the trip down Rosie's memory lane. 'Now *he* was a total psycho. Rosie, do you realise that if Cara and I hadn't staged that intervention at the salon, you'd be walking around with—'

'I know, I know,' Rosie interrupted, 'a bloody great tattoo of his name right on my—'

'Ahem,' Ashanti coughed delicately.

'You make me sound like a total slapper,' Rosie sulked.

'Not at all, hon,' Ashanti soothed. 'But you must admit that you do fall rather hard and . . . um, shall we just say, very quickly?'

'And you can't deny that you pick men who are guaranteed to give you a hard time,' Cara chipped in.

Ashanti nodded sagely. 'Anyway, Rosie love, the point we are trying to make here is that given some of the losers you've put up with in the past, maybe you need to approach your next relationship . . . differently. You know, like go out with someone that worships *you* for a change, instead of vice versa. Okay, so old Spaniel might have crap timing at movies, but you've got to admit that he treats you like a queen and thinks the sun shines out of your you-know-where. Would it really be such a bad idea to give him a proper chance?'

Rosie stared at her feet, looking the picture of gloom. 'Dad still isn't over that middle-of-the-night saxophone serenade. He moaned for weeks that his ears were ringing from the shock, and he swears the cat's still traumatised. I honestly think I'd be taking my life into my hands if I told him about Sean.'

Ashanti gave an impatient tut. 'Never mind your dad, kiddo. What do *you* want?'

'It's not that simple,' Rosie said. 'Look, there's more chances of pigs flying than my father letting Sean anywhere near the house.'

'Sean, eh?' Ashanti winked at Cara. 'Did you get that? Not Spaniel anymore . . . Sean. Oh, and talking about flying pigs, have you taken those jeans back to the shop yet?'

Rosie squirmed uncomfortably and Ashanti tutted in exasperation.

'I'll take that as a no, then, shall I?'

'I *did* go back, but that cow of a sales assistant was having a go at another girl trying to return something. Literally everyone in the shop was staring at her. It was so embarrassing and, well, it just didn't feel like the right time.'

Cara sighed. 'Rosie, give me the jeans and *I'll* take them back. I'm not a lawyer but surely there's no way she can refuse to refund your money. You've never even worn them!'

Rosie still looked glum, but she shook her head stubbornly. 'No, it's fine, I'll do it. It's— would you two please stop looking at me like I'm a complete wimp. I've said I'll do it, and I *will!*'

Cara and Ashanti exchanged glances, knowing the chances of Rosie standing up for herself, whether against unscrupulous boyfriends, an overprotective and overbearing father, or an aggressive shop assistant, were close to zero.

Rosie swallowed the rest of her tea in silence and then glared at Cara. 'Okay, if we've finished with pick-on-Rosie time, it's my turn. What's going on with you and Ryan?'

Cara blinked, taken aback by the sudden charge. 'Nothing,' she said automatically. She reached for her cup and swallowed the cooling dregs. 'Absolutely nothing. So, Ash, how does it feel to know you can perform again?'

Ashanti raised an eyebrow. 'Nice try, but Rosie's got a point. Why have you let that snake back into your life?' She glanced at Rosie. 'Sorry, love, I know he's your family, but . . .'

'Never mind about that, it's her I'm worried about. Cara, *do* you want to get back with him?' Rosie asked, sounding worried. 'You always used to say that you two were destined to be together and Ryan was your soulmate. Do you still think that?'

'Look, it's complicated . . .' Cara's voice faltered at her feeble response, but nothing about Ryan or the feelings he generated was simple. 'Yes, Ryan and I have history but why would I even be with Henry if I still believed Ryan's the man for me? I didn't ask Ryan to come back, and I've got enough problems keeping things on track with Henry without my ex-boyfriend complicating things.'

Ashanti pounced. 'What problems? I thought you and my lawyer were solid.'

'Your . . .? Oh, never mind,' Cara sighed. If it kept Ashanti happy to think she had Henry at her legal beck and call, then so be it. Rosie still looked anxious, and Cara put down her cup and paced up and down the room as she tried to assemble her confused thoughts into a coherent sentence. The uncomfortable truth was that despite her best efforts, Dexter's words were still lodged in her mind. There were so many differences between her and Henry and although they were happy now, would it last? She'd been happy with Ryan too and look what happened. Could she really put herself through more heartbreak?

'Well, okay, maybe not problems exactly, but definitely a dilemma. I like Henry. I mean, I *really* like Henry. A lot. But we're so different! First off, I'm a city girl. A weekend is doable, but what if I can't hack the whole country-living thing?'

'You do know there are Black people outside London, don't you?' Ashanti said dryly.

Cara ignored her and carried on pacing. 'Secondly, Henry's the only son and he's probably going to inherit the estate which means I'm going to have to live out there.'

Ashanti sucked her teeth. 'Aren't you getting a bit ahead of yourself, hon? Not to mention killing off the poor bloke's dad after you've only just met him.'

Rosie chipped in. 'You've just been having a go at me to give Sean a chance, so how about you do the same for Henry? You're nuts about him, and after everything he's done for you, he obviously feels the same way.'

'Yes, but just 'cos we're together now doesn't mean it will last. Being together isn't the same as belonging together.' Cara hesitated. 'Okay, I hate to admit it, but sometimes I wonder if Dex is right?'

Ashanti snorted with derision. 'Can I just say that if you're taking relationship advice from Dexter, right there is where you're going wrong.'

'Ash, how long are you planning to keep up this I-hate-Dexter act? You're not fooling anyone. We all know how much you're missing him,' Rosie piped up, sounding unusually stern, and Cara grinned as Ashanti looked nonplussed.

True to form, she recovered quickly and gave Rosie a glare. 'This isn't about me. We're talking about Cara, remember? And weren't you the one who brought up Ryan in the first place? Right, so let's get back to the point.' She turned her gaze onto Cara, who groaned as the interrogation commenced. Peppered with questions from both sides, she waited for a lull in the barrage to speak.

'Of course Henry is lovely and, yes, he makes me very happy. But realistically, how long can it last? You haven't seen where his family lives. It's a massive mansion – and let's not forget his grandfather is a frigging *earl*!'

'That's hardly his fault,' Rosie pointed out. 'We don't get to choose our families. Don't you think I'd have disowned Ryan years ago if I had the choice?'

Ashanti shook her head impatiently. 'Cara, Henry's old enough and smart enough to make his own decisions and looking at the way he bends over backwards to make you happy, I don't see him doing anything to change that. Just because Henry didn't go to school in Kilburn or live on a council estate, how does that make it a problem? It's not like you're living on the margins yourself, is it?' Ashanti added impatiently as she gestured around at the African sculptures and artistic black-and-white framed posters that decorated the walls of Cara's living room.

Cara plopped down on the sofa, propping her head against the throw cushion made from the Kente-patterned fabric Grandma Maggie had gifted her. What was so hard to understand about the gulf between her background and Henry's? Wasn't it obvious that you could like – even love – someone and yet have little in common with them? If she could see that now, it was only a matter of time before Henry realised it too, and although she was still furious at Dexter for his judgemental comments, it was difficult to banish his remarks when they reinforced the niggling doubts nesting in the recesses of her mind. And yet, she reasoned, who in her right mind would walk away from someone as perfect, as loving, and as supportive as Henry, and especially for reasons she couldn't even clearly articulate?

'It's okay to let yourself be happy, hon,' Ashanti said softly as she took in Cara's troubled expression. 'Being with someone different doesn't have to be a bad thing. Even people from the same backgrounds have problems. Just look at me and Dex, for God's sake, and even though Ryan went to the same school as us, look how *that* turned out.'

With that, she sat up and slipped her feet back into her heels.

'Where are you going?' Cara and Rosie protested in unison.

'Ash, I pulled a sickie so we could all hang out this afternoon. You've only just got here,' Cara scowled.

'Sorry, girls, but I need to rest my voice. I'm singing at Mocktails tonight and Colum feels so badly about encouraging Elliott that he's given me a double slot. Rosie love, why don't you invite the Spaniel along?' Seeing Rosie's expression, Ashanti tacked on, 'Sorry, I meant invite *Sean*.'

Ashanti bent to gather her assorted carrier bags, still babbling away until Rosie coughed loudly and deliberately. She gave Ashanti a stare, her silence speaking volumes. Although Cara hadn't said a word, Ashanti ducked her head, suddenly not quite able to meet her eyes. It took a moment, but then she looked up and, after a slight hesitation, she tossed back her hair and her dark eyes flashed defiance.

'I didn't *ask* you to sort it, you know.'

'I know,' Cara agreed gravely.

'I could have got myself out of it without your help,' she added.

'Of course.'

Ashanti stood up, and Cara rose to her feet simultaneously. They stared at each other for a long moment without either saying a word. Then with what sounded suspiciously like a sob, Ashanti dropped the bags and flung herself into Cara's open arms. They held each other tight and after a moment, her voice muffled by Cara's shoulder, Ashanti mumbled, 'Thanks, Cara.'

Cara swallowed hard and blinked back her tears. Ashanti never explained and never apologised, but she knew how close she had come to losing her music and everything she had worked for.

'You're welcome, hon.'

Ashanti broke away, wiped carefully under her eyes, and picked up her bags. 'I'll see you guys tonight. By the way, Cara, I've invited Henry to the club. If he's going to be part of the gang, he needs to experience how the other half lives.'

Rosie reached for her jacket. 'Wait! I'll come down with you. I'm going home to pick up those jeans and take them back to the shop.' She slipped her arms into the jacket and tossed back her hair. 'And you can both take that look off your faces. I'm fed up with everyone thinking I'm pathetic.'

She slung her handbag over her shoulder and took a deep breath. 'Besides, I'm going to need that refund to buy Dad a bottle of scotch, 'cos he'll want a stiff drink after I've told him I'm going out with Sean.'

27

SUNDAY BLUES

It wasn't the best Sunday Cara had ever spent with Henry. In fact, as she reflected later, it was unquestionably the worst. The plan had been to spend the morning in bed with bacon rolls and coffee, followed by an afternoon on the sofa watching back-to-back episodes of *The Sopranos,* Henry's favourite show.

The morning part had started well enough with the warm butties and only slightly cool lattes Henry had sprinted down the road to buy from Greggs. Their leisurely breakfast had given them a chance to catch up on the past week and for Cara to recount the horrors of the wildlife charity fundraising dinner Paula had entrusted to her, and which Julio once again managed to sabotage, starting with the banners he had set up around the ballroom inviting the five-hundred-pound-a-head guests to 'Help Us Save the Cheaters'. Following the sumptuous dinner, the video link-up Julio had been charged with organising with the cheetah sanctuary outside Johannesburg had been halted when two of the endangered wildcats charged at the terrified camera operator during the live interview, forcing him to climb a nearby tree. To add insult to injury, as Cara explained to a convulsed Henry, Paula – who had overridden Cara's protests about using Julio for such a prestigious event – had been so mortified by the fallout that she'd refused to speak to Cara for the rest of the week.

Still laughing when his phone buzzed, the urgency in his senior partner's voice had been enough to send Henry scrambling for his trousers, searching for his car keys, and disappearing through the door, promising to return as soon as the crisis was resolved.

With Henry gone, Cara had cleaned her flat, and an hour later was camping on the sofa in her now-spotless living room with her laptop, a mug of tea and a plate of Jaffa cakes. Eventually tiring of celebrity gossip, she put her laptop aside and stretched out on the sofa, staring at the newly dusted mantelpiece displaying the scenic print of Little Duckworth that Fleur had sent her and wondering why she felt so unaccountably at a loss. Before Henry, when her Saturdays had usually been spent either running an event, hanging out with her girlfriends, or visiting her family, Cara had always welcomed the solitude of her Sundays. Now, she realised, it was hard to remember when Sundays hadn't included Henry, and after only a few hours without him she felt bereft. Far from being comforting, the insight brought a deep sense of disquiet. If being with Ryan had taught her anything, it was that depending on *anyone* was exactly what caused problems because they either left you or died . . .

Uneasy at the sombre direction her thoughts were taking, Cara slipped off the sofa and wandered into the kitchen. Opening the fridge, she took out the bottle of wine she had been cooling for lunch and poured herself a generous glass. She took a gulp and topped it up before settling herself back on the sofa.

◆ ◆ ◆

It felt like minutes and yet, when Cara glanced at the clock, it was almost three o'clock. There was still no word from Henry and the wine she had continued drinking had left her feeling distinctly light-headed. The Jaffa cakes she had eaten earlier had taken the edge off her appetite but hadn't been enough to blunt the effects of the alcohol and when her phone rang, she reached for it, hoping desperately it was Henry calling to say he was on his way back.

'Hi, Dexter,' she said brightly, trying not to sound disappointed.

'Cara, have you heard from Ryan?' Dexter sounded unusually brusque, and she pulled herself upright on the couch, feeling slightly unnerved when the room swirled gently with the movement.

'Not since I hung up on him – again – yesterday. Why?'

Dexter sighed. 'He was on an overnight job, and I've just had a call from Pete. The client's phoned in to say they still haven't received their goods and we've both been trying Ryan's phone, but it keeps going to voicemail. I just hoped you'd have some idea where he might be.'

'You mean Ryan's out there with your van and your customer's goods and he hasn't so much as called you?' She didn't bother to disguise her incredulity.

Dexter hesitated. 'We don't know what's happened,' he said reasonably. 'He could have been in an accident or broken down on the road somewhere. If his phone battery's dead—'

'More likely it's a case of Ryan screws up again. But then, what else would you expect?' she retorted, slurring her words slightly despite her efforts.

'Are you *drunk*?' Dexter sounded astonished.

'No,' she insisted weakly, shaking her head as if he could see. The move was a mistake as the room tilted sharply, and it took her a minute to re-focus. 'I've had a couple of glasses of wine, tops, but that's not the issue. I warned you that taking Ryan back was a mistake, but you, you just let him get back into your head . . . and, and your heart, and . . .' she tailed off as she lost track of the point she was making.

'Are you sure it's me you're describing, and not yourself?' Dexter asked drily. She bristled at the insinuation, but he cut her off with a curt 'I'll talk to you later'.

Cara held her breath for almost a full minute, releasing it in a whoosh when she felt her face about to explode. Stumbling to the kitchen, she poured a little more wine to calm her agitation. The utter *nerve* of Dexter to suggest she still had feelings for Ryan. She was sick to death of trying to explain to her brother that she had moved on. And why had he called her about Ryan, anyway? The man was *his* bloody employee!

Cara tossed back the wine in her glass and weaved her way back to the sofa, taking the bottle with her. Was Dexter right and had she allowed Ryan past her defences, she wondered uneasily? Ryan had certainly not let up on his pursuit, and his daily calls insisting they needed to talk were ratcheting up her anxiety. She had released the fox into the hen house by letting Ryan into her flat, and now, faced with the potential of carnage and flying feathers, she knew she only had herself to blame. She took another sip of wine and, for a surreal moment, imagined herself in the dock being interrogated by a stern-faced Henry in a black gown and white wig.

I remind you that you are under oath. Now, did you let Ryan back into your life?

That's not exactly what happened.

Really? Did you or did you not willingly *allow your former boyfriend entry into your flat?*

Imagining a sceptical judge and jury listening to her attempts to pin the blame onto Mrs Aggarwal, Cara groaned out loud.

She and Henry should have stayed in their bubble and kept the world out. And why, why, *why* did Ryan have to come back and ruin everything? She had been fine until he showed up again, and now she didn't know which feelings to trust. She didn't want Ryan back . . . *did she*? Or was she just so afraid to trust anyone that she was self-sabotaging her relationship with Henry? *Oh God!* There was a reason she avoided thinking about him. It was just too hard. Ryan reminded her of everything she had loved – and lost – and that memory was fuelling her fear of trusting her heart again and making things work with Henry.

As Cara continued to drink and berate herself, for the first time in a long time she could feel the dark fog descend and swirl around her and once the crying started, she couldn't stop. Feeling raw and exposed, she was powerless to stop her mind from drifting back to the lost period, the months of agony following Ryan's abrupt exit from her life. It was a time she rarely dwelled upon, so frightened was she of its power to pull her back into the grief-stricken pit out of which she had so painfully clawed her way. She didn't want to, but she could feel herself spiralling into that place again. *Will this ever end?*

She dashed away the tears flooding her eyes, but, as fresh ones took their place, she let them fall, defiantly pouring the rest of the bottle into her empty glass. Far from numbing the pain that seemed to be squeezing out every breath of hope and happiness inside her, the wine pressed down heavily on her chest until she was struggling to breathe. Henry doesn't deserve the mess that's me, she thought sadly. *Face the truth, Cara, it's never going to happen for you.* What was the point of going through the stress of trying to make a relationship work when she was never going to be happy? It was time to admit that Ryan had ruined her for love, because if she couldn't make it with kind, loving, generous Henry, what the hell made her think she would ever be able to love *anyone*? Despite everything she'd tried, Ryan's return was fast unravelling the tapestry of her new life, and she didn't know how to make it stop.

28

In Vino Veritas

The early promise of afternoon sunshine had transformed without warning into dark, heavy thunderclouds that brought the torrential rain lashing at the windows behind the drawn curtains. Unearthing a forgotten bottle of wine from the back of the cupboard, Cara had continued drinking throughout the afternoon and lay curled up on the sofa. Other than a text, she hadn't heard anything further from Henry and as the alcohol-fuelled afternoon wore on, she had sunk deeper into despondency. Finding it impossible to close the Pandora's box she had opened, the long shadows cast by the aftermath of her break-up with Ryan engulfed her and she surrendered to the dark memories.

Exhausted from repeated bouts of tears and emotionally drained, Cara didn't appreciate quite how drunk she was until she stood up to answer the doorbell to Henry. She staggered out into the hallway and leaned against the wall for a moment to steady herself. Pressing the button to release the main door into the building, she waited until she heard the door slam below before opening her door and then stumbling back to the sofa and wrapping the throw around her like a protective cloak. Moments later, she heard her front door open and footsteps crossing the hallway.

'Cara? What's wrong? Have you been crying?'

She squinted up at Henry, trying to clear her befuddled brain enough to dredge up an intelligent response. 'You're soaked. Is it raining?'

He shrugged off his jacket. 'It's pouring, but never mind that. Why are you looking so . . . so sad? Have you had bad news?'

'No, not really,' she mumbled. 'Dexter called in a panic about a delivery Ryan was supposed to make, but he's got lost . . . or something.'

Henry gave her a strange look and then glanced at the almost empty bottle on the table. 'Okay,' he said cautiously. 'But is that a reason to sit here on your own getting drunk and upset? Have you had anything to eat since I left?'

'No, I'm not hungry.' She shook her head, instantly regretting it when the room whirled like an out-of-control spinning top. Perversely, his concern only served to make her feel resentful and she pulled the throw tighter around her and muttered, 'Sorry if I'm disappointing you, but we're not all stiff upper lip types.'

Henry raised an eyebrow and moved to sit on the edge of the armchair opposite her, looking baffled. 'What are you talking about?'

Trying to keep the Ryan-shaped weeds from strangling the shoots of her new life had failed dismally, and Cara shrugged listlessly. 'What I mean is that we're different. We react to things differently. We behave differently. I don't fit into your world, and I don't see that ever changing. Let's be honest, I couldn't even get through two days without embarrassing you in front of your family and friends.'

Henry released an impatient sigh. 'Will you stop harping on about that blasted croquet lawn! Do you really believe that my parents or their friends are so shallow that they're going to judge you on one stupid accident? Is *that* why you're sitting here feeling miserable?'

Why the hell was he being so deliberately obtuse? She stared at him, and a rush of frustration-fuelled adrenalin shot through her. 'Your family is such a *stretch* from mine. Your grandfather is an actual earl, for God's sake! I grew up dodging drunks and gangs on a South Kilburn estate while you were living in a mansion – with tennis courts, horses, and a croquet champion mum. I went to the local comprehensive and you've only ever seen the inside of the best schools in the country. I mean, just look at us! I work for a poxy events company and you're this amazing super-smart lawyer taking on major corporations and winning millions of pounds in settlements. How can this, *us*, possibly work?'

Henry listened to her impassioned outburst without expression and Cara stared at him, distressed at having to say it, and yet knowing that what she'd said was the truth and willing him to acknowledge it.

'So, what exactly are you telling me, Cara? That because we had different experiences in our childhood, we can't be together?'

'It's not just about our childhoods,' she shot back. 'I don't belong in your world. Do you think Primrose would have been so daft as to run across your mother's croquet lawn in heels? Of course not!'

He nodded slowly, his voice gently probing. 'So, what you're saying is that I should be with Primrose and not you, is that right?'

He sounded so understanding and non-judgemental that she had a momentary flash of insight into why he was such a brilliant lawyer. He probably used that tone to lull witnesses into thinking they were simply having a chat in the dock until, before they knew it, they were admitting to stealing corporate secrets.

As it was, his question had thrown Cara off track, and she gave a ragged sigh. With the conversation racing downhill, she was beginning to sober up fast. Her earlier decisiveness about ending things, bolstered by the Dutch courage brought on by the wine, was faltering in the face of resistance. Why was Henry making this so difficult? Wasn't it tough enough having to face the fact they were doomed as a couple without him deliberating over her words like some impartial judge?

She tried again. 'No-o, maybe not Primrose exactly. But someone like her. Someone who knows what to do and how to behave around your people.'

'*My* people? What exactly does that mean?'

'Sorry,' she muttered, feeling increasingly wretched. 'I don't mean to sound like . . .'

'Like what? A snob? Too late.'

She ran trembling fingers through her tangled curls, trying to find a way to head the conversation away from the increasingly scary turn it was taking. 'Henry, I'm not ashamed of where I come from and I'm not suggesting there's anything wrong with your background, either. But you've got to admit that we're very different.'

He stood up and walked across to the window. 'If it's because I happen to think that so-called class differences don't matter in the slightest if you genuinely care about someone then, yes, we *are* different,' he said evenly.

He pulled back a curtain and looked out onto the street, the dull thud of heavy raindrops against the window filling the silence. Then Henry turned around and although he sounded calm, she could hear the emotion simmering beneath his words. 'And by the way, where does love fit into all this? Or is that also conditional on the size of my family's home or the name of my school?'

He walked across the rug to sit beside her on the sofa. 'Cara, I don't deny for a moment that our lives up until now have been different, but what you seem to overlook is we have so much more in common if you choose to see it, not least the fact that we both come from loving families. I don't see anything wrong with us having different lived experiences and, to my mind at least, we're great together *because* of our differences, not despite them.'

'Henry, please don't misunderstand me,' she said tremulously. 'Your parents and your family are lovely, but we're always going to come up against people like Arabella Wynter. I'm not one of the shiny-haired, pearl-wearing girls with a posh accent that everyone expects you to bring home. I'd have to change so much about myself to be with you, but the thing is I *like* who I am, and I don't want to be made to feel less than because I don't shop in Kensington, and I didn't go to private school.'

'*I* like who you are, too!'

'Well, then, surely you can see it's impossible and that it's only going to end with—'

'With what?' His voice was dangerously quiet. 'With you getting bored of me? Don't you think *I* sometimes wonder if I'm exciting enough for you? I mean, if we're being candid, patent lawyers are hardly the sexiest men alive. I can't lay on the charm with your family like your ex, and I have almost no idea about reggae or drilled music . . .'

'Drill,' she interrupted absently, and he smiled faintly.

'There you go, see what I mean?'

She sighed and made to turn away, but he pulled her back to face him and she shivered at the naked pain in his eyes.

'Cara, I know there are things you haven't shared with me, and I've never pressured you because I meant it when I said I'm here to help with whatever you're going through. No matter what it is, I will understand – believe me when I say you're not the only one who's gone through tough times.'

'Henry, I—'

'Please, let me finish, there's something I need you to know. After my accident, I was . . . I thought I was going to die, and there was a point where I desperately wanted to. I couldn't move, Cara. I was trapped inside my body and too helpless to do even the most basic things for myself. When the doctors admitted they didn't think I would ever walk again, I— well, let's just say if I had been physically able to do it, I wouldn't be here today.'

Shocked, Cara gasped and covered her mouth and Henry looked down at the floor, his expression bleak. 'I hate talking about that time, but the one thing regaining my mobility taught me was not to waste my life or throw away anything good that comes into it. You're the best thing that's ever come into my life and I wish I knew what else to say or do to make you understand that our differences don't matter to me in the slightest, but this is all I have, Cara, this is me.'

He looked up at her, his eyes suspiciously bright, and shrugged with an air of finality. 'I've told you everything that matters and if you're still not willing to trust your heart with me, then we're over before we really, properly, began. We're good— no, we're great together, and if I'm ready to take a chance on us and do whatever it takes for us to work, why aren't you?'

Cara struggled to hold back the tears. This was all going horribly wrong. She hadn't meant to hurt Henry, and she so wanted to let go and trust him enough to tell him everything, but she was too scared of being sucked back into that pit. It had been so much easier to focus on their differences and hope he would accept that, but it was clear he didn't. Which, once again, left the problem down to her to sort.

Fighting the overwhelming desire to release her fears and burrow into his arms, she said dully, 'Maybe our differences don't matter to you, Henry, but they matter to me. A lot.'

For a long moment Henry stared in silence at Cara's unyielding expression and then he stood up abruptly.

'I think I'd better go,' he said curtly. 'It's obvious I've been barking up the wrong tree for the past few months. I'll see myself out.'

She watched him stride towards the door, his back ramrod straight, and the word escaped her before she could prevent it.

'*Henry!*' She scrambled off the sofa and rushed towards him, stopping short at the look of fury in his eyes. Henry didn't get angry, at least, not with her. His calmness and self-control were among the many things she loved about him, but there was no sign of either in the face looking down at her.

'What is it, Cara? Anything else you forgot to add? Any other knives you'd like to stick in before I go?'

Stricken, she gasped in horror. 'Please, Henry, you mustn't—' She reached out to touch his arm, but he jerked it away.

'Don't! You've had your say. You're entitled to your opinion, but you are *not* entitled to tell me what I must or mustn't feel!'

She pressed her knuckles against her mouth, biting back a sob. What the hell had she done? Henry was ashen, his lips a pale, angry gash against a white canvas. She had never seen him look so furious.

'Do you think you're the only one who's taking a chance, Cara? Do you have any idea what it's been like for *me* to navigate new territory? Do you even appreciate how far out of my comfort zone I've gone for you – for *us*? Before I met you, I hadn't eaten anything hotter than a bloody chicken korma, but even making a complete prat of myself at lunch with your parents or dealing with your brother's disapproval didn't stop me from wanting you. I'd have humiliated myself a hundred times over if it meant being with you.' He stopped and took a deep breath. 'Not even risking my spine again to save your sister's dog made me think twice about us.'

She stepped back, stunned by the words being hurled at her. Not giving an inch, Henry stepped forward, his eyes trained on hers. 'Yes, our backgrounds are different but that doesn't make mine better or worse than yours; it just makes it different. You, however, have decided to be both judge and jury about this relationship, no matter how I feel about it. I don't get it, and it seems to me that you are a complete mass of contradictions. You like my family, and yet they're not good enough for you. You claim not to feel intimidated by anyone or anything, but here you are allowing idiots like Arabella Wynter decide if we should be together or not. So, if I'm not the snob, is it that you are a coward? Is *that* the problem? After all, let's face it, that's your obsession, isn't it? Sorting out everyone's problems? So, tell me, Cara, when did *we* become a problem that you needed to sort?'

'Henry, I'm sorry . . .' Cowed by the unfamiliar savagery in his tone, Cara tried to pacify him, but it was much too late.

'Don't be. It seems your brother was right – or did you think I hadn't picked up on Dexter's not-so-subtle code that I'm all wrong for you?'

Cara winced. 'Henry, my family *really* likes you. Mum thinks you're wonderful and after saving Logan, you walk on water as far as Manon's concerned. As for Dex . . . well, it's just that he's really close to Ryan and—'

'Ah, yes, the ex.' Henry cut her short with a mirthless laugh. 'Well, I'm sure good old Ryan will be happy to hear the path is clear for him to come back. God knows he's tried hard enough to show me how attached he is to your family, just in case I hadn't got the message.'

Embarrassed by his forensic analysis of the situation, Cara squirmed.

'Ryan doesn't think before he speaks sometimes. It's just the way he is,' she countered feebly. As soon as the words were out of her mouth, she knew they were a mistake.

'Are you actually *defending* his behaviour?' Henry looked incredulous.

'Of course not! I'm just saying that . . .' She couldn't bear the cold, biting tone Henry was directing at her, and desperately wishing she had kept her mouth shut, Cara tried to keep her tone neutral. 'I only meant that things are a little complicated with me and Ryan.'

At first Henry said nothing, and then he spoke as if he were thinking out loud, 'You know, Cara, I have to wonder if any of this is actually about me.'

'What do you mean?' She looked at him fearfully, wondering what was coming next.

He shrugged. 'What am I missing here? How obtuse am I being? This isn't just about my family owning land or my grandfather having a title.'

Cara froze and held her breath.

'It's about Ryan, isn't it? You want him and I'm in the way.'

'No! Henry, *no!*' Cara protested, her voice trembling. Anguished that he could imagine she was simply looking for an excuse to return to her ex-boyfriend, she reached out a hand, but Henry backed away, his eyes suddenly so bleak that Cara felt a physical pain in her heart. Her throat was thick with unshed tears and when she opened her mouth, no sound emerged.

Henry shook his head slowly. 'I should have seen that coming, shouldn't I, given how everyone reacted to me being with you. Whatever the two of you had must have been incredible, and it's bloody obvious you're still not over him.'

'That's not true!' she choked, her eyes swimming with tears. 'I *don't* want Ryan and there's nothing between us—'

He held up a hand to cut through her stumbling explanation. 'Nothing? Really, Cara?'

270

Then Henry smiled, a smile so sweet and so sad that Cara could almost hear her heart shattering inside her. Taking a step towards her, his eyes scrutinised her stricken face with such intensity that it felt like the last time he would ever look at her.

'I wish I could believe that, but I don't. Even if you don't want him, there's something unfinished between you. And whatever happened, you've never chosen to share it with me. My darling Cara, whether or not you want Ryan, you clearly don't want me.'

She was crying now, fresh, hot tears coursing down her face. '*No*, Henry! You don't get it! I-I just thought it would be better for us to talk about this, about us, a-and figure things out now before it gets too hard.'

'It's already too hard, Cara,' he said sadly. 'I've never walked away from a fight in my life, whether it's in a courtroom or outside it. But I only take on battles where my intervention is welcome. I'm prepared to fight for someone who chooses me and who wants me for who I am, not because she can't have someone else or because she needs a shield to protect herself from her feelings for her ex. If you want Ryan, then go for it, but I can't stand around and watch. The one thing I want – wanted – from you, Cara, was to be your first and *only* choice, in the same way that you were mine.'

Henry picked up his jacket from the back of the chair and it was as if a gush of ice-cold water had suddenly been injected into Cara's veins. *What have I done?* Abandoning any pretence at control, she flung herself on him, winding her arms around his neck and sobbing.

'Don't, Henry! Please don't go . . . you don't understand!' She couldn't let him leave. Not like this. But he gently disentangled her arms from around his neck and she felt the warmth of his body move away from hers, leaving her chilled and alone.

The gentle kiss he placed on her cheek felt even more crushing than his whispered 'Goodbye, Cara.'

29

LIVING HISTORY

The heavy showers had lessened in intensity and the silence in the living room amplified the sound of raindrops tapping against the window. In the hush, the muted television flickered silently, the light from the screen providing the only illumination in the darkened room.

Cara plucked another tissue from the depleted box on her lap and blew her nose hard. It was almost nine o'clock and she had scarcely left the sofa in the hours since Henry's abrupt departure. She was still in shock at the finality of his parting words, and she prayed for the numbness that had taken over her to continue, knowing that when it wore off, she would feel more pain than she could imagine.

The sound of the doorbell came as a harsh intrusion into the silence, and she froze. She knew instantly from the impatient double buzz that it was Ryan, and her first instinct was to ignore him until he went away. As usual, his sense of timing was impeccable in its wrongness. Not only did she feel horribly raw from the conversation with Henry, but with a blotchy face, red eyes and a blocked nose, she was in no fit state to be seen by anyone. The bell sounded again and still she refused to move. Then she gave a long, deep sigh and dragged herself to her feet. This had gone on too long and cost her too much. *I need to get this over with once and for all.*

There was no response when she pressed the entryphone button and by the time she trudged down the stairs and opened the front door, Ryan was already at the end of the path. He turned when she called his name and his face brightened into a knowing smile as he strode back with long, loping steps. As he approached, the puppy-dog look that had once charmed her now only prompted irritation. He obviously thinks he's got me right where he wants me, Cara thought resentfully. Why did I ever think he was confident when he's just bloody cocky!

Making his way up to the top step where she stood waiting, he placed a hand that felt far too proprietary on her shoulder, and she stiffened.

'Now what have I done?' he asked, widening his eyes with a feigned innocence that immediately put her back up. Taking her silence as forgiveness, he unleashed the crooked grin that was guaranteed to melt any woman's heart. *Well, not this woman and not this time.*

'You'd better come in,' she said brusquely. She tramped up the steps to her flat, not bothering to turn and check if he was behind her, and returned to the living room and her sofa. Ryan stood in the doorway, his smile faltering as he took in her dishevelled state and the rain of tissues scattered on the floor.

'Have you called Dexter about that delivery?' Cara asked without preamble. 'He sounded frantic when he rang me earlier.'

Ryan flushed and ducked his head. Good, he deserves to feel bad, she thought vengefully. She had no intention of reassuring him that her brother had been more worried about his friend than his missing merchandise.

'There was a bit of a mix-up with the address on the order and I took the delivery to the wrong shop,' he admitted. 'I've spoken to Dex, and he's had one of the other lads take the goods over to the client.'

'You can sit down if you like.' Cara waved towards the empty armchair, stifling a pang as she remembered its most recent occupant.

His eyes narrowed as he took in her blotchy face and the discarded tissue box. 'You've been crying.'

Ten out of ten for observation. She bent to pick up the pile of used tissues by her feet and dumped them into the empty tissue box.

'You never cry.' He sounded accusatory and she shook her head impatiently. Whether she cried or not had absolutely nothing to do with him.

'Never mind that, Ryan. Why are you here?'

'To see you, of course.' He sounded surprised. 'Cara, I meant what I said. I'm not letting you go again. Did you think I was kidding about us getting back together?'

'And did you think *I* was kidding when I said it's never going to happen?' she retorted, and then sighed deeply. The man had been in her flat for less than five minutes and she already felt weary. All she could think about was the look in Henry's eyes as he'd walked away and instead of the peace she craved, here was Ryan doing his best to drive her crazy by trying to recreate history.

He was looking at her enquiringly and it belatedly dawned on her that his lips had been moving.

'Did you hear a word I just said?' he asked.

'Yes, I did,' she lied, trying not to sound defensive.

Ryan looked sceptical. 'Okay, so then answer me. Are you crying because of Henry?'

She stared at him dumbly, too afraid to open her mouth in case she burst into tears, and he shuffled forward in the chair until his face was only inches away from hers. She could feel the warmth of his breath on her cheeks, but this time there was no frisson of anticipation on her part and not even the tiniest shiver of desire. On the contrary. Now she was forced into such close proximity, she marvelled that she had never noticed before quite how close Ryan's eyebrows were to each other. It would take only a few rogue hairs for the two arches – well, they were more like dashes really – to merge into one thick black line above his eyes.

'So, has Manon forgiven you yet for nearly getting her dog killed?'

Her discomfort at having him so close made her sound sharper than she had intended, although part of her was curious about how he was taking his fall from grace.

'I think it'll take some time,' he admitted, settling back into the chair.

She gave a weak smile to show she meant no malice and when he grinned in reply, just for a moment she saw the old Ryan, the teenage boy she had loved for so long. Before everything else that had happened.

'So, Cara, can we talk? I mean, properly?'

She was too drained to argue with him and she also knew Ryan would never leave her alone if she didn't hear him out.

The halting explanation that followed was patently intended to evoke sympathy, but Cara didn't care. She listened to the words spilling from his mouth, not bothering to comment or even argue because, as usual, Ryan had somehow found a way to make it all about him. *How could I have ever wondered if this man had changed?* Ryan imagining himself to be the victim was beyond her. When he finally ground to a halt and she gave no response, he looked at her oddly.

'Did you get all of that?'

She shrugged. 'Yes, I heard everything you said. That's what you wanted, isn't it? For me to listen to you? Well, I did.'

' . . . and?'

' . . . and what?'

Ryan exhaled heavily and ran his hands through his hair. 'Jesus, Cara, I just bared my soul to you! I told you stuff that I've never shared with another living soul. Could you at least *look* like you care?'

'Are you kidding me?'

Ryan blinked. 'What?'

The lassitude blanketing her fell away and she looked him straight in the eye. She tried to keep a grip on her emotions, but it was a losing battle. In the space of twenty minutes, she had moved from irritation to mild annoyance to lethargy. Now she was incandescent with rage, and it took every ounce of her rapidly diminishing self-control to stop herself from smacking him hard across the face. Her voice trembled with unbridled fury and contempt.

'How bloody *dare* you, Ryan?'

Visibly shocked, Ryan reared back as she leaped from the sofa, far too agitated to remain seated.

'Cara, sit down and let's discuss this sensibly,' he protested.

Further infuriated by his tone, Cara's no-swearing policy flew out of the window as she let rip with a torrent of abuse. Ryan lowered his head until she fell silent. Then he looked at her and his expression moved from perplexed to comprehension.

'Is all this because you're still upset about the baby thing?'

Caught unawares, Ryan's question was like a blow to her stomach. She gasped for air like a boxer on the verge of victory suddenly sucker-punched by his opponent. She lowered herself onto the sofa and buried her head in her hands, too shocked even to cry, and when Ryan touched her shoulder tentatively, she flinched and pulled away.

'Don't! Do NOT touch me!' she screamed, overwhelmed by the pure, undiluted pain flooding through her.

Taken aback by the ferocity of her response, he sat back with a bewildered frown. 'Why are you getting so emotional? It was ages ago!'

The baby thing? 'For Christ's sake, Ryan! Is that *really* how you choose to refer to the child we so nearly had? Tell me, is that what you told yourself that made it all right for you to just walk away? That all you were leaving behind was *the baby thing*?'

He shifted in the armchair and her eyes blazed scorn at him as her words tumbled out. 'Even now, look at you. Still acting like you're the only one awful things ever happen to. '*I was in a bad place, Cara.*' '*Everything was closing in on me, Cara.*' '*I couldn't handle it, Cara.*' *You* couldn't handle it? What about me, then, huh? Did you ever stop to think about how I had to handle everything on my own when you decided to push off?'

He opened his mouth, but no words emerged. Enraged beyond measure, she screamed at him. 'Answer me! *Did you*?'

Ryan shrugged defensively. 'I offered to go to the clinic with you, didn't I? I got the money together. We could have sorted it without any fuss. You're the one who didn't want to go through with it.'

Her head was pounding with the emotions she had repressed for three long years and her breath came in short gasps as it fought for space with the anger that filled her chest. 'You're unbelievable, do you know that? So, once again it's *my* fault? Because at the time, you couldn't even look at me, but that's what you said, remember? '*You've got to get rid of it, Cara. I'm not ready. How could you let this happen?*'

'Look, I'm not saying it's your fault but . . . you didn't go ahead and have it, so you obviously decided to get rid of it anyway. Maybe if you had done it sooner, I'd have stayed— Cara, *for God's sake!*'

She wouldn't have believed it possible to feel any more rage, but watching him stammer through his pathetic attempts at self-justification, a red mist of pure fury descended. Utterly livid, she seized the empty wine bottle on the table by the neck and advanced towards Ryan.

'You heartless *bastard*!' she screamed. 'I went through *hell,* and you have the nerve to use words like *it* and *the baby thing* to me? You think *you're* a victim in all this? I'll tell you what you are – a narcissistic, self-absorbed, empathy-lacking *sociopath*! This is all just some game to you, isn't it? You didn't come back to London because you love me, because you don't have the first clue what love means. You just waded back into my life to see whether you could get me back if you tried hard enough. It didn't cross your mind whether I was happy with someone else because the only thing bothering you was the idea that I could be in love with someone who wasn't you! You – you selfish, *selfish* motherfu—!'

'*Christ, Cara!* Calm down, will you?' The colour drained from Ryan's face as he scrambled to his feet and backed away. At the look on her face, he raised a hand and added hastily, 'Sorry . . . I'm *sorry*! Please, just put the bottle down.'

She stopped and stared at him, taking in the tall frame, square jaw, perfectly chiselled cheekbones, dark-lashed languorous navy eyes and the silky black hair she had played with more times than she could count. And suddenly she felt . . . nothing. Absolutely nothing.

She thought about the years spent trying to bury the pain, the ban she had instigated against any mention of his name, her panicked fears about his return, and it all suddenly felt like a colossal waste of time. She had suffered so much because of this egocentric man-child who was incapable of accepting responsibility for anything, whether it was a lost consignment or an unplanned baby. Nowhere in Ryan's long-winded, self-justifying speech had he acknowledged that he had royally messed up and caused her pain, let alone explained how he planned to fix it. Now, watching him recoil from her, it was blindingly clear Ryan's concern – just like before – wasn't that he'd hurt her, but how he could escape unscathed. As the realisation dawned, Cara's rage dissolved, taking with it the last emotional thread binding her to Ryan.

Relaxing her grip, she eyed the bottle she was clutching, not quite sure how it had got there. She looked up to catch Ryan's shell-shocked expression, and seeing herself through his eyes, she almost felt sympathy for him. It must be hard to comprehend that the person standing poised to attack him was Cara, the warrior who had fought battles for him, not against him. The strong, capable fixer he had always relied on to sort out his problems, the protector who had kept his secrets and taken the blame for his actions. She could understand his shock because wasn't that how she had also seen herself? The young girl trying to be strong for her mother after her father's sudden death, the determined teenager taking on the burdens of resolving first Dexter's, and then, Ozzie's escapades. Being the fixer had become what she was known for, but what no one, Cara included, had realised was that beneath the capable exterior was a little girl living in fear of life moving beyond her control and terrified of a day when there would be a problem she couldn't handle. And who could know that it would take one unplanned pregnancy to destroy the identity she had so carefully crafted, and that unexpectedly losing her baby only days after Ryan bolted would not only break her heart but strip her of the essence of her identity, making Cara the problem that needed fixing. The memory of the lost period and the herculean effort it had taken to pull herself out of the depression that had swamped her for months after losing her baby hit her with fresh intensity. But from Ryan's flippant choice of words and the stubborn set of his mouth, he clearly had no idea of the impact of his actions, and any desire Cara had to tell him how she had lost their child disappeared. Ryan had never wanted the baby and would no doubt even manage to make her miscarriage all about him.

For years, she had tried so hard to control everything around her by taking charge of other people's problems, Cara realised sadly, but the man cowering in front of her was a painful reminder that you couldn't fix people simply because you could imagine a better version of who they were. Which made it even more ironic that Ryan's return had dredged up so much grief and left her so insecure about her own judgement that she had seized on any excuse to push away the one person who had never looked to her to fix anything. Remembering the heartache she had caused Henry, Cara dropped the bottle on to the table in anguish and folded her arms tightly around her as if trying to hold together the broken pieces of her heart.

With the makeshift weapon now out of harm's way, Ryan drew a deep breath. 'Cara, I truly am sorry.'

'I don't believe you,' she said woodenly. 'And even if I did, I don't care. Thanks to you, I've lost the best thing that ever happened to me.'

She had been a monster to Henry, and she couldn't blame him for leaving, but none of it would have happened if Ryan had only stayed away. She seized his arm and propelled him to the front door. Ignoring his unspoken plea, she held it open, her eyes bright with angry tears.

'Goodbye, Ryan.'

'Cara, I'm begging you! Give me a chance and let's work this out. This is *us*, remember? We're—'

'We're *not* destiny, Ryan. We're history! Don't *ever* come here again.'

With that, she pushed him out, slammed the door and walked away without looking back.

30

Sibling Rivalry

The office grapevine was buzzing with the news that Useless Dave had been issued with his final written warning, and, consequently, Paula had been on the warpath all morning. After snarling at the intern and reducing him to tears, she'd called an impromptu departmental meeting, most of which was spent hurling abuse at her team for failing to meet their admin processing deadlines and threatening at least half of those present with the sack.

When, at midday, Paula uncharacteristically took her lunch hour and stormed off the premises, the chastened staff members heaved a collective sigh of relief before promptly taking to their phones to check the office WhatsApp group for the latest odds on Dave surviving the week.

Free at last to check her mobile for any missed calls, Cara stared dejectedly at her handset and wished she hadn't. The last few days had dragged by without so much as a text from Henry, and she was feeling increasingly desperate. Unable to help herself, she quickly dialled his office line, hoping to think of something to say to him by the time he answered, only to reach his PA who explained apologetically that Henry was still in Stuttgart. Ending the call, she slumped into her chair with a sigh.

'Trouble in paradise?' Ben's gelled quiff reared up from across the partition and his bright-blue eyes shone like a curious parakeet's as he took in her downcast expression.

Cara shook her head automatically, then reconsidered and nodded dolefully. 'You could say so,' she admitted. 'I've made a complete cock-up of things and now Henry's buggered off to bloody Germany and I can't sodding make things right.'

Ben's lips twitched with suppressed laughter. 'Um, how's that no-swearing policy coming along?'

She tutted and then brightened as her phone lit up with an unknown number. Perhaps it was Henry calling from his hotel! But although the brittle voice with the clipped vowels sounded familiar, it took Cara a few seconds to process who it was, and a few more to wonder why Henry's sister was calling her.

'*Imogen!* Is that you?'

'That's what I said, isn't it?' came the irritated response.

Cara inhaled and counted to three . . . and then five. How could one sibling be so sweet, and the other such an imperious witch?

'How can I help?' she asked calmly. Although it seemed unlikely, it was still possible that Henry had asked his sister to pass on a message.

There was a moment's silence and then, 'Actually, I was wondering if you'd heard from Ozzie?'

'Ozzie?' Cara echoed, confused.

'Yes, Ozzie.' Imogen sounded even more irritated.

'Er . . . no, not for a couple of days. Why?' Suddenly recalling her brother's 'I'll-call-you' gesture to Imogen at the party and his subsequent evasiveness, she groaned silently. What had he done now?

'We had a bit of a . . . um . . . disagreement the other day, and he's not answering his phone.'

Cara's heightened emotions provoked an unexpected wave of compassion for the other woman and her voice softened. 'Look, Imogen, whatever is going on between you and my brother is none of my business, but I think it's only fair to warn you that Ozzie can be a bit of a . . . how do I put this . . .?' She racked her brains. 'Player' pretty much summed it up, but Ozzie *was* her brother, after all.

Imogen's brisk tone broke into her mental tussle. 'Cara, relax, I'm not some wide-eyed, soppy teenager. I know exactly what Ozzie's like so there's no need to try and spare my feelings. I just wanted to find out if you'd spoken to him and if he was alright, that's all. I've no doubt he'll get in touch when he's stopped sulking.'

The line clicked off and Cara blinked in shock and slowly set the phone back on the desk. Perhaps Ozzie had finally met his match. Although the thought of Imogen with her brother was . . . *urgh!*

Rebuffing Ben's attempts to cajole her into betting on Useless Dave's future, Cara focused on crafting an apologetic email to Julio's latest victim. It was proving a challenge to find the right words to explain why the dancing dog act their highly disgruntled – and now former – client had booked to charm the guests at his wife's sixtieth birthday party had been replaced by a troupe of semi-naked male dancers. Although neither his wife nor her friends had voiced any complaint, the retired colonel had been apoplectic with rage, giving Paula yet another excuse to rant. Interrupting Paula to point out that Julio had been hired only at Paula's insistence had been met with a stony, 'No buts, Cara. You should have personally double-checked. You know what Julio's like!'

It was mid-afternoon when the office grapevine confirmed that Useless Dave, courtesy of *two* pairs of Premier League tickets this time, had survived to fight another day. With all bets – and Paula

– quietly settled, the rest of the day dragged by until it was time for Cara to leave.

◆　◆　◆

Coming out of the pub after drinks with the team to celebrate Ben's win on the office sweepstake, Cara made a quick detour via the supermarket before heading home. It was almost nine by the time she trudged down her road juggling two bulging shopping bags and the bag of greasy chips she'd bought to soak up the rum and cokes she had consumed.

As Cara stopped to cross the road, the headlights from the passing cars flashed over a solitary figure sitting on the wall in front of her house. Her first thought was that it was Ryan, but then another car drove past, and its powerful beams lit up long legs, a dark curtain of hair and the look of naked misery that only a teenage girl could produce.

'*Fleur!*' Cara gasped. 'What on earth are you doing here?' Checking quickly for oncoming traffic, she crossed the road, her bags bumping against her legs in her haste, to wrap her arms around the girl who promptly burst into great, gulping sobs.

'What's happened? Are you hurt?' Cara demanded. She stepped away and grasped Fleur's arms while her eyes scanned the girl's slight figure. But, other than a large hole in one knee of Fleur's leggings, there was no sign of anything amiss.

Fleur shook her head and stared mutely at the ground. Despite her frustration, Cara forced herself to remain calm, reminding herself that shouting at teenagers typically only provoked silence.

'Fleur, it's late and you shouldn't be out here alone. What's going on?' she asked softly, her brain trying to grasp the fact that Fleur had been sitting on her own and exposed to Kensal Green's finest on a Friday night. Between Imogen's bizarre phone call and now this, Henry's family was shaping up to be just as mad as her own.

Fleur peered up at her from beneath her fringe, her expression at once scared and defiant. 'Well, you *did* say I could visit you at any time.'

'Yes, and I meant it. But you should have rung me first. What if I wasn't coming home tonight?' Cara reasoned, trying not to sound as exasperated as she felt. 'Does your mother know where you are?'

Fleur's guilty expression was answer enough, and Cara sighed. 'Come on, let's get inside and call her. She must be frantic.'

Ten minutes later, after placing a reassuring phone call to a panicked Lady Isobel, Cara and Fleur sat side by side on the sofa with a plate of soggy chips between them.

'I'll make up the sofa for you in a bit. You must be tired, and your mum won't get here until the morning,' Cara said, dipping a chip into the pool of ketchup on the side and swallowing it in two bites. She glanced at Fleur who was beaming at the sight of her framed Little Duckworth print on the mantel, seemingly unfazed by any dark thoughts about how her adventure could have ended.

'You know, I can appreciate you were upset, but at the very least you should have let your mother know where you were,' Cara chided gently.

Fleur's smile faded, and she nibbled morosely on a chip. 'I know, but I was just so furious with her that I had to get away and, by the time I'd calmed down, my phone battery had died.'

Cara despatched another chip. 'So, what's brought all this on?'

'Mother offered to take me into Cheltenham so I could get some new jodhpurs for the county trials. The next thing I know, we're in some stupid shop buying school uniforms for Pemberton Hall!' Fleur's voice rose high with indignation. 'I couldn't believe she'd blatantly lied to me! So, when I went into the changing room and saw there was a fire exit at the back, I used it to leave the shop before anyone could stop me. The train station was only a few minutes away and I had enough money on me to get a ticket to London, so I did.'

Cara almost choked on the chip she was about to swallow. 'Fleur! That was hardly the best way to deal with the situation. Do you have *any* idea how your parents must have felt not knowing where you were? Anything could have happened to you!'

Looking suitably crestfallen, Fleur pushed her long hair back from her face and munched silently. Cara gestured towards the rapidly depleting pile of chips. 'You can finish them if you like. I'll find some sheets and bring you the spare duvet.'

As she made to stand up, Fleur pushed the plate to one side and hurled herself onto her, winding her arms tightly around Cara's waist. For a moment, they sat in silence with Cara gently stroking the younger girl's hair.

'I'm sorry for being such a pain in the arse,' Fleur said eventually in a muffled voice. 'I didn't mean to scare Mother, honest. It's just that she never listens to me! She thinks I'm a nuisance and she's just looking for a chance to get rid of me. I thought if I could get Henry to talk to her, she might change her mind about boarding school but when I went to his flat, he wasn't there.'

Cara sighed. 'Fleur, I honestly think you're looking at things the wrong way. You're not a pain in the— well, you know. I'm glad I was here for you, but I just hope because you came here to me that your mum doesn't think I encouraged you to do this. I'm not exactly her favourite person, especially after what I did to her croquet lawn.'

Fleur shook her head vehemently. 'No, it's not that. Mother always gets a bit weird if a girl starts getting close to Henry. That's why he never brings anyone home – you're the first girl he's talked about in ages.'

Remembering Henry's warning about his mother during the car ride on their way to Oakley Manor, Cara shrugged. 'Well, mothers can get very possessive about their sons.'

Fleur shook her head again. 'No, Mother's just terrified of another woman messing Henry around after what happened with Sophie when he was ill—' She broke off and yawned widely.

Sophie?! Cara looked down at the top of Fleur's head, desperate to know more but feeling too guilty to pump the exhausted teenager for information. Resolving to drag all the details she could get out of Fleur before she left for home the next day, Cara tried to get up, but Fleur yawned again and burrowed further under Cara's arms.

'Thanks for taking care of me. You're so kind, and I didn't want to go to Imogen's. She can be such a cow sometimes.'

Cara tried hard not to laugh. 'Fleur! You can't say that about your sister! I know you two have your differences, but she loves you and wouldn't want anything bad to happen to you.'

'See? You're *so* much nicer than her! Especially after she poured vodka into the drinks at that birthday party you organised. I heard her on the phone talking to one of her friends about it. Just 'cos she's always wanted Henry to go out with boring Primrose doesn't give her the right to mess you around.'

Cara's brain exploded in shock. *Imogen* was the one who'd spiked the drinks at Tabitha's party? *The total bitch*! Poor Jasper hadn't been to blame, after all, she seethed, furious with herself for having tried to save Imogen from Ozzie's careless clutches. How could anyone be so evil as to deliberately intoxicate a bunch of teenagers and sabotage her supposed best friend's party just to get her own way? Cara felt a brief pang of sympathy for clueless, malleable Primrose who couldn't see past Imogen's beauty and status.

' . . . I knew *she'd* have a go at me for running away, so I came here instead. Please don't be angry with me.'

Cara sighed and continued stroking Fleur's hair. She would deal with Imogen later or, even better, leave the backstabbing she-devil to Ozzie's tender mercies. Right now, she still had a rebellious teenager on her hands, and she wasn't looking forward to tangling with Lady Isobel who quite clearly wanted Cara as far away as possible from her son. Despite Cara's best efforts to relinquish the role of fixer-in-chief, it was proving a lot harder than she had anticipated.

31

FAMILY FEUD

Lady Isobel looked very much like she had left home in a hurry. In stark contrast to her usual elegance, the sleeveless white blouse she wore was crumpled, and her tailored navy trousers bagged around her knees. Her blonde hair was scraped back into a ponytail, and her only jewellery was a single-strand pearl necklace and matching stud earrings.

'Oh, Fleur, darling, thank God you're safe!' she breathed with relief, sweeping through the door into Cara's flat to wrap her daughter in a tight embrace. Fleur stood stiffly in her mother's hold and, after a moment, as if sensing her daughter's resistance, Lady Isobel stepped back, her beautiful violet-blue eyes looking weary.

'Darling, I know you were upset, but running away like that was really foolish. We were frantic, and Daddy was on the phone to the police when Cara called. Fleur, anything could have happened to you!'

Her voice was hoarse with exhaustion and there was no mistaking the anguish in its polished tones. Fleur looked up, her eyes meeting Cara's steely gaze and its uncompromising *I told you so* message, and, looking sheepish, she dropped her eyes down to her scuffed trainers.

'I'm sorry you were worried,' she mumbled. 'I shouldn't have run off like that. But I *did* text you when I was on the train to say I was fine before my phone battery died.'

'Yes, darling, but you also said you were on your way to Henry's, and I knew he was abroad because I'd only just spoken to him. Imogen was out with a friend when I rang her and said she was nowhere near her flat. Fleur, you're fourteen years old, for heaven's sake! You've got no business going off like that without permission. London's a huge city and can be dangerous.'

'Well, I got here fine, didn't I?' Fleur muttered in defiance.

'And you were jolly lucky that Cara was in,' her mother replied heatedly, her face flushed with anger. 'What if she had been out when you got here? *Then* what would you have done?'

Cara looked from mother to daughter and prudently decided to intervene. 'Um, Lady Isobel, can I make you a cup of coffee or tea? You must be exhausted after leaving home so early.'

'Thank you, Cara. Some tea would be lovely.'

'Why don't you take a seat? I won't be long.' She ushered the older woman into the living room and towards the sofa. Lady Isobel sat down, her back stiff and her knees pressed primly together as her gaze swept over the Ikea bookcase in the corner and the brightly coloured African prints and framed movie posters on the walls.

Fleur threw herself into the adjoining armchair and pulled her legs up under her. Strands of her hair had escaped its makeshift bun, and she nibbled on a stray tendril, keeping her eyes firmly fixed on the floor. Having offered her apology, it was clear she had decided on silence to register her ongoing protest.

Cara went into the open-plan kitchen and selected an oversized teacup with splashy red poppies and a matching saucer from the cupboard, threw in a teabag and waited for the kettle to boil. It was too early in the day to offer Henry's mother anything stronger, although she suspected Lady Isobel was going to need more than PG Tips to deal with the teenage crisis that had reached its head.

Meanwhile, Lady Isobel was studying her daughter intently. After a few minutes, she cleared her throat and spoke slowly, as if picking her words carefully.

'Fleur, darling, you must be sensible. Despite what you think, I'm not punishing you by sending you to a good— no, a *wonderful* school. Daddy and I just want the best for you.'

Fleur stopped chewing her hair and frowned ferociously at her mother. 'Daddy's not the one insisting I go to Pemberton Hall, it's you.'

'That is simply not true! Your father is just as keen as I am for you to use your fantastic abilities. Just because he doesn't want to be the one who says no to you and leaves it to me to be the disciplinarian—'

Lady Isobel caught herself, her breath coming as fast as if she had just finished a race.

Cara walked into the silence and deposited the brimming tea-cup onto a side table, discreetly slipping a folded wedge of paper under one of the table legs to shore up the slight wobble.

'Would you like some sugar with that?' she asked politely.

'No thank you, Cara. It's fine as it is,' said Lady Isobel. She gave the tea a cursory glance and fiddled with the string of pearls around her neck, her brows creased in anxiety.

'Fleur . . .' Cara perched on the arm of the sofa and adopted the cajoling tone that usually succeeded in getting Logan to release a shoe from between his teeth. 'Your mother's come all this way for you, so why don't you hear her out.'

Lady Isobel threw a grateful glance in Cara's direction before turning her attention back to her daughter, who had scrunched her thin frame into the armchair. Fleur listened without interruption, her expression growing more thunderous as her mother carefully explained the virtues of Pemberton Hall. When Lady Isobel eventually paused for breath, Fleur scrambled red-faced out of the chair to face her squarely.

'It's not *about* the stupid school, Mother! Don't you get it?' She spat her words out in a fury, and Lady Isobel looked at her in bewilderment.

'Darling, I don't understand. If going to Pemberton Hall isn't what's upsetting you so much, then what is?'

Fleur's eyes filled with tears, and she rubbed at them awkwardly with her fist. She choked back a sob and turned an accusing glare onto her mother. 'I know I'm in your way, and that's why you want to send me away to boarding school. You've *never* wanted me! I'm the accident child that came along just when you thought you could have your life back. If you hadn't had to stay at home and look after me, you'd have been a champion croquet player by now.'

Her mother gasped. 'Where on earth did you get that idea?'

'It's what you said! I heard you telling Mrs Wynter that it was your duties at home that had kept you off the county team.'

'Darling, that's simply not true! Yes, yes, I know that's what I *said*, but you can't possibly imagine that I meant—'

'You just want me out of the way so you can travel around the country for your silly croquet tournaments. You don't care about me or what I want at all!' With that, Fleur turned on her heel with a loud sob and rushed out, slamming the door hard behind her.

Cara winced as the sound reverberated around the small living room and she felt a pang of sympathy at the expression of devastation on the older woman's face. Lady Isobel was clutching her necklace and looking utterly wretched.

'Oh, Fleur,' she whispered as tears rolled down her pallid cheeks.

'She's just upset. She doesn't know what she's saying,' Cara said softly, her heart going out to Lady Isobel as she wrapped her arms around herself and shrank into the sofa.

'I *did* use those words, but I really didn't mean any of them. It's just that Arabella Wynter is so boastful and such a bore, always going on about what a wonderful croquet player she is. I love croquet, but it was silly of me to suggest I would have been a more successful player if I'd been free to devote more time to the game. I should have realised Fleur overhears everything and been much more careful with my words.' She shook her head and pulled a tissue from the pocket of her trousers to wipe her face. After a moment, she added in a wistful voice, 'But I did so want to shut that stupid woman up.'

Despite the gravity of the situation, Cara couldn't help the grin that tugged at her lips. Remembering how awful Arabella Wynter had been to her, she couldn't blame Henry's mother for attempting to take the woman down a peg or two.

'Lady Isobel, it's none of my business, but why is it such a problem for Fleur to stay on at the local school? If she's happy there and gets to see her horse whenever she likes, I don't see why it's such an issue.'

'Because Pemberton Hall is very sought after and has turned out some of the country's most successful women.' Lady Isobel reached for the teacup beside her and took a few short sips before setting it down.

Cara picked her words with care. 'I'm sure the school is excellent and everything, but if it's not what Fleur wants—'

'Oh, of course, you wouldn't understand,' Lady Isobel cut in impatiently, and Cara raised an eyebrow. The older woman flushed, and added, 'No . . . I don't mean— What I'm trying to explain is that—'

'—someone who went to a local comprehensive in North London can't possibly understand the advantages of a superb education at a top girls' school?' Cara parried, her sympathy for Henry's mother rapidly evaporating.

'No, I certainly didn't mean to imply anything of the sort! What I couldn't expect you to know, and therefore understand, is that Fleur is very, *very* bright. The truth is that my daughter is extremely gifted academically and a near genius in terms of her IQ, although it's hard to believe given what's just happened. Fleur will benefit enormously both from the level of teaching and the educational resources they have at Pemberton Hall. I know she's happy at the village school, but her teachers admit they can't challenge her and what they have to offer just doesn't compare. Cara, I love my daughter very much indeed and I don't want her to throw away the opportunity to make the most of her talent.'

She fiddled with her pearls once again as her voice rose in agitation. 'Oh, how I wish we'd never bought her that stupid horse!'

She blinked back tears and, for the first time, Cara saw Henry's mother in a completely different light. Despite her title and enormous wealth, the woman sitting on her sofa wasn't a sophisticated and rather intimidating aristocrat. She was simply an anxious parent trying to do her best for her intransigent teenager. *Just like Mum does every day with Manon and Thaddeus.*

'Is there no way to compromise on this?' Cara asked gently. 'I do see why you'd like Fleur to go to that school, but if she refuses to cooperate, she'll end up being chucked out anyway which would be far worse, surely?'

Lady Isobel looked up and a reluctant smile found its way onto her pale lips. 'It would indeed be far worse.'

She sipped her tea and for a few minutes the two women sat in silence. Then Lady Isobel set her empty cup on the table and nodded as if she had reached a decision. 'It's not ideal as we would really like her to have the full boarding experience, but I suppose we could consider enrolling Fleur as a weekly boarder so she could come home at weekends.'

Before Cara could comment, the door to the living room was flung wide open and Fleur burst in. 'Really, Mother, could I?' she begged. 'Please say yes! I'll agree to go if it means I can come home at the weekends to see Caramel.'

Her mother gaped in astonishment. 'But how did—?'

Cara shrugged in apology. 'Sorry, I should have warned you the walls are paper-thin in this place.'

'So I see. Fleur, for goodness' sake calm down! I'll have to discuss it with Daddy first.'

'He'll be fine about it. He always says yes to you!' Fleur exclaimed with exuberance. She flung herself on the sofa and threw her arms around her mother's neck. 'Thank you so much, Mummy! You're the best, and I really am sorry about running away. It was awful of me. I heard everything you said to Cara about loving me, and I love you too.'

Cara watched Lady Isobel's harried expression melt away. She returned her daughter's embrace tentatively, as if afraid the rare and unexpected display of affection would suddenly be snatched away.

After a moment, Fleur released her mother and jumped up to fling her arms around a startled Cara. 'Thank you *so* much. I don't know what I'd have done if you hadn't been here. Henry's incredibly lucky to have you.'

Fleur beamed at her mother. 'I'm going to get my stuff from Cara's room and then we can go home and tell Daddy the good news,' she said with jubilation before skipping out of the room.

After a moment's silence while they both tried to digest what had just happened, Lady Isobel cleared her throat. 'Fleur's right, you know, Cara. Henry *is* lucky to have you. You're very good for him.'

It was Cara's turn to gape, and she resisted the impulse to look outside the window for flying pigs. Even after destroying the woman's precious croquet lawn, Lady Isobel Fitzherbert believed it was *her son* who was lucky to have Cara! And could his mother's timing have been any worse?

Too stunned to beat around the bush, she blurted out the words before she could stop herself. 'It's very nice of you to say so, Lady Isobel, and I do appreciate it, but sadly, I don't think Henry would agree with you. We've had a bit of a . . . um . . . falling out and . . . um . . . I don't think we're going to be able to work it out.'

She tried to swallow the lump that had appeared in her throat by the end of her sentence and blinked rapidly as she struggled to retain her composure.

'I find that very hard to believe, Cara,' Lady Isobel said, looking doubtful. 'Henry hasn't been this cheerful or carefree for years.' Her eyes narrowed, and her voice sharpened. 'I can't imagine *he* would be the one who'd want to end your relationship.'

The unspoken accusation hung in the air and Cara sighed. 'It's not that I don't care for Henry . . . it's just . . . it's complicated,' she muttered helplessly, instantly recoiling from the flash of scorn that crossed Lady Isobel's face.

'Cara, I don't say this lightly but Henry has been through a great deal, and I simply can't bear the idea of him being hurt again. My poor boy had the most dreadful time after the accident.' Lady Isobel twisted her pearls and her eyes misted over. 'We came very close to losing him, and I don't just mean physically. When it looked likely he would be paralysed, Henry just seemed to give up. It's honestly a miracle he came through it all, especially after Sophie broke things off . . .'

She shook her head as if to clear away the dark thoughts. 'Anyway, that's all in the past. The only reason I'm bringing it up is because while it might appear my son has lived a charmed life, he's had more than his fair share of heartache.'

For a long moment she looked at Cara intently, then her face softened. 'When we first met, I might have appeared a bit, well, distant. Goodness knows, Henry gave me a telling-off after your visit for not being as welcoming as I should have been and for making such a fuss about the damage to my croquet lawn. Cara, I can only apologise if my attitude has added to any challenges you've encountered as a couple, but I hope you've come to understand why I might appear overprotective of my son. When you came to Oakley Manor, I could see straightaway how much he cared for you, but, after what happened with Sophie, I had to be sure you felt the same way about him. Since meeting you, Henry has been happier than he's been for a very long time, so, Cara dear, whatever's gone wrong between the two of you, please try and sort it out.'

Lady Isobel leaned forward to cover Cara's hand with her own. 'And I'm so very grateful to you for taking Fleur in last night. I dread to think what would have happened to her otherwise.'

With that, she glanced at her watch and exclaimed, 'My goodness, is that the time? We're going to have to rush back. I've got the vicar coming over for tea this afternoon. Mrs Soames is off today and I promised him cheese scones.'

Cara crossed the hallway to fetch Fleur, her mind in a whirl after Lady Isobel's confession.

'—and Mummy says I can be a weekly boarder, isn't that *amazing*?' Fleur was in Cara's bedroom babbling into her mobile while stuffing her jacket into her duffle bag. She grinned at Cara as she opened the door. 'Okay, Jess, I've got to go now. I'll call you when I get home. Bye!'

Cara leaned against the door frame as Fleur picked up her bag and turned to her with a mischievous smile. 'I'm so glad you're with Henry. You're brilliant, and you're a much more *useful* sister than Imogen.'

Cara burst into laughter and playfully tweaked the girl's bun as she walked past. 'You'd better not let Imogen hear you say that. Come on, your mother's waiting.'

Watching Fleur on the sofa next to her mother, munching happily on Jaffa cakes while waiting for a cab to take them to the train station, Cara almost pinched herself. And yet, there it was. Henry's world and hers had finally collided, and as far as she could see no one appeared any the worse for it.

After seeing off the Fitzherberts, Cara snuggled into the sofa marvelling at the turn of events. Money and titles clearly made no difference to family dramas, and the past twenty-four hours had obliterated the picture-perfect scenario she'd imagined was Henry's life. For all their wealth, the Fitzherberts were just as dysfunctional as any normal family. Even more satisfying was mentally replaying Lady Isobel's acerbic comments about Arabella Wynter.

But, as Cara reflected, her biggest problem remained unresolved. Despite finally winning his mother's approval, Cara didn't have the first idea how to make things right with Henry.

32

'LET ME COUNT THE WAYS . . .'

Staying up half the night talking to Fleur had taken its toll, and Cara was dozing in front of the television when the sound of the doorbell jerked her upright. Still half-asleep, she walked to the door and peered groggily at the face looking up into the security camera. She pressed the entry button and opened her front door, standing to one side as the thud of footsteps climbing the stairs grew louder.

'Hello, Dexter.'

Her brother strode past her and walked straight into the living room without a word.

'Why don't you come in?' she murmured to his disappearing back. *Now* what was wrong? Feeling drained at the thought of yet another Nightingale/Grant drama, she trailed after him and found him sprawled on the sofa, TV remote in hand. She watched in silence as he chopped and changed channels, making no attempt to speak to her. When he finally settled on motor racing, Dexter kept his eyes fixed on the action taking place on the screen, the frown he had come in with not budging an inch.

'You missed meeting Henry's mother and younger sister. They left about an hour ago,' Cara ventured. Her bright tone only served to deepen his scowl.

'What a shame.' Sarcasm dripped through his words like water through a colander. 'Big congratulations on joining their family, milady. Do I bow before addressing you now?'

Cara abandoned her attempt at appeasement. 'What exactly is your problem with Henry? I mean, seriously, *what* has he ever done to you?'

Before he could speak, she rushed on, 'Well, as you hate him so much – no, let me finish – as you hate him so much, you'll be delighted to hear that he thinks we should break up.'

Dexter's eyes narrowed. 'Why? Does he think he's too good for you?'

'No, he doesn't think he's too good for me,' she retorted impatiently. 'Give me some credit, will you? Why would I go out with someone who thought that?'

'So why, then?' Dexter looked baffled. 'I'll admit he's not exactly my idea of, well, you know. But if you like each other that much . . .'

Cara sat beside him, resting her head back against the cushions to stare at the ceiling. 'I told him I was worried that because we're so different, it won't work. And then, of course, Ryan's been doing his best to cause confusion and make Henry feel like the rebound guy. Henry didn't believe me when I said he wasn't, and we haven't spoken since.'

She turned towards her brother with sad eyes. 'We had a huge falling out, Dex, and I'm scared he won't come back.'

'Honestly, I just don't get it.' Dexter looked utterly perplexed. 'Cara, you're a good-looking girl. You could have your pick of the men around here. Why *Henry*, for God's sake?'

'Why Henry?' she echoed, incredulous at the lack of sympathy from her own brother.

'Yes, why him? I'm sorry, but I can't believe you'd go from someone like Ryan to that . . . that posh boy!'

'Oh, so just because Henry's family is rich, there's no way that he could be a good partner for me, right? I admit I had my own preconceptions before I met them, but at least I've tried to be open-minded, so what does that say about *you*, Dexter? That you're so prejudiced you can't see past any of the superficial stuff?'

'Look—'

'No, *you* look! You asked me, so I'll tell you!' Exasperated at Dexter for unfairly judging Henry, Cara got to her feet and marched up and down the living room, her words tumbling out as if an emotional dam had burst.

'Why Henry? Why *not* Henry? I couldn't stop thinking about him for months after our first meeting even though we'd barely spent any time together. Have you any idea how lucky I was to find him again in this massive city? And when I did stumble across him, I practically crunched the bones in his foot into a pulp with my size sevens and instead of yelling at me or making a fuss, the first thing he did was protect me by apologising for putting *his* foot under *my* bloody Doc Martens!'

Cara stopped pacing while she struggled to find the right words. 'I was drawn to him from the first time we met, but I think that's why I fell so hard for him when I saw him again. Because who does that? Who the hell is so sweet and so kind that they put a complete stranger's feelings ahead of a ton of pain? I'll tell you who the hell *doesn't*, shall I? Your precious Ryan. Because that's what you're really wondering, isn't it? The question you really want to ask isn't "Why Henry?", it's "Why not Ryan?"'

Dexter scratched the stubble on his chin. 'Okay, I wasn't going to go there but since you brought it up, then tell me. How could you have dropped Ryan so easily, Cara? Because I know if you hadn't pushed him away, he'd never have left us.'

'Is that what you really think, Dex? That *I* made him leave? That I made Ryan leave *you*?' Cara stared at her brother in dismay fighting to keep her emotions under control. Her mind flew back to their childhood when Dexter and Ryan's friendship was the stuff of legends. The two had been inseparable since a fight in the school playground had ended in a draw, provoking sufficient mutual admiration for the eleven-year-old Ryan to subsequently declare Dexter to be his 'best mate of all time'. When Dexter had turned to one of the gangs in their local estate to fill the void caused by his father's sudden death, it had been Ryan who pulled him away before he got too caught up in their increasingly dangerous activities to back out. Even after an unexpected kiss that surprised them both had led to Cara and Ryan becoming a couple, the relationship between the two men had remained unbreakable.

'He was my best mate, Cara. You knew he was like a brother to me,' Dexter muttered, the accusation in his voice striking her heart like a hammer blow.

Caught up with managing her own emotions after Ryan left, Cara had never fully appreciated the extent to which Dexter had also felt abandoned. Now, hearing the pain in his voice, she also finally understood how much he blamed her for it, and she felt the sting of tears prickling behind her eyes. Was she forever doomed to pick up after Ryan?

She blinked back the tears. She had let this go on long enough and it was time to end it. She went to sit beside Dexter and, resting a hand on his knee, she looked him straight in the eyes.

'Do you remember the day Ozzie rushed out of his photo shoot to run that delivery down to Portsmouth for you – that day Mick got food poisoning and all the other drivers were out on jobs? Remember how Oz didn't stop long enough to clean off his make-up even though he knew he looked a total prat and the loaders at the depot would all take the piss, but he did it anyway? The reason he drove that van was because you would have lost the client if the delivery didn't get there by close of business. *That's* what brothers do. They are there when you need them. What they *don't* do is walk off and leave you in a fix because they're not paying attention to where they're supposed to deliver a consignment or because they simply can't hack it anymore. No matter what Ryan does, you've always forgiven him, but you don't know him, Dex, not really. You don't know the real Ryan because if you did, you wouldn't dream of asking me that question.'

She stood up with a sigh and walked over to peer out of the large bay window while she collected her thoughts.

'Dexter, I didn't leave Ryan.' She turned back to face her brother. '*He* left *me*. No, I promise you, it's true.'

'What are you talking about?' Dexter said hesitantly. 'That can't be right. He said—'

'Oh, I can imagine what he said. Probably the same story he told me the other night when he was rewriting history. You know, how he desperately wanted us to be together, to go travelling around the world and have fun, how I refused to leave my job and my new studio flat and go with him, yada, yada, yada. Am I right? The truth is, Ryan was petrified. The whole travel thing was simply his way of avoiding having to grow up because he knew I wanted to settle down and if he stayed, I would expect him to become the man he was terrified he could never be. So, when his pleas and his begging didn't work, he ran.'

Her eyes were wet with tears and her heart felt wracked with pain as the memories flooded back. She took a long, juddering breath before she continued, her voice soft in the still, quiet room.

'But not before I told him I was pregnant.'

She could almost feel the shock radiating from Dexter, and she turned away, unable to bear the unspoken reproach in his eyes.

'I'm sorry, Dex, but I couldn't tell you. At the time, I couldn't tell anyone; I could barely think straight. All of you thought I was devastated because I'd finished with Ryan, but I was simply too ashamed – of him and of me – to confess the truth that our great love story was just a delusion. It was way too humiliating to admit the man I'd been with since I was sixteen was a flake who'd left me knowing I was carrying his baby.'

Dexter sat frozen in his seat, which was just as well since Cara hadn't finished. Now she was finally confessing the secret that had haunted her for years, she owed Dexter the whole truth. 'You thought losing Ryan was why I couldn't get out of bed for weeks and couldn't even speak for a month, but he wasn't the reason I was so depressed. Losing my baby exactly one week after Ryan left was the reason.'

Saying it out loud to her brother brought a shiver of shock mingled with relief. She had buried the truth so deeply and for so long that even relating what had happened felt unreal. The first month had been the worst. The pain, at first physical, when the tiny acorn of life having settled in the wrong place had abruptly ripped itself away, and then the emotional anguish that invaded every cell of her body, leaving her mute. By the second month, barely eating and struggling to sleep, she had finally accepted the help of her concerned doctor and distraught mother. The pain had faded over time from a raw laceration into a dull, hopeless ache, but although she'd survived, Cara knew she would never be the same. Forbidding any mention of Ryan's name, she had instead focused on her work, unable to imagine ever giving her heart away again. Until Henry.

Dexter hadn't moved a muscle and his eyes glistened as Cara finished speaking and returned to sit beside him. He cleared his throat and, for a tense moment, the only sound in the flat was the loud ticking of the clock on the mantelpiece.

'Why didn't you say anything, Sis?' he asked softly. 'If I'd known, I'd have hunted him down and beaten the crap out of him.'

Cara smiled wanly. 'Only Mum knew the truth. I called her from the hospital, and she came round to mine every day for weeks. Ashanti guessed, which is partly why she hates Ryan so much, but she swore never to bring it up unless I wanted to talk about it. Mum, on the other hand, didn't let up. She begged me to tell you, Dad and Ozzie the truth. She said I'd never really heal if I didn't talk to the people closest to me, but I couldn't bear to discuss it and I made her promise not to tell anyone. In the end she agreed, but she insisted that I see a counsellor to help me come to terms with the miscarriage. She was right, as usual. It took a while, but I did get better.'

Dexter smiled wryly in agreement. 'That's Mum all over. I remember when we were kids and Jimmy Owens robbed the newsagent behind the estate. She warned me to stay away from the Boxers and I remember giving her lip until she just stared me down and said, 'Do you know that a gang is where cowards go to hide?' She told me later that it was something she'd heard somewhere, but it really made me sit up. When you think you're a hard man and someone calls you a coward . . . well, it's about the worst thing you can hear, especially at that age.'

He took her hand and held it gently between his. 'Enough about me. I'm sorry, Sis. Really, truly sorry. I wish I'd known what you were going through. I just thought—'

Cara sighed. 'I know. You assumed I had ended the relationship because you couldn't believe Ryan would ever have done it. I didn't argue because it hurt too much to think about what I'd lost and so it became the narrative. Cara dumped Ryan and she doesn't want to talk about it, but you know what, Cara's also had a breakdown because she loved him so much, so let's give her space.'

Dex stared at Cara dumbly, and she shook her head slowly. 'I felt so torn and so guilty, Dex. I hated myself because even after he'd left, a part of me still hoped he'd realise he had made a massive mistake and come back. Ryan was my first love, and we were supposed to be forever, and then when he didn't . . . and then the – the baby . . .' She paused and took a breath. 'I felt dead inside. Everything around me felt dark and hopeless and it was like I had nothing to live for.' She suddenly remembered Henry's words and was struck by how eerily similar the impact of their different traumatic experiences had been. How could she not have seen this and understood how much more they had in common than she'd given credit? Once again, she silently cursed herself for pushing him away.

For a few moments Dexter and Cara sat side by side in silence, and then Cara said quietly, 'I really loved him but the Ryan you knew, the Ryan we all thought we knew, was so much more damaged than we realised. All that business with his dad's addiction and his mum sending him away to live with Rosie's family really affected him. I think he was terrified that if he tried to settle down and start a family, he wouldn't be able to hack it and he'd turn into his father.

'It wasn't all his fault. I made excuses for him and let him off the hook so many times because of his awful childhood, but other people have had it worse and still turn out to be decent human beings. I've lost count of how often Ryan stood me up or would promise to do something, forget about it, and then look at me with his big blue eyes and charm his way out of pissing me off. Not to mention the projects he started and never finished – you wouldn't believe the number of times I bailed him out of one crisis or another because he'd run out of cash or messed someone about.

By the time you took him on as a driver, he was close to being bankrupt.'

Dexter looked incredulous. 'Why didn't you ever say anything? I just thought you and Mum were being hard on him. I knew he could be a bit, well, you know, unpredictable, but you never said things were that bad.'

'Dexter, I love you, but you are so overprotective that sometimes telling you stuff can be more stressful than just dealing with the problem myself. When Ryan left, even though I was devastated he didn't love me enough to stay, a tiny part of me felt relieved that I didn't have to take care of him anymore. Until I lost the baby. *That's* when I fell apart.' She gave a mirthless laugh. 'Even his baby wanted to leave. *Everything* about Ryan was dark and painful and sad. That's why I couldn't talk about him and why even hearing his name was difficult. He represented pain, shame, loss, sadness . . . everything I have tried not to dwell on anymore. Which is why I'm so angry at myself for opening the door to him, however briefly, when he came back.'

Dexter wrapped his arm around her and, resting her head against her big brother's broad shoulder, Cara felt a sense of peace steal over her. She should have told Dex the truth a long time ago. Being honest would have swept away his rose-tinted glasses and neither of them would have let Ryan ruin things once again.

As if he could read her thoughts, Dexter gave her shoulder a gentle squeeze. 'I wish you had told me what was going on. You know I always have your back.'

'I know, but – as ever – I thought I could fix it. Ashanti and I talked about it and decided not to tell you the truth and shatter your illusions about Ryan. You two were so close that we knew you'd be gutted if you heard what he'd done. Maybe we were wrong, but at that point he was out of our lives and after everything you'd gone through when our dad died, I couldn't bear to see you hurt again. But Ryan's still coming between us and still hurting us both and it makes no sense to continue lying to you.'

'Cara, has it ever occurred to you that you don't always have to be the one who sorts things out?' Dexter said gently with a smile in his voice. 'I'm not a fourteen-year-old boy you have to protect from a bunch of yobs anymore.'

'Then don't keep messing up and I won't need to,' she protested.

Holding her shoulders, he turned her to face him, a grin lighting up his ruggedly attractive features. 'That's not going to happen, so don't use me as an excuse. Look, life is about messing up,' he held up a hand to stop her before she could jump in, 'and *learning* from it. Despite what you think, I've reflected a lot on the way I handled the whole Barry Sykes situation and I know that if you hadn't talked him round, I could have been in serious trouble. I said it then and I'll say it again, I'm grateful you stepped in and persuaded that piece of crap to drop the assault charge. But, Cara, here's the thing. You're my younger sister and *I* should be protecting you, not the other way round. So, let's make a deal. You stop trying to fix me and everyone else, and I'll try a whole lot harder to stop creating problems.'

Cara stared at him for a long moment and then nodded. 'Does that mean you'll patch things up with Ashanti?'

Dexter leaned back, crossing his legs. 'I was planning to do that anyway. I'm just trying to find a way to get her to hear me out without slamming the door in my face.'

Cara giggled. 'Well, don't give up. She misses you badly and she needs you, even if she'd rather chew on broken glass than admit it. You two are made for each other – you're both nuts!'

Dexter chuckled and then his expression sobered as he looked over at her. 'What about you, Sis? What do *you* need?'

Touched by the tenderness in his voice, Cara stood up to distract herself from the tears threatening to return. Standing by the window, she looked down at the people milling up and down the high street and her eyes fell on an elderly woman in an orange sari clumsily steering a loaded shopping trolley. She watched her navigate her way along the pavement for a few moments and then faced her brother.

'You know, Dex, when I met Henry, all I knew was that here was this amazing man who I could be myself with and just have fun. Of course, I knew we had different backgrounds but none of that mattered in those first few weeks when it was just the two of us. It was like we'd made this unspoken pact not to talk about our pasts or even our families and just leave all our baggage outside our bubble. Which was just as well because once we let the outside world in, God knows there were enough people ready to point out our differences.'

Looking embarrassed, Dexter turned his eyes away and Cara smiled. 'You were right about one thing, though. I didn't really know Henry, not at first. I knew he was gorgeous and fit, and that I fancied him like mad and being with him felt fantastic, but once we were outside our bubble, it began to feel more and more like we were too different to last. Which was probably why when Ryan came back, despite everything he'd put me through, for one tiny moment he felt . . . *familiar*, you know, not intimidating like Henry's world.'

Cara leaned against the windowsill and crossed her arms. 'After what happened with Ryan, I didn't think I would ever trust another man, but Henry made me see that there *are* good guys out there. Since the moment I met him, Henry has never let me down. He never says he'll be somewhere and then not show up or promise something and then forget he ever said it. Henry cared enough to trail around the shops for hours until we found exactly the right birthday present for Mum even though I found out later he absolutely hates shopping. He helped Ashanti out at his own risk, not to mention risking his actual life to save Logan from being run over.'

Dexter remained silent as if recognising her need to let it all out, and, after a moment's reflection, Cara went on. 'Being with Ryan was like being swept along by a crazy, tempestuous current. It's exciting but also unpredictable and a bit scary, which makes it easier to go along with the flow than to swim against it. But being with Henry is like . . . like being on a warm, buoyant wave that holds you up so you can enjoy the experience without being afraid you'll drown. With Henry, I can be one hundred percent myself, and he doesn't expect me to be perfect or strong or the fixer. He's the kindest, most generous person you can imagine, and you know what I'm only just realising, Dex? *He* fixes things for *me*. Sometimes, it just takes one good person to make the bad things go away, and that's what Henry does for me – or did, until I was stupid enough to push him away. So, there's your answer, Dexter. That's "why Henry?" *That's* why I love him . . .'

She tailed off, then smiled in wonderment, her heart soaring as if finally released from an anchor weighing it down. Suddenly everything was crystal clear, and she stared at her brother. 'I do, Dex. I love him. I *really* love him!'

The clock ticked quietly in the silence that followed. Then Dexter nodded his head slowly and looked her dead in the eye.

'So then, what are you waiting for, Sis? Sort it out.'

33

A RUM IDEA

'You're an idiot!' Ashanti said bluntly. 'Girl, you know I'll always be your ride or die, but as far as I'm concerned my lawyer walks on water.'

Cara glared at her, beginning to regret the impulse that had prompted her to summon her best friends. Ashanti had grudgingly abandoned a half-written song to turn up at Cara's flat with an out-of-breath Rosie who'd been obliged to cut short her evening Zumba class.

Surveying her unruly council of war, Cara tried to get the conversation back on track. It was all very well deciding you wanted your boyfriend back; figuring out how to do it was a completely different matter. Instinct told her that Dexter's suggestion to just talk to Henry wouldn't be enough to convince her estranged boyfriend that she knew what, or who, she wanted. Henry's former girlfriend had abandoned him after his accident and that would surely make anyone distrustful. Simply marching up to Henry to tell him he'd got the wrong end of the stick and that she loved him wasn't going to do the trick. Hence the emergency after-work summit with the girls which, so far, was proving less than successful.

Cara counted to five under her breath and tried again. 'I *know* Henry's wonderful, but that's not the point. What I need from you two are ideas to help me persuade him that he's the man I want.'

As if Cara hadn't spoken, Rosie asked tentatively. 'Are you sure you didn't push Henry away because you still love Ryan? You and Ryan always used to say you were destiny.'

'Do I *look* like I need my head examined? I'm so over Ryan, I can't tell you.'

Ashanti gave a sceptical hoot and Cara threw her an impatient glance. 'Okay, so I got a tiny bit confused, and for a teeny moment I did wonder if there was still something there. But he hasn't changed, and it didn't take me long to see that Ryan 2.0 was just an older version of the original.'

'I could have told you that if you'd bothered to listen to me,' said Ashanti, her voice thick with derision.

'I know, but . . . I just thought . . . Oh, never mind! What's important is that I'm finally over it.'

'You should have shown him the door the minute he showed up. Didn't I warn you we needed a strategy?' Ashanti's face was the picture of self-righteousness as she continued to hammer her point home and Cara gritted her teeth in silence. Ash had never been one to shy away from saying *I-told-you-so*.

Rosie nodded. 'She's got a point, Cara. We all know you've got a weak spot for my useless cousin.'

Cara rolled her eyes. 'Again, can we stick to the subject, please? That was then and this is now. If anyone's my destiny, it's Henry. Seriously, do you know how wild the odds were against us ever seeing each other again?' She paused and sighed dreamily. 'I knew the moment I laid eyes on him at the gala that we *must* be meant for each other.'

Then she snapped to attention. 'Now, what can I do to convince Henry that I'm over Ryan? I need a big gesture to prove Henry's my number one choice!'

The blank faces looking back at her didn't offer much hope of a solution and, after a long pause, Ashanti looked at her watch and cleared her throat.

'Um, love you and all that, hon, but we've been here for almost two hours. I don't mean to be unsympathetic, but I've got to finish the lyrics to my new song *and* learn the chords before Thursday night.'

Cara sighed with frustration. That was a giant pizza and two bottles of wine down the drain. 'Fine, you can go! Don't worry about me, I'll think of something. As usual.'

'You know, you could just talk to Henry and tell him the truth,' Rosie offered. 'Sometimes you simply have to face up to your fears and go for it.'

Ashanti did a double-take, and Cara spluttered. That was rich coming from Rosie! Although, in fairness, Rosie also looked like she had no idea where her words had come from.

Ashanti jumped up. 'Right, I'm off! Cara, I'm sure you'll think of something. If not, we can have another brainstorm at the club on Thursday. In the meantime,' she gestured towards the container next to the empty pizza box, 'go easy on the ice cream. You're not going to find your missing self-esteem at the bottom of a Ben & Jerry's carton. Trust me, all it'll do is make you fat.'

Ignoring Cara's indignant gasp, Ashanti picked up her bag before throwing out casually, 'Oh, and Dexter's coming along on Thursday.'

Her words were met with a stunned silence. Rosie was the first to recover, and she stared at her friend in astonishment. 'You guys are actually *speaking*?'

'Not all of us are idiots.' She gave Cara a pointed look. 'Dex was the first person I wanted to call when Henry told me I was a free agent, which means I must still love him. So, last night, I decided to ring him and, as it turns out, he was already in his car and on the way to my flat.'

'Wow. And you didn't get into another argument?'

'That's the weird thing . . . he was really chilled. You know, like he used to be. Cutting him off must have done the trick because something's finally got through to him.' Ashanti's voice bubbled with happiness and Cara shook her head in amused resignation. Trust Ash to save her bombshell announcement for when she was about to walk out of the door!

An hour later, having finished the first bottle and most of the second bottle of wine on her own and still with no strategy forthcoming for Operation Reclaim Boyfriend, Cara was slumped against the cushions, trying not to slide off her sofa. 'I think we need another drink to help give us some ideas, don't you?'

Rosie, curled up in the armchair opposite, nodded at Cara's empty glass. 'It's getting late. Don't you think you've had enough?'

Cara snorted. 'I called us together to help me sort things out and I have to say it's been a bust so far.'

Rosie held up a placatory hand. 'Fine, if you think getting plastered will help, then go right ahead. But you can count me out because I've already blown my calories for today.'

Knowing that drinking alone was a very bad idea didn't stop Cara from opening the bottle of rum sitting in her cupboard. After a few shots, she could barely hold her head up.

'Listen, I'm going to leave so you can sleep off all the booze,' said Rosie, taking in Cara's bleary expression. 'Do you want me to get you some water first?'

'No! Don't go yet.' Cara frowned. 'I'm per-perfectly sober, thank you very much. Just 'cos my stubborn boyfriend won't listen to reason doesn't mean . . .' She stopped, having lost the thread of her sentence. And then she had a flash of inspiration. Of course, she should phone Henry! He was too much of a gentleman to hang up on her and if she didn't have to look at him and get distracted, she could explain everything properly. Feeling much better now she had a solution, she tried to spell out her brainwave to a sceptical Rosie.

'Bad idea, Cara,' Rosie sighed. 'You really should get some sleep before you do anything silly.'

Ignoring Rosie's frown of disapproval, Cara pulled her phone from her bag and called Henry's number before she lost her nerve. After several rings, it clicked to voicemail and she cleared her throat. Having fired herself up to speak to him, she wasn't ready to admit defeat.

'Henry, this is Cara. Of course you know it's me . . . but well, anyway, the thing is . . . I can't stop thinking about you and how we left things. I'm not saying it's your fault or that I blame you or anything . . . because I don't, of course!'

She paused, trying to get her thoughts together. This wasn't proving quite as straightforward as she had imagined. She tried again. 'What I'm trying to say . . . and not very well . . . ha-ha . . . that's rum for you. Not that I've had that much. Okay, just a few shots, but that doesn't mean I don't know what I'm saying. Which is, ahem, what I mean is . . . I really—'

There was a loud bleep before she could say another word, and the line went dead. Cara stared at her handset in disbelief. How *dare* his phone cut her off? *And* just when she was getting around to making her point! Rosie had been watching in silence, her expression a blend of horror and deep pity.

'The stupid voicemail cut me off before I could say anything! Can you *believe* that?'

'Maybe it didn't record,' Rosie offered, sounding unconvinced.

Cara's eyes lit up hopefully. 'Really?'

Rosie had never been good at lying and after hesitating for a split second, shook her head.

Cara's face fell. *Bloody hell!* She had to fix this before Henry thought she'd lost her mind. She was just about to tap his number again when Rosie prised the phone out of her hand. '*There* we go! It's no use glaring at me because I'm just trying to save you from making an even bigger fool of yourself. Trust me, you'll thank me tomorrow.'

Cara scowled, but when Rosie remained unmoved, she shrugged and tossed back the last drops of rum in her glass.

'Maybe you're right,' she conceded with a delicate burp. 'Always best not to talk to people who are sober when you're not. You sure you don't want another drink?'

34

CHOICES

Cara's head was throbbing along to the heavy rock concert playing in her skull. Her eyelids felt like they'd been weighted down with a stack of coins and her tongue was so dry, it felt glued to the roof of her mouth. She groaned and lowered her head to rest it gently on her desk. It was a miracle that her alarm had somehow cut through the thick fog of sleep that had engulfed her after she'd eventually crawled into bed, and she had no idea how she had found the strength to shower. Ironing the lightweight cotton dress that she'd planned to wear to work had proved a step too far which was why, despite the unseasonably warm day, Cara had arrived at the office in slashed camouflage trousers and wearing a pair of heavy combat boots.

It was now almost two weeks since she and Henry had last spoken, if that was the right word to describe the scene that still made her shudder whenever she replayed it in her mind in the irrational hope it might turn out differently. The sound of a chair scraping across the floor broke through her semi-comatose state and she angled her head to find Ben leaning over the partition, studying her.

Pushing her hair out of her eyes, Cara glared up at him. 'What are *you* grinning at?' The last thing she needed was judgement from her annoyingly chirpy-looking colleague.

'Looks like someone had one too many last night,' Ben observed virtuously.

Cara groaned pitifully, and he relented. 'Okay, I'll be nice and grab you a bacon butty from downstairs. Just make sure you cover for me if Paula asks!'

About to argue, Cara's stomach rumbled loudly, and she nodded, wincing as the rock band in her head started up again. 'Thanks, Ben. Oh, and don't forget—'

'Yeah, I know. Ketchup, not brown sauce.'

'*Extra* ketchup.'

One greasy bacon butty and two mugs of coffee later, Cara's stomach was appeased. Her head had quietened, but the ache in her heart was unbearable, and ten minutes after her department had been hauled into the MD's impromptu all-staff meeting, Cara had had enough. Malcolm's motivational speech was leaving her uninspired, un-uplifted, and unable to concentrate, and ignoring Paula's astonished glare, she slipped out of the room.

Back at her desk, Cara looked around the deserted office. The silence echoed her emptiness and she felt like crying. Knowing what Malcolm was like with a microphone in his hands, the meeting was likely to go on for some time and maybe she should take the bull by the horns and call Henry – but sober this time. She reached for her phone, still struggling to work out what she could say that would erase the look in his eyes on the night he'd walked out. When nothing came to mind, Cara stared at her handset in misery and dropped it back onto the desk. What if, as far as Henry was concerned, this was really it? Her eyes burned with unshed tears as she faced the very real possibility that she and Henry were over. She had spent so long trying to fix other people's problems that it had taken Ryan's reappearance to brutally expose how much she needed to fix her own. By letting Ryan over her doorstep and under her skin instead of leaving him to the tender mercies of Mrs Aggarwal's one-woman Neighbourhood Watch, Cara had made the worst decision ever, and sabotaged the most important relationship of her life. Henry was worth a hundred Ryans, and she desperately needed to let him know that and fix the mess she had created.

An idea began to form in her mind. *Maybe, just maybe, I can sort this.* The beginnings of a smile crept onto her face. Sure, the idea was a little crazy, but then, desperate times and all that. The only problem was that the one person she knew who could help at such short notice was only slightly shy of certifiable.

Cara picked up her phone again and made the first call, crossing her fingers hard when it went through. With a sigh of relief, she made a second call and, following another short conversation, raced out of the office, stopping only to leave a hastily scribbled Post-it on Paula's desk.

Under normal circumstances, it would have been the kind of morning that Cara relished – sunny but not too hot and an azure-blue sky that held no hint of cloud. But as she stood on the pavement outside her office in the middle of the morning, the weather was the last thing on her mind. Finally reaching a decision appeared to have eased the worst of her hangover and her earlier lethargy was forgotten. She would deal with her bolshie boss later, Cara decided, hurrying towards the Underground. After all, even Paula would find it hard to argue with Cara's claim of suspected appendicitis.

By the time she emerged from Shepherd's Bush station, the sun was high in the sky and the temperature had shot up. Cara's skin was damp underneath her long-sleeved black t-shirt and her feet felt hot and sticky in the heavy boots she had pulled on in her drunken haze. Ignoring the sweat prickling her scalp, she dashed up the stairs to Julio's office.

He was waiting for her, and she flopped into a battered arm-chair near the door. There was no sign of Gina and other than the usual clutter of half-open boxes and assorted gadgets, he was alone.

'Julio, I need you,' Cara pleaded, once she had caught her breath.

His face brightened and he hurried to kneel beside her. He leaned in hopefully and Cara pushed him away with an impatient tut.

'No, I mean I need your *help!*'

Julio's face fell, but then with a philosophical shrug he stood up and walked over to a tiny fridge to extract a bottle of water, which he handed to her with a good-natured grin.

Cara accepted it gratefully and after several gulps she paced up and down the office explaining her predicament. To his credit, Julio listened without interruption, nodding slowly when she got to the part where his expertise came in.

'I know it's really, *really* short notice but I have to do it today. *Please*, Julio?' she begged.

'You have come to the right place. For matters of the heart, Uncle Julio is your man!'

Cara looked at him anxiously, knowing she was taking a huge risk. 'Do you think you'll be able to pull it off? Honestly, Julio, be straight with me. This is too important to mess up.'

'*Querida*, have faith! Uncle Julio will never let you down,' he shamelessly declared. Gesturing for her to take a seat on his rickety visitor's stool, he punched out some numbers on his desk phone and, putting the call on speaker, he leaned back in his chair. After a conversation in rapid Spanish accompanied by much animated hand-waving, Julio ended the phone call with a self-satisfied smile.

'The timing, it is very critical because Emilio needs the equipment for another event later today. But he owes me many favours and he cannot say no to Julio.' He reached into a drawer and pulled out a notepad and pen. 'Now then, if it is to work as you wish, this is what we must agree, so listen carefully.'

Twenty minutes later, with a skip in her step and only a trace of her earlier hangover, Cara returned to the Underground and jumped onto the first train that roared onto the platform.

It wasn't until she'd navigated the maze of streets outside Bank station and was standing outside the revolving glass doors belonging to the law firm of Carradine, Jarvis & Knott that Cara felt the first stirrings of doubt. She looked down at her crumpled top and distressed combat trousers and gnawed on her lip with uncertainty. Leaving aside the fact that she looked a hot mess, what if she was about to make a colossal mistake? She paced up and down the pavement in an agony of indecision until she remembered Dexter's words. *Sort it out, Cara.* Taking a deep breath, she squared her shoulders and pushed through the doors into the lobby of Henry's office.

Marching up to the security desk, she signed her name in the visitors' book before taking the lift to the twelfth floor, as instructed, where the bright reception area with its huge windows offering magnificent views of a sunny London reminded her instantly of Primrose's office. After a brief conversation, the receptionist gestured towards a cluster of leather armchairs. 'Please take a seat while I give Fenella a call.'

'I phoned a little while ago to check. He *is* still here, isn't he?' Cara asked with apprehension. The receptionist nodded, and a few minutes later a dark-haired woman in a fitted navy dress appeared.

'Hello. I'm Fenella Walker, Henry's assistant. You must be Cara,' she said with a smile.

Cara jumped up and shook Fenella's outstretched hand. 'I'm so sorry to barge in like this, but I really need to speak to Henry. It's *very* important,' she stressed, as she noted the woman's frown.

'I'm sure it must be,' Fenella murmured agreeably. 'It's just that he's about to go into a meeting with the partners and—'

She broke off to scrutinise Cara's flushed face and then said, 'Come with me.'

Cara trailed meekly behind as Fenella led the way through two sets of double doors and around a maze of corridors. Neither of them spoke until the PA knocked on a heavy door and pushed it open. Cara's heart was thumping in her chest as she followed her into the room, her heavy boots sinking into the thick-pile carpet. Henry was seated behind a huge desk scribbling notes on some papers in front of him and when he looked up, Fenella stepped aside, leaving Cara staring straight at him.

For a moment, there was complete silence. Cara scoured his face, at once elated to see him and fearful of what he might say. His eyes looked tired and without their usual sparkle and his hair appeared a little longer. When he leaned forward to drop his pen into a holder, his fringe fell into his eyes, and she had to clench her fists to stop herself rushing forward to smooth it back.

Henry continued to stare at her, but it was impossible to tell what he was thinking. Without breaking eye contact, he stood up and came round from behind the desk, and Cara held her breath as he walked towards her. Was he going to listen to her or throw her out?

Fenella cleared her throat and broke the tense silence. 'I'm sorry to interrupt you, Henry, but I thought perhaps you might have time for a quick chat with Cara before you join the partners' meeting?'

'*Please*, Henry,' Cara said breathlessly. 'It's important, no, it's *vital* that you come with me. Now.'

He glanced at his watch and then resumed his scrutiny, and she flushed with embarrassment, suddenly conscious of her shiny face devoid of any make-up, her ripped trousers, and the half-tied black boots that looked as out of place in Henry's plush office as a rump steak at a vegetarian dinner.

'I gathered from the . . . erm . . . interesting message you left on my phone last night that there was something you wanted to tell me,' he said finally. He paused and then enquired casually, 'Are you still drunk?'

Was she imagining a slight softening of his jaw and a flicker of amusement in his eyes? She shook her head vigorously, immensely grateful Rosie had seized her phone and stopped her from having another go. Drunk-dialling hadn't exactly been her brightest idea.

Fenella had been observing the interchange with interest. 'Henry, if you need to go, I can make your excuses to the partners and reschedule the presentation?'

Henry's gaze was still on Cara and the plea on her face. After a moment he nodded. 'Thanks, Fenella. Please tell them that something . . . *vital* has come up and I'll be back a bit later.'

Fenella left the room, giving Cara an encouraging smile on her way out. Henry shrugged on his jacket and led the way back to the lift and neither he nor Cara said a word during the descent to the ground floor.

When they emerged onto the street, Henry turned to her and raised a quizzical eyebrow. 'So, where are we going?'

She looked at her watch. 'London Bridge. We need to go now, but I'll explain everything when we get there.'

It was lunchtime in the City and Cara forged ahead, weaving a path through streams of tourists with oversized backpacks and office workers clutching sandwiches and plastic containers of salad. She was unfamiliar with the maze of narrow cobbled streets between Bank and the Monument, and it was left to Henry to gently steer her down a side alley and towards a major junction with several sets of traffic lights. Arriving at London Bridge, they walked along the historic bridge until Cara came to a standstill at what she guessed was the halfway point.

Henry looked at her expectantly, and this time there was no trace of the smile she thought she had seen earlier. She took a deep breath and willed herself not to lose her nerve.

'Your mother came to my flat last weekend.'

'I know. She told me what you did for Fleur.' He hesitated and then added, 'It was very kind of you to take her in and help mend the rift between the two of them.'

Cara shook her head. 'Fleur's a lovely kid and, besides, it was nothing compared to you risking your life for my sister's dog.'

After a moment of silence, she stared down at the ground and then said quietly, 'Your mum told me about a girl you were seeing and what happened with her after your accident.'

When he didn't reply, she looked up anxiously. Had she upset him by reminding him about the woman he had loved? But Henry showed no sign of distress. On the contrary, a faint smile hovered over his lips.

'It was wrong of me not to tell you about Sophie, especially after accusing you of keeping secrets about Ryan.' He frowned, as though trying to recall something long forgotten. 'Sophie was a nice enough girl. I suppose you could describe her as a— what did you call it before? Ah yes, a shiny-haired, pearl-wearing type of girl, but she couldn't get away fast enough after the accident. I can't say I blame her, after all we'd only been going out for a couple of months, and she hadn't signed up for a boyfriend with a poor chance of ever getting back on his feet again.'

Henry's rueful smile didn't quite mask the flash of pain that crossed his face. 'Although she was hardly the love of my life, we had been getting along well before it all happened and watching her walk away at a time when I couldn't, it was . . . well, I suppose it was the final straw. I already felt completely worthless and after she ended our relationship, life seemed pointless.'

'I know what that feels like,' Cara said sadly. 'Wanting to lock yourself away so you don't have to speak to anyone, and you can just disappear.'

For the first time since her unceremonious arrival at his office, his eyes seemed to soften. He drew her aside to avoid the stream of people walking past and bumping into them and she leaned against the cool stone wall of the bridge, her eyes drifting down to the river of grey water flowing below. She shivered despite the heat of the midday sun and then turned back to face him.

'Cara, tell me what happened,' he said gently.

She looked deep into his eyes and, seeing no judgement there, she nodded. Pouring out the story of the unexpected pregnancy, Ryan's abrupt disappearance and losing the baby proved easier than she had feared. Henry listened, giving the occasional nod but making no attempt to interrupt. As she spoke about the dark, lost period of her life, she could feel something almost physical shift inside her. By the time she'd finished, she felt at once empty and cleansed, as if someone had reached down and lifted away a burden that had sat quietly within her for years.

'I know you wanted to help me, Henry, but it isn't easy to ask for help or admit when you're struggling mentally, especially when I've grown used to seeing myself as the strong one who sorts out everyone else's problems. But I'm the one who needs sorting out this time, I'm afraid.' She gave him a small smile. 'I was trying to keep everyone happy but, unfortunately, it had the opposite effect. Covering up the truth about Ryan only made Dexter blame me and become bitter and angry. Even Manon felt abandoned and decided Ryan's selfish decision was all her fault.' She took a deep breath. 'So, you'll be pleased to know that I've finally got it through my head that I don't owe it to anyone to fix their life, even if I could.'

Henry nodded slowly. 'You only tried to shield your family because you love them so much, but that left you carrying all the blame as well as the devastation of losing your baby. That's an awful burden to bear, Cara. I see now why his coming back affected you so badly and why you've been struggling about us.'

Looking up at the man standing before her, Cara's heart swelled with relief that she had finally found the courage to share the one thing holding her back from fully giving her heart to Henry. Why had she ever assumed he wouldn't understand how much her devastating loss had impacted every action she had taken since?

'Ryan caused so much damage and seeing him brought it all up again and made me doubt myself. At the time, it felt like you and I had so much stacked against us, and I knew I couldn't handle the pain if we didn't work out. So, rather than take that risk, I created a tangle of excuses to protect myself.'

Cara glanced at her watch and looked upwards and then returned her gaze to Henry. 'Mum told me ages ago that I should tell you everything. She knew from the beginning you were special, and she insisted you would understand.'

'She's a wise woman,' he agreed. After a moment's hesitation, he asked, 'So . . . how do you feel about Ryan now?'

Cara shrugged. 'Honestly? I don't feel a thing. I think the real feelings I had for him died a quiet death a while ago, but it took me a little too long to recognise that, which I suppose is why you didn't believe me.'

He still doesn't. Although Henry had listened carefully to every word, he didn't look persuaded, and Cara felt a jolt of panic. Even after baring her soul, Henry still didn't accept she was serious about him! And where the *hell* was Julio? It was well past the time they'd agreed. She took a few calming breaths and tried to relax, and then glanced up once more. Still nothing.

'Oh God, oh God, oh God,' she mumbled under her breath. *Please*, Julio, she begged silently, don't let me down. Not today. Not for something this important. She focused her gaze on the river and concentrated on breathing in and out slowly and deeply, counting to five as she took in and released air from her lungs. *Christ, I am so screwed!* This was it. There was no Plan B. Everything had ridden on Julio's idea working out and she closed her eyes in utter devastation. It was her own fault for trusting him, knowing what he was like, and now here she was, standing on a bridge with a world-class patent lawyer she had dragged out of an important meeting and feeling like the prize idiot Ashanti had called her.

'What on *earth* is that?' Henry squinted upwards in astonishment and Cara's eyes flew open. She looked up to follow his gaze and gave a loud whoop, punching her fist in the air. *I take it all back, Julio*, she thought joyfully, jumping up and down in excitement as a tiny plane buzzed across the sky almost directly above them.

However, it wasn't so much the plane that had caught Henry's eyes, or those of every passer-by on the bridge. It was the white banner streaming behind it with the words 'I choose YOU, Henry Fitzherbert!!!' in big black lettering.

It was now or never, and Cara took a deep breath. 'Henry, please, *please* listen to me. Ryan is my past. Until I met you, I never knew I could feel like this about someone. The only reason I'm glad Ryan came back is that it's given me a chance to get closure on everything that happened between him and me, but I don't want him back. I only want *you*. I *love* you!'

The small aircraft circled and then flew off into the distance, the banner fluttering in its wake. Clearly stunned into silence, Henry ran his hands through his hair, the breeze playing through the silky blond strands.

'I'm so sorry for barging into your office and messing up your day, but I had to show you and not just tell you,' Cara pleaded, staring at him with eyes wide with anxiety.

'Please say something,' she begged when he continued to stare at her wordlessly. 'The only other option apart from the plane was for me to skydive with coloured flares. I'm a bit scared of heights, but I'll do it if that's what it takes to convince you that I know what, and who, I want. I mean it, Henry. I *really* choose you.'

For a moment, he frowned as he appeared to weigh her words and then his face cleared and he laughed, pulling her tightly against him to kiss her, his lips warm and achingly familiar.

Smoothing back the cloud of curls tumbling over her face, Henry twirled a lock around his finger. 'God, you have *no* idea how much I've missed doing this!'

He kissed her again, oblivious to the City workers walking around them with barely a glance or the group of giggling foreign tourists who stopped to surreptitiously take a picture of the fair-haired man in a smart suit enjoying a passionate embrace with the slender brown-skinned girl wearing heavy boots in blazing sunshine.

Henry kissed her over and over and it felt like coming home. Cara clung on tightly, wanting to hold on to him forever and wondering how she had ever thought she could be without him. But there was still unfinished business, and eventually she pulled back and gently stroked his fringe away from his flushed face. She traced his jawline lightly, feeling the warmth of his skin and the faint rasp of stubble beneath her trembling fingertips.

'Henry, you still haven't answered me,' she said breathlessly.

He reached into his jacket pocket and pulled out a small glass bottle.

'What's that?'

'Hot pepper sauce,' he grinned. 'I've been sprinkling a little on my food every day for the past couple of weeks. If I'm going to be part of a family that eats chilli peppers like they're Smarties, I figured I'd better get used to it.'

'*Oh!*' Speechless, she stared at him while her whirring brain took in the implication of his words. 'You mean . . .?'

He kissed the tip of her nose and dropped the vial back into his pocket. 'You didn't really think I would walk out of your life, did you? There is no way I'm kissing our dream goodbye. I had meant to give you time to sort out your feelings, but, after listening to your mad message last night, it struck me that waiting on the sidelines while you turned into an alcoholic wasn't the best strategy.'

He folded her into the gentlest of bear hugs. 'Before you turned up at my office, I'd already decided to come over this evening to talk some sense into you and tell you what I'd said before wasn't true. I will *always* fight for you, even when you can't fight for yourself. I love you, Cara, and from the moment you landed on my foot against all odds, I promised myself I would never lose you again.'

'*Ooh!* You—! Why did you make me suffer so much when you knew all along you wanted to be with me?'

He grinned and kissed her lightly and, at the touch of his lips on hers, her indignation instantly subsided.

'Oh, Henry, I really *do* choose you,' she murmured.

The noise of the traffic receded into the distance and the people pushing past them could have been invisible as his eyes looked deep into hers.

'Caramia Nightingale, I choose you, too.'

A MESSAGE FROM FRANCES

Thank you so much for taking the time to read my book. If you enjoyed Cara's story, please take a moment to share your thoughts with a short review. Even if it's only a line or two, I would really appreciate it. If you'd like to hear about my future releases, then please subscribe to receive my regular newsletters:

https://francesmensahwilliams.com/newsletters

You can also follow my author page below:

https://www.amazon.co.uk/Frances-Mensah-Williams/e/B008VGSXRM

Although Cara's family is fictional, the Nightingale-Grants aren't a million miles away from my own drama-filled clan. Growing up in London with my parents, four brothers and a sister, our house was always open to visiting 'aunties' and 'uncles' from Ghana and elsewhere, as well as friends who came to visit and often ended up staying! Much like Cara, my extended family is a mini-United Nations with family members originating from Africa, New Zealand, Britain and Europe. In writing Cara's story, I wanted to show the joy of being part of an exuberant and inclusive support system which, despite its dramas, always brings the love.

Telling Cara's story was a delight and I'd love to hear your thoughts about it. Please do get in touch with me via my Instagram, Twitter, Facebook page or website.

Thank you!

Frances x

https://twitter.com/francesmensahw
www.facebook.com/francesmensahwilliams
https://www.instagram.com/francesmensahw
www.francesmensahwilliams.com

BOOK CLUB QUESTIONS

1. Who is your favourite character in the book, and why?
2. What feelings did Cara's journey evoke in you?
3. Which scene was the most memorable, and why?
4. How big a part do you think abandonment plays in the story?
5. Did you identify with Cara's dilemma of sustaining a relationship with someone who appears to be very different to you?
6. What key points do you think the author was trying to get across in writing this story?
7. Which aspect of the book did you most relate to?
8. How would you compare Cara and Henry's families?
9. Did you find the cultural references believable and did any of the characters remind you of anyone?
10. If this book were a movie, which song would make a great soundtrack?
11. If you had to cast two people to play Cara and Henry, who would you choose?
12. Have you read any other books by this author and, if so, how did they compare?

ACKNOWLEDGEMENTS

As ever, I remain in awe of the many stages through which a book must journey as it moves from an idea to a story and then all the way to the finished product. It truly takes a village to walk that first draft of a manuscript through its transformation into a novel which – as every author hopes – readers will connect with, enjoy and talk about.

My sincerest thanks to everyone who accompanied me on this incredibly exciting and exhilarating journey.

My agent, Rukhsana Yasmin, I can't thank you enough. Your warmth, wisdom and sense of humour – not to mention fantastic agenting skills – have been invaluable every step of the way. My thanks also to Gyamfia Osei for your enthusiastic support and inspirational ideas and to the Good Literary Agency for championing diverse voices.

A huge thank you to Hannah Bond for loving this story from the outset and welcoming me into the Amazon family and to my editor, Leodora Darlington, not only for leading the brilliant team that transformed the manuscript into a book, but also for your insights and challenges which have only made it better. Thank you also to Laurie Johnson for your exceptional editorial skills and super-helpful guidance.

My thanks to everyone who reviewed the manuscript for your feedback and brilliant suggestions. Henry, I so appreciate the time you spent talking me through the perils of entertainment contracts and any errors are mine.

Finally, love and thanks to my family near and far, my tribe of sister friends, my rock of ages, Chux, and my beloved girls, Seena and Khaya.

ABOUT THE AUTHOR

Photo © 2021 Abi Oshodi

Frances Mensah Williams CBE spent her early childhood between the USA, Austria, and Ghana before settling in the UK. An avid scribbler, her acclaimed first novel *From Pasta to Pigfoot* was published in 2015 and the sequel *From Pasta to Pigfoot: Second Helpings* in 2016. Her third novel *Imperfect Arrangements* (2020) was followed by the *Marula Heights* series of standalone novellas, *River Wild* and *Sweet Mercy*, set in contemporary Ghana.

An entrepreneur, Consultant, Executive Coach, and TEDx speaker, Frances is also the author of three non-fiction careers books and the publisher of careers portal www.ReConnectAfrica.com. She is a passionate advocate for skills development and has written extensively on careers and business relating to Africa and the African diaspora. She has received awards for innovation in business and skills development, culminating in the CBE awarded by Queen Elizabeth II in the 2020 New Year's Honours List for services to Africans in the UK and in Africa.